WHAT WILL YOU DO WHEN:

—Money is barely worth the paper it is printed on

—Transportation slows to a virtual halt

—Government services break down

—Cities default

—Banks close their doors

—Crime rises astronomically

—The social fabric is ripped to shreds

—And panic is everywhere

This is not a science fiction nightmare. It is a sober scientific forecast based on unassailable facts. *It is what you have to be prepared for.*

Now you can be.

AFTER THE CRASH
How to Survive and Prosper During
the Depression of the 1980s

Recommended MENTOR and SIGNET Books

AFTER THE CRASH

How to Survive and Prosper During the Depression of the 1980s

Geoffry F. Abert, Ph.D.

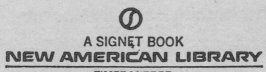

A SIGNET BOOK

NEW AMERICAN LIBRARY

TIMES MIRROR

This publication is designed to provide the Author's opinion in
regard to the subject matter covered. It is sold with the
understanding that neither the Publisher or Author is engaged
in rendering legal, accounting or other professional service.
If legal advice or other expert assistance is required, the service
of a competent professional person should be sought.

This is an authorized reprint of a hardcover edition
published by Bradford Press

SIGNET, SIGNET CLASSICS, MENTOR, PLUME, MERIDIAN AND NAL BOOKS
are published by The New American Library, Inc.,
1633 Broadway, New York, New York 10019

First Signet Printing, February, 1980

3   4   5   6   7   8   9

PRINTED IN THE UNITED STATES OF AMERICA

Contents

Section One

WHAT'S HAPPENING HERE?

CHAPTER ONE

What's Happening to the Good Life?

The American dream never seemed closer than in the 1950's. Resounding victories against a major depression and a world war provided reassurance of the indomitable American ability to overcome difficulties. Unparalleled prosperity was emerging. Opportunities existed for all. A contemporary television program has captioned this era, "Happy Days."

The fifties was an era of progress, prosperity, and positive prospects. This, indeed, was the stuff of which dreams were made. Twenty years later, a popular song summarized the mood by its title, "The Class of '57 Had Its Dreams." We were a generation who didn't believe in limits. We could fine-tune the economy, make the world safe for democracy, eliminate poverty, and explore outer space while enjoying a drip-dry, perma-press, split-level life with instant cake mix, coffee, and affluence. All we had to add was water and dollars.

What was wrong with the formula? Why has our diet of instant gratification given us economic and physical malnutrition? Why have those bright, cheerful dreams of the class of '57 become nightmares of running in place? Where are the snake-oil salesmen who offered us gleaming promises with gilt-edged guarantees?

This book will give you some answers. It will explain how and why the American dream has gone sour. It will show how the mightiest nation in the world traded its natural birthright for a bowl of pottage and a quick fix. More importantly, it will show how to cope with the Frankensteinian monster that we have created.

I have no grand design to save the world. Frankly, I believe that it is too late for us to avoid the economic crisis that looms just ahead. I know that the steps required to cope with our economic dilemma are politically inexpedient. Our leaders lack the courage to lead because they know that their constituency wants simple, painless answers. Anyone with even a reasonable claim to leadership knows the two immutable laws of economics: there are no free lunches and no simple solutions.

Is There Really a Problem?

Right now, you may have some reservations about the whole thesis of this book. You have a vague, general feeling that things aren't exactly right. You may not be moving ahead as fast as you would want to, but your income is higher than anyone in your family has ever made before. You have more cars, a bigger house, more gadgets, and bigger payments than you ever thought possible. It's true that you are not saving as large a percentage of your income as you once did and your debts are enough to be frightening whenever you happen to think about them, but that's the new American way.

For the next few minutes, take a tour with me to some of the major U.S. institutions: the government, American cities, and the family. We also will review the status of key subgroups such as workers, youths, and blacks. Our tour will conclude with a brief survey of a country that has traveled a little farther down the same road on which we seem to be headed. Let's explore the myth and reality of American progress and prosperity.

YOUR UNCLE IS BANKRUPT

Americans believe that "big is better." By this measure, we have a magnificent government. The federal government alone spends an amount equal to almost twenty-five percent of the nation's total production of goods and services. The government owns 760 billion acres—⅓ of the nation's total land. Uncle Sam also holds title to 405 buildings that cost $91 billion to construct. Additionally, the annual bill for rent on another 54,000 office buildings runs to $663 million. In other words, the U.S. government occupies the equivalent space of 96 Sears Towers—the world's tallest building, with 110 floors. To handle the paperwork generated by federal regulations and procedures, 211,000 clerks, typists, and secretaries are employed. A major portion of their work involves processing 4,504 different federal forms. The material generated by these forms each year would fill eleven Washington Monuments.

In 1950, government cost $1,600 per family. Now, the cost is close to $9,000 per working family. This means that the average family spends between five and seven months per year working simply to pay all of its direct and hidden taxes. In the Dark Ages, the serfs were required to spend only three months working for their masters. During the rest of the year, they were free to work for themselves.

Specialists in the White House have estimated that the cost of useless and wasteful regulations by federal agents is over $130 billion per year, the equivalent of more then $2,000 annually for every U.S. family. A recent study by Dr. Murray L. Weidenbaum for the Joint Economic Committee of Congress showed that government regulations have added $666 to the price of a new automobile and between $1,500 and $2,500 to the cost of a new home. The Office of the Inspector General reported that the Department of Health, Education and Welfare misspent between $6 billion and $7.4 billion in fiscal year 1977 because of waste, fraud, and abuse. Four billion dollars were spent unnecessarily on health care programs, including Medicare and Medicaid payments for unnecessary surgery, hospital studies, and X-rays. Other authorities estimate that the total theft and fraud against federal agencies could run as high as $25 billion per year. Some dramatic examples include:

—One firm was paid to paint 2.4 million square feet of space at GSA headquarters in Washington. The entire building has an area of only 1.9 million square feet. Some GSA building managers are accused of having received as much as $300,000 annually for their part in repair and maintenance shenanigans.
—The Cook County (Chicago) Welfare Queen is charged with using six aliases to draw more than $150,000 in allegedly illegal welfare payments. A graduate student at the University of Illinois, in criminal justice, she had applied to law school asking that application fees be waived because she was indigent. Indicted on 613 counts of theft of Medicaid, Food Stamp, Aid to Dependent Children programs, she was arrested in the Criminal

Court Building where she had gone to interview a judge as part of her graduate studies.

—In South Florida, a community council that received $1.3 million in job training funds diverted $22,000 to a privately run service station, paid money to a staff "psychologist" with no degree, and made loans to friends and family members.

—In Maryland's job training program, nine young women were paid $145 per week to attend a ballet school. The wife of a dentist received $11,000 a year in payments under the Comprehensive Education and Training Act.

The National Taxpayers Union estimates that there are over 900,000 "totally ineligible" welfare recipients receiving regular payments. They also point out that $250 billion has been spent for foreign aid including money for the United States to provide financial assistance to both sides of a conflict in fourteen wars during the past twenty years. Excessive red tape, inept management, poorly trained front-line personnel, and careless investigative policies are costing taxpayers billions of dollars each year.

The U.S. economy is still productive. It generated goods and services at the rate of $2 trillion in 1978. But remember the public debt in the United States is approaching $1 trillion and annual spending in Washington is approximately $500 billion.

President Carter's description of this $500-billion budget for 1979 as "lean and tight" is hardly accurate. If you started out at the birth of Christ spending $690,000 a day, you would have just now succeeded in getting rid of $500 billion. Yet, we will be spending that much in a single year, and many authorities feel that the figure will double in less than a decade. In order to get rid of $500 billion this year, the government will have to spend an average of $951,000 a minute or $57 million an hour every day including holidays and Sundays.

You will notice that I am spelling out words like *billion* and *trillion*. They require so many zeros that they are distracting to the average reader. Let me provide a couple of additional reference points for these sums. If you were to spend $1,000 a day, a billion dollars would last for 2,738 years. Multiply that times 500 to see how much money Washington spent in 1978.

If you were to lay end on end 1 trillion dollar bills, they would stretch 4 million miles beyond the sun—which, for those of you who have forgotten junior high science, is 96,-909,000 miles away.

We spend $85,000 per minute to pay interest on the national debt. At the present rate of real and inflationary growth in the cost of government, public spending at all levels will be $1.75 trillion by 1995, about 3½ times the 1975 level, and the average tax burden per family will be over $16,000. The total cost of government divided by the anticipated 60 million families would average $29,000 per family. Does this convince you that governmental spending cannot possibly continue to grow as it has?

What Do You Owe?

Recently, I received the following invoice:

TAXPAYER'S LIABILITY INDEX (prepared by)
National Taxpayers Union
325 Pennsylvania Avenue, S.E.
Washington, D. C. 20003

DEBT OR LIABILITY TERM	GROSS COST	YOUR SHARE
	Public Debt	
Public Debt	$ 721,000,000,000	$ 9,012
Accounts Payable	$ 80,000,000,000	$ 1,000
Undelivered Orders	$ 332,000,000,000	$ 4,150
Long Term Contracts	$ 15,000,000,000	$ 187
Loan and Credit Guarantees	$ 209,000,000,000	$ 2,612
Insurance Commitments	$1,733,000,000,000	$ 21,662
Annuity Programs	$5,900,000,000,000	$ 73,750
Unadjudicated Claims International Commitments & other Financial Obligations	$ 43,000,000,000	$ 537
	$9,033,000,000,000	$112,912

Somehow a national debt of almost a trillion dollars or even liabilities of approximately $9 trillion don't concern me as much as the fact that my personal stake in all this is almost $113,000. It bothers me even more when I realize the small percentage of people in this country who can be counted on to pay their liabilities. One prominent political figure has suggested that more people vote for a living than work. According to the North American Newspaper Alliance, over 120 million people are largely dependent on tax money. This includes government employees, the military, welfare recipients, public pensioners and dependents of these groups—almost 60 percent of the total population.

A President who campaigned on his promise never to lie to the American people has abandoned his campaign pledge to balance the budget for 1981. The Office of Management and Budget admits that a deficit of around $10 billion by that date is likely. Leonard Santow, Senior Vice President of the J. Henry Schroeder Bank and Trust Company and a consultant of OMB, thinks that the deficit in fiscal 1979 will rival the peace-time record deficit of $66 billion set in 1976. He also believes that it will rise to about $70 billion in 1980. Computer projections by Data Resources, Inc. show that if the Administration gets hit by just a few hard breaks such as continued rapid increase in food prices or imported oil, the deficit could explode to $220 billion in 1987 alone. In the 1970's, federal deficits have totaled $338 billion.

Budget Bloat

You may be interested in a few of the items in the current budget. Civil service and pension budgets have increased sixfold during the past two decades to a total of $20 billion annually. President Carter recommended $85 billion in grants to state and local governments for 1979. Since 1972, aid to education has more than tripled to $3.2 billion. The largest single program in the federal budget is Social Security. Since 1965, the number of Social Security beneficiaries has jumped from 20 million to 34 million, while average monthly benefits have tripled. In the same period, welfare rolls have grown from 4 million to 11 million, while the average annual benefit per recipient has risen by 50 percent. Since 1970, the number of Medicaid recipients has increased by more than 8 million and the number of people receiving food stamps has quadrupled to 16.7 million. At the same time, the average benefit has jumped by 86 percent for Medicaid and 150 percent for food stamps. From $17.5 billion in 1965, social security will probably cost around $133 billion in fiscal 1979. You may not notice it, but $20 billion here and $133 billion there—and before you know, you're talking about some real money.

If the volume of dollars spent is depressing, the ineptitude with which it is spent is even more frightening. Everyone is concerned about the excessive profits earned by the giant oil companies. Yet the first year's budget for the Department of Energy was $10.6 billion. In order to protect you from the oil companies, the federal government is spending more than the total profits of the fourteen largest petroleum companies and about two-thirds of the total industry's profits. Another way of looking at the same information is to say that the new agency to protect you is going to cost the equivalent of four cents per gallon for all gasoline consumed in the United States.

If you want to be picky, you may want to know why Congress has authorized $375,000 for a Pentagon study of the Frisbee, or $125,000 to find out why some people say "ain't," or a $29,324 authorization for a study of the mating calls of the Central American Toad. (Compared to other projects, this one sounds like a real bargain.)

The Federal Trough Is Sweeter

As the preceding paragraphs will indicate, whoever is minding the store in Washington isn't practicing the best concepts of fiscal and social responsibility. Federal employees are not known for their dedication, productivity, or efficiency. Yet their pay and benefits are enviable:

—According to the Civil Service Commission, the average government employee in Washington earns $18,965 per year. The average employee of private business earns less than $10,000.

—The average employee of the Federal Government gets 50 percent more paid time off than the person working for private business.

—Government employees are exempt from Social Security, which means that they pay approximately $1,000 per year less in federal taxes.

—Federal employees can retire with full pension at age fifty-five—a decade sooner than the typical employee in private enterprise.

A study by the General Accounting Office confirms that government employees get paid more for doing less. For example, claims processors working for the government handle

2,500 claims per year. Those working for private companies process more than twice as many—an average of 5,700 claims per year. In addition, the government processors earn $21,600, while those working for private industry average only about $15,000. In ten years government white collar workers have received twelve raises that have boosted their pay 94.8 percent. Small wonder that there are seventy-six applications for every federal opening.

CRISIS IN THE CITIES

After the turn of the century, Sam Lewis and Joe Young had America singing, "How're you gonna keep 'em down on the farm . . ." After seeing the wonders of cities such as Paris, New York, and San Francisco, it seemed that people would be foresaking the farms in droves. For a while this was true. The good life could be found in cities, where there was easy access to good shopping, quality education, exciting entertainment, and lucrative employment.

Today, the exodus from the farm to the city has reversed. People, especially the well-to-do and middle class, are leaving the city because of its problems. Crime is out of control, taxes are exorbitant, and education is a farce. Many cities have become virtual jungles. As Dr. George Sternlied of Rutgers University says, "You can't support the poor without the rich. Every time some taxpayer moves out of the city, the poor are left even poorer, and this is what is happening in every large city in America."

While the public rebels against taxes, cities throughout the country are literally wearing out. The evidence of this deterioration is easy to spot. We have become accustomed to streets and expressways pocked with potholes and cracks, signs above bridges warning us that they are unsafe, public buildings and schools in disrepair, sewers frequently backed up and clogged, aged equipment, and dangerous water systems.

According to the Congressional Joint Economic Committee, paying for maintenance and improvements in public works "may be the single greatest problem facing our nation's cities." As an illustration, New Orleans has a major sewage problem. According to the Director of the Sewage and Water Board, "Our antiquated equipment just isn't doing the job.

We are still using some equipment that we first installed in 1896—and we purchased it secondhand from Philadelphia." The sewer system in Pittsburgh still has brick sections that date back to 1877. Such antiques are not uncommon throughout the East. In some places, wood-lined mains are still in use. About 150 million gallons of water a day are lost in Boston through leaks.

The Environmental Protection Agency estimates that municipalities would have to spend $96 billion to build the facilities necessary to meet requirements of the 1972 Water Pollution Control Act. To prevent pollution from industrial waste waters would cost another $54 billion.

A Rocky Road Ahead

The Federal Highway Administration estimates it would cost $23 billion to replace the more than one hundred thousand bridges that are officially classified as dangerous. In New York City, more than 1 million potholes are filled each year. Despite this effort, there were more than 35,000 lawsuits that involved defective sidewalks and potholes during the past seven years. These have cost the city more than $61 million in damages.

At current funding levels, New York City would complete replacement of their obsolete sewer system in 300 years. Parks specialists recommend that major repairs on public parks be based on a twenty-five year replacement rate; Manhattan is operating on a budget that allows for a nine hundred year replacement cycle. If the current level of city services is to be maintained, citizens are going to have to pay more than they are currently doing. There is no evidence that they are either willing or able to handle this burden.

American cities owe a staggering total of $200 billion in municipal debts. There is no historical precedent of any debt of this proportion having been paid off. Debts of this magnitude have always been repudiated—and no one is in a better position to do this than a government. Debts will continually be refinanced until no one is willing to accept the obviously empty pledges to pay and investors are left holding worthless paper. We have seen this happen in New York, and it will be repeated in cities across the country. *Business Week* magazine has editorialized:

New York's troubles are harbingers of a broader problem . . . the problems of New York City are not unique. By 1980, every one of the thirty cities in the United States with a population of more than one million will be in financial distress to some degree. These big cities are in big decline. They are all adding services and increasing public payrolls while the economic base deteriorates.

The Bronx Cheer

Economic commentator Howard J. Ruff has suggested that the South Bronx section of New York City is a microcosm of what will be happening across the country. This area has a population of about one-half million. In the 1960's, the job market became soft and welfare roles grew by 500 percent. When the unemployed head of a household took a job, his welfare benefits dropped one dollar for every dollar earned. Since the job was not likely to be terribly pleasant or significantly better paying than the welfare dole (the highest in the nation) many welfare recipients decided not to work at all. Today, almost 30 percent of the families are on some form of welfare. About half of the sixteen to twenty-one-year-olds have dropped out of school and almost two-thirds are unemployed.

In the last six years, burglaries went up 700 percent. There have been over 70,000 fires—about thirty every night. A third or more of these can be attributed to arson. Still, neighborhood welfare offices post notices that any tenant burned out of his apartment automatically will be entitled to a grant of up to $3,000 to cover the cost of new clothing, furniture, and moving. Burned-out families go to the top of the waiting list for public housing projects.

For those people who are determined to work, getting back and forth from their place of employment is an exercise in survival. It's just a matter of time until they are preyed upon by a mugger, junkie, or one of the eighty-nine organized street gangs in the neighborhood. Observers have described the scene as "battle-scarred and bombed-out."

If you live in any city of a population of over one million, how long has it been since you have walked (or even driven) through the worst ghetto in that city? If you aren't adventurous enough to take a firsthand observation, merely check the fire, police, and emergency room records next Monday morning.

THE DEATH OF A DREAM

A May, 1978, cover story of *Newsweek* magazine concluded:

> ... hardly anybody doubts that the nation is in trouble. In a Gallup poll released last week, 54% of the national sampling named inflation as the nation's worst problem—up dramatically from 33% just four months earlier.

Workers who earned $5,000 in 1960 must make $11,000 today just to stay even. Most of this increase is made necessary because of inflation. At higher income levels, tax increases sharpen the bite. Someone who earned $50,000 in 1960 would have to make three times that much today to keep his family's standard of living even. The Conference Board, a New York based economic research organization, suggests that in 1978 a family needed $34,065 of income to have the purchasing power of $19,751 in 1970. Cambridge Surveys (President Carter's polling organization) reports that, "In 1977, 25 percent of the public said there was no way to stop inflation. A year later the proportion was 50 percent."

While Chapter Three will provide much greater detail about the history and national impact of inflation, I do want to show you what has happened to the budget of the "average American family" in the past five years (see Table 1-1).

While I recognize that few of my readers will be "average" Americans, I find it almost impossible to believe that half of the families in this country are able to exist on less than the "moderate budget" suppositions of the Labor Department. While I find the official figures depressing by themselves, they fail to reveal three vitally important factors. They are:

1. *It is almost impossible to get by on what the "average family" is supposed to spend.* In developing this composite picture, analysts at the Bureau of Labor Statistics assume that the family's toaster lasts twenty-three years, that the vacuum cleaner is replaced once every fourteen years, and the television set will be around for a full de-

Table 1-1
The Impact of Inflation on Family Budgets

CATEGORY	1971	1977	Percentage Change
Food (this includes every grocery bill, restaurant lunch, and Big Mac)	$47 weekly	$ 79	+ 62%
Housing (mortgages, furniture, utilities, repairs, and cleaning)	$219 monthly	$ 335	+ 52%
Transportation (buying, insuring, repairing, fueling, and parking)	$964 yearly	$ 1,472	+ 53%
Clothing and Personal care (everything from lingerie to lipstick for the woman; business suits to jogging shoes for the man; back-to-school clothes and T-shirts for the children); beauty or barber shop and dry cleaning	$1196 yearly	$ 1,559	+ 30%
Medical Care (health insurance, doctor and dentist visits, prescriptions, cough medicine, and supposedly, allocations for braces, and hospitalization costs not covered by insurance.	$612 yearly	$ 985	+ 61%
Entertainment and Education and other Family consumption (KISS records, newspapers, television sets and repairs, vacations, movies, education expenses).	$684 yearly	$ 909	+ 33%
Misc. (X-mas gifts, life insurance, union dues, and other occupational expenses, etc.)	$560 yearly	$ 763	+ 36%
Social Security and Disability Taxes	$419 yearly	$ 961	+129%
Personal Income Taxes	$1366 yearly	$ 2,342	+ 71%
TOTAL	$10,971	$17,106	+ 56%

cade. The husband of this family buys one year-round suit every four years and a topcoat every eight and a half years. The family buys a two-year-old car, which it keeps for four years. The husband takes his wife out to a movie once every three months, and the two children will get to see a flick every four weeks.

For this family, the American dream is a cruel joke. With the cost of a year at a private college averaging $5,110, and state universities averaging about half as much, their children would do well to commute to a local community college. Their teeth had better be good, because this budget doesn't allow for a $1,800 orthodontist bill. Vacations, at best, will mean a steady diet of roadside hamburgers and cheap motels. Because of rampant inflation, the only way to keep up or to move ahead is to take an extra job, but more about that later.

2. *The inflation rate for necessities is rising faster than anything else.* A study by the Exploratory Project for Economic Alternatives reports that, "the annual rate of inflation for the four basic necessities (food, housing, energy, health care) was 44 percent greater than the annual inflation rate for non-necessities." If your major purchasing problems concern the choice of a new yacht, country club membership, or even an electric toothbrush, you may not notice inflation as much as if a significant portion of your budget goes for essentials.

3. *While your money buys less, the government takes more.* A fifth essential (in addition to food, housing, energy, and health care) has grown faster than anything else. According to official figures, taxes and Social Security deductions have grown more (up 85 percent) since 1971, than any other category. The government is responsible for rapid inflation in all categories, and it benefits most from the increasing cost of everything.

The total cost of government is significantly higher than those figures suggest. In reality, government now costs the average family more than food, shelter, and clothing combined. Do you wonder why people are more upset about the taxes today than at any time since the Boston Tea Party?

. . . THE BEHINDER I GET

There are a few categories of workers who have managed to stay ahead of inflation. These include: coal miners, auto workers, and disabled veterans. Other groups, such as retail clerks, school teachers, bank employees, construction workers, and farmers have lagged behind. If you wish to look behind the official figures released by the Department of Labor, you will find that the average wage earner has not kept up, but, in fact, has lost ground when you take into account the taxes he has to pay, the quality of goods and services received, and the number of dollars required to purchase necessities. Dr. Claud Raines of Temple University has concluded that the purchasing power of the average worker's paycheck peaked in 1965.

The Economic Unit of *U.S. News & World Report* has estimated that inflation and higher tax brackets reduced the "real" income for the average American family between 1973 and 1978. Consumer prices rose by 46 percent during this period. A $50,000-a-year executive in 1973 would probably be making $73,000 in 1978. Despite this $23,000 raise, inflation would have cost him $16,295, and a higher tax bracket would reduce his true income by another $9,509. Instead of making $23,000 per year more, he has actually lost $2,804 in buying power. An average production employee who is married with two children would have moved from making $7,550 per year to $10,600. Yet the real income would be down $188. A single pensioner living on Social Security would have gained $885 because of benefit increases, but lost $911 to the inflation tax.

Surprisingly, middle-level executives have been especially hard hit. According to a survey by David Kraus of McKinsey & Company, an internationally respected management consulting firm, the real pay of middle-level executives dropped an average of 27 percent between 1964 and 1976, when taxes and inflation are considered. During this time, middle managers were receiving the smallest annual increases of any group of employees—averaging only about 3 percent per year.

Dr. Franz Pick, a leading monetary analyst for over thirty years, concurs. He points out that between 1940 and 1975 dollar wages have increased nearly 570 percent. The inflation index would reduce this increase to a real improvement of about 75 percent. According to Pick's research, between 1940 and 1975 the real purchasing power of the average worker's income dropped almost 9 percent. My own analysis of Raines', Pick's, and official data leads me to conclude that the real purchasing power of the average worker increased almost 60 percent between 1940 and 1965. Between 1965 and the present, however, the income for middle-class families who have not supplemented their earnings by extra jobs has lost about a third of their purchasing power. For many, extra jobs have provided the only means of staying up with the treadmill of inflation.

Moonlight Sonata

The number of individuals holding two or more jobs is currently approaching 5 million. During the 1970's, the number of moonlighters has increased almost 20 percent and the number of women holding multiple jobs has doubled. Moreover, the average family today has 1.7 workers in it. About half of the families making $17,000 (the 1978 median income) do so only because two members of the family work. Moonlighting, working wives, exhaustion, persistent worry, and fighting over money is the spotlight that shines through the picture window of middle-American homes. We dream of upward mobility, affluence, and getting ahead, but in reality we find ourselves quibbling with children about their allowances, skipping an annual physical check-up, and cashing in insurance policies. Epidemic advances in alcoholism, drug addiction, divorce, and early heart attacks are not unrelated to financial pressures created by this race for the good life.

In the long run, not just individuals, but all society loses to inflation. Tensions between labor and management, between the government and the people, and eventually between social and economic classes become dangerous. "These tensions," says Gardner Ackley, professor of economics at the University of Michigan and onetime chief economic advisor to President Lyndon Johnson, "are destructive of the social and political fabric." Ackley adds, "The significant real cost of inflation is what it does to morale, to social coherence, and the people's attitudes toward each other."

"Middle-class earners feel rotten because a lot of them have not kept up with the median," says economist Rudolph G. Penner of the American Economic Institute. "The polls show that the general public is compassionate over the poor, but that is easier when your own share of the economic pie is growing. When your share is not growing and benefits are seen rising for the disadvantaged, there is bitterness."

In the past this bitterness has been kept in check because the United States emerged from short-term setbacks with a sense of increased potential for everyone. In mid-1978, *Business Week* concluded:

> . . . Now the economic outlook is clouded, inflation is no longer waning, and the country could be headed into the worst period of economic and social dislocations since the civil war.

The Rainy Day Is Here

With the ravages of continuing inflation, it is not surprising that Americans are finding it almost impossible to save. In the past decade, the percentage of income allocated to savings has dropped by 33 percent. While some Americans do manage to put aside some money (5.1 percent), the rate is among the lowest in major industrialized countries. Canadians save almost 10 percent of their income. In Great Britain and West Germany, the savings rate is almost 14 percent; in France it is over 16 percent, and the Japanese save 21.5 percent of their after-tax income. The American inability to save suggests the meager resources that we have to fall back on in case of personal or national financial problems. It also indicates that it will be very difficult for a country to secure the needed capital for new jobs throughout the future.

By the way, in the next decade we will need almost 27 million new jobs. This works out ot almost 72,000 new jobs each week if the people entering the job market are to find employment. It appears certain that there will not be enough capital to create these needed jobs.

While Americans are finding it hard to save, we are experiencing absolutely no difficulty in borrowing. In 1977, individuals took on nearly $143 billion of new debt, a record increase that raised total outstanding personal debt above the trillion-dollar level for the first time. These private debts range from charge accounts to student loans to home mortgages, and in July, 1978, totaled $1 trillion, 162 billion. This comes to approximately $4,748 per person. The largest amount (62 percent) is for home mortgages.

A House Is Not A Home

Today, two of every three American families own their own homes, a far higher proportion than in many other industrial nations. While foreign visitors may be shocked by the squalor of big city slums, they are awed by the conveniences and comforts of the houses where middle-income Americans live. But achieving the dream of home ownership exacts a demanding price. Sixty percent of the first-time house buyers are families in which both husband and wife hold jobs. Many couples have to make the choice between having a house or a child—and more than ever before, they are choosing the house. More than half of all married women with school-age children hold some type of job. Couples with no children under age eighteen now make up 47 percent of all families. In the first six years of the 1970's, median family income (in inflated dollars rather than buying power) rose 47 percent, while the monthly cost of owning a home increased over 100 percent. The cost of utilities and property taxes are rising just as fast as housing prices.

One of my students, who grew up in Santa Barbara, California, said that his parents purchased a tract home in 1954 for $16,000. On a VA loan, they only had to put up $1 as a down payment. In 1978, they sold this same house for $104,-000. Within a single year, the average housing price rose in San Diego 30 percent. California is always unique, but this dramatizes what is happening on a smaller scale throughout the nation.

While a significant number of problems facing the American family are economic in nature, the pressures often manifest themselves in other ways. The family itself seems under attack because of changing moral values and contemporary stress. The U.S. divorce rate is the world's highest. Thirty-eight percent of all first marriages fail. Forty percent of the children born during the 1970's will spend part of their childhood in a single-parent family. Almost 20 percent of all children under eighteen are now living in single-parent families, and remarriage has created new family units for approximately 18 million stepchildren.

PERIL IN THE PEPSI GENERATION

Children are learning the harsh realities of contemporary life at a very early age! There are almost 500,000 babies born each year out of wedlock (15 percent of all births). Most of these are to women in their teens and early twenties. Fifty percent are to teenagers. The Department of Health, Education, and Welfare believes, "There is definitely a high correlation between out-of-wedlock births, welfare costs, and many of our most pressing social problems."

One major impact is the $11.7 billion spent yearly in federal, state, and local aid to families with dependent children, the welfare program for poor families with no father at home. The Urban Institute in Washington has conducted research that suggests that women who begin the drift toward dependency as teenage mothers cost taxpayers about $6 billion a year in welfare payments.

Depending on which state they live in, most teenage mothers with one illegitimate child can qualify for payments of $100 to $150 per month. To the average mature, middle-class citizen, this doesn't seem like much. But to a fourteen- or fifteen-year-old ghetto teenager, it is a bigger allowance than she has ever received. She will probably continue living at home and qualify for food stamps, thus her food may cost only one-fourth of the regular price. She and her child can receive free medical care and she may have regular homemaker service to help with domestic chores. In many cities, free day-care services are available. Despite this financial support, these mothers usually have no effective model for mothering. Consequently, they reinforce the behavior patterns that led them into dependency and repeat this destructive cycle with their own children.

University of Maryland sociologist Harriet B. Presser has studied the characteristics of unwed mothers and reports that half of them are in school when they become pregnant and half of these drop out. Nearly two-thirds have no high school diploma and only 44 percent have any work experience. As a result, only half are able to get even temporary employment during the first four years of motherhood. Ten percent of all girls between fifteen and nineteen get pregnant. Within a year of giving birth, one-fourth of these teenage mothers are pregnant again.

While writing this book, I realized how serious HEW was about the problem. The office of research at my university sent out a memorandum reporting that the agency was requesting research proposals "designed to explore the reasons for teenage pregnancy." Although I am not a sociologist, I think I have a sneaking suspicion how teenagers get pregnant. Unless some basic law of biology has been repealed, the process by which teenagers become pregnant is remarkably similar to the process by which other people achieve this condition. According to the HEW study, 80 percent of all black, unmarried girls and half of their white counterparts have had intercourse. Moreover, only 30 percent of the sexually active teenagers use contraceptives.

Teenage marriages are twice as likely to fail as marriages where both partners are in their twenties. Teenagers are more frequent crime victims than adults are now or were during their younger years. Murder is the second leading cause of death among Americans between the ages of fifteen and twenty-four. Forty percent of high school students have been the victims of violent crimes such as robbery, assault, or murder.

A 1978 report by the Ford Foundation notes that the number of juveniles arrested for violent crimes such as homicide, rape, robbery, and assault rose 293 percent during the past fifteen years and is increasing at more than double the rate of increase in the adult arrests for violent crimes. In large cities, the courts probably deal with less than 5 percent of the violent crimes committed by juveniles. While youth violence is more extensive in large cities, surburban and rural crime is increasing even more rapidly. Research in rural and small town Oregon shows that one-fourth of all boys were caught committing crimes at least once during their adolescence.

Education was once used as the means of improving one's lot in life. Today, the quality of education and intellectual attainment seems to be declining. Prospects for jobs, even if an education is obtained, are discouraging. Until recently, there was good evidence to support the claim that a college education paid off financially and helped a person become a better informed citizen. Today, the financial value of a college degree, especially in the arts or humanities, is in question. The estimated rate of return on the money spent for college fell from 12 percent in 1969 to about 6 percent at present. (This figure is computed from projected lifetime earnings of the college graduate minus tuition and other costs such as lost income while in college.)

Today, about one-third of men graduates and two-thirds of women with college degrees are taking jobs unrelated to their academic majors. In the early 1970's, the rate was 10 percent and 13 percent respectively. In a *New York Times* article, Fred Mechinger has asked, "Will we turn out useless and therefore disgruntled graduates? Will the United States repeat the dangerous example of Germany and Italy in the 1920's—create an unemployed, alienated, and politically menacing proletariat?" This rhetorical question is based on the fact that one-third of the SS officers in Nazi Germany had Ph.D.'s. There is clear evidence of disenchantment among men and women who face menial jobs or unemployment. For in addition to their frustration of lost income, they must also accept the loss of social status and their claim to the "good life." Thirty percent of all workers are "underemployed"—that is, their qualifications exceed the real requirements for the job they are currently holding.

Enrollment in public schools across the country dropped 2.3 percent between 1971 and 1976, but the cost of education rose 56 percent during the period. Between 1962 and 1977, the scores on the Scholastic Aptitude Tests (a standardized examination taken annually by 1.5 million high school juniors and seniors) have dropped over 10 percent. The valedictorian at a Washington D.C. high school was shocked to find that his SAT scores just weren't high enough to admit him to a local college. At Ohio State University, 1,700 of the 1977–78 freshman class of 7,100 had to take remedial English, and 2,-000 had to take remedial Math (and even Ohio State doesn't have that many varsity athletes). Federal funds are being expended to teach high school students how to read. Some states are passing competency requirements that suggest that high school seniors have to be able to read and write before they can receive their high school diploma. In 1978, Joseph Califano, Secretary of HEW, pointed out that in the last three years the number of Americans rating the public schools as good or excellent has fallen almost 25 percent.

There may be good reason for the general distrust. The two largest school districts in Texas have begun to give proficiency tests to prospective teachers. At the initial testing in Houston, 150 applicants took the widely used Stanford Achievement Test. One-third scored below average eleventh grade level in English and about half performed below that level in Math. In Dallas, 849 prospective teachers were given a similar exam. Over a third failed to achieve what school system administrators viewed as acceptable scores. To compound the embarrassment, a reporter gave the same exam to a group of students at one of the leading private schools in

Dallas. These high schoolers significantly outperformed the teaching prospects.

Drug addiction, alcoholism, and unemployment are epidemic among teenagers. At an early age, some of the brightest decide that they cannot cope with the world that has been created for them.

THE WORK ETHIC IS OUT ON STRIKE

I have already shown that the earning power of the average American worker has declined. This may be partially because American workers aren't producing the way they once did. American ingenuity and productivity used to be the envy of the world. Something has gone wrong with the productivity and quality of American industry. Part of the problem may be due to the rigid and sometimes arbitrary hiring and safety standards imposed by the federal government. Some of the failing may be due to bad management and some to creaky old factories. It is also clear that significant portions of the labor force have lost the American work ethic. Whatever the reason, the United States now lags behind most of the other developed countries in its growth of manufacturing productivity. Some observers feel that this problem stands at the very center of the inflation issue. In the first two decades following World War II, American industrial productivity grew at an annual rate of 3.3 percent. Since 1973, the rate has dropped to 1.3 percent.

In almost 40 percent of the key industries studied by the Department of Labor, productivity actually declined. Official productivity figures reflect a combination of new technology and worker initiative. Higher prices for material and labor make it difficult for companies to invest in new capital. In 1978, American business spent nearly $100 million to meet new pollution controls and safety regulations that reduced growth of productivity by 25 percent. Unions oppose new equipment that they fear will cause a loss of jobs. The sum result of what has taken place during the past decade can be expressed in the following table:

Annual Rates of Productivity Growth

Japan	6.8%
Denmark	6.6%
West Germany	5.3%

Italy	5.3%
France	5.2%
Sweden	4.5%
Canada	3.5%
Britain	2.5%
United States	2.3%

You won't be surprised to learn that the quality, as well as the quantity, of output has declined. In 1977 and 1978, Detroit had to recall more cars than they sold. As we saw earlier, the Bureau of Labor Statistics assumes that the average family's toaster will last twenty-three years and the vacuum will be working for fourteen. Where can you find products like these? Most modern products break down even before planned obsolescence sets in.

Problems with productivity and product quality affect all sectors of society. Whether you look at unemployment, income, welfare dependence, or any other measure of the quality of life, minority groups seem to reflect the worst of the statistics. If you accept the evidence presented thus far about the problem of the middle class, think about the plight of the people who have little hope of achieving that degree of status.

THE FUTURE IS BLEAK FOR BLACKS

While there have been significant gains in the number of middle-class black families, it is obvious that despite the best efforts of the war on poverty, the great society, civil rights legislation, and forced busing, black families are still experiencing economic problems of even greater magnitude than any other segment of American society. Recent progress in the war on poverty has not included many members of the black community. The number of blacks classified as poor in 1977 rose to almost 8 million individuals. This was the highest level in a decade. Real income for black families is estimated at $9,563—the lowest level in almost a decade. The ratio of black family income to white family income has dropped to 57.1 percent. In other words, the average black family makes only a little more than half of the median family income for whites.

The unemployment rate for blacks is twice that of the general population. Among adult males, the unemployment rate for whites is 4 percent, for blacks, twice that. Among white teenagers, unemployment is 14 percent; for black teenagers, the rate is an unbelievable 39 percent. While 14 percent of people below 18 are black, they account for 22 percent of all juvenile arrests and 52 percent of all juvenile arrests for violence.

Almost 40 percent of all black households are headed by women. In the past decade, illegitimacy has risen from 25 percent of all births to 50 percent of all black children born. Two of every five black children in the country are receiving financial assistance from welfare from the Aid to Dependent Children Program. In the past two decades, black suicides have risen by 33 percent—almost three times as fast as the rate for the rest of the population. Homicide is the leading cause of death among black males under thirty.

The black section in any major city is a tinderbox. Poverty, prejudice, grandiose promises, and unreachable dreams are a highly flammable combination. For every successful black who has escaped the ghetto prison, there are ten who have seen the promised land but found that they can't pass the entrance exams. The real villain in this tragedy is the slick-talking politician who bought votes by making totally unrealistic promises. In some ways, the obvious hypocrites were less dangerous than the well-meaning simpletons who tried to fulfill their promises when resources were not adequate. These ill-fated programs so clogged the financial machinery of the economy that real progress was impeded.

The statistics mentioned earlier in this section merely confirm the hypothesis that the "American Dream" is more illusionary for blacks and other minorities than the mainstream of U.S. society. This frustration, coupled with resentment that has built up for decades, has created a highly explosive situation in almost any city with a sizable minority population. We'll see in Chapter Four how this may be ignited in our depression scenario.

THE ITALIAN CONNECTION

Many observers believe that some of the shadows of the future for the United States may be seen in what has taken place in Italy.

Like the United States, Italy enjoyed an economic boom in the 1950's and 1960's. The boom has run its course, and large numbers of Italians, especially young people, feel that they are the victims of broken promises and empty dreams. Of 1.6 million unemployed Italians, 63 percent are under thirty and a fifth of these have university degrees.

In 1977, reported crimes in Italy rose 7.5 percent over the previous year to a total of 2,009,000. Eighty percent of these crimes remain unsolved. Kidnappings for profit and politics total ninety in a single year, and since 1970, kidnappers have netted $175.5 million in ransom money. A plague of riots, lootings, kidnappings, and bombings has contributed to the new "Dark Age" in Italy.

Much of the violence is the work of 115 identifiable political movements. Ninety-four of these groups belong to the far left. The remaining twenty-one can be classified as neo-fascist right. There were more than 2,000 terror-connected bombings in Italy in 1977, almost double the number reported for the previous year. In one year (1977), police seized 11,441 small arms, 937,711 bombs, and almost 15,000 pounds of explosives. Industrial sabotage and arson caused over $55 million worth of damage to factories. University students rioted and damaged computers and laboratory instruments in protest over bleak job prospects. Security devices and hiding have become major growth industries. Businesses that specialize in making ordinary cars into armor-plated fortresses have a back-log of orders. Costs range from a $7,000 conversion fee for a compact Fiat 127 to $30,000 for a Rolls Royce. There are approximately four hundred firms employing a private army of over 20,000 security agents who hire out as bodyguards for $150 to $230 a day. Trained German shepherds sell for almost $6,000, and Italians bought $7 million worth in 1977.

More and more wealthy Italians are moving out of the country, or at least setting up another residence. As might be expected, their government has made it difficult for them to take enough resources with them to support themselves in the manner in which they would like to become reaccustomed. Many have succeeded in spite of the law forbidding them to take more than $580 in lire out of the country. Recently, there has been a major crack-down. In April, 1978, actress Sophia Loren and her husband, Carlo Ponti, were charged with having illegally transported several million dollars abroad.

Several familiar ingredients are in this description: the end of an economic boom, high unemployment (especially among

the young), restrictions on personal freedom, increasing inflation, crime and violence, as well as the agonizing death of a
dream of a better life.

Without doubt, Italy is farther down the dangerous road
we are traveling. Yet our depression will not replicate the
latest decline and fall of the Roman Empire. Stay with me
and we'll review the unique handwriting on the wall that
describes our own fearful future.

CHAPTER TWO

Signs of the Times

The decision to write this book occurred on Monday, February 27, 1978, as I was reading the *Wall Street Journal*. On the first page of this single issue, I noticed the following headlines: The U.S. Moves To Bolster The Faltering Dollar, Lack of Confidence Is Cited; Jimmy Carter Is Getting Worried About the Stock Market—First Democratic President Since World War II To See A Falling Stock Market In The First Year After The Election; Prolonged Market Declines Foreshadow Recession; Some Church Bonds Plunging Into Default—Investor Losses Mount; Machine Orders Fell In January; Bankrupt W. T. Grant Trustee Agrees With Twenty-Six Lenders On A Settlement Of $650 Million; Manufacturers Hanover Trust Is Focus Of Union Hostility; Coal Pack Proposal Faces An Uphill Battle for Rank-and-File Ratification; The Swiss Government Moves To Curb Foreign Demand For Its Franc.

When a single issue of a traditionally conservative and positive publication such as the *Wall Street Journal* chronicles these kinds of problems, then it becomes obvious that something is afoot. For several years, as my horizons broadened, I had been concerned about economic trends. This single day's summary of financial news prompted me to do more intensive research. I was amazed to find that almost every segment of society was reporting equally discouraging indicators for the future. The more I looked into it the more pervasive the pessimism appeared to be.

I had no desire to become a prophet of doom. I have chuckled, as I am sure you have, at the cartoons of be-whiskered guys in robes and sandals walking the city sidewalks with their placards announcing the impending end. That isn't my self-image . . . and yet, the more widely I read, the more fields I explored . . . the more consistent be-

came the warning cries of the leading spokesmen in each
field.

ALL ROADS LEAD TO . . . ?

My research leaves me with the inescapable conclusion that
we are racing toward catastrophe on several separate but
related routes: monetary and fiscal policy, government spending (especially welfare), pollution, overregulation, food supplies, defense, crime, education, and morality. I don't see an
approaching *end* of the world, but rather a time of dramatic
reversal of things we take for granted. The upheavals will be
so great and so unanticipated that they will alter the majority
of the social structure we know today. It is quite likely that a
few simple preparations and adjustments by those who anticipate the future will result not only in survival, but prosperity
in the brave new world that follows.

Success has always favored those who could read the signs
of coming events and make appropriate adjustments even
though everyone else was ignoring (or even laughing at) the
warnings. Remember, it wasn't raining when Noah first
started to build his ark. His neighbors ridiculed him for over
a hundred years as he began to build that monstrous boat in
his back yard. You too may be laughed at if you begin now
to make preparations for a very difficult kind of life style.
My task in this chapter is to consider the evidence. The decision and the action, of course, have to be your own. I can
only share with you the evidence that has convinced me that
special preparations are essential.

THE HISTORIANS: STUDY THE PAST
OR BE DOOMED TO REPEAT IT

Scholars who study the cycles and stages of history are not
very encouraging about the future of Western civilization.
Historians can contribute a perspective that most of us lack
because they are *by necessity* in the habit of looking at centuries and millennia rather than the short term to which we
are most accustomed. Nevertheless, when an historian
describes a likely result of a national trend and then it doesn't
happen immediately, the warnings may be discounted.

There are several key examples of the general population's
inability to think long term. One is the well-known work of

Professor Arnold Toynbee on the traits of Ancient Rome in its declining days. Since Toynbee's ideas were first advanced in the 1930's, their impact has gradually reduced with each passing year. "I've heard that stuff about Rome and America all my life," responds a friend today, "and the country is still here and doing just as well or better than when Toynbee first came out with it."

What that friend is overlooking—what so many of us overlook—is the insignificance of the mere forty or fifty years in the history of a nation. Americans have often pointed in derision at the changing governments of France, Italy, and "banana republics." Yet we forget to compare our 200-year history with the 2,000-year history of most European countries. There is most definitely confirmation in history of the basic principles and national cycles suggested by Toynbee. What's more, those same principles were proposed by Plato and others from much earlier days and have been reinforced over and over again.

Platonic Prophecy

Plato's description of the cycle said that the first national stage was the emergence and power of one person (either a dictator or a monarch). As time passes, this one person's power is spread among a few (either with the consent of the one or against his wishes). More rulers are included as the nation moves to a position of democracy (in which the majority are ruling). As the abuses of democracy proliferate, the minorities begin to seek their own through unlawful means (which leads to corruption or anarchy). As these conditions of lawlessness become more prevalent and more threatening to the majority, the stage is set for the reintroduction of a dictator or anyone who will take charge, short-circuit the troublesome individual rights, and restore order and security. With this dictator in power, the cycle begins again.

Over fifty years ago, the German philosopher Otto Spengler predicted "The Decline of the West." Basically, he agreed with the cycle described by Plato. He also added the idea that as the people gained a victory over the aristocracy, there would also be a victory of the city over the country, money over principle, and of the immediate gratification over tradition. These forces, he felt, would ultimately lead to primitive conditions that would replace civilized life. Of the advanced countries such as England, France, and the U.S., he concluded that "Race suicide set in long ago."

For our purposes in this book, we can begin by surrendering any hopes that humans are solving the cyclical problems. The trappings and settings with which each new generation surrounds itself may look different, but the basic flaws of greed and selfishness and violence remain to maintain the historic cycles. Mankind seems to encounter the same basic problems whether he wears a toga to Rome or dacron polyester to Washington. Don't waste your own planning time hoping that humans will do better. Plan—by the assumption that the cycles are set. If things *do* change for the better, you will be even better off than you planned. If not, you and your family will be as well prepared as possible to enter the next stage of evolution.

The Roman Tradition and U.S.

The similarities between the histories of Rome and the United States may already be obvious to you. Consider, for example, that Rome's time ran out when she:

1. got most of her people off the farms and into the cities where they more rapidly communicated counterproductive demands and disastrous panics;
2. found herself importing more than she was exporting;
3. became burdened with social welfare efforts to support the masses who were becoming harder to please and ever more antagonistic;
4. allowed a single essential group to take control (in Rome, it was the army. For us it could be the military-industrial complex, the labor unions, or simply the poor);
5. saw the emphasis on the "people to be pleased" move down from the aristocracy to the middle class and then to the lower class;
6. had everybody adopting the values of the lower classes instead of modeling after and aspiring for the upper classes;
7. suffered continuously escalating inflation and the resulting public assumption that such economic spiraling was normal and natural;

8. was unable to provide general safety and protection for the citizens because of ever-increasing groups that took the law into their own hands;

9. declared that every member of society was equal and deserved to have whatever any other member had;

10. had a rise in superstitious beliefs, astrology, religion, and any other escape philosophies that promised a better world to come;

11. entered a time of political purges and revenge;

12. was faced with reluctant trading partners in other countries of her world;

13. lost a steady stream of food and essential supplies because of weather reverses;

14. gave up the pursuit of artistic and technical superiority; and

15. began a final era of corruption and intrigue that left a society in which no one could be trusted or depended upon.

Of the thirty-two civilizations the earth has seen, Toynbee says that over half have collapsed and half of the rest are in a terminal condition. The distinguished historian himself concluded after his impressive study ". . . Death the Leveler will lay his icy hand on our civilization also." There is little purpose to be served by our debating the likelihood that our own nation will succumb to these same weaknesses. The indicators are present in our situation without question. The next five years will reveal whether or not society has been able to learn the lessons of history or will simply repeat them. In either case, you will need to be prepared. You will be wasting valuable resources and earning power if you withdraw into a state of readiness too quickly. On the other hand, you want to plan your trajectory so that you are prepared for the worst just before the worst arrives.

The American historian Crane Brinton has analyzed four major historical revolutions. These are the French Revolution, the American Revolution, the Russian Revolution, and the Glorious Revolution of England in 1688. Crane found that conditions preceding each of these revolutions had a striking degree of commonality. Among these were the presence of bitter class antagonisms, ineffective operation of governmental machinery, potential approaching bankruptcy of the government, and a loss among the ruling class of confi-

dence about their traditions, with many members of the upper class moving over to support the values of attacking
groups. All these conditions sound strikingly familiar to the
observer of Western civilizations.

The evidence is overwhelming that our present system of
dealing with populations and their subgroups has built-in
self-defeating characteristics. There will definitely be a nation
between the Atlantic and Pacific during the 1990's, but it is
almost certain to have a different personality from the one we
know today.

THE FUTURISTS: THE FLOWERS OF ALL THE TOMORROWS LIE IN THE SEEDS OF TODAY

In view of the serious trends in world population growth,
food shortages, and political tension, maybe we should arrange to get the best minds in the world together and give
them free rein and plenty of resources to explore the possibilities and tell us what to expect and how to prepare for it.

It's a good plan, but it's already been done. The findings
were documented, startling, and almost totally ignored. The
whole effort was valuable in its ability to prove that the majority of humanity will not listen to sensible warnings. You,
on the other hand, may have the kind of individual drive to
prepare for your part of the world winddown predicted in
1972 by the prestigious Club of Rome.

This highest-level think-tank was founded by Aurelio Pec-
cei, an Italian economist and management consultant who got
his start as an expert by making Olivetti an international corporation. He invited the participation of the best brains in the
world from business and scientific endeavor and began in
1968 an organization with the purpose of exploring the most
basic issue confronting society: survival.

With a quarter-million-dollar grant from Volkswagen, the
Club of Rome gathered data that could have impact on the
world's future survival. The data included both hard statistics
and subjective judgments from many of the world's best thinkers on the various component topics. All this information
was fed into the giant computer at M.I.T. with an intricate
program that could not only simulate the major ecological
forces at work in the world, but also compensate for the interlocked nature of these influences. For example, the growth
of human population requires more food and less pollution.

We cannot have more food without increases in industrial products to facilitate natural growth methods. More industrial process results in more pollution and fewer natural resources. Pollution ultimately interferes with everything and, according to the computer projections, everything winds to a halt with the survivors living a sort of primitive agricultural life trying to grow crops in the medians of deserted interstate highways and to capture rainwater next to poisonous, polluted rivers.

It sounds like the ravings of a wild science fiction writer, and yet these projections have been verified and crosschecked by countless computer runs. The findings have been questioned, but never successfully denied. My feeling is that they may have been overly optimistic. Common sense dictates that there has to be an end to the use of raw materials that cannot replenish themselves.

Limits to Growth?

The Club of Rome's revelation that may prove harder for the American people to accept is the idea that continued growth is literally going to kill us. *Growth* has become a religion with our economy and it is almost impossible for us to imagine an economic problem that cannot be solved by continued growth. If a company is selling its product below costs, there is no way that the difference will be made up in volume.

According to the Club of Rome report, economic population growth has to stop almost immediately, or shortly after the arrival of the next century the population, food production, and pollution curves, along with the supply of natural resources, will converge for a catastrophic collapse. The life style of those who survive will center on getting food and maintaining life at the simplest possible levels.

What about the Happy Ending?

At about this point in the story, we are accustomed to the introduction of the happy ending. We are prepared to hear a voice say, "However, if we will *stop* doing these things and *start* doing these we will be able to avoid the events that have been described." Unfortunately, there are no happy endings in these predictions of the future. In fact, the computer analyzed various alternative situations and in every case came back with discouraging results. What if there are other undiscovered reserves of natural resources (perhaps under the oceans)? The computer answers that industrialization will accelerate with runaway pollution. What if new technological devices are found to control pollution? Population would soar, and soon the land's food-producing ability would lose out. What if pollution were abated, the birthrate halved, and food production doubled? Even then, responds the computer, the pollution generated to produce and process the food will ultimately outdistance the earth's ability to assimilate it.

There is no happy ever after. It appears that if the M.I.T. models are correct, we may have already gone too far down a self-destructive path toward unrelenting growth. The next steps can only be those of compensating, not correcting. The breakdown of society and of the life support systems in major portions of this planet is inevitable—possibly by the end of this century and certainly within the lifetime of your children.

Recently the Club of Rome was pressured to reexamine its data. Pressure applied when the results of the study first came out caused the same research team to come out with a modified set of conclusions. They suggested that possibly if the rich nations began to give very large amounts of aid to the poor nations, it would be technically possible for us to avoid the kind of prospect described in the first report's limits to growth. If you analyze the data carefully and read between the lines, you will find that according to their projections sometime in the early 1980's we will reach a point of no return. Without control of population growth and economic growth, events will be set in motion that simply cannot be reversed. Eventually some major adjustment (i.e. worldwide famine or war) will be necessary to rebalance the relationship between supply and demand of the world's life-sustaining material resources.

Lest it appear that this entire case rests upon the Club of Rome study, two other major futurists reached the same conclusion while using different procedures. In his follow-up to his global best-seller, *Future Shock*, Alvin Toffler describes an *"Eco-Spasm"* that has the potential of destroying the life style that made his prior book so successful. Like any sensible observer of global trends, Toffler concludes that adapting to the manmade marvels projected in *Future Shock* may not be the world's greatest challenge. Instead, he comes back to the hauntingly familiar theme of survival.

An Italian computer wizard and systems expert, Robert Vacca, has predicted the collapse of technology and of modern life in his book, *The Coming Dark Age*. Vacca shows how all the major systems on which we depend (transport, electrical, garbage removal, postal, telephone, and so on) are hopelessly overloaded, poorly planned, badly managed, and about to crack. While his homeland shows ominous signs of this breakdown, Vacca believes that the collapse will be signaled by the major failures (between 1985 and 1994) in the United States and Japan. A collapse in one system will instigate a collapse of another, and then another—until the catastrophe becomes worldwide.

Signs to support this thesis are already apparent. These include massive power failures, fuel shortages, chronic traffic jams, deteriorating mail services, and paralyzing garbage strikes. Commenting on Vacca's book, the world's most famous science fiction writer, Isaac Asimov, said, "I have never read a book that was at one and the same time so convincing and so frightening."

THE ECONOMISTS: A DISMAL SCIENCE BECOMES MORE DISMAL

In April, 1978, the *Futurist* magazine featured an important article entitled "Smith, Marx, and Malthus—Ghosts to Haunt Our Future." The article explored the kinds of society envisioned by three key economists, Adam Smith, Karl Marx, and Thomas Malthus. While the first two presented economic models for activity (neither of which is currently in use anywhere in the world, although we assume that Smith's model is the foundation for the "free-societies" and Marx is the patron saint of communist countries), Malthus was the most predictive. Known as the "Gloomy Parson" because of his dreary vision, Malthus presents a cruel future dominated by the specters of famine, pestilence, plague, disease, and war. Reverend Malthus saw a world driven by uncontrollable forces. While I was a student of economics in the 1950's, my professors ridiculed the naivete of Malthus's pessimism. Today, his concerns are widely shared by two growing camps of economic analysts, contemporary Jeremiahs and mainline economists.

The best hope is that there will be a series of minicollapses during the next thirty years that will relieve some of the strain and pressures on the overburdened support system of the *planet*. This is what I expect will happen during the next decade. I genuinely believe that a severe crisis during the 1980's is preferable to a complete global collapse in thirty or forty years. Our culture has adopted the philosophy of "Fly now and pay later." The time has come for us to make the payment. It will be painful for us to settle our debts, but if we fail, our debts will settle us.

The Modern Jeremiahs

In the Old Testament, a Jewish prophet named Jeremiah incurred the disfavor of his people by constantly lamenting the imminent downfall of his culture. Today, an impressive number of modern Jeremiahs with conservative economic backgrounds are bowing at a golden shrine and prophesying of "tribulations and desolations." Chances are this is not the first book that you have seen decrying the coming calamity or suggesting ways to survive it. The mails are filled with newsletters from a host of prophets who provide regular doses of personal opinions, evidence of trends, and tidbits of sound advice. Several of these publications are reviewed in the appendix of this book.

The new Jeremiahs do practice what they preach. The gold-silver doctrine was dramatized by Harry Browne, author of the best-seller *You Can Profit from a Monetary Crisis*, when he told a *Newsweek* reporter, "When we are in the middle of the crisis, a pound of beef may be selling for $80 million—or two silver coins. The next week, the price will be $80 billion—or two silver coins. People will realize it's not worth using paper currency and they'll switch to other media of exchange."

Browne, whose writing and investment success has enabled him to take his own advice, recently sold his lavish $250,000 home in the mountains overlooking Vancouver, British Columbia, and moved to Switzerland. He maintains a wilderness retreat from economic disaster stocked with a year's supply of food and other essentials for independence and survival. Janes Dines, who authors the *Dines Letter*, is also contemplating a move to Switzerland before the major political shift "either to the far right or the far left" that he expects to occur following the huge market shake-up "and the fall of all pension systems and the Dow Jones."

The author of *The International Harry Schultz Letter* publishes two other reports on a monthly basis. The first is *Gold and Other Currencies,* which deals with how international events affect the gold market. This four-page document sells for $10.00 a copy. He also publishes *Exodus,* a monthly eight-pager (sells for $13.00 a copy) that explores options that are available to individuals seeking foreign havens.

Schultz's consultation fee is $1,250 per hour during the week or $2,500 per hour on Saturday or Sunday. (Fees payable in advance.) If you have a question that can be answered within three minutes, Schultz has a special $100 "quickie" rate, but anything above that becomes $312 for his quarter-hour rate. Although maintaining several plush residences around the world, Schultz has identified Amsterdam as a place where he feels he will be better situated to meet the coming crunch.

Among the newest and most successful members of the tribe is Howard J. Ruff, a California-based Mormon, who edits a bi-weekly newsletter, produces his own television program (carried by about sixty stations), and maintains a staff of thirty to help answer his nationwide WATS line, do research, and plan for conventions. *The Ruff Times* has over 45,000 subscribers who pay $105 a year to read Ruff's insight about the plight of the cities, investment or financial strategies, and the importance of a two-year food supply. Ruff reports that his subscription rate runs .4 of 1 percent of mailings. With 45,000 subscribers, that means that he has sent out over 10 million pieces of direct mail.

Other newsletters zero in on tax havens, the purchase and holding of gold and silver, the avoidance of taxes, the best times and places to consider if you are going to leave the United States. I have personally read and reviewed more than twenty of the leading newsletters. Many of them I have found quite helpful in doing research for this book. The appendix summarizes the major features of several of these.

As I will stress throughout the book, the nature of any prediction or advice is that it remains ultimately a guess about what is going to happen. Maybe an educated guess, but it has to be a guess. Any advice can aid you only as long as you maintain perspective about your information source. No expert is able to perfectly foretell the future and outline exactly what you need to do to come out on top. You can, however, benefit from the principles that are distilled from the experience and research of individuals who devote their full time to assessing economic trends and developments.

While the modern Jeremiahs generate a great deal of publicity, it is only a minor overstatement to say that the conservative economist (especially the so-called "Chicago School" of monetarists) are unanimous in their opinion that the monetary policy of the United States is leading us toward a collapse of the system. Most prominent among these is Milton Friedman, the Nobel laureate, who for decades has pointed out the irresponsibility of fiscal and monetary practices of the United States.

The predictions made by the conservative economists are supported by disturbing revelations about the manipulations of the Federal Reserve System to expand the money supply and thus guarantee continued inflation. They point to the juggling acts of U.S. banking and make us wonder how any bank can keep from being dangerously overextended in the middle of the "rob-Peter-to-pay-Paul" approach that is standard operating procedure. They talk about the millions of dollars in U.S. accounts that come from the Middle East and, if moved suddenly, could topple the system. (This possibility has been explored in Paul Erdman's best-selling novel, *The Crash of '79*). They make convincing scenarios for the set of events that could create the setting for a downfall of the economy's ability to withstand failures of banks and major corporations.

Mainline Economists

Underlying all the arguments of the conservative economists is the background of the Depression of 1929. Some disturbing comparisons can be made between the monetary policy of our time and those just prior to that crash. Frederick Von Hayck, Nobel Laureate of 1974 and one of the world's leading economists, accurately predicted the crash of 1929. Now he describes a coming world economic collapse as something that everybody should more or less take for granted. "I used to think it would not come for many years," he maintains, "but now I think I might live to see it." Hayck made that statement recently at seventy-seven years of age.

William Simon, certainly not a moss-bound academic, left a $2–3 million-a-year partnership with Wall Street's Salmon Brothers to join the Nixon administration as Secretary of the Treasury in 1973. He continued in the highest levels of government policy-making through the Ford administration. While in Washington and since retiring from government, Simon has been one of the staunchest defenders of the free marketing system. In a far-ranging interview with *Reason* magazine in February, 1978, Simon said,

> We are in a position now where half the people in America work for a living and the other half vote for it . . . We have been going through minicollapses for the last twenty years—going through exaggerated boom-bust cycles, with ever-increasing unemployment, ever-increasing inflation, and ever-increasing miseries for the people. If you are looking for a grand collapse that ultimately is going to come as a result of all these shocks, don't worry, it will come if we just continue to follow these insane policies (fiscal and monetary policies) . . . Within the first few months of the Carter administration, I sold every stock I owned and I wouldn't buy a stock right now with *your* money.

Few economists can match the establishment credentials of Robert L. Heilbroner. He is a past president of the prestigious American Economics Association, author of several best-selling economic books, including the widely acclaimed *The Worldly Philosophers*, and numerous scholarly publications. As late as 1970, he was a spokesman for economic optimism about the potential for the U.S. and world systems. Intervening events have, however, forced him to change his perspective. His book, *An Inquiry into the Human Prospect*, describes a future that is dismal on almost every front.

Heilbroner describes the same problem areas that other writers mention, but goes on to point out that human beings have proven themselves unable to heed warnings . . . unable to deny themselves in the present to avoid certain future catastrophes. His conclusion:

> If then, by the question "Is there hope for man?" we ask whether it is possible to meet the challenges of the fu-

ture without the payment of a fearful price, the answer must be, "No there is no such hope."

The "fearful price" that Heilbroner foresees includes "wars of redistribution," "pre-emptive seizure," "the rise of social tensions in the industrialized nations," and a number of other experiences that will allow mankind to survive, but only at the drastic renovation of the life style we know today. Like most others who have delved into the future, Heilbroner comes again and again to attack a concept that is dear to modern man's heart, but at the same time the root of his survival dilemma. Growth is one of our society's favorite opiates, but the future-oriented thinkers of our time have almost unanimously identified growth as a concept that can kill.

During the 1920's a Russian economist, Nikolai Kondratieff, developed and published a set of statistics indicating that capitalist countries were subject to fifty-year cycles of growth and decline. He accurately predicted the great depression, but alienated the Marxists because his long-wave theory suggested that capitalism would bounce back. As a reward for his research Kondratieff wound up in Siberia. In Western circles, the reception of his ideas was only slightly warmer. More recently, with another fifty-year cycle nearing its conclusion, a number of other observers are reexamining his ideas. One key scholar is J. W. Forrester, an MIT professor who invented the random access magnetic memory for computers. Forrester is world famous for his computer simulations of complex organizations. With his colleagues at MIT, Forrester has put together a new computer model that indicates that we have passed the peak of another Kondratieff Wave and will probably face a prolonged period of economic disarray. Forrester warns about the danger of a breakdown of political stability as well as economic difficulties.

Basically, Kondratieff's hypothesis is that the free world economy fluctuates in an economic cycle that peaks every forty to sixty years. Recent scholars have tried to pinpoint the peak at fifty-four years. This long-wave concept is tied to wars and depression. At the bottom of the peak, there is usually a war. The cycle will move up following a war for approximately twenty years. At the peak of this period of peace and prosperity, there may be another period of war. The peak is followed by a sharp decline and a plateau that will usually last between seven and ten years. After this warning period, everything moves downhill for the next twenty or so years.

Many observers feel that 1974 marked the initial decline and that the remainder of the 1970's can be viewed as the plateau period preceding the major decline. David Rhodes in his *How to Survive a Spastic Economy* and R. E. McMaster in *Cycles of War* have provided popularized descriptions of the Kondratieff theory. McMaster adds the specter of civil war as part of this depression scenario. As he points out, "Civil war occurs most often when there is a highly centralized government, when the nation is geographically large, and the culture is heterogenous. Civil war can be triggered by government's failure to fulfill the expectation of minority groups, or when the necessities of life are in scarce supply."

THE PHYSICISTS: CLOSE ENCOUNTERS OF A FEARFUL TYPE

While the economists have been trying to predict the tangibles of the future by the intangible philosophies and trends of the present, the physical scientists have been inferring some of the future's intangibles from some of the tangibles of high probability.

Is Your Underarm Deodorant a Global Threat?

We have heard about the ozone layer now until it is old hat. It was in the early '70's that scientists like Dr. Harold Johnston of the University of California at Berkeley began announcing to us that fleets of high-flying jets or sequential detonations of several nuclear bombs could create holes in the ozone layer that sits up twenty-five miles in the sky and screens out lethal ultraviolet rays from the sun. Next, we got the word that fluorocarbons in aerosol cans could also erode this protective shield. Whenever a scientist makes a startling finding, the news media can usually find someone who will interpret the facts differently. Galileo had the same problem. The result in the case of the ozone layer is that we have all now heard the story both ways (imminent danger vs. very little danger at all) until we are confused enough to push it out of mind. The person on the street figures that ozone, for good or bad, is 25 miles up and totally out of his control. It's a good example of the normal human response to a warning. We assume that it's out of our individual sphere of influence and that the government will no doubt fund an extensive study of it and that eventually it will be replaced as the topic of current panic. Perhaps such an attitude is the only rational procedure when the topic is the bomb or the ozone layer. But when the prophets are giving their opinions about the matters that we can influence (or that we can compensate for), then we owe it to ourselves to listen thoughtfully, utilizing the input that has documentation and the ring of truth.

Does the Fault Lie in the Stars?

In Shakespeare's *Julius Caesar*, we are told:
Men at some times are masters of their fate.
The fault, dear Brutus, is not in our stars,
But in ourselves, that we are underlings.

Today, highly respected physicists who specialize in astronomy are suggesting that the stars (or planets) may have something to do with the problems we face. For some time, there has been a feeling that the positions of galactic bodies have an influence on everything from weather to blood pressure. Just exactly what is influenced by alignments in the solar system is unknown. However, there is no denying that the near future holds some of the most ominous planetary movements of many years. *In 1982, we can look forward to something that only happens once every one hundred seventy-nine years:* an alignment of all the planets on the same side of the sun. Ordinarily the planets are spread out so that they surround the sun. There is considerable fear that this togetherness will produce unaccustomed pulls on the earth. We know that the pull of the moon and other bodies in our solar system can influence ocean tides and earthquake activity. The added pull of the Jupiter line-up will also be occurring at a time when the sunspot activity on the sun will be unusually great.

According to *The Jupiter Effect*, a book by two highly respected astronomers, John Gribbin and Stephen Plagemann, this combination of influences will produce huge disruptions in the earth's upper atmosphere. There will be a shift in the winds, modifying rainfall and temperature patterns around the globe. Even more frightening is the concern that all this change will cause winds that can slow the earth's rotation just enough to mess up the works. *The Jupiter Effect* anticipates severe earthquakes in all the places where the earth's crust is already in a strain—the most obvious being around Los Angeles and San Francisco. Although not specifically mentioned by Gribbin and Plagemann, other high-probability quake areas in the United States include New York City and Memphis, Tennessee, as well as Japan and Italy abroad.

Almost every self-respecting prophet or mystic has predicted a giant (already overdue) earthquake in California. One does not have to be too brilliant to predict that if there is a major California earthquake, it is going to be a serious one due to the high densities of population in the state. Hardly anybody argues with the California earthquake idea anymore. The debates are more aimed at *when* it will happen and just *how bad* it will be. The people of California—in their own characteristic relaxed style—have continued on with their way of life with little consideration for the impact of an almost certain killer earthquake.

According to this theory, California can look for the earthquake in 1982. Jeane Dixon said it would hit in 1983 and Edgar Cayce predicted (in 1940) that it would hit before the end of this century. And if you are one of those who is skeptical of human seers, you'll take little comfort in knowing that when all the available data was poured into the giant UNIVAC computer, the resulting analysis indicated that the Southern California earthquake was mathematically long overdue.

THE ASTROLOGERS AND THE AGE OF AQUARIUS

The predictions of the "Jupiter Effect" were first set forth in 1974 and seem to gain in influence every year—especially in serious astronomical circles. Astronomers generally want to make it very clear that their discipline is a distinct branch of physics and not to be confused with astrology. Although they both study the stars, astronomers feel that theirs is a respectable branch of the physical sciences and that astrology is merely a part of the occult and of no significant consequence.

Nevertheless, because of the increasing popularity of astrology and the obvious conclusion that anyone who studied the stars would be concerned about the consequences of the unique planetary alignment of the 1980's, I began to do a little research in this area. In my inquiry, I was fortunate to make the acquaintance of Joyce Greer, first vice-president of the Congress of Astrological Associations, an international federation of groups involved in the study and practice of astrology. Ms. Greer does not fit the typical stereotype of astrologer. She is an attractive, vivacious wife of a university professor. She holds a Master's degree in Education and is a pleasant, intelligent person to talk with. I told her of my own writing project and asked if she could collect some information on the immediate future from the vantage point of astrological documents. Her report to me was surprising, primarily because of its consistency with other reports that I reviewed in preparing this chapter. Greer's own analysis was supplemented by two key astrological documents: Frances Sakoian and Lou S. Acker, *The Astrologer's Handbook* (Harper & Row, 1973) and Geoffrey Dean's *Recent Advances in Natal Astrology—A Critical Review 1900–1976* (Para Research, Inc., 1977).

One of the reasons that astrologers see validity in the unhappy predictions of the "Jupiter Effect" is that there will be several major planetary sign changes in the 1980's. Ancient astrological documents are calculated from a *geo*centric standpoint, which means that the earth is placed at the center of the solar system, rather than a *helio*centric perspective, which places the sun at the center. With the use of an Ephemeris (a document which provides daily descriptions of planetary positions throughout the past and future), it is obvious that the planets are coming closer and closer together, and on November 1, 1982, the planets will be at their nearest juncture. All nine planets will be contained within 63 degrees and 42 minutes of the ecliptic. In other words, all nine planets will be packed within a little more than one-sixth of the total perimeter.

In studying major eclipses that have occurred and will occur in the future, astrologers note that there will be a total of seven eclipses during 1982 (four solar and three lunar eclipses). This has only happened twice in this century—in 1917 and 1935. Eclipses have long been considered by astrologers to be connected with earthquakes and all kinds of natural disasters. For that reason alone, 1982 would be a year of concern for astrologers.

There is also a common belief that any time a planet changes from one sign of the zodiac to the other major changes will take place. When the rock musical *Hair* sang about the changes in the "Age of Aquarius," it was reflecting the consensus of astrological literature. People born in the broad transitional period between the Piscean age and the Aquarian age—basically between 1975 and 2000—"will experience the greatest upheaval of human civilization in recorded history." Between 1970 and 1984, the planet Neptune is said to be in the sign of Sagittarius. According to the *Astrologer's Handbook*, this means that there will be:

> a period when the need for high religious and spiritual values will find positive expression. There will be a return to God and a desire to spiritualize the larger social order. Mystical and occult subjects will be gradually introduced into the university curriculums. Religions will put more stress on man's contact with God through his inner being.

We have seen evidence of this transition with an amazingly rapid concurrent growth in both evangelical religions and an interest in mysticism and the occult.

The transition from the sign of Sagittarius through Capricorn (between 1984 and the year 2000) is even more frightening. This is described as:

> a period comes in which world governments will be in chaos, and economic and political structures will be brought to their knees. Out of this chaos and suffering will come true spiritual responsibility and discipline that will be expressed in practical dealings. People will no longer have the luxury of abstract Sagittarian spirituality. In order to survive, they will be forced to incorporate spirituality into their practical lives. New forms of government and political concepts will be brought into being out of necessity. The end of this period will produce the beginning of world government.

Neptune will enter the sign of Aquarius along with Uranus about the year 2000, which marks the real beginning of the Aquarian age. At that time a new civilization will be born based on enlightened humanitarianism and on a science using new technology and new forms of energy. This will mark the beginning of a thousand years of peace, which was spoken of in the biblical book of Revelation.

The last of the three major sign changes that will occur during the 1980's is when Pluto moves from the sign of Libra into the sign of Scorpio in 1984. Prior to this change, astrologers believe:

> . . . man must renew his consciousness of responsibility for his fellows if world destruction is to be avoided. As part of this awakening, new concepts of marriage, law, and justice will be developed. If the necessary regeneration in personal, national, and international relations does not occur at this time, worldwide chaos and war will ensue during Pluto's transit through Scorpio. During this period, we must learn to settle domestic and foreign disputes by law and arbitration rather than by armed conflict if civilization is to survive.

Once Pluto makes its move into the sign of Scorpio between 1984 and 2000, the projection is even more bleak:

> world-wide conflict is likely to reach a peak of intensity. Regenerate or die will be the order of the day because Pluto rules Scorpio, the sign of death and regeneration. There is no other planetary sign position of such potency. This period marks the final death gasp of the Piscean Age. Time will have run out on human folly and there will be no choice but to face the consequences. As the Biblical book of Revelation says, "Unless these times are shortened, there would be no flesh saved." The greatest danger of plague, famine, and atomic biological warfare will occur during the last twenty-five years of the twentieth century—from 1984 until the end of the century—the human race will be forced by dire necessity to regenerate itself, in preparation for the Aquarian age and the year 2000.

These projections are based on long-term revolutions and orbits. Many of the transits described for the planets are not likely to occur any more often than once every two or three hundred years. Many of the dates were written long before and without knowledge of the other prophecies by experts in other areas (i.e., the "Jupiter Effect," etc.). It becomes immediately apparent that some bad times are "in the stars" especially clustering around the year 1984. The probabilities include plague, famines, and warfare.

THE CLIMATOLOGISTS: EVERYONE TALKS ABOUT THE WEATHER . . .

You've heard the old adage, "Everyone talks about the weather, but no one does anything about it." Historically this statement may be true. For centuries, people talked about the weather and, fortunately for us, frequently recorded the kind of weather conditions they experienced. In recent years, a science of forecasting the weather has begun to emerge. Recently, that science has become critical for topics much more significant than planning a weekend picnic. Nations across the world are beginning to get some rather disturbing messages from the weather phenomena of the past five years. Record cold waves in the winter and extensive droughts in the summer are not merely unpleasant, they are potentially devastating to the world's economy. Weather scientists at the Institute for Environmental Studies of the University of Wisconsin and other key centers have become quite concerned about the evidence that appears to emerge from their analysis of historical and contemporary weather patterns. The verdict is good news and bad.

The bad news is that the earth's weather is undoubtedly getting colder. The good news is that colder winters around the world could be the one thing that could reverse the downhill economic direction of the United States. While none of us is going to welcome longer, colder winters with deeper snows, we can still take some consolation. Under such conditions, the United States would become the dominant food-producing nation in a world that is not only hungry, but absolutely unable to grow enough food. According to special reports prepared by the CIA, the country that has the food is going to hold all the cards in the next five years.

Of course, every advantage has an accompanying disadvantage. What do we do when we have all the food and the frozen, starving leadership of less fortunate nations decide they have little to lose by holding a nuclear gun to our heads. The pressures of hungry masses on the judgment of otherwise sane leaders could be devastating. When the pressure begins to rise, do we give the food away, or sell it, or exploit its power to control the way other cultures must behave? Do we require birth control practices of those who will receive our precious food? How many people are we willing to allow to starve so that we can maintain the standard of living to which we have become accustomed?

The evidence points to the fact that we will not really have the option of keeping our present standard of living. The winters of 1977 and 1978 treated all of us to extremes and dilemmas we had never encountered before:

1. Two-thirds of our country experienced the coldest winter temperatures on record.
2. Twenty-six feet of snow fell on upper New York state. Over a million citizens of Buffalo found themselves paralyzed under a record fifteen-foot accumulation. The city of Boston was completely incapacitated and looters ravaged shops and food stores.
3. Icy temperatures visited Florida long enough to almost wipe out a $125 million citrus crop.
4. Key rivers were blocked with ice for the first time in this century. Lake Erie froze solid.
5. With unseasonable cold striking points as far apart as Pittsburgh, Nashville, and Jacksonville, heat waves and droughts attacked ski slopes and winter farming areas.
6. People began to wonder if the bad weather was a fluke or an ominous trend that was coming to be a permanent fixture.

A careful investigation of the historic records of temperatures and snowfalls has now begun to reveal the unhappy news. Climatologists tell us that this weather is not "abnormal"—what we have enjoyed for the past fifty years was abnormal.

In a comprehensively researched, scholarly publication, Nels Winkless, III, and Iben Browning confirm the fact that climate in the past fifty or so years has been the warmest and most productive in several centuries. They predict that the world will soon return to harsher, more normal conditions. They also suggest that the predicted changes in climate can cause some severe disruptions in food production with accompanying political and economic pressures on countries. In fact, the twenty-eight scholars who have published significant

papers on climatology in recent years, twenty-three are in
agreement that the earth will be cooler in the next decade
than it has been in the past few years. Thus, it appears that
the weather is now beginning to return to the normal state of
long, frozen winters. We may not like it, but the earth's climate cycles were in existence long before our civilization
came along and, if it's time for another Ice Age, there is little
we can do to stop it.

We've enjoyed "unseasonably good" weather during the
past half-century and now we are headed back into a cold
cycle that can be expected to extend hundreds of years into
the future. The extent and impact of this trend on you and
your family can be quite easily deduced. You may want to
store food and other supplies that will enable your survival in
the more likely event of being trapped in your house for a
long period of time. You may need to insulate and weatherize your home for the eventualities of colder temperatures
and loss of outside power support. Or—you may decide that
your home deserves to be sold as you seek warmer regions of
the country where the temperatures promise to be colder, but
not paralyzing.

When does it all happen? It has already begun, but some
weather predictors with sparkling records are pointing to the
winter of 1981 as the first one that we are going to have
trouble believing. Joseph Goodavage, an astro-meteorologist,
predicts a 1981 winter of 20-foot snowdrifts in New England,
followed by weeks of constant sub-zero weather, polar air
masses sweeping deeper into the southern regions than ever
before, low temperatures that stay so long that they drain all
our resources, and steadily worsening weather climaxing in
the late 1980's with the most disastrous deep freeze in history.

THE THEOLOGIANS: IS THE END
FINALLY AT HAND?

A bumper sticker on a psychedelic van put it this way,
"Jesus Is Coming Soon . . . And Is He Sore!" A growing
number of popular religious personalities are building their
followings on light they claim to be able to supply us on the
Bible's prophecies for the future of mankind.

Hal Lindsey is the leader of the apocalyptic club. His
books on prophecy have sold over 15 million copies, and he
stays in demand as a speaker around the world. Lindsey

doesn't claim that God tells him directly what will happen. His deductions come from continuing comparisons between the Bible's veiled prophecies of the events leading up to the end of the world and the events of our daily world news. Though Lindsey's conclusions have their skeptics among the more scholarly theologians, his ideas have quite obviously caught the imagination of a great many readers around the world. He estimates that some 8 million people stand with him in an apocalyptic interpretation of the following political, economic, and geographical trends:

1. The growing isolation of Israel will force it to work out a mutual defense pact with the European Common Market, which will cause:
2. Black Africa to align with the Arab world against Israel.
3. A tenth nation will join the Common Market, making it fit the biblical description of the ten-horned beast described in Daniel and Revelation.
4. The beast will be led by the "Anti-Christ," an electrifying speaker who will be possessed by Satan, after miraculously surviving a head wound. Possessing almost superhuman intelligence, he will become head of a world confederacy.
5. This world confederacy will assign code numbers for every person on earth. Each number will incorporate the 666 that the biblical prophecies established as the identity of the Anti-Christ. The numbers will be tied into computers that can read them by ultraviolet light and cut off the ability to buy and sell for those who are out of favor in the cashless, electronic banking society.
6. Famines will increase due to climate changes and create great international tensions and crises.
7. There will be a great increase in killer earthquakes.
8. The power of the United States will decline and there will be a shift in the balance to Europe.

Hal Lindsey says that these events will (in his opinion—not in prophecy) all take place before the year 2000. Although he has been sharply critical of Jeane Dixon, Lindsey's predictions have the ability to mesh loosely with those of the best-known prophet of our time. According to Ms. Dixon, the world must return to a life of faith and prayer or else the next half-century will include:

1. a catastrophic world earthquake in 1980,
2. invasion of Israel with battles until 1988,
3. Russian occupation of Israel leading to:
4. a nuclear war between Russia and the U.S. in 1999, with "fear for the survival of all mankind,"
5. the victorious allied armies will then fight Communist China for nineteen years,
6. culminating about the year 2020 with the apocalyptic battle of Armageddon,
7. The Allies will win and usher in the reign of the Anti-Christ, who will be in full command of the world.
8. The years 2020–2037 will hail the second coming of Christ. The surviving Jews will spread his gospel throughout the world.
9. The new Judeo-Christian faith will usher in unprecedented human happiness and good will beyond the year 2037 . . . after which Ms. Dixon's visions cease.

YOU: THE ULTIMATE ANSWER

I realize that some religious readers will be offended by what they interpret as the humanistic emphasis of this section heading. I respect the sincere conviction of my religious friends who believe that the only solution to the problems that lie ahead is for God to intervene in our behalf. My personal religious persuasion is that God will not repeal the law of consequences that He set in motion. Rather, my hope is to remain open to receive guidance about how to direct my affairs now and throughout the future. I do not expect a miraculous vision of a still small voice in the night. I believe that by being receptive to truth from all sources, I will receive the direction that is needed.

Once you have evaluated the varied, yet similar, prophecies by the experts of many disciplines, I believe you will be impressed by the frightening prospects of the next decade. The visions of the future are not identical, but they are similar. According to probability theory, the true nature of any universe tends to be near the center of observations that fall on either side of it; thus, the phenomenon of the bell-shaped curve. I don't expect to see the fulfillment of all the prophecies mentioned in this chapter. Depression, famine, violence, and natural disasters have, however, been recurring themes. These, it seem, form the center of the bell-shaped curve and have an extremely high probability (in my opinion, 90 percent probability) of being realized by 1986—and a 60 percent probability of changing our world dramatically by 1984.

For many years, the period around 1984 has been an object of considerable fascination. George Orwell used it as a target period and, even though the exact events he predicted are unlikely, the year is likely to be a time of tremendous change.

Among the various popular, futuristic novels, Ayn Rand's *Atlas Shrugged* presents a scenario that I find very appropriate for this time. She describes a society where the producers become tired of bearing the burden of everyone else. They finally refuse to continue shouldering this heavy burden. Of course, the book's title refers to Atlas's mythical duty of bearing the world on his shoulders. The shrug is the prophesied result when Atlas finally gets tired of doing his share and everyone else's too. In the novel, the producers go off to a place called "Hidden Valley" (perhaps a survival community like those discussed in Chapter 11?) where they are able to work and not worry about the lazy and irresponsible. Is it possible in a society where 10 percent of the population pays 50 percent of the taxes . . . where 70 million taxpayers work to support 150 million people who pay no taxes . . . that a significant number of citizens are almost ready to shrug?

Regardless of what everybody else is saying about the future, you can tell that things are not quite right. This is a gnawing kind of concern that tells most people today that there are harder times ahead. That's the reason you picked this book up and the reason that you may be one of the few to prepare for the coming stresses. Your own intuition tells you that we have gotten off the track and that there are some dark days ahead. This book is designed to show some of the ways that these hard times can be handled in a way that will be more pleasant for the people who are willing to read and heed the signs of the coming times.

CHAPTER THREE

Why Has the American Dream Gone Sour?

When Tennessee Ernie Ford went to the top of the Hit Parade with his song called "Sixteen Tons," it was before the era of the protest song. People just liked the beat and the bitter-tough soliloquy of a poor coal miner trapped in the economic death grip of the company store—loading sixteen tons a day and getting deeper in debt.

When the song came out in the boom-time fifties, the record-buying middle class was not worried about its soul being taken over by any company store. Of course, most families did have a gradually growing debt that Sears liked to call a revolving charge account. But, why worry? Everybody has to owe money to have the things he needs.

It's no wonder the fifties have found their place in nostalgia as the happy days. They occurred just as the nation was whizzing to the top of an exciting roller coaster. The ride was still fun and the "spend what you are going to earn" myth was still keeping us up to our ears in bright, shiny things. What we didn't know then was that there was no track at the other side of the roller coaster's summit.

If we thought we were speeding going up, we will hardly believe the acceleration on the way down. The speed on the way down is not fun, though, because of the obvious fact that we cannot continue without a crash. At this moment, we are just before another slight incline and then the final descent into a catastrophe where we will finally pay for all the lunches we thought were free.

On a national and individual basis, we are overextended—a nice economic term for being broke! The American dream has gone sour. We finally succeeded in cutting free from the old-time, hard cash morality of our grandparents. We finally convinced ourselves and the world that "you've got to spend money to make money." Unfortunately, we worked right

54

through that cliche and coined another that said "you can spend tomorrow's money today."

As we dig our fingernails into the rail of the roller coaster car hurtling downward, we can't understand what went wrong. We can't understand why our nation's economy no longer leads the world . . . why the dollar is starting to do those things that only the foreign currency used to do. Why don't the other nations love us anymore . . . didn't we give them millions? And why isn't the capitalism that people used to criticize for being so efficient continuing to give us worry-free goodies . . . what ever happened to the self-correcting promise of competition and free enterprise?

GETTING AHEAD: THE EMPTY VICTORY

The family sits down to take its medicine and spend an evening with the budget. It's a job nobody likes since it always ends up with the inescapable conclusion that we are spending more money than we are making. We go over the figures again. We check our computations. How can we possibly be in trouble? People who make what we make used to be rich. Really!

Remember when you were first married? Remember how much you made then? And you not only got by, you were probably saving a little money as you went. Now, how, in the name of common sense, can you be making five, six, or seven times more than you were then, and be going down the tube? It just doesn't make sense. You are not that wasteful. You buy only the things that you need. You are constantly talking about the ways to cut back, and yet you are getting in deeper every week.

For a housewife, the trip to the grocery store is the most discouraging part of the week. For a politician, the budget sessions and economic questions are the ones you'd rather miss. Either way, most people are stuck with the simple fact that there's not enough money for all the things you *need* . . . much less the other things you *want*. If you want something and there's no cash in hand, you can buy it in some non-cash fashion and never even consider the alternative of waiting or, perish the thought, doing without.

In today's economic jargon, most of the encouraging news is that "the rate of price increase has slowed somewhat." It is still increasing—the good news is that it has slowed somewhat to get its breath. As consumers and voters, we never question that the cost of things will go up. We just busy ourselves with trying to figure out when and how much.

What is it that causes this feeling of helplessness? Why is it literally futile to try to get ahead today? Why is there such an empty victory at the end of the battle for a raise, a better position, more fringe benefits, or an effort to save? Why can't you win, and, more important, will things get better or must you expect to continue on the treadmill to financial ruin? Something inside tells you that it cannot logically go on indefinitely. But how can it end? Things have always gone up and up. Perhaps they will do so indefinitely. Maybe your only task is to simply stay flexible enough so that your mind does not snap with the $300 loaf of bread, the $75,000 economy car, or the $20 trillion interest payment on the national debt each year.

THE DEVIL WITHIN AND THE DEVIL WITHOUT

There are two major causes for the dizziness you may feel whenever you try to comprehend our economic situation. One is a personal devil inside each of us, and the other is an even larger demon who rages outside. Unfortunately, neither seems to be under the control of anybody.

The internal troublemaker has been on the lips and pens of theologians and philosophers forever and ever. It is the predictable, but still puzzling, enigma known as "human nature." Mankind seems to possess a germ of laziness and dishonesty that hopes against hope that you can really get something for nothing. As children grow up (in any century) parents and societal cliches provide regular reminders that you have to work for what you get, the cream will rise to the top, and the free lunch is always gonna cost you. We hear the words, partly believe, but never completely drown out the inner voice that starts babbling whenever we are onto a sure thing, in on the ground floor, coming up on the chance of a lifetime, or hearing sleigh bells on the roof. When opportunity (or temptation) knocks, humans seem to forget all the things they have righteously maintained, and run wild in carefully rationalized idiocy.

Human nature allows us to rant on and on about the ridiculous, irresponsible movement in which Washington is selling us down the economic river by printing paper money that is two parts money and ninety-eight parts paper . . . and then, in the next breath, to make personal plans to spend today the paycheck we expect to receive eight months later. Human nature is the puzzling humor that lets us laugh and say "who cares" while doing something that we know is financially suicidal. None of us wants to give up our flawed human nature because, even though it gives us daily pain, it is still our membership card to the global fraternity. Misery loves company, and the cadre of people overpowered by human greed is growing every day.

Is it fair to blame human nature for the obviously worsening situation of our economy? Since human nature has been around for millennia and the economy has only been staggering for less than a century, how can we pin the blame on human greed? The answer is simple. There was a time when society held on to the brakes that protected us from letting base human nature run wild.

Since the Constitution was framed and up to the early years of this century, the term *Christian nation* was acceptable in polite conversation. That didn't mean that everybody was a Christian, or even a church-goer. It just meant that, generally speaking, everyone was under the restraint of a social disapproval system that was closely tied to the old-time religion. That religion may not have come from God, the Bible, or even the church. It may have been an intricate weaving of Ben Franklin's sayings, Horatio Alger's stories, and the precarious season-to-season life on the farm. Whatever its composition, it provided a set of brakes to slow us up and to say "no" when we were about to go for something that would hurt us.

If the idea of religion offends, we might just as well say that, until World War II, we were, as a nation, far more willing to be guided and restricted by the accumulated wisdom of the ages. Obviously, there have been get-rich-quick schemes as long as there have been people, and P. T. Barnum knew long before World War II that there was a "sucker born every minute." Prior to the world homogenization process that began with that war, the old-time values and warnings were still assumed to be good. Only in the last fifty years has moral goodness gone on the rack and badness been given such terrific press. While the positive and negative fringes of society are always going to be far apart, the central trust of our national character has shifted. This has turned a rising host of people loose in a world that automatically devalues anything old, trusts its feelings more than its history, and praises doing what you want to rather than what you ought to.

So culprit number one is a familiar one—the devil within, and collectively we have abandoned the old restraints and no longer benefit from the accumulated wisdom of the past. In fact, we are proud of a newfound ability to stand on our own, distrusting tradition, and making our own decisions. But, as a nation, we are more in trouble than ever before.

Devil number two is both familiar and unknown. *Inflation* is a word that is worn from daily use; but few citizens realize what causes it, what it causes, and how little about it we are ever allowed to know. How many times have we heard someone say, "I remember when I bought my first car . . . paid $250 for it . . . but saving that $250 was like saving $2500 in this day and time."

Inflation—you know the feeling. But what is it? How is it that you have a pocket full of dollars that would have made you a high roller a few years ago, and today that roll of greenbacks will hardly get you lunch and a trip home? If you prefer to see the positive side of the situation, you may assume that while everything does cost twice what it did, everyone seems to have twice as much. The actual numbers tell a less encouraging story. We are not just using bigger numbers in the same ratios—things do cost more and, for most people, income doesn't grow as fast as prices and tax brackets.

Suppose you crawl up on the beach of a deserted island. Correction: an island that is deserted, except for one coconut vendor. The stock in his coconut stand is composed of 100 coconuts, priced at one fish each. You feel confident that, as an expert fisherman, you should be able to satisfy your need for coconuts. You catch a fish and buy a refreshing and delicious coconut. Life won't be too bad on this island. There are plenty of fish and an ample supply of coconuts. Next day, the vendor tells you that the coconuts will now cost two fish each, since the supply is dropping. You don't like it, but there is nothing you can do. You fish a little longer and enjoy the same coconut satisfaction. Next day the price is up again, but this time you tell the vendor that you have established a new monetary standard and in the future two rocks from the beach will equal one fish. If the vendor accepts your notion, he is a fool (but no bigger fool than the U.S. public and the host of foreign buyers who have accepted the dictum that paper is as good as gold). The cycle continues, but there is no feeling of ease because of the obvious fact that no matter how many fish or rocks you have, there are no more coconuts. In fact, there is an ever-decreasing amount of the basic resource.

The word *inflation* has the sound of hot air filling a balloon. Balloons are relatively simple, but our understanding of monetary inflation leaves us wondering. Actually, the same thing happens. When you blow into the balloon, you appear to create a bigger balloon—but you don't. You are in reality only stretching the same balloon over a bigger area. There is no additional rubber in the balloon, only hot air to make the same amount of rubber appear to go farther. Of course you cannot stretch the balloon indefinitely. Hot air can push the balloon beyond its limits, and the hot air of inflation is pushing the economy beyond its limits.

INFLATION—GETTING LESS
WHILE EARNING MORE

The reason we have economic problems today is that we quit doing what we were doing when we didn't have these problems. "Thanks a lot," you say, "what does that double talk mean?"

There was a time when inflation was not the problem that we have now. The beginning of the problem corresponded directly to the beginning of some specific policy changes. Specifically, we left the gold standard and started printing paper that said it was gold. This was about like calling a rock from the beach a fish. It makes you feel wealthy, but it creates no actual wealth.

The deficit spending disease began to spread at the point the nation said, "Either we are going to have to spend money we don't have, or some of us will have to do without." That simple change in policy created the fantasyland roller coaster that was so exhilarating through the 50's, but is now becoming a terrifying nightmare. At first, it was fun for the nation to spend money it didn't have. People in need were getting what they wanted. Everyone seemed to have more, and there was still the optimistic anticipation that eventually we would be able to pay it all back. The hope of being in the black again enabled us to maintain our self-respect at the begin-

ning. But, as we have continued to spend more and more that
we did not have, gradually, like a junkie who accepts his
need for larger and larger fixes, we have come to think that
life in the red is normal.

It was a simple habit to acquire. And, once a policy of
monetary inflation was adopted, carrying out the policy was
taken out of our hands. Government grew. It seemed natural
to take over and administer the care of people in need and
protect us from every danger. After all, someone had to keep
the nation safe for deficit spending. The cycle continues today as the bureaucracy, the politicians, and the taxpayers
look for someone else to bail them out of their baffling problems. More than anything else, everyone wants to avoid the
personal pain required to kick the habit and fix what is
wrong. We are all desperately overextended in debt and
hoping that there will be some way to get right again without
pain or sacrifice or surrender. It is not possible. We are where
we are because we have put off for years the daily sacrifices
and discomforts of getting along. The price must be paid—either a day at a time (which is called life) or all in one terrible lump (which is called the crash). Balloons can only
stretch so far.

The only *cure* for inflation is a depression! A depression,
as a few of you can remember, is a terrible thing to go
through. It hurts and makes people work hard for almost
nothing. In that sense, it is merely an overcompensation for
the cause of inflation—the desire to not work and have almost everything.

Some politicians will suggest that there are simple cures
like tight money or high taxes. These do tend to push us
gradually back in the right direction, but they never last long
because these policies also tend to get the politicians un-elect-
ed at the next election.

Inflation is a necessity for the survival of big government.
The government gets a raise every year because of inflation.
Then with that over-the-counter raise in its pocket, it
proceeds to get an under-the-counter raise. It works like this.
Under the guise of closing the tax loopholes, the politicians
hammer out a tax reform. It is popular because we can all
picture those dirty, old rich guys who use the loopholes to
avoid paying taxes. We assume that the reform is to stop all
that. But the opposite is true. Tax reform to help the poor is
easy on the government because the poor pay no taxes. The

bottom 50 percent of the taxpayers pay only 17 percent of the taxes. But, they also swing 50 percent of the votes. It doesn't cost much for the government to buy half the votes.

The contrast is that the top 10 percent of the taxpayers pay 50 percent of the taxes. This is true in spite of the myths about the rich guys having all the fancy tax lawyers who keep them from having to pay any taxes at all. The deception in the whole tax numbers game is that the middle class is so much larger than any of us realizes. The top 10 percent of taxpayers, which we might suspect would be mostly millionaires, includes families who make as little as $23,420 a year. It is the middle class who pays the taxes in America. The people who make from $10,000 to $25,000—because there are so many of them—are the ones whose taxes must not be cut if Uncle Sam is to get his regular raise. The politicians can make the news with a tax cut (that sounds good) for the poor (that sounds good) and never really affect the middle class (who pay the most taxes but are hardly disposed to talk against relief for the poor).

The very rich, on the other hand, represent only a few votes and do indeed pay taxes. Of the 1,149 taxpayers who earn more than a million dollars a year, the average tax payment was $1,011,317. A million dollars is a lot of taxes to pay for government services you'll never get to use. To most citizens, the term *tax reform* sounds like the rich are going to have to pay more taxes. But the real purpose of closing loopholes is to enlarge the tax base. The current effort is attempting to do this by redefining personal income to include fringe benefits and capital gains and by reducing deductions. Enlarging the tax base will raise everyone's taxes, but it will hit the middle income brackets the hardest.

When the federal income tax system began in 1914, it was sold to the people as a tax for rich people only. At the beginning, it did hit a mere, 350,000 citizens—less than one-half of one percent of the population. Unless you earned the equivalent of $117,000 of today's dollars, you never had to worry about taxes at all. But gradually the thresholds were lowered and the tax rates were raised. Today, the bottom bracket has to fork over twice the percentage that the rich had to pay in 1914 and no income is exempt from reporting. Between 1914 and 1975, the population of the United States grew by 120 percent. During the same time the number of individual tax returns filed each year grew by 23,800 percent.

We are running out of new people to tax. That simply means that more money will have to be extracted from the producers.

Paul Craig Roberts shows us the impact of our inflationary tax system by describing a hypothetical person who is earning $6,240 a year. In 1976, he would have paid no taxes. But after 45 years of 5 percent inflation he would be earning $56,077 a year and have a $17,019 tax bill (at present rates). His after-tax income in 2021 would have a purchasing power equal to only $4,345 in 1976 dollars. The higher inflation, the worse it would be, because he would reach the higher brackets even sooner.

Because the man on the street cares little about the intricate explanations of national fiscal policy, politicians have been quick to manipulate the percentages and tax bases instead of imposing the alternative solution. The other way of getting money is to raise taxes. This method is clear to everybody who receives a paycheck, and so government is naturally going to avoid this obvious, unpopular method. If the politicians can get the extra money they want without raising the official tax rates, that sounds perfect. After all, you should be thankful that you are earning so many dollars. Once every few years (as in 1978) we can even have an insignificant cosmetic tax-cut. This way everybody will win—right? Wrong. Everybody cannot win. And the deceptive manipulation of taxes merely postpones the unpleasantries. From a selfish viewpoint, it may seem justifiable to postpone the unpleasantries. If we were only trying to save our own skins, we could take the easy way out and let our successors pay the bill. That is exactly why we are in the spiraling mess we are in—because the past generation and those in authority now have selfishly taken the easy way out and have now retired, leaving us to pay the bill.

A BRIEF HISTORY OF THE CRUELEST TAX

There is little encouragement when you look at the history of inflation. Like heroin, inflation is not a new addiction. It has existed in many societies and for many centuries. It has not always existed, which counteracts the idea that inflation has always been with us and is inevitable. However, when inflation *has* existed in history, it has always been caused by the same types of human weakness. Someone avoided the unpleasantries and left them to be handled by those who came after. And, without fail, the unpleasantries did get handled. The bill always gets paid and somebody always loses. History tells us that we have the option of either biting the bullet each day or swallowing the bombshell all at once.

Nero Fiddles While Inflation Burns

By our political standards, Nero was not a bad leader. He was well liked by the people because he was always giving the exciting shows at the Coliseum and providing public works and services that cost far more than people paid in taxes. What more could the people want? What could be better than a leader who charged you 10 denarii in taxes and gave you twenty denarii back in goods and services? What would have been better was honesty—even honesty that painted a bleak picture.

No accounting was ever done of Nero's fiscal income and expenditure. Historians suspect that in the beginning Nero was able to do his wonders by simply paying for them out of his own pocket. Admirable, but laying the groundwork for future problems. Next, Nero discovered that if the rich were found guilty of treason, condemned, and executed, the state could confiscate their wealth. He did so. (Today we accomplish the same goal by confiscatory estate taxes.)

Nero's final stroke of fiscal genius set a precedent that has been emulated in every economy in trouble. In A.D. 60, he changed the nature of the coins the Romans used. There had always been forty-two gold coins to one pound of gold and eighty-four silver coins to one pound of silver. Nero discovered that by mixing in baser metals, he could make each pound of gold produce three extra gold coins and each pound of silver produce twelve extra silver coins.

It was like creating money from nothing. It was the literal devaluation of the money, and it has been repeated by nations in financial trouble ever since. The United States has devalued its dollar on several occasions, most recently in 1972, and, unofficially, 1978. Like Nero, we devalue because we want more than we can afford. This is a none too glorious tradition in North America.

When the colonists started a revolution to gain freedom from England, there was not enough money to pay for the war. The rebels used their printing presses and printed up a supply of money that paid for the war but left the American money worth only about one-fortieth its face value. The expression that something is "not worth a continental" grew out of these times when there was American money with nothing to back it up.

Don't Save Your Confederate Money

The Civil War in America produced its own horror stories of inflation. The Union paid for its side of the war by printing up $450 million in special bills that gained the nickname "greenbacks." The greenbacks ended the war at a value of seventy-four greenbacks for one real dollar. People were pretty upset when the issuing government began refusing to accept them as payment. The government paid its debts in greenbacks but wanted real dollars when it was paid.

The Confederate States in the Civil War cranked out over $2 billion on their printing press. When the war was lost the Confederate money was all people had. Its value was so low that it took one thousand of them to buy a barrel of flour.

After the Civil War, the U.S. government eventually bought back all the greenbacks for gold. It was difficult. It put a lot of strain on the economy. Many people were out of work, since there were so few dollars available for the same amount of goods. It was a painful time, but it put the U.S. dollar on firm footing in the world's money market. The dollars then continued to gain in strength because the people were working hard to get the country moving again after the war. There was a steadily increasing productivity. A lot of new and valuable commodities were being created, grown, and manufactured. With that creation, there was strength behind the new dollars that were printed.

Inflation: Prelude to the Goose Step

The most spectacular inflation story is that of the Germans in the years following World War I. Germany's industry and agriculture were destroyed, and there was nothing to swap for the goods needed from other countries. At the same time, the truce placed a reparations payment on the Germans they could not possibly meet. The value of the German mark began to drop. One mark had been equal to about twenty-five American cents in 1914, but by 1923, one American dollar would equal 4 million marks. This meant that the prices of things in marks were almost unbelievable. Prices were going up so fast that many companies would pay their employees three or four times a day so that they could spend the money before it lost its value. In order to supply enough marks for this madness, more than two thousand printers and three hundred paper mills were working twenty-four hours a day to supply bank notes to the Reichsbank. Eventually, there were bills in general use for 1 billion marks and for 1 trillion marks. This unbelievable time finally began to stabilize when the Dawes Plan eased the payment of Germany's war debts. However, it was out of the dissatisfaction in Germany that Adolph Hitler found a foothold and eventually led Germany into World War II.

A Fast Deal on Dollars

In the United States, the strong, well-founded economy became the basis for more and more risk taking. The stock market was rising so continuously that many people began to speculate on the rising stocks. They would purchase shares of stock with money they did not have. Then the stock would rise in value, and they would sell, pay the money they had borrowed, and make a handsome profit. It was easy money. Everybody got into the act. More and more people bought more and more stock with money that wasn't real. The banks loaned out more money than they actually had, since it was all on paper anyway and no one ever called for the real money. As the market's rise hesitated, everybody seemed to panic and sell. The market stopped going up, so people stopped making profits and could not pay what they owed the banks. The banks were in trouble already when everybody got worried and rushed to take their money out of the bank. In effect, the people demanded more money out of the banks than the banks had. The crash that occurred in 1929 left banks broke, individuals in financial ruin, and the government seemingly helpless to get things moving again. People were out of work—they couldn't buy till they were working again—and the companies couldn't hire them until people started buying again. It was a depression of the most basic kind—the sort that is necessary to get things level again. The government could have suffered with the people, tightened the belt, and ridden out the depression as it did following the

Civil War. Instead, it took a turn from which we are yet to recover.

In 1933, Franklin Roosevelt took office. He adopted the economic policies of John Maynard Keynes (pronounced kaines), an English economist. Keynes' basic idea was that there was no reason for countries to have to back their money with gold. In fact, Keynes suggested that the responsibility of government was to get the ball rolling by spending money—even if the government was broke. His plan was to create money by deficit spending.

Roosevelt bought the idea. He took control aggressively and pumped money into the economy by creating government jobs for millions of Americans in public works. It was good news—people were going back to work. There was money in circulation again and the wheels of the economy began to turn. The wheels spun faster and faster. At least, they appeared to spin faster and faster. In reality, there was more money around but not that much more productivity.

Roosevelt became one of the most popular presidents ever. People were happy. They were working. They weren't too happy about the way government and taxes were growing. And they didn't like the fact that they were paying more all the time for the same goods and services. The inflation roller coaster had been boarded. The inflationary ascent would be gradual at first, but ever increasing. Nobody stopped to recognize that the idea of spending money without having it had been tried repeatedly in the economic history of the world—and had never worked.

What We Haven't Been Told

When Keynes recommended that nations "spend their way back to prosperity," it sounded good. Most drunks like the idea of taking a couple of snorts to end a hangover. The prescription seemed to work at first. But the inflation that was begun at that time may eventually be the final undoing of America's economy. Priming the pump was one thing. It is quite another to continue to prime the pump (and other countries' pumps too) after the water has begun to flow. Too much pump priming means that everyone gets soaked!

People and their governments have simply become unable to say no. When we want something, we buy it regardless of our debts or ability to pay. What difference will more debt make when you never plan to pay? The government borrows money to meet its obligations. When those loans come due, it borrows more money to pay. By 1978, the interest alone on the national debt was $21 trillion.

Because the politicians want the American public happy at any cost, the figures that would reveal the alarming trends are doctored on a continuing basis. The official Consumer Price Index (CPI) is published every month by the Department of Labor. It calculates and explains the monthly changes in the prices of all items forming the CPI. This comparison system began back in 1934. It gradually increased each year. By 1947 the index (which considered 1934 to 1939 to equal 100) was faced with a comparative index of 159. Because a 50 percent increase is terrible politics, a little statistical lie was told and accepted. 1947 became the year to which we would compare all subsequent years. Thereafter, the year of comparison has been changed at regular intervals. *If we were still stuck with comparing to 1947 levels, we would have to announce a CPI of about 445 percent in 1979.*

Most people don't realize that the statistics get this cosmetic treatment every decade or so. But one suspects that, if the true figures were revealed, there would not be much of a public outcry. There would be many words, but little impact. Inflation is an addiction that our nation does not want to take the cure for. We will content ourselves with inaccurate statistics and myths like "things do cost more, but we all have more" rather than pay the price of reversing the trend.

WHY WE WON'T LEARN

Inflation is the mutual enemy. You will never hear anybody stand up and say that inflation is a virtue and makes life better. But history makes it quickly clear that the voting public demands the inflation-producing behavior of its elected representatives. A president could, for example, decide between reduced inflation next year and one million additional people unemployed. Not much of a choice! One alternative would halt inflation and end a political career. The other alternative would continue the spiral of inflation, reduce the price of the dollar, and spell slow death for all.

The anathema against putting people out of work is relatively new. Prior to the Roosevelt era, there was no general assumption that everyone deserved a job or had any innate right to a given income or standard of living. The processes of protecting every person from every eventuality have increased the size of government and fed the fires of inflation. The year after World War II ended, Congress passed the Full Employment Act, stating that the government would vigorously promote two goals that were and are basically inconsistent—price stability and full employment. Ever since that time we have opted for the full employment half of the equation whenever there was a conflict. That's not totally bad. It is based on the very humane idea that it is better for everyone to hurt a little than for a few to hurt a lot. Unfortunately, the number of people who are willing to give has declined in inverse relationship to the people who want to get.

Throughout the history of the world, nations have followed wars with inflation, and then deflation until things stabilized. Thanks to Keynes' theories and the United States' world leadership, World War II and the Vietnam War have been followed by nothing but runaway inflation. The inflation has been worse. Does it stand to reason that the deflation when it comes—and it must come—will be worse?

As the rate of inflation increases, everyone thinks he is getting more. But average price increases of 2 percent in the 1950's, 2.3 percent in the 1960's, and 6.1 percent in the 1970's produce no more goods and services—just higher prices for the same goods. Can you accurately say, though, that as long as most people *feel* good about the economy, the economy is good? Of course not. Aspirin never cures a headache. It simply keeps us from feeling the pain that in the case of real disease would be a valuable warning to us.

When a major employer like Lockheed or Penn Central goes broke, the government has two options again. They can let the mismanaged company go under (putting thousands of voters out of work), or they can bail the company out (with dollars the country doesn't have). Sound economic direction would say, "It's sad, but the company is not justified by the economy. It will have to die." Popular politics would say, "We are already in debt. What difference will a little more debt make. Besides—my brother-in-law works for that company."

Inflation becomes an international way of life. If the Arabs charge us more for oil, we no longer consider responding by marching in with troops and tanks under the pressure of

some international affront. Rather, we now pay the price—
and charge them higher prices in return. It's automatic—the
oil costs us more so the things they need are going to cost the
Arabs more. Air conditioning and computers are going to
come at higher and higher prices.

Inflation is much more popular than any world leader will
ever admit. More than anyone else, the U.S. government benefits from inflation—at least in the short term. Inflation
means that massive debts can be repaid in cheaper dollars.
Moreover, a 10 percent rate of inflation brings about a 16.5
percent increase in government revenues. Inflation pushes
people into higher tax brackets and they send an even larger
share of their shrunken dollars to Washington. No wonder
governments prefer inflation to unemployment! If people
complain enough about their taxes, politicians will decide that
they can gain some mileage from a cosmetic tax cut. After a
national outcry against taxes (including the wide-ranging
reactions to Proposition 13 in California), Congress decided
to provide some tax relief in 1978. Despite the provisions of
this law, most people will pay more taxes in 1979. The new
law wasn't designed to offset increases in Social Security
payroll taxes scheduled for 1979 nor the effect to pay raises
and inflation that lift people into higher tax brackets. According to the Joint Committee on Taxation, a married couple earning $30,000 in 1978 (with two children) could
expect to pay $179 more in income and Social Security taxes
in 1979 than they did in 1978. Inflation is popular because it
provides a device for staying popular with the electorate. The
man on the street needs a financial fix and wants to believe
that he has more money when he actually has less. Inflation
is only unpopular with those who recognize the historic economic implications. A fresh fix seems to make everything more
pleasant, but each cycle requires a bigger dose. Breaking the
habit sounds so simple. There seems to be little reason to
worry. In reality, the addiction is frequently lethal for a culture.

When you blow a tiny balloon full of hot air, it inflates.
Reverse the flow of air and you have to swallow a lot of unpleasant carbon dioxide. Continue blowing in the air—the
balloon won't get bigger but the space it must cover will—
and the balloon will find its own way of relieving the undue
stress. However, after the balloon (and our economy) fixes
itself, it will never be the same again.

CHAPTER FOUR

The Worst is Yet To Be

When the romantic poet Robert Browning contemplated the future, he wrote in "Rabbi Ben Ezra":

> Grow old along with me!
> The best is yet to be,
> The last of life, for which the first was made.

In addition to his poetic genius, Browning was an optimist. He also lived in an era where a positive view of the future was much more reasonable than it can be today, even for the star-crossed lovers. The best I can offer you is "come read along with me, for the *worst* is yet to be." In this chapter, I will provide you with a general scenario of how the crash of the 1980's will probably occur. This vision is not based on hallucinogens or a crystal ball. Instead, it reflects the accumulated lessons of a life spent observing and participating in the economic determinations of our time. This analysis is based on a consideration of practically every written projection of the future. I have discounted a great deal of it, and stirred in some knowledge of the historical responses of other societies when confronted with the same dilemmas we face. All of this input has been filtered through my own common sense and judgment—two key traits that each individual must develop if he or she is to wade through the flood of gurus, seers, and saviors to survive the coming trauma. This is an important scenario because it has a direct relationship to the type of preparations you will want to make. In considering the possibilities for the coming decade, my vision is not an extreme one. Some observers believe that the catastrophe will be so great that only 20 percent of the total population will survive. They foresee an era of runaway famine, pestilence, plague, and massive armed violence. If this is your vision, you will need to make much more extensive retreat provisions.

I feel that this is a reasonable scenario because it will provide the flexibility to deal with a situation more intense than I anticipate, while at the same time providing personal and financial advantage if conditions do not deteriorate as drastically as I anticipate.

The drama I anticipate is presented in three acts: act one is the short-range future—the next five years; act two presents the midterm view from five to twelve years; and the final act describes the long-range future from approximately twelve years and beyond.

THE SHORT TERM: TOMORROW HAS BEEN CANCELED

With the problems that our society faces during the next few years, there may be a temptation to cancel the first act. Unfortunately, it's a little too late for this to happen. The curtain is already going up. The action takes place against a background of *inflation*. While this is a symptom of economic problems, it also is a causative and will be responsible for many of our other difficulties. I expect inflation to average between 7 percent and 10 percent for a couple of years and then rise steadily until 1984, when I expect it to get completely out of hand.

This brand of inflation is not the old variety that brought with it full employment and appearances of prosperity. In fact, unemployment will be a major problem, especially among the young and minority groups in the country. Concurrently, we are going to become increasingly aware of an inability to meet the social crises of the people. It will become apparent that government-led inflation will be putting people out of work as inflation grows so high that the absence of discretionary income eliminates the demand for many pleasant, but nonessential, purchases. Attempts to help the retirees, the unemployed, and other poor people stay up with inflation will only fuel its fires.

Before very long, everyone will recognize that the government's efforts to solve problems by throwing piles of money at them don't work—and those piles of money will be in even greater demand as the number of problems multiply. Already Gallup polls have confirmed the fact that the man on the street recognizes that inflation is the number one problem of this country. Soon, the public's pessimistic opinion will be further confirmed by obvious deterioration of the physical forms of public service. The quality of roads, schools, public transportation, and safety services will decline further as the price for maintaining even the status quo skyrockets. No, these losses in effectiveness will not come about through cutbacks in government spending. There might be some hope if a cutback occurred. If the government, like a wise and caring parent, would call a family meeting to explain that we have just run out of money and are going to have to "make do" with less until time and thrift get us back on our feet—then there might be hope. Unfortunately, the promises of myopic politicians have made the majority of people unwilling to accept even temporary cutbacks as long as the printing presses at the Treasury Department are working. Thus, governments at all levels are prohibited by pride and politics from admitting failure. The result will be ever-increasing deficits and doles of newly printed paper dollars to treat the symptoms. Despite press conferences and pronouncements of progress, the obvious reduction of the quantity and quality of services is going to create a sour attitude on the part of the taxpayer—sour and becoming rotten very quickly.

Less Service for More Money

The level of police and fire protection will have to decline because of the inability of municipalities to pay the rising bills for declining skills. The faster inflation grows, the less likely there is to be any remaining fat to be trimmed from the police, fire, or garbage collection operations. City councils will have to choose between purchases of modernized equipment or higher pay for existing personnel. Equipment purchases usually get press coverage, but they do not lead to contented personnel or satisfied, well-served clientele. Given a choice, most of us would rather have a working police force with old walkie-talkies than the best-equipped strikers in the United States. But that choice is still a dilemma, and either alternative provides a decline in the level of service at the time that a demand for these services will reach critical highs.

Whatever Happened to Private Enterprise?

While public agencies are taking their licks, the activities we mistakenly refer to as private enterprise will be suffering similar throes. We seldom stop to think of the extent to which many private companies are dependent upon government contracts, purchases, and protection. We can no longer support the fantasy that the role of government is merely to provide necessary protection to its citizens and to stimulate private activity. We have already passed the point where one out of every three Americans is on the public payroll. Gradually, the strength of the private sector has been sapped by the same disease that has eroded the moral fiber of our individual citizens. The private sector no longer has the strength to "save" the public. Businesses that do not sell all of their output to government purchasers certainly depend for buyers on at least one of every three customers who are dependent on the government. Capital and credit will become two critical criteria for business survival. Already, the quality of U.S. plant and equipment has slipped well below that of many international competitors. Firms are asked to depreciate their assets on the basis of prices that are obsolete immediately. Most companies are not able to finance "sinking funds" to offset the deterioration of their equipment, and the typical depreciation allowance simply does not provide enough money to purchase replacements when they are needed. Many observers feel there simply is not enough capital to maintain industrial productivity in the next decade.

In order for business to prosper, sufficient credit and capital must be available to finance new ventures and expansion of successful activity. While we can anticipate a strong demand for capital, there will be a relatively weak supply to meet this need. As a result, interest rates will be quite high. Extremely large sums of money will be needed to finance pollution controls, energy developments, modernized transportation, making factories more efficient, and salary increases for workers. Because of increased inflation and higher deductions for social security, income taxes, and other public services, our personal savings will drastically decline. This, of course, will reduce even further the amount of capital available for business borrowing and investment.

U.S. News & World Report has estimated that the United States faces the monumental challenge of creating an average of 72,100 jobs every week until 1986. This means that 3.5 million jobs per year—in addition to those that will open up because of retirement and death—will be needed to provide work for individuals seeking jobs for the first time, workers displaced by machines, and those listed as unemployed. Simply creating these new jobs is an almost impossible task. The challenge becomes even more frightening when we consider that it means the country needs to create twice as many jobs as the economy created during the 1960's, without further fueling the fires of inflation.

As it becomes more difficult and expensive for people like General Motors and IBM to borrow money, imagine how consumers' credit will be affected. As interest rates for mortgages and car loans skyrocket, you will see a recession in the housing interest that will filter throughout the rest of the economy and accentuate the problems of unemployment that we mentioned earlier.

The Demise of Middle-Class Affluence

As we pointed out in the first chapter, middle-class affluence has already become something of an illusion. As an individual consumer, you will continue to spend larger and larger percentages of your income to obtain the basic necessities such as food, housing, and energy. Very little money will be left to spend on frills such as travel, entertainment, dental work, and medical checkups. If you have thought that you have been on a treadmill, running hard to just stay in place, imagine the sensation as the treadmill continues to gather speed.

Due to dreams of "The Great Society" and "The New Frontier," we really believed that we could eliminate poverty and make everyone prosperous. The black, the young, the middle class all bought the notion that everything was going to be better. Even education no longer offers an avenue to a better life. Numerous college graduates are finding it almost impossible to find employment. Enrollments are dropping in the liberal arts as students move to more practical disciplines in hope of being able to find a job.

We can see evidence of growing disenchantment among men and women who face menial jobs or unemployment who, in addition to their frustration about lost income, must accept the loss of anticipated social status and their claim to a good life. The near future is almost certain to see greater hostility and suspicion directed, not only against the government, but also toward others who are seen as being wasteful and nonproductive. The gulf that already exists between the rich and the poor, the black and the white, even the doers and the watchers, will accelerate. Indeed, all the stress points of human relations can be expected to intensify when critical financial stresses are introduced. The seething discontent of both sides of the economic equation will lay a foundation for some event that will trigger the collapse. Rising inflation has already created social tensions that fill our social atmosphere like an invisible gas vapor waiting for some chance catastrophe to strike a match. Severe weather—extremely cold winters and shorter growing seasons and droughts in the summer—will create scarcities, and higher prices for food that will further aggravate social discontent.

The Straw to Break the Economy's Back

Between 1982 and 1985, I anticipate the catastrophic event that will trigger the collapse. It could be the bankruptcy of several large banks or the default of two or three cities on their bond obligations. It could be a plane crashing into a key electrical relay station in New York, Chicago, or Boston during the middle of a winter storm that sets off a chain reaction resulting in a nationwide paralysis of transportation and communication. Another major possibility is a series of natural disasters such as earthquakes striking two or three major cities at the same time. Nuclear blackmail from some minor power becomes more likely every day, even though this trigger is less likely, in my opinion, than the other alternatives.

Almost without exception, the equipment and procedures that are highly touted as modern means of meeting urban disasters can be immediately crippled by the obstruction of public roads or by the removal of power. The national interstate highway system was justified by the rationale that they were primarily for purposes of defense and public safety. Many Californians can testify that a relatively minor earthquake can raise or lower the slabs of concrete in an expressway by eighteen inches and render the freeway impassable to any vehicle other than tanks. How well will modern fire engines or police cars perform in a city with its streets clogged with cars that have run out of gas and are stuck in a twenty-inch blizzard? How many of our gasoline-powered vehicles can function when there is no electric power to run the gas pump? Not only is our security highly vulnerable to a multitude of likely natural disasters, we are even dependent on highly vulnerable emergency equipment and contingency plans.

The components for paralysis already exist in most cities with populations above 2 million. The only thing that remains is for the right combination of catalytic agents to come together at an appropriate time.

Chaos in the Cities

Several of our large cities have already been through blackouts and lived to laugh about them. But we have not yet seen the impact when several metropolises are hit at the same time, and it all arrives in the middle of the policemen's January strike. The domino effect will rock the entire country. We can count on public disorder, looting, and the essential outside authoritarian solution to the chaos.

Economist Thomas Muller, of the Urban Institute in Washington, lists several "municipal danger signals." These include: substantial long-term out-migration, loss of private employment, high debt service, high unemployment, high tax burden, increasing proportion of low-income population. Do you know any major city that doesn't have a perfect score on this list of imperfections?

Americans were shocked at the looting in Watts over a decade ago and more recently during the blackouts in New York City and the 1978 snowstorm that immobilized Boston. We used to assume that these types of civil disobedience were reserved for less sophisticated nations. But every day we move into a more desperate condition than we have ever been in before. Many people identified with Howard Beale, the deranged newscaster in the movie *Network*. They are "mad as hell" and don't plan to take any more. More importantly, people believe that authority is probably wrong. No longer is "our friend the policeman" respected as a public servant with the public well-being at heart. Today, public servants are assumed to be out to serve themselves first, last, and always. Last year about thirty cities experienced a police or fire fighter strike. At the local level, they're caught in the crunch, too.

We should well expect that during the very critical first

days when urban America is really beginning to fold and
people have begun to get the idea that they are on their own,
looting will become the order of the day. Those whose conscience might discourage them will be able to rationalize that
the supermarkets and gas stations have taken more than their
shares for years and that looting is only evening the score.
Besides, they will reason, the big companies can stand to take
the losses anyway, and they probably have insurance to take
care of it. Supermarkets will be hit hard and fast. Rioting will
break out quickly. You should expect to see some type of
guerilla warfare and massive sabotage, as those who got to
the store late proceed to take it away from those who looted
early in the day. (Secondhand looting is easy to rationalize;
imagine the simple mental steps required to justify stealing
something from someone who stole it in the first place.)

Food and welfare riots will continue. Remember that the
riots of the 1960's were triggered by relatively minor events.
Howard J. Ruff reports that he has encountered massive fear
on the part of white surburban Americans that this will trigger massive black militance and signal the beginning of a
race war. Given the dependence of much of the black population on public funds, the high rate of crime and unemployment among black teenagers, the growing alcohol and drug
addiction as well as the "hate whitey" rhetoric of the past,
this vision isn't difficult to conceive. Yet Ruff makes two excellent points concerning the containment of this activity. He
believes that the resulting violence will be contained within
the city limits. With a ghetto six miles across with one-half
million population, there is a twenty-eight-square-mile area
with a population density of almost 18,000 people per square
mile. Obviously, every ghetto resident will not be ready to go
on the war path. The "attack" group will be mostly adult
males and teenagers on the loose. If 100,000 people decide to
spread out in a radius of fifteen miles from the center of the
ghetto, they have to occupy 706 square miles, leaving only
141 people per square mile. A forty-mile radius reduces the
intensity to twenty raiders per square mile. The further you
move out from the ghetto, the less of a threat exists.

As Ruff points out, full-scale rioting, looting, and burning
in the context of a full-blown depression and monetary crisis
". . . will be a tragedy for America's black people, as the
numbers and the guns are against them." Violence and looting in the ghettos will probably die down within one to three

weeks when there are no more food stores to loot and liquor stores' supplies run out. Spoiled food and stolen liquor are not a sustaining diet. Street-wise blacks will realize that they can't hide in a white community so they will come back to their own environment where their survival skills prove more valuable.

The intensity of the initial reaction will probably stimulate many urban whites who have managed to hold on to some of their money to exodus toward small cities that they believe will be safer. There will be a short-lived boom in land, farm equipment, and home furnishings. Although the intensity of the initial looting and rioting will subside, violence and robbery will become increasingly common. I believe that Ruff is mistaken in his assumption that people living more than fifteen miles from a ghetto will be relatively safe during this crisis. Already, the suburbs are being plagued by a dramatic increase in burglary and theft. People who have to satisfy a drug addiction (or even an addiction to food) learn quickly that you can't steal money from people who don't have it. They will, consequently, move in increasing numbers to any area where they believe that people still have food or other valuables. Such criminal acts will be driven by more desperation than is typical today. I expect a great deal of violence on the part of perpetrators and the victims.

Hungry People Are Not Polite

Food shortages will remain critical. We have become a nation where few individuals can grow or kill their own food—even in the best of times. As the chaos spreads and the meaning of money becomes less clear, food itself or old silver coins will become the best medium of exchange. People will revert almost overnight to some of their basic drives for the basic requirements of food, water, and shelter.

As the initial rash of looting, burning, and violence subsides, authoritarian control will be imposed in an attempt to sustain life and public safety. Another totally unbelievable stage will be entered. For a relatively short period, prices will accelerate to unimaginable levels due to the scarcity of food and other necessities. In this period of runaway inflation, people who have supplies of paper dollars will buy any kind of luxury good that is available because they see the prices rising so quickly. This will be a very short-lived boom. During this period, I would encourage you to unload your paper dollars as quickly as possible. You may be paying $500 or $1,000 an ounce for gold, but it will hold its value better than any of the gadgets you might buy.

Black markets will return us to the sort of unbelievable prices we have heard of in post World War I Germany, but never could quite believe. But we *will* believe them when the only way to get a loaf of bread and a quart of milk is to pay out sixteen dollars in greenbacks or one gallon of gasoline or two genuine silver quarters. This last sentence suggests how the transition from runaway inflation to a full-blown depression will take place. Prices in paper dollars will continue to skyrocket for a while, but concurrently, there will be a second and much lower tier of prices for real money.

The stock market will plummet out of sight—after having produced at least one late inning rally over 1000, which will keep some people thinking that the market will muddle through. But it will be some time before it becomes a reasonable place for prudent investors.

There will be another attempt at price controls and official action to force people to make goods available. But these approaches have never been able to control the black markets that spring to life almost automatically whenever there is a low supply and high demand. Paper money will be a highly suspect medium of exchange. Initially, the government will try to force people to accept and use paper dollars. However, most merchants will learn to say the requested item is "out of stock" and save it for the buyer with gold or silver. Shop owners will quickly learn that, no matter how many dollar bills they receive for an item, inflation makes it impossible to buy replacements for that price. The natural stability of gold and silver will return regardless of government monetary policy. It always has.

Even before the final crunch of the crisis arrives, the dollar bill will continue to falter on the international scene relative to the more stable currencies of Switzerland, Japan, Germany, and Holland. This will mean that we will be able to sell our goods abroad, but it will be very difficult to buy foreign-made items. Foreign-made cars and parts will be extremely expensive and anything else made abroad will be hard to purchase.

Two other significant developments on the international scene are almost inevitable. We can expect an increase in the terrorist activities of other countries, and their spread to the United States has already begun. We need to reckon with the existence of groups throughout the world who view themselves as united in behalf of the creation of international chaos as a step to international renovation. The "Revolutionary Army" has volunteers in practically every country throughout the world. There have been at least two training schools for revolutionary activity within the United States where recruits are taught the basics of guerilla warfare, terrorism, and even torture. Additionally, we have thousands of disillusioned Vietnam veterans who have been taught these concepts in an optimum laboratory environment. It isn't hard to understand why someone who was prevented from entering a career while times were good, and who was trained and armed efficiently and then sent out to fight in a godforsaken quagmire where he was told to be careful not to win, might resent a society that returned him home where it was difficult to find a job and then asked him to endure the cruelest inflation in the history of the country. Remember, too, that the more than 460,000 in the Air and Army National Guards have ready access to high-powered, sophisticated weapons of destruction. Those who prophesy marauding bands of terrorists sweeping through the countryside may have only a slightly exaggerated picture of future events. You can rest assured that terrorists in this country will have financial and moral support from their comrades throughout the world.

The other international development is the likelihood of one or more bad crop years abroad, which will lead to certain famine and create pressures in the poorer nations to consider a nuclear blackmail. They would have little to lose by demanding food from the United States in exchange for sparing the District of Columbia. Some observers cite the probability of nuclear blackmail as being as high as 40–50 percent within the next five years.

THE MIDTERM: THE DARKEST BEFORE THE DAWN

In ancient Egypt, Pharaoh was warned that his country was to endure seven years of great suffering. Only by making provision for these seven lean years could his country survive. And only after enduring this period of deprivation could the Egyptian nation go on to achieve its ultimate destiny. Similarly, I believe that this country must endure seven years of full-scale depression with large numbers of people unemployed, shortages, and the pervasive inability to get many necessities. Luxuries will be only bitter memories for all except a fortunate few who have been able to preserve portions of their predepression resources.

Cities will deteriorate rapidly and to overwhelming degrees. Criminal elements will prove more dependable than police, and there may be a revival of the old protection games. Citizens will be afraid to walk the streets of most American cities. Services within the cities will become almost nonexistent. There will be rampant fear, hostility, hunger, and despair.

The government will attempt to provide control, but neither the National Guard nor the military forces will be able to restore order once the public at large becomes convinced that its survival is not the primary interest of these authoritarian forces so representative of the government that let them down before.

A Perpetual State of Emergency

To stave off a complete collapse of order, the president will be forced to use some of the emergency powers at his disposal. Most people do not realize that the president has "near dictatorial" powers to issue orders changing the course of foreign and domestic affairs. Often this can be done without consulting Congress. The most impressive weapon in the president's arsenal is the broad power given him under the "National Emergency" provisions. It is with this authority that presidents have issued wage-price controls, imposed import taxes, called out troops to deliver mail during a postal strike, and reorganized the nation's banking system. Under emergency circumstances the president can at any moment:

1. call up retired or reserve members of the armed forces and send them anywhere he chooses.
2. seize foreign ships in U.S. waters and requisition and arm private ships.
3. restrict production of explosives.
4. refuse the right of any person to leave or enter the United States.

5. take back former Federal installations that have been transferred to state and local governments.

Any time the President declares a state of emergency, there are more than 200 laws that permit him to take decisive action without waiting for the approval of Congress or anyone else.

In case you may wonder what constitutes a state of emergency, the answer is that one exists whenever the president says it does.

Survival and Security for the Duration

The people who will function best during this crisis will be those who have had experience in taking care of themselves, whether on a farm or in an urban ghetto. Flabby members of the middle class will probably suffer more than anyone else. Contrast between this desolate period and the past will not be as great for the poor, who have always had to worry about survival. The middle class, on the other hand, will survive only with deliberate preparation and practice for the time of stress.

The development of citizens' police groups to protect subdivisions and neighborhoods is likely. Security is already a major expense for American business. During the next ten years, it will surely increase in an attempt to protect against increased robbery attempts and crimes of vengeance or simple hostility. This latter category will be the characteristic crime in the war of the "haves" and the "have-nots." Racial and class hatred will become more pronounced during this time.

The "subterranean economy" will become significant as more people do business and never report it or swap products between themselves with no money changing hands and no resulting tax records. This will be a time when individual initiative and ingenuity will once again be rewarded in America—not with wealth but with survival.

During this period, it is likely that churches will become very introverted. Religion will offer solace for the righteous, but will tend to ignore the "heathen"—which will mean everyone else. "True believers" will find unity and brotherhood in their abhorrence of the wicked who are responsible for this calamity. When any group wants to deny responsibility for mistakes, there is always a convenient scapegoat. Familiar sermon themes will be "God Helps Those Who Help Themselves" and "If a Man Won't Work, Neither Let Him Eat."

The mood of the times will make the country susceptible to a popular takeover by a demagogue who appeals to the popular paranoia and offers a simplistic solution to the nation's plight. I fear that Hitler's rise to power on the frustration of people racked by runaway inflation will be a tempting model. A charismatic leader will have a unique opportunity to rise on the political front of the country as popular opinion is drawn to anybody who can optimistically, enthusiastically, and authoritatively present a way out—even at the surrender of some previously treasured civil rights and national values.

During this period, people who live on farms will be in the best shape of all. This will not be equally true for people who live *near* farms as many commuters do today. They will be isolated from the place of earning and yet unprepared to create a self-sustaining farm on their half-acre with split-level home and pool.

Farms will rise in value, but not price, for a couple of obvious reasons. They have food that will be in demand. But, more importantly, farm life tends to imbue its people with a greater degree of self-sufficiency. Small towns, with their closer social ties and more conservative values, will see less suffering than the major urban areas that are so totally dependent on public services.

Some manufacturing and service businesses will do surprisingly well, even though there is limited money around. Luxury merchants who prospered during the hyper-inflation will fold, but those providing basic services will prosper. Individuals with skills will do well. Diplomas and certificates that *say* you have skills will be as worthless as paper dollars inless these pieces of paper have solid backing. Survival may depend on real and required abilities that are useful enough that people will value them more than their limited financial resources.

Many of my former colleagues in academia will find that idyllic university towns are not suitable locations for riding out the storm. Since most of the jobs in these towns are oriented around a university that may close (and certainly cut its staff to the bare bones), it will be hard to make ends meet unless the town has more seed stores than pizza parlors.

Over all, the surest place to be in the midterm crisis is on a farm, where there are self-sufficient people with plenty of preparation and substantial practice at keeping wishes in line with means.

THE LONG TERM: THE DAWN OF A NEW DAY

Just as gold or iron ore is made more valuable by a fiery refining process, human beings are also able to grow as a result of suffering. Many psychologists feel that there is very little emotional growth without pain. If this is true, as I believe it is, this period of refining will strengthen our national character and provide hope for the future.

While it is doubtful that the United States will ever again have the degree of world dominance it knew during the 1950's, there is hope there will be an even greater nation. As the country works through its problems and some of our individual expectations are scaled down, we can anticipate a repudiation of national debts and a start over again with at least a modified gold standard.

People will eventually find themselves returning to an "old-time" morality, with the pace being slower, simpler virtues being emphasized, greater respect for nature, and more reliance and trust in the free market system rather than a naive trust in the power of government to solve our individual or collective problems.

This does not imply that there will be a return to life as it existed around the turn of the century. Technology will still be with us. Computer and laser technology will eliminate much of the repetitive nature of manufacturing activities. New forms of energy will be utilized that are less damaging to the environment. I anticipate that solar energy will be even more widely used than is currently anticipated.

We will emerge from the crisis holding fast to the idea that reward should be directly related to how much a person is willing to contribute—not what their educational credentials are or what status symbols they possess. While there will be compassion for those who are unable to work, there will be much less sympathy for people who choose not to contribute to society. Because of the thorny problems of how to deal with the innocent children of irresponsible parents, I believe that society will conclude that parenthood is not an inalienable right, and consequently there will be many more cases where parental rights are terminated in order to break the cycle of dependency. Punishment for crimes will seem more severe compared to current standards. We will, I hope, have learned a lesson that there is an immutable law that people must reap what they sow.

There will be less emphasis on growth. We will be more content with smaller cars, smaller houses, and fewer status symbols that serve no purpose but to merely demonstrate wealth. Skills will be respected more than useless knowledge. In the words of John Gardner: "A country which respects a poor philosopher more than a fine plumber is in trouble. Neither their ideas nor their pipes will hold water!"

In this period of time, we will move toward an emphasis on the *complete* individual versus the *specialized* person. A person who is able to take care of his problems—whether it be a leaky faucet or a faulty relationship—will know prosperity, peace of mind, and respect of peers.

Sex roles will be far less pronounced than they have been in the past. Household tasks and contributing to the economic well-being of the family will be shared by all family members. The family itself will be forced back to oldtime closeness by the common survival needs of its members and memories of the past.

Although the last chapter of the book will emphasize our ability to *make* the future a positive thing, I am basically optimistic about the long-term prospect. There will be a great deal of suffering in the short and midterms for people who are not prepared—and a great deal of painful readjustment is going to be necessary to get the nation's economic ecology in balance again. A certain amount of suffering will be healthy, but you and I won't be stricken by the worst of it if we plan ahead.

In the 1990's, life will not be as rosy as it was in the "happy days" of the 1950's. The average standard of living will not be as high and few people will have the luxury of the naive optimism as in the recent past. We will still be plagued by climatic problems, but there *is* light at the end of the tunnel we are going through. Whether or not you and I make it into the light will be determined by our wisdom as well as the way those around us react to the trauma of the times. The sad events that have been described in this chapter are the specifics of the "abominations and desolations" suggested in Chapter 2.

On the international level, there will be a massive number of people who will die of starvation and exposure. The big question in the long term is how we are going to fare with the world's suffering. There may be events over which we have no control. There may be power plays that make it impossible for us to go back to this period of tranquility. The Soviet Union, because of its vast store of natural resources, extensive space, and because of its military power may emerge as an even more significant world power than it is today. A lot will depend on how aggressive their tendencies are and whether or not we are able to develop a position of strength while fighting off the monster of inflation. Already the Soviets have taken command of the seas as voter pressure to cut naval expansion in the United States has cut the lead the American navy had maintained for years. The major result of SALT negotiations seems to have been to weaken the military posture of the U.S.

It is likely that as we rise from the ashes of economic collapse, we will seek a position of strength based on soundness and wealth and integrity rather than the "might makes right" philosophy that seems to have motivated us during the early days of the Cold War.

Section Two

HOW TO ACHIEVE PROSPERITY AMID POVERTY

CHAPTER FIVE

What Will Happen To Your Traditional Investments?

The fact that you are reading this book indicates that you are one of the minority of thinking people who can see through the disastrous impact of tradition on day-to-day activities. Without becoming a jaundiced cynic, you've learned to carefully evaluate the enthusiastic investment recommendations that you regularly receive. It never hurts to ask a few extra questions or to seek the undisclosed bias that influences the person making a recommendation. Have you ever wondered why your stock broker almost always says your portfolio needs more stocks or bonds? Has he or she ever recommended that you buy a "no-load" mutual fund? An insurance agent may do a computerized analysis of your financial situation, but almost inevitably will conclude you could use a little more whole life insurance—not term insurance, but the more expensive, more commissionable whole life policies.

Even some of the very excellent advice given by such astute advisors as Harry Browne and Howard Ruff tend to reflect their own individual background. For many years, Harry Browne was affiliated with Economic Research Counselors and was involved in setting up Swiss bank accounts for persons who resided on the West Coast. Similarly, Howard Ruff's emphasis on the possibilities of famine in this country is somewhat influenced by his years as a nutritional counselor representing Neo-Life, one of the nation's largest food storage companies, and his role in setting up Reliance Products Company.

One of the major advantages of this book is the relative degree of objectivity that it provides. As a professor and consultant, I had to evaluate a vast amount of material relating to each of the subjects discussed in this book in order to make recommendations to students and clients. Nevertheless,

I have never received income from any of the investment media that are being discussed.

To be perfectly fair, I need to point out that a person who has spent several years representing a particular investment media is much more likely to know the intricate details of that particular concept than I am. In writing this section of the book, I have attempted to steer a middle course, assuming that the reader is neither a completely uninformed oaf nor a supersophisticated multimillionaire. I will not take time to explain the difference between common stocks and preferred stocks since I assume that anyone who is willing to invest in a book like this is already sophisticated enough to make some good decisions concerning his or her financial objectives. And since the book is aimed at a wide audience, I don't intend to explain the difference between puts and calls, selling short, and straddling an investment. There are a number of excellent specialized books and consultants who are willing to provide this type of assistance. My feeling is that if you wish to use some esoteric investment technique, you will be better off in talking to a professional in that area. This book is designed to give you some general guidelines—some principles that will help a person with above-average intelligence plot a practical course during the coming period of financial disorder and uncertainty.

Traditions are a valuable part of our society. They give stability and the ability to remember lessons learned by our predecessors. Any tradition, however, is cursed for those who accept it blindly. Traditions can help you if you accept their wisdom while questioning their assumptions and applications. They can destroy you personally and financially if you swallow them indiscriminately.

In this chapter, I will review the traditional means of investing. I will discuss the likely results of continuing inflation on the standbys like banks, bonds, and the bull market. I will also ask you to consider the likely results of devaluation and other natural disasters.

Most investors seek absolutes when looking for an investment philosophy. If this is your goal, you'll find plenty of books and advisors who will tell you the "one best way." Doubtless you've heard people say, "Bank accounts are insured, they're solid as the United States"; or "The stock market reflects the health of the nation"; or "Treasury bills are as safe as the federal government." Frankly, none of those cliches is particularly reassuring to me. Even in the best of times, such absolute statements lead to narrowmindedness, inflexibility, and inability to learn. In these troubled times, such cliches will almost certainly lead to financial ruin.

If you're assuming that this chapter will tell you specifically how much to invest and where, you're looking for the impossible. There are people who will be willing to give you the certain answers you seek. But I am writing to people I hope will be my friends after we have worked through the problems of the next decade or so. My conscience requires me to give up any hope of simplistic formula for financial success. Even if I was willing to dole out simplistic answers, they could hardly be expected to be trustworthy as each case has its constellation of specific circumstances. The key to financial success or failure requires the proper understanding of your resources, goals, and temperament. This chapter will be full of principles and concepts that can enhance your ability to evaluate investment options. But, ultimately, your challenge will be to filter out all that you've learned through your own intellect and judgment, then weigh the apparent consequences against your gut-level feeling for what is best for you.

You'll never get where you want to go by blindly putting all your eggs in the most highly touted basket. You cannot follow any one advisor's counsel to the exclusion of all others, your own common sense, or your emotional evaluation of the situation under consideration. I will attempt to share with you my experience and insight concerning several major investment media. I'll even provide some guidelines for various sizes of investment portfolios and timetables to keep in mind. But you are the star of the show when it comes to planning and determining your investment future. When you think about it, would you really want it any other way?

FRUIT JARS AND BANKS

You would probably be surprised if you could know the number of people who have buried money in their backyards, packed it away in fruit jars, or hidden it in mattresses. On March 20, 1978, the *Wall Street Journal* carried a front page article about the "Subterranean Economy." As the name implies, subterranean economy is the part of our nation's economic activity that cannot be seen. Peter Gutmann, an economics professor at City University of New York, estimates that the activity of the subterranean economy currently exceeds $200 billion.

A significant portion of the subterranean economy is devoted to illegal use. According to Gutmann, this currency also "lubricates a vast amount of non-reported income and non-reported work." In all probability, continued inflation, high taxes, and pervasive government regulations will guarantee the continuing growth of this component.

Additionally, large numbers of people are simply hiding away currency because they do not trust banks. In some instances, they do not trust the banks to protect their income. In other cases, it is because they do not trust the banks to keep their possessions secret from the government.

The traditional middle-class response to stories about misers and pack rats is that these people are leftovers from the Great Depression and simply don't know any better. It is generally assumed that if you have any money at all above your immediate needs it ought to "at least" be in a savings account where it can be safe and earning a little interest. Perhaps this is true if you are talking about the $156 in the PTA's checking account. However, the bank is one of the poorest locations for any sizable amount of money that is supposed to be working or even safe.

An important distinction that is seldom made by investment advisors is that some savings are mainly needed to provide emergency back-up while others are thought of as investments. Banks and other savings institutions are probably the best ways to store dollars that must be kept liquid and ready to jump into service in the very near future. But if the money is considered to be an *earning* investment—one that is made up of dollars that are not critical to week-to-week survival—then the savings account ranks at the bottom of the list of places to put your money. Banks are probably currently a safe place to deposit money that you are going to need in the short-term future. As I will point out, however, you need to be alert to signals that will indicate that it is time to take anything you have out of the banks.

Those who defend banks and savings and loan institutions like to point to the fact that their deposits are "fully insured." The letters FDIC and FSLIC are featured in every commercial or saving account book because people feel at ease knowing that the government's Federal Deposit Insurance Corporation and the Federal Savings and Loan Insurance

Corporation guarantee up to $40,000 of the account. By putting multiple accounts in the names of various family members, you can have a very large amount of your savings insured in this manner. Once a person is infected with the Federal Insurance idea, he or she can glibly respond to any subsequent mention of a high-return investment by saying, "I know there are places where I can earn more, but I need to know that my money is safe. I'd rather have my sure 5 percent than some pie-in-the-sky 14 percent on a less secure deal."

Unfortunately, the savings accounts are not as guaranteed as you have been led to think. The FDIC has its name on the line for something in the neighborhood of $750 billion worth of bank deposits. However, the FDIC has only about $6 billion in its insurance fund. There is legislation allowing FDIC to borrow an additional $3 billion if necessary, but that's it. There is $9 billion to protect $750 billion. That means that of every $1,000 you have in one of those guaranteed accounts, only $12 of it is fully protected.

The best strategy, of course, is to have your savings in one of the first banks to go under. For obvious public relations reasons, FDIC is going to be on the spot in a hurry doing everything possible to inspire public confidence by paying back dollar for dollar. But FDIC cannot survive very many bank failures in a row. When the Franklin Bank failed in 1974, the FDIC paid out $4 billion. I can assure you that the public smiles of FDIC were masking the private knowledge that $4 billion was more than 40 percent of their total insurance fund.

Obviously, it is just in jest that I recommend finding the next bank to go. You should use banks for the things they can do well for you but not be tied to them by traditions. It is highly unlikely that when things start to collapse, the banks will go out in one united flash rather than one by one according to strength. Few people realize it but the nation's banking system is dominated by no more than fifteen banking groups, most of them controlled by giant holding companies. Though that may seem strange to you, stop and think where *your* bank gets its loans. The pinnacle of the pyramid is in New York City and the domino effect is all set for one spectacular chain reaction. The Chairman of the Senate Banking Committee admitted in 1976, "A relatively limited economic setback could result in the failure of some of the nation's largest banks."

Not only are the banks interlocked to pull each other

down, they are not even individually sound. They are in fact made out of money that does not exist—not just living on borrowed money, but living on nonexistent money. Suppose you be the bank—I'll give you a $1,000 deposit. You turn around and loan out $750 to someone. How much is your bank worth? $1,000? Not the way bankers see it. You have $1,000 in deposit and $750 in outstanding loans. That's $1,750! Maybe you can even borrow additional funds on the strength of the numbers. Our banking system is sophisticated, but it is still involved in this same kind of exercise—creating money on paper and even loaning out the blank spaces between the lines of figures in their ledgers. And this practice doesn't scare me as much as the shaky loans that have been made to U.S. real estate speculators, almost defunct municipalities, and questionable foreign operations.

Even if banks were as strong as we have always been told, they are lousy places to get a return on your money. Anytime the rate of inflation in the economy is greater than the interest you are earning, you can be sure that the end result is a loss for you. Your savings passbook will *say* you have more dollars but the purchasing power of the total will be less than the purchasing power of the money you originally deposited.

Banks can help you. The cash you stash in the fruit jar may even have its appropriate place in your financial plan. Banks are valuable in the day-to-day handling of money and rainy day savings for emergency use. If you wish to put money in a fruit jar, remember that currency draws no interest and will lose value daily. While I would recommend something more secure than a fruit jar, be sure that any money you squirrel away is "real money"—that it has some gold and silver content. More about that subject, however, in the next chapter.

In summary, you should neither trust banks implicitly nor distrust them altogether. Keep close to your bank until danger signs (such as a few bank failures or the default of a couple of cities on their bond obligations) tell you that you should be losing interest in them. Use them for your day-to-day dealings, but look elsewhere for a place to develop your money's greatest earning power.

THE STOCK MARKET

The first thing to remember about the stock market is that

you are competing with some of the most intelligent and sophisticated money managers in the world. Pension funds, insurance companies, and trust departments of banks account for a majority of the trades made each day. These funds are managed by teams of full-time professionals who follow every piece of financial news, often monitored by sophisticated computer systems, to anticipate the impact of any news events upon the performance of various stocks. In other words, it's awfully hard for the average dabbler to outperform the market—or the funds.

One popular method of being in the stock market without competing with the professionals is to work with the professionals via mutual funds. By pooling your funds with many other investors, you can hire experienced professionals to buy and sell a large, diversified portfolio of stocks and bonds. You can even choose funds that reflect your particular investment philosophy. There are funds that emphasize income and those that emphasize capital growth; funds that stress old-line, blue-chip firms; and funds that concentrate on relatively unknown over-the-counter stocks. You pay your money and take your choice.

At face value, mutual funds seem to have a great deal going for them. There is the security of being in a large group, the security of a professional investment team and the security of a diversified placement of money. It must be remembered, however, that no mutual funds have consistently outperformed the market. There have been many short-term managers who have provided dramatic returns to their investors. When you put them all together, they tend to move in the general direction of the overall market.

If you want to be "in the market" but have neither the time, patience, or confidence to play the role of the swashbuckling risk-taker, mutual funds may be for you. If you want to give your money the no-holds-barred potential to hit the sky or drag the bottom, invest in one or two stocks at a time. Somewhere in all the literature about the stock market, someone needs to admit that one of the factors that encourage people to participate in this gigantic crap roll is that it is exciting fun. You really don't have to go to Las Vegas or Atlantic City to gamble. Moreover, you can gain the added dignity of being a member of an exclusive club with a dramatic history. The fact remains that there is a bit of the Walter Mitty in each of us. Everyone wants to strike it rich by following in the grand tradition of the Rockefellers and Kennedys.

To admit that the stock market can be fun is not to exalt it or condemn it. My purpose is merely to provide better perspective. The funds invested in the market should be discretionary funds. The market is the last place for money that you and your family may need in an emergency.

If a person has any significant assets (a minimum of $50,-000 to invest), he or she might be wise to have a portion in the stock market, particularly in small, local companies that have a potential for growth. Rather than going by the sound of a corporate name or the national advisement services, the sage stock trader will look to small companies that he or she knows something about. Ideally, you can find a regional company that is in some field that is likely to do well during the period of a faltering economy. For example, certain companies in agriculture and energy are going to have good prospects even when the nation's consumers begin to tighten their belts. These types of "basic human needs" stocks are the surest bets. And the more basic the company is, the more potential they have. In other words, I'm not as optimistic about the long-term future of the nutritionless convenience food companies as I am about companies that are involved in planting and harvesting real food.

By emphasizing regional companies, the small investor has a chance of being at least as knowledgeable as some of the competition he faces. One of the few individuals I know who has been consistently successful in the stock market is a person who, several years ago, decided he wanted to live in the Sun Belt because of personal convenience and because of his belief in the future of the region. While living in San Antonio, Texas, he had to travel to Houston and Dallas frequently. He found that a new company, Southwest Airlines, was offering transportation between these cities at approximately half what the established airlines were charging. Socially, he had an occasion to meet an attorney who was representing Southwest Airlines in many of their dealings. When he had satisfied himself that this company had a sound management, he was also convinced of the validity of their idea. He bought their stock at 3½ in 1974 and sold at 22 in 1975. About the same time, he was involved in a project with Church's Fried Chicken. Although the company was experiencing some problems at that time in closing out some of their unprofitable operations, he recognized that their concept and management were basically solid. During the slump of 1974, he bought the stock at $7 per share and kept it until it had risen to $58 in mid-1978 (after a three for two stock split a year before).

In 1976, he moved to mid-Tennessee and became impressed with a local catalogue showroom. A Nashville-based company, Service Merchandise, was one of the largest catalogue showroom merchandisers in the United States and was expanding rapidly. He bought their stock at a little under $10 in 1977 and sold it in mid-1978 for $27. He also learned that a Memphis-based firm, Federal Express, was considering going public in 1978, and did a little investigation to find out about the dramatic growth of this operation. Since the need for overnight delivery of key papers and packages was obvious due to the faltering U.S. Postal Service, he bought as much of the stock as possible when it was first issued to the public in April of 1978 at $24 per share. In about five months, the stock was selling for more than $60.

The rules this investor has successfully utilized are summarized as follows:

1. Emphasize companies you know something about.
2. Choose companies that perform or deliver a worthwhile product or service.
3. Watch for young companies that have a record of growth (or evidence that they are making a dramatic turnaround).
4. Prefer stocks priced under $25 per share (It is easier for low-priced stocks to double than for high-priced stocks.)
5. Divestment is as important as investment. (Don't expect a stock to double in value every year. Sell when you've earned a reasonable return. Don't be greedy.)

David Rhoads estimates that 65 percent of an investor's profit from being on the right side of market moves and 25 percent of his potential comes from picking the right industry. You should still remember that each stock reflects the fortunes of an individual operation and in all cases anticipation is the key to market success. While you hope that the stocks will outperform the market, it is an unusual company whose stock moves in opposition to the market. If the nation appears to gain even temporary control over inflation, the market will move ahead aggressively. It appears that as long as inflation is above 6.5 percent, the market will not move ahead, on an average, faster than inflation. I, and several other advisors, feel that there is one more bull movement left in the economy before the tremendous collapse. Harry Browne recommends the use of warrants to gain leverage on the up-side movements of the markets, while limiting the amount of money you can lose in a stock market crash. A system for evaluating and choosing warrants is developed in his latest book. While I prefer to choose stocks in smaller companies that will outperform the averages even during a bear market, Browne's ideas about using warrants are worthy of consideration.

In March, 1978, stocks were selling at what appeared to be a frightening low. In reality, the prices were even lower than most people realized because of the inflation factor. While the Dow Jones Industrial average was around 740, the purchasing power value was 60 percent below its 1966 level. If you try to stay up with the stock market, don't make the mistake of using only the Dow Jones Industrial Index. This is the most widely quoted index. Yet, it is based on only thirty old-line, blue-chip stocks that most of my readers will not be interested in. For overall assessment of the market, the New York Stock Exchange Composite is a much better reading. If your portfolio emphasizes stocks that are traded over the counter, the NASDAQOTC Composite is a better index. Since the Dow Jones Company publishes the *Wall Street Journal*, you would expect the Dow Jones Average to receive special attention. Yet, the next to the last page of each *Journal* contains several indexes that are much better suited to monitoring the activities of your portfolio.

For the next year or so, I would not rule out participation in the stock market. But you should be very specific about the kind of money you are using for these investments. Keep emergency funds and survival money in more protected areas. If you have remaining money that you wish to use for short-term investments, then do your homework and take a risk.

Consider Your Taxes

If you are one of the millions of people who are finding themselves in constantly higher tax brackets, be sure to consider the advantages of taxfree municipal bonds for your short-term portfolio. These bonds, which are promissory notes offered by various municipal agencies, pay a return that is not subject to federal or state income taxes. The higher your tax bracket, the more this feature can mean to you in April. For example, a married couple with a taxable income above $39,200 is currently taxed at a rate of 45 percent. That means that a municipal bond that pays 6 percent provides the same return as a corporate bond or other investment that yields almost 11 percent.

Unfortunately, municipal bonds are no longer the conservative domain of "widows and orphans" who wish to commit their money for long-term periods of time without worry or concern. The financial solvency of large cities is certainly suspect. As with many other investments, pick your choices with care and, by all means, stay clear of bonds for cities such as:

New York	Cleveland	St. Louis
Detroit	San Francisco	Honolulu
Philadelphia	Los Angeles	Baltimore
Boston	Memphis	

If you prefer to let someone else evaluate municipals for you, there are several municipal bond funds that provide regular taxfree income. There is a ready market for units of these funds should you decide to sell, but you may have to accept a slight loss in your capital.

YOUR INSURANCE INVESTMENTS

Even if you don't own stock in Prudential or Metropolitan Life, you probably have a significant portion of your investment funds tied up in insurance. Most people don't understand that a major part of the premium for ordinary life insurance is an incredbily poor investment.

When looking at insurance dollars, you should recognize that there are two major objectives to be achieved through insurance. The first is protection for your family in the event of an "untimely demise." With both partners in a marriage capable of working today, that term basically means while there are small children at home.

The other major objective is to provide liquidity for your estate. If your *taxable* estate is only $100,000, your heirs will owe $18,200 plus 28 percent of the amount over $80,000. If your taxable estate is $1 million, your estate will have a tax liability of $345,800. Even most millionaires don't have that much cash sitting around. In fact, for individuals whose net worth is tied up in real estate or business interests, the estate tax bill may be a very significant problem. In many instances, this need has caused people to sell valuable business interests or real estate holdings at losses in order to meet their liability.

Either of the two reasons mentioned above is a legitimate reason for putting money in life insurance. The old argument that insurance is a good way to force you to put aside for a rainy day is totally fallacious for anyone with the good sense and discipline to read this book.

To meet family needs for a young wage earner, there is no question that term insurance is by far the best alternative. Young people who need an insurance agent to force them to put some money aside for investment deserve the 3 or 4 percent return they receive.

Since not many people like the idea of sickly 3 or 4 percent return, this fact is not highly publicized by insurance agents. There is a simple solution but it requires a measure of self-discipline. Instead of buying an ordinary life policy, buy the same amount of term insurance. Find out the difference in the two premiums and then invest that difference as regularly as you would have paid the insurance company.

Consider, for example, the case of a thirty-five-year-old male (the rates are the same for a forty-year-old female because of her higher life expectancy) who needs $100,000 of protection until his two children are grown. Using 1978 rates of one large company, he can spend $303 per year for a twenty-year term insurance policy, or $1,718 per year for a whole life insurance policy. If the individual's protection needs end at the conclusion of twenty years, he will have a cash value of approximately $29,580 in his ordinary life insurance policy. On the other hand, if he takes the difference between the premiums and invests it—even in municipal bonds that yield 6 percent—at the end of twenty years his nest egg will be worth more than $51,000.

Another factor to consider when taking out insurance for protection needs is a cost-of-living adjustment. For example, some policies give you an option each year to purchase additional insurance that will keep your coverage comparable to the amount you had when you bought the original policy. For example, a major insurer recently provided a policy holder with a notice about his term insurance that read, "For the year beginning May 1, 1978, you have $26,880 as the contractual amount of insurance under this policy. During the period used to measure cost of living changes for this policy, the Consumer Price Index increased by 49.63 percent, making $13,370 of insurance available to you for the coming year in addition to the contractual amount. The year's premium for this additional insurance is shown above."

If your objective is to provide liquidity for your estate, an important way to gain maximum advantage is through *minimum deposit insurance*. Under this arrangement, you take a whole life policy because you want it to last for all your life—not just a specified term. If you pay the full premium in four of the first seven years of the policy, you can in the other years borrow against the cash value of the policy to pay the premiums each year. This has three valuable results. First, the rate of interest is very low for this loan (6 percent as opposed to 9-10 percent if you borrowed elsewhere) and the interest is tax deductible. The premium is fixed so you always pay back with inflated dollars, which makes the cost less than it would appear. Finally, the overall cash outlay is quite low. For a $100,000 policy, the average annual net outlay for a person in the 50 percent tax bracket will be approximately $400 per year (see Table 5.1). This is still not quite as good a buy as term insurance.

THE GOOD EARTH

There is probably no area of investment that is more victimized by the traditional cliches than real estate. You have heard the old saws that "God has quit making land but he's still making people" and "real estate prices always bounce back eventually."

These little ditties sound good, but there are plenty of examples of ways they have been proven wrong recently. The U.S. population has hovered near the zero-growth level since 1973.

Land prices that have suffered after a particular speculative wave may come back up in the long run, but as the New Deal economist Maynard Keynes once said, "in the long run we are all dead." There are a startling number of locations in urban centers where demographic shifts have left property owners with holdings that were useless for the production of income or capital gains. Most major cities have areas that

TABLE 5.1

Example of Minimum Deposit Life Insurance

Age 35 Male

WHOLE LIFE POLICY							FACE AMOUNT BASIC PREMIUM	$97209.00 $ 2120.38
Year	Net Annual Premium*	Loan Interest* 6 Per Cent	Paid By Loan*	Annual Cash Outlay*	Net Annual Cash Outlay*	Cumulative Loan*	Guaranteed Cash Value	Net Death Benefit*
1	2121	0	731	1390	1390	731	778	96478
2	2121	44	1553	612	590	2284	2430	94925
3	1969	137	1645	461	392	3929	4180	97460
4	1915	236	0	2151	2033	3929	5930	99210
5	1862	236	0	2098	1980	3929	7680	100960
6	1810	236	0	2046	1928	3929	9526	102806
7	1756	236	0	1992	1874	3929	11276	104556
8	1706	236	8406	6464CR	6532CR	12335	13123	97997
9	1655	740	1736	659	289	14071	14970	98108
10	1605	844	1736	713	291	15807	16817	98219
11	1561	948	1645	864	390	17452	18567	98324
12	1516	1047	1737	826	302	19189	20414	98434
13	1473	1151	1645	979	403	20834	22164	98539
14	1432	1250	1736	946	321	22570	24011	98650
15	1393	1354	1644	1103	426	24214	25760	98755
16	1358	1453	1736	1075	348	25950	27607	98866

TABLE 5.1 Cont'd.

Example of Minimum Deposit Life Insurance

Age 35 Male

FACE AMOUNT $97209.00
BASIC PREMIUM $ 2120.38

WHOLE LIFE POLICY

Year	Net Annual Premium*	Loan Interest* 6 Per Cent	Paid By Loan*	Annual Cash Outlay*	Net Annual Cash Outlay*	Cumulative Loan*	Guaranteed Cash Value	Net Death Benefit*
17	1326	1557	1736	1147	368	27686	29454	98977
18	1298	1661	1736	1223	392	29422	31301	99088
19	1275	1765	1737	1303	420	31159	33148	99198
20	1256	1870	1736	1390	455	32895	34995	99309

Summary to Age 55

Net Surrender Value at 53   1365*

Years	Average Annual Gross Outlay	Average Annual Net Outlay 50% Tax Bracket	Annual Surrender Net Cost 50% Tax Bracket
1-5	1342	1277	482
1-10	565	418	300
1-15	691	401	284

have been literally abandoned by owners rather than pay the taxes that already exceed the earning power of their property. The number of these urban wastelands will certainly increase during the next decade.

Studying migration trends can be helpful. At the present time, it appears that people are moving away from the large cities. The Conference Board, a New York-based business and economic research organization, recently predicted the metropolitan areas with populations above 2 million will decline during the next decade. Conversely, they suggest that cities with populations between 100,000 and 2 million will experience considerable growth. Personally, I would prefer to risk my money (and life) in cities that are closer to the 100,-000 level—particularly if these are in the so-called Sun Belt. It's not merely that the weather is better in these locations, they're going to be safer and have lower energy costs. Consequently, jobs and business opportunities are more likely to be found in these situations and along with them, a demand for housing and office space.

For many people, their home is the largest single investment they ever make. While I believe it is a mistake to view a house as an investment, certain real estate principles need to be considered in making this purchase. Many individuals make the tragic mistake of computing their net worth based on the appreciated value of their house. This has the intoxicating effect of making them appear to be much better off than they really are. As things now stand, you might be able to sell your house for a substantial profit. But what would you do about another place to live? Chances are you would buy an even more expensive house in order to "move up" the materialistic ladder. Once inflation runs its full course and we are faced with a massive deflation, that overpriced house will offer only shelter as a major advantage and little hope for further capital gains.

Consequently, you should choose a house based on your plans to live in it. I would further recommend that you not buy the largest or most expensive house you can afford. Large houses cost a great deal to maintain today. But with the increasing cost of energy and other services, maintenance is going to be a major problem throughout the future. Repairs and upkeep, as well as energy, make a big house a questionable investment—unless you have a big family. The place you live in is a necessity—not an investment.

What then about real estate as an investment if you have funds beyond these that are required to provide lodging? Here we're talking about income-producing real estate and property held for potential appreciation. Like every other investment, your success in making these investments depends upon your ability to assess the changing situations and time your commitments correctly. If you already own rental units in locations that are safe for the long term, you would be well advised to hold onto them. I wouldn't recommend shopping for a new acquisition, however, because it will be very difficult for you to get a long-term return on the inflated price you would have to pay at present. If your rental units are in a location that you think might be shaky for the long term, start looking for a buyer who is less realistic about the long-term economic future of this country.

As far as I'm concerned, the bloom is off the rose as far as holding raw land for appreciation. In early 1978, *Business Week* reported that farm prices were already declining in certain parts of the Midwest. In Kansas, for example, irrigated farmland that reached a peak value of $1,200 an acre in 1975 was being offered for $800 or $900 an acre two years later. As a general rule, it's a good time to start unloading some of your nonliquid investments. Prices will probably go a little bit higher during the next couple or three years, but as Robert Preston has suggested, "It's better to be a year early than a day too late." If you are able to convert your money into gold or silver that will continue to appreciate with inflation, you'll find yourself in a very enviable situation when real estate prices hit the bottom—probably in another six to eight years.

Incidentally, if you happen to have some basic carpentry and plumbing skills, buying distressed properties will continue to be a wise move during depression times. Find a property that has been on the market for a while and needs repairs, make a very low down payment and quickly spruce up the property, keeping the improvements primarily cosmetic and noticeable to prospective tenants. Don't redecorate to your own tastes, but to the standards of comparable units in the surrounding neighborhoods.

Since you've put a small amount of money into the property, you can allow the rent to make the payment, support the upkeep on the property, and pay your increased taxes. Since you can depreciate the house as a business expense, this will provide a limited tax shelter. Most of the innumerable books on how to make big money in real estate suggest this approach with the profit from each transaction becoming the down payment for the next, larger investment. If this has been your plan during the past, the next few years will be a good period for you to take a brief rest from your labors so that you can start over when prices are lower and prospects are brighter.

In facing our cloudy future, debts pose a complex dilemma. With inflation moving rapidly ahead during the next few years, there is an incentive to borrow as much as possible and to pay back the obligation in "cheaper" dollars. If your income doubles, it would appear to be relatively easy to pay off a debt that may have been almost too much for you to handle at the time it was made. If, however, the costs of food and energy have tripled in that time period, paying off the debt may be even more difficult in the future than it is at present. The other major problem with debt is what will happen when inflation tops out and is followed by the almost inevitable deflation or depression. With an ordinary home mortgage, all of the buyer's assets are pledged as security against that debt. If the borrower is fired from work and defaults on the house payment, the lender can foreclose on the mortgage. If the proceeds aren't enough to discharge the obligation, the mortgage-holder can get a deficiency judgment and take other of the homeowner's assets. This feature is typical in most debt agreements. Be wary lest all your possessions be subject to seizure for the satisfaction of any debt that may default. Unless you carefully read your loan agreement, you may not be able to simply let the bank or finance company take back the item that you borrowed against.

Have your attorney check all of your loan agreements to see what options are open to your creditors in the event you are unable to make any of the payments. Then work with him to restructure your debts so that you can protect yourself as much as possible. On future obligations, be sure that you have limited your liability to the property under consideration. This may be done with a sales contract, a purchase money mortgage, or a clause specifically inserted in the loan agreement that identifies the limit of your liability. A sales contract merely says that the title stays with the seller until he has finished paying for the property. You can resell the property under certain conditions, but if you are unable to make future payments, you simply return the property back to the original owner. You lose your down payment and whatever else you have paid toward the mortgage, but your other assets are protected.

A purchase money mortgage is a loan that is made by the seller of the property. Instead of using a third party such as a bank or savings and loan association, you may be able to persuade the seller of the property to make a loan directly to you. In this instance, the seller is protected because of your down payment and the inherent value of the property. Even if the seller still owes some money on the property, you may be able to make a down payment that will cover his indebtedness. Then, the only debt you will owe is to the seller. In other instances, you may be able to "assume" the mortgage. Frequently, under this arrangement, you will be able to limit your liability to the property itself. If, for example, you assume a VA "guaranteed loan" the individual you bought the property from still maintains a degree of liability. This means you should be extremely careful if you happen to have obtained a government guaranteed loan and wish to sell the property to someone else.

If you are able to obtain the services of an attorney who will work with you to protect your finances in the event of economic distress, his fees will be a worthwhile investment. If an attorney, no matter how prestigious the firm, tries to tell you that you don't need to worry about things like this, look around for somebody who's willing to work for you. The best attorney is the "can do" type who will work things out for you, rather than telling you all the things that are impossible. You may want to look for a one-armed lawyer who isn't always saying "on the other hand . . ."

SOCIAL IN-SECURITY

When the social security system was first set up (1940), there were 130 wage earners for each beneficiary. Currently, there are 3.2 wage earners for each beneficiary of the social security system. Official projections indicate that by the year 2000, the rate will drop 2 to 1. That means that if social security were the only welfare program, every two individuals would be supporting a third. And of course, social security is not even intended as welfare. It was designed as an insurance program, but no insurance company could be licensed that

operates with the kind of fiscal irresponsibility of the social
security system. Pat Buttram once said, "Look at it this way
. . . if there wasn't so much money deducted from our pay-
checks for social security, unemployment insurance, and
pension plans, maybe we wouldn't need social security, unemployment insurance, and pension plans."

Figures released by the Social Security Administration reveal that nearly a third of a million workers have served notice of withdrawal from social security systems in 1976. This
was a 1,600 percent increase over two years before. The Social Security Administration says that it will resist any attempts to liberalize the withdrawal procedure. This, according
to their spokesman, would only "imperil our already weak-
ened trust fund."

Boyd Crabtree has published a little booklet entitled, "How
to Drop Out of Social In-security." In this booklet, he points
out the many defects in the social security system and suggests that people simply request exemption from participation
in social security as "conscientious objectors." His argument
is based on the fact that members of certain religious orders,
such as the Amish, are exempted. Additionally, the 1972 Social Security Amendment granted exemption to Christian
Science practitioners since they would not participate in or
receive benefits from the social security program. IRS Form
4361 or 4029 can be used to seek this exemption. Crabtree
argues that other citizens can write requesting exemption because of the conscientious objection to the system. If you are
interested in more details of this program, his address is provided in the bibliography.

I personally wish Mr. Crabtree and his followers the very
best. It is certainly appropriate to consider the cost and consequences of making a frontal attack on a major agency of
the U.S. government. You need to be prepared to spend a
great deal of time in defending your position. In all probability, the legal costs will be significant. Don't be surprised if
your income tax forms are audited on a regular basis. You may
even hear strange clicks on your telephone when you answer.

In reflecting on that last paragraph, I must confess that it
sounds a bit cowardly. Perhaps the only solution to the problems such as social security will come if enough people are
willing to stand up for what they believe and accept the unpleasant consequences. This is basically what happened in this
country in 1776 and shortly thereafter.

CHAPTER SIX

Best Bets for Your Money

The basic dilemma confronting each investor is the trade-off between risk and return. Every investment in an uncertain world involves risk. Generally speaking, we expect our return to increase in relationship to degree of risk. This simplistic formula assumes that an investor can anticipate the returns from a particular investment and accurately estimate the risk involved. There is also the assumption that the wise investor knows to put the right kind of money into an appropriate investment. He or she never puts grocery money into long-term or highly speculative investments. Neither is it prudent to keep stashing money in a low-yield investment when safety is not the primary consideration.

Every investor must recognize that the basic principles that existed ten or twenty years ago are no longer valid today. If circumstances are substantially different today than when you first learned your investment principles, you need to re-evaluate your principles and the premises on which they are based.

An awareness of the concurrent economic crisis and the impending collapse can provide you with a keenly focused sense of perception that all investors should strive for. More than ever before, you should be exactly sure *which money* is going into a particular investment and what return you expect that investment to generate for how long a period of time.

While this singlemindedness will add strength to your pursuit of specific goals, it will also mean that you must have the courage to move contrary to traditional investment philosophies. For example, you may put retirement funds into gold certificates rather than the common stock of blue chip companies. Or you may pay record high prices for diamonds even though you are not particularly interested in jewelry.

On application of the new perspective suggested by this

book you can expect some scorn from some of the very experienced professionals in the investment field. Unfortunately, their experience will have been gained in the wrong era to assess the performance of the emerging economy. Even more difficult for you to handle will be the difficulty in shaking free of the investment instinct that you evolved when growing up in a prosperous America.

In many ways, the self-discipline to cope with the challenge to your commitment will be a preview to the type of determination that will be required for long-range survival. Living through the actual depression will be much easier for people who have had the determination and stamina to survive the trauma of preparation. In an athletic contest, a great deal of attention may be directed to a final free throw or extra point attempt. In reality, those crucial plays are no more important than all of the previous plays that led up to the final climactic moment. Similarly, the final stage of your survival plan may involve a dramatic move to a survival retreat or some other highly significant activity. Still, your game plan leading up to that final moment is just as important as the grand finale. As you move toward that critical moment, expect considerable conflict between your long-range strategy and objectives and your short-term instincts. The difference between you and other investors will be that they expect the future to follow in the footsteps of the past. The timid souls who choose to run with the herd fail to see that circumstances have rendered time-tested cliches invalid and dangerous. The old principles are very quickly becoming cliches. Can you remember when people used to say that something was "sound as a dollar"?

The national outlook would not be so frightening if we merely had to worry about the gradual shift of our national fortunes. Even though inflation is a demoralizing, dehabilitating malady, economic strategy might help us cope with its impact for another decade or so. Predictable changes are much easier to handle than major surprises. In assessing the future, we need to be prepared for what Peter Drucker has called the major "discontinuities." In my opinion, these may be brought on by a widespread famine associated with severe climatic changes, earthquakes, or a major breakdown in the electrical system so that a heavily populated segment of the country is without power during a heavy winter blizzard. Rampant frustration and economic weakness resulting from chronic inflation combined with such a catalytic catastrophe will create changes that only the most prepared will be able to handle.

Our Deadly Assumptions

Most investment philosophy and most business disciplines, including economics and marketing, are based on the assumption that everybody will continue to experience higher standards of living—indefinitely. Against all logic, we expect to continue an unbroken stream of economic progress even when we see evidence that the progress has already ended. We assume that somehow there will be an availability of resources for investments and paying inflated bills for food, shelter, energy, and government. We also believe that there will be sufficient natural resources to meet this demand that a higher standard of living would create. In spite of obvious shortages in several key areas, we plan for "progress" that would place even higher strains on our natural storehouses without paying an exorbitant price for this recklessness.

Another assumption is that we can predict and control the economy. We seem to think that our civilization is basically stable and that the immediate future will dependably mirror the past. If the study of history teaches us anything, it shows that historical themes repeat themselves but *never* with dependable predictability.

As suggested previously, there is a common misconception that any changes that take place will evolve gradually. This reminds me of the assumptions we make about being in an automobile accident *until we actually are in one.* You have probably watched those slow-motion movies of dummies being bounced around inside the test cars. Somehow, the slow motion is deceptive and you can imagine having time to brace for such an impact and ride out the crash without injury. But when you are in your first real crash, you realize that it does not occur in slow motion. Indeed, it happens faster than your eyes and brain can register impressions. It's over before you know what hit you. Many victims never know they hit the dashboard—they merely begin to wonder first why there is suddenly blood on everything.

You can anticipate this type of shocked disbelief when you experience an economic crash. There will be no slow motion documentary accounts before the fact, no last-minute chance to brace for the crash. Rather, you will wake up to discover that yesterday's rules no longer apply. The crash will have happened and left its victims injured before they have a chance to see it coming. As the collapse nears, the government will initiate a last ditch media campaign of lying optimism in a final attempt to turn the tides. Our leaders at the FDIC will be telling us that first bank failures have been paid off in full. They will calm our fears with their confident news conferences on the very night before massive bank closures and the FDIC announcement of its own bankruptcy.

Don't waste time trying to explain your mistrust of the system to your stock broker, insurance agent, or most business friends. The ones who will understand or even listen will be few. More likely, they will lock arms and reassure themselves by unanimously denouncing your pessimism. They will hurry to remind you that the American system will "always find a way" and even profit in the development and marketing of the new ways. They may tell you that too much negative talk about the economy can become self-fulfilling and that you have a moral obligation to the country to express confidence in the system by staying in your traditional investments and letting this invincible system heal itself. Just save your breath. The majority of your friends are too afraid to see what is happening. They are unwilling to see that growth cannot possibly continue indefinitely and that the limits of growth are becoming apparent in almost every aspect of our society. A major readjustment is inevitable: there is going to be a re-alignment of the goods, services, and values in our world. You will never explain it to your friends, but, if you have read this far in this book, you may have the kind of objectivity that allows you to see and prepare for history's most obvious surprise.

Despite the "selective deafness" of the majority, your major responsibility is to set your own house in order and prepare for the problems you see on the horizon. In this chapter we will discuss the investment approaches that are capable of preserving your wealth whether the system collapses or continues. You have everything to gain and nothing to lose by shifting into an inflation-resistant, crashproof form of investing. This is as logical as it can be, but don't try to explain it more than once to people whose heads are stuck in the sands of foolish optimism.

The Meaning of Money

Have you heard the story about the three wealthy playboys who were trying to impress a pretty blonde at a cocktail party? One lit her cigarette with a $50 bill. The second lit her cigarette with a $100 dollar bill. But the fellow who took her home was the one who lit her cigarette with his personal check for $1 million!

He knew (whether she did or not) that it was only paper that was worth nothing. Incidentally, there are about 200 million people in the United States who appear to be as gullible as the naive blonde in the story. Money only has value because of what it represents. Dollar bills began steadily losing their value when the United States quit letting each dollar bill represent a specified amount of gold that was kept on deposit in the U.S. Treasury. Without increasing the supply of gold, the government increased the number of dollars. Somehow, public valuation of paper money always manages to adjust itself to stay in step with the true value of the paper. For example, the purchasing power of one workday or hour is a valid yardstick that remains fairly constant no matter what somersaults paper money might take. It still takes the average worker approximately the same number of working hours to buy an ounce of gold as it took ten years ago, even though the pay for that hour is expressed in much larger numerical terms.

Historically, money usually is relatively rare, has real value of its own, is easily carried, is widely accepted everywhere, and does not deteriorate. Money is most often not sought for itself but for the power it represents. You can exchange it for many specific things that you want.

Picture yourself as a shepherd in the old days before greenbacks. Someone visits your flock and wants one of your sheep. He offers to trade you an ivory zither for a sheep. Since you don't play the zither, you are reluctant to make the trade, but your visitor eventually convinces you that the zither is going to be quite usable to people so you let him have the sheep. When you go to town to purchase a new toga, the tailor tells you that he has no use for the sheep since he has given up making woolen togas. You try to convince him to trade you a double-breasted robe for the ivory zither. He finally agrees even though he doesn't play the zither and has no intention of learning to play. That zither has become *money* in this basic society. Though it has some value as an instrument, it is really just moving from person to person representing value—the value of a sheep, a toga, or whatever the tailor trades it for. Somewhere along the line, folks are going to get tired of carrying their zithers around. They will leave them with the local zither-keeper who will give them a receipt on a piece of paper that can be redeemed for one zither. From this point, people can trade that piece of paper for one sheep or one toga. Major problems will begin, however, when the zither-keeper gives out more than one piece of paper for the same zither. Then, if the tailor is smart, he's going to require *two* zither notes for one toga. And you will expect *two* zither notes for one sheep. There is only a certain amount of value around. Calling it twice as valuable doesn't make it so. The value of any money is held in natural check by the real value of the thing it truly represents. If the zither-keeper keeps printing worthless receipts, people will eventually quit giving two hoots for them. Perhaps this foolish zither-keeper will help you understand why the U.S. dollar has lost so much ground on the international market.

When Is Money Not Really Money?

In 1939, one dollar of U.S. currency could buy 2½ ounces of silver or twelve loaves of bread. In the forty years that have passed since those "good old days," the quality of the dollar and the quality of the bread have both deteriorated. Today it takes about $14 to buy the same approximate amount of silver or bread (if you want bread with comparable quality without the empty calories or chemical additives that most of today's bread contains).

As I write this, a quality loaf of bread costs 95 cents per load (it will almost certainly be over a dollar before you can read these words), and silver is selling at $5.80 per ounce. The conclusion is obvious. Compute your wealth in dollars and you will never know for sure how much you have and you'll never be able to predict your future wealth or what you will be able to buy in a few years. Silver or other "solid currency," on the other hand, remains an almost consistent monetary element—one that *gains* in relation to the dollars and *holds* in relation to the goods and services to be bought.

This illustration about silver, dollars, and a loaf of bread capsules the way in which silver, gold, and other hard currencies remain a solid way of providing protection. There are several currencies in the world today that have some direct relationship to gold. Of those, the Swiss franc, while not having the highest degree of gold backing, is probably the most stable. For a beginning portfolio, some form of currency that has both gold backing and also is recognized as a medium of exchange is desirable. Later in this chapter, some sample portfolios will be suggested, reflecting this component.

For anyone with additional assets, the investment commodity with *security* to equal its fame is gold.

THE GOLDEN RULE

The use of ivory zithers as money somehow never got off the ground. But since 4000 B.C. mankind has been fascinated by the glimmer of gold. Gold has always had its own intrinsic value as a metal for fashioning things; its greatest appeal since the beginning of history has been that everybody *perceives* it as money.

Gold is virtually indestructible. If you have visited an exhibit featuring King Tut and his possessions, you will know that gold holds its beauty and rich appearance century after century without interference from moths, rust, or corrosion. Even though our nation has officially abandoned the gold standard, the phrase "good as gold" holds its impact long after the demise of "sound as a dollar." When large American banks saw their dollars shrinking, many of them began switching more of their assets to gold. And if you wonder where excess petro-dollars go, you may be interested to know that the Arabs are the world's largest purchasers of gold today. Those who have the option of any of the investment avenues are, without exception, depending on gold as the sure thing to hold value through thin and thinner times. Gold has been called a "magic time machine" because it is the one commodity that can dependably transport wealth from the present, across uncharted chaos, and into the world of the future where economic waves have finally been calmed.

Why the Fabled Appeal of Gold?

As a metal and as an investment, gold can do things tha' other metal can never do. It is one of the most malleable permanent, and beautiful of metals. And, despite the deman(by dentists and the jewelers who are using it in record quanti- ties, the supply is diminishing. The world no longer produce: as much gold as it used to—the productivity peak wa: reached and passed a few years ago. The demand continue: to grow, yet there are no new gold fields being discovered or mined. The great majority comes from either South Africa (60 percent) or Russia (30 percent). Either of these coun- tries could clamp down our gold supply completely should they decide this were to their political advanatge. Our nation could be denied a supply of gold at any price. In this event, we could probably find suitable substitutes for the industrial and jewelry applications of gold, but the international economic consequences would be frightening. We could find ourselves completely out in the cold—without gold.

Invariably, countries that are under a threat of impending political turmoil experience a sudden rush in the buying and storing of gold. This has happened recently in Italy, France, and the United States. Private citizens have been buying and storing gold—even at what appears to be highly inflated prices. Though the traditionalists ridicule purchasing gold at the current high prices, alert citizens in France, Italy, and the United States are purchasing and salting away gold. They know that if there is any money that can safely get them to the other side of their nation's crisis, it is gold, mankind's most historic money. Of course, the Italian-French rush for gold may tell us something else as well. If those two countries cave in to eurocommunism as it appears they will, the strength of NATO will be badly crippled and the blow could radically change the balance of both political and economic power in the world.

Another reason for gold's appeal is its scarcity. All the gold that has ever been produced in the entire history of the world could fit comfortably in a large barn. Its rarity is part and parcel of its myth.

In 1946, at Bretton Woods, New Hampshire, a new inter- national monetary system was established with gold as its basis. Its primary purpose was to keep the U.S. dollar close o the gold standard since all the participating nations recognized the pivotal nature of the dollar. The system lasted until 1971, when the United States could stand it no longer. The temptation to print two certificates for every ivory zither was just too great and the U.S. left the gold behind and rushed off into a sunset of inflated (and therefore deceptive) prosperity.

The appeal of gold is a fact of life. The factors we have discussed can help us understand it but none will explain it fully and simply. The one most persuasive reason is that gold has gained too much strength (through many centuries as the world's ultimate money) to ever be replaced or unseated due to some minor historic occurrence like the economic collapse of a single century.

Owning gold will cost you a bundle of paper dollars, but that paper bundle is going to be worth a lot less next year. If you are investing to turn a healthy profit, gold is probably a good buy even at $250 or more per ounce. And if you are worried about the ultimate direction of the U.S. economic policy, remember—gold has never defaulted.

Once you are sold on the idea of gold as a hedge against disappearing money, your basic questions are how do I get some and where do I put it? With the exception of a few television ads for Krugerrands and regular ads in the *Wall Street Journal* and other financial publications, the gold market has remained largely the arena of the insiders. The mental image of yourself driving a lift truck with several pallets of gold ingots will soon disappear as you consider the density and price of this truly precious metal. You will have to be in the best top one-half percent of investors to buy more gold than you can carry. And if you have these resources, you'd be much too smart to carry it anywhere. You would more likely "take possession" of it by signing a paper that causes it to be moved a few inches in somebody's vault and labeled with your name.

While this is sound strategy for major purchases, I must warn you against the dangers of trusting anyone with a vault and a receipt book. If you want to own over $100,000 in gold, consider the advantages of storing it in a Swiss bank, where your worries of financial failure or government seizure are much less realistic.

There are numerous ways you can purchase gold today. There are plenty of people waiting to make a profit when you are ready to buy. Once you begin to consider the ways you

might wish to make your purchase, you need only request
free brochure and the sales representatives will begin to tele
phone to give you the latest tips and recommendations. Som
of the major alternatives are discussed in the following pages.

Gold Coins: Gold coins are an outstanding medium of ex
change that will become immediately visible in the event of
collapse of the established currencies. There are some 10 mil
lion Krugerrands in the United States and a large number o
other gold coins. Dollars will still be used after the crash, bu
it will take astronomical numbers of them to equal the buy
ing power of a single gold coin. Buy a gold coin today—i
will cost you more than a couple of hundred paper dollars
When the crash comes, you'll be swapping that single gol
coin for a food supply, wardrobe, perhaps even a car.

While gold coins are not likely to become a total mediun
of exchange, they will most certainly enable you to purchase
necessities when merchants begin to turn down offers of dol
lars in any amounts. It may be hard for us to imagine, bu
quite likely that day is coming when "all the paper money i
the world" will not buy what you need. If you don't believe
it, ask some old Germans what they used their money for ir
the 1920's.

There are two basic categories of gold coins when you be
gin to consider owning them. The coins that are of specia
value to coin collectors have numismatic value and thei
prices are set by a combination of the amount of gold ir
them and their rarity as collectors' items. If your primary in
terest is getting the most gold protection for your money, you
will probably avoid the numismatic treasurers since you may
be hard pressed to find a wealthy coin collector in the midst
of social chaos. During a crisis, the rarest gold coin might be
reduced to the value of its gold content.

There are, however, a number of coins that are minted and
available today in coin shops, banks, and even some depart
ment stores. Because they are current coins, the premium to
be paid to buy them tends to be far less than for the antique
and rare coins. The term *premium* refers to the extra amount
above the face value of the coin that you may pay as profit
and handling costs to a dealer. The more coins you buy, the
less premium you should have to pay.

Of those coins available to Americans, the surest bet is the
South African Krugerrand. It is the only gold coin that is still
in use as currency and therefore can be traded in at any bank

or that day's value as set at the Reserve Bank of South Afica or the prevailing value of its gold content. The Krugerand's popularity and convenience is that it contains almost xactly one ounce of gold. Its price is therefore extremely imple to follow and compute. Generally, you should not exect to pay more than ten percent premium above the quoted rice of gold on one of the major exchanges to buy Krugerands. They will store easily and allow you to carry a signifiant amount of purchasing power when you begin your etreat.

Other current gold coins that sell at attractively low premiums are the Austrian 100-crown piece that contains just less han a full ounce of gold and the Mexican 50 peso that has a it more than an ounce. Most of the other coins tend to have prohibitively high premiums for the limited amount of gold content—for example, the American $20 "double eagle" that contains less than an ounce and carries a premium of around 70 percent. On the other hand, you could purchase double eagles in 1973 for $195, and today coin collectors gladly give about $400 for them.

Some coins of numismatic importance have premiums as high as 575 percent. If your interest is beating inflation and assuring the security of your wealth, you want the coins that will have low premiums, high credibility, and immediate liquidity after the crash.

Gold coins are not the best, or even the first, thing to buy for escaping with your money, but they certainly have their appropriate place in your survival portfolio. Their primary weakness is that they are worth so much that they are not likely to be very good at purchasing bread and milk when you have to have them. But gold represents the near ultimate in doomsday security and, when you are buying gold for the crash, I don't think there is a more efficient, flexible, secure, liquid way to get it than in the form of gold coins. They don't come cheap, but neither does survival.

Bullion: Gold bullion evokes exciting images of Wells-Fargo and the Old West during the mid-1880's. Gold is exciting to see, touch, and own—but it has some major disadvantages relating to security.

The disadvantages of bullion are that you do have to pay for storage, insurance, shipping, and assaying—either when you buy or when you sell and sometimes on both occasions. There are a lot of carrying costs associated with owning bul-

lion. On the other hand, if you have substantial resource
these costs may be justified in order to store a lot of wealt
with little worry about devaluation. In the short run, you ma
have bullion with the conventional storage places. But, if yo
have more than $200,000 in gold, you should begin moving
to private storage or a Swiss bank. If you expect to store it i
a Swiss bank, then you should make your purchases fror
that bank in the first place (see Chapter 8). In this manne
you will save the costs of assaying, shipment, and insuranc
and pay only the minimal storage charge.

Buying Part of a Gold Mine: One of the easiest ways t
get into the gold business is to purchase stock in one of th
world's gold mining companies. Shares may range in pric
from less than $10 to over $100. This process works like an
other stock ownership.

While some advisors talk about gold stocks as an inflation
proof investment medium, I generally don't recommend then
because of three basic kinds of uncertainty that can influenc
the success of the stock. The first factor is the stability (o
lack of it) of the country in which the company is located
Most gold mining operations that you can invest in are lo
cated in South Africa, where the political turmoil and uncer
tainty makes it a rather shaky investment. Secondly, there i
the question of the firm's management capabilities and how
well they are able to utilize the valuable resources they con
trol. My final reservation deals with the overall problems o
the stock market. Many negative factors can influence the
price of a stock that have very little to do with the nature o
the investment. During a bear market, factors that may dis
count a stock's price might not have any relationship to the
real value of the ownership represented by the shares o
stock. For that reason, I'd recommend moving into some ac
tual ownership.

Futures: While investing in the futures of gold and silver
is very different from buying future contracts for soybeans or
pork bellies, all these contracts are technically classified as
commodities. By utilizing the commodities market, you can
put some of your dollars for speculation into precious
metals.

The commodities market was developed to help farmers
eliminate some of the risk in the production of their products.
Cattle ranchers or cotton planters can make agreements to
sell their crop at some specified time in the future. This elimi-

ates some of the uncertainty associated with estimating probable return for their time and effort. It also enables them to do a better job of determining the amount of a crop to produce. Commodity traders are willing to make advance agreements with farmers because they think the price at the time the commodities are available will be higher than the price they negotiate through the futures market.

In a similar way, you can agree to sell gold that you own or to buy gold that you may wish to acquire at a specified price on a specific date in the next couple of years. Gold futures are less a barometer for production than a place where some very high gains and losses can be made in the area of predicting the price of gold. Basically, it is a form of speculation. Ninety-five percent of the people who speculate in commodities lose their money because of the wide swings and fluctuations in the futures market. The producers and the specialists are the people most likely to find this market useful.

If you recognize that precious metals do experience wide fluctuations, you can study the charts for long-term directions and get a feeling for whether or not it is a bull or bear market. Overall, the market for precious metals is going to move in an upward direction, but there will be a number of adjustments as we move through the treacherous "80's". I expect the price of gold to exceed $300 per ounce by the mid-1980's. Still, there will be a number of sharp downward movements in its climb.

As an example of how future markets work, suppose that you had decided to buy gold futures in April, 1978. This would have been optimal time to buy because prices were temporarily depressed. If you were following the news, you probably recognized that this was merely a temporary adjustment in the overall upward progress of gold prices. Although I usually favor more conservative investments, I decided that this was an ideal time to take advantage of the market's adjustment. By merely callnig a local stock broker, I bought some futures for June of the following year. As the price of June, 1979, futures rose, I had several alternatives to consider. Since the basic trading unit of futures is 100 troy ounces, every dollar change in the price of an ounce of gold creates a gain or loss of $100. Consequently, each movement of $10 in the price of June, 1979, futures earned a $1,000 profit on each contract. When extensive speculation seemed to be driving the price up too fast, I sold out for $258 per ounce in October—a profit of $7,300 per contract. As I had anticipated, prices peaked shortly thereafter and corrected down to $202 during the next months when I decided it was time to buy back in. Prices may drop a little more after this book goes to press, but I believe that gold is a good value at these prices and will move back up. If I had held onto the gold for more than a year, I could have sold the future to someone else and my profit would have been viewed as a capital gain—thus qualifying for a lower taxation rate. Of course, I could have held the contract until it matured in June, 1979, at which time I would have been entitled to take delivery of 100 troy ounces of gold at a price of $185 per ounce, even though the market at that time should still be well over the purchase price.

One minor disadvantage of buying gold futures is that a monthly fee for insurance and storage is included in the quoted price. This explains why a futures price for one year from the present is always more expensive than the futures price for six months from the present. This is not because the price of gold is going to go up every month. There is simply a recognition of the storage cost associated with holding gold.

On the other hand, the purchase of a gold future represents the least expensive method of gold ownership. Compared to other forms of buying gold, a futures contract affords low transition cost, relatively inexpensive, safe storage, and ease of disposition (no inspection required and immediate liquidity available). The carrying charge associated with your contract can be recovered for the unused portion of time if you sell before maturity.

Most futures are purchased on approved margin accounts. This means you only have to put up about 10 percent of the money represented by your contract. In the preceding illustration, I contracted to buy 100 ounces of gold for a total price of $18,500 in about thirteen months. For each of these contracts, I had to put up less than $2,000. If the market goes down significantly, you may be asked to put up enough money to "cover your margin." This means that if the price of my July future had dropped below $167 per ounce, I would have to deposit some additional funds in my margin account.

During the past year, the range of gold futures contracts had been between $292 per ounce and $160.50. This type of fluctuation is almost always present in the market. The entire situation is hazardous. My own rule of thumb is, "Never buy when the price is within 90 percent of the season's high." Some people do make money by making purchases at record highs, but I feel better buying gold coins at high prices than gold futures. Generally, motivation in purchasing coins is very different from speculating in futures. Unlike coins, futures are not a medium for long-term buy-and-forget investment decisions. If you have the patience to wait for market fluctuations, the futures market can be a stimulating place to put some of your speculative dollars. The biggest temptation for you to watch for is the tendency to become euphoric about the paper profits that you may be able to make on your first purchase. If you time your purchase near the beginning of an upward swing in prices, it is easy to see your original investment double or triple in a short period of time. On my April, 1978, purchase of futures for the next year, my original investment tripled in three months' time. There is a strong temptation to keep redoubling your bets until the market downturn catches you heavily leveraged with high-priced contracts. It takes a special kind of discipline to take your profits and keep a substantial amount of your resources liquid for a time as you wait for another downturn. Of course, if you are interested in storing bullion, but don't wish to take immediate possession, properly timed purchases of gold futures might be an attractive way to accomplish this objective.

Options: On June 1, 1978, the sale of gold options became illegal in the United States because so many people selling the options were unreliable. One spokesman in the industry said that there were basically "bucket operators who had a telephone, a brochure, and a willingness to sell options." However, when the buyer was ready to exercise the option, the operator had disappeared.

Because of the abuses and the inability of the law to control the situation, options have been outlawed as of this writing. Of course, this will be appealed and my prediction is that they will become legal again in the early 1980's but will be much more extensively regulated, and only the larger, more reputable, companies will be able to make a profit and still meet government restrictions. Options can still be purchased through Swiss firms like Valeurs White Weld of Geneva.

The bottom line of any gold section of any book is "gold is good." It is a sure bet for getting your wealth across the time chasm from one side of the collapse to the other. Own some gold—it is a value holder. However, there are some other commodities you may also need to round out your portfolio, silver for daily bread—and diamonds for the road.

LOOK FOR THE SILVER LINING

The history of silver's value is a representative story of economic theory with special emphasis on the relationship between price and supply and demand. For thousands of years, silver maintained a fairly consistent relationship to gold. Between ten and fifteen ounces of silver could be counted on to equal one ounce of gold. But the respective supply factors and new industrial uses for silver began to change that tie.

In the 1800's, the United States knocked the price of silver off its even keel and the metal has never recovered its old relationship to gold. In 1890, the Comstock Lode in the American West began to flood the silver markets of the world. Eventually, the number of ounces of silver required to equal an ounce of gold rose to forty. Then, with the 1930's Depression, the number rose to seventy. Since that time, the rate has declined as the value of silver in relation to gold has risen steadily because the supply of silver is now being used up instead of simply stored and swapped.

The United States government has been a major manipulator of the value and availability of silver. For years, the government agreed to contracts that purchased silver from western mines at prices far above the going price in the rest of the world. This resulted in the U.S. government being the leading stockpiler of silver and therefore a key factor in the world price. The pattern-changing policies that evolved thereafter appeared to be erratic and contradictory, but almost always made sense at the time. Basically, the government was storing and releasing silver at different rates in an effort to keep its silver coins at a fairly consistent value. The effort finally became unmanageable because the use of silver in the industrial world began to increase so dramatically. Now, the U.S. government has lost its silver stockpile and the world is heading into an unavoidable silver shortage.

While silver is a positive hedge against inflation, it is also a very promising speculative investment because of several prevailing conditions. The simple facts are that the world is using up over 400 million ounces of silver a year while it is producing a little over 200 million ounces! The difference is being made up from the silver stockpiles of the world and they are just about empty. The largest stockpile is probably in India, where silver jewelry remains the most prevalent national method of storing individual wealth. The future is unsettled in fields like photography, electronics, and pollution control since they are dependent on a ready supply of silver. The one certainty is that they are going to be paying higher and higher premiums for the disappearing metal.

Silver is not an inexhaustible resource. We are rapidly approaching the end of its availability. The U.S. Treasury finally had to give up minting silver coins because people were likely to melt them down for their silver content, which far exceeded their monetary value.

If you have silver—hold it. If you get a chance, buy it. It will be easiest to handle in the form of coins, but you will find that silver tableware and silver trays will continue to appreciate in value. Some authorities even suggest that old x-rays (which are coated with silver) will eventually become objects of value.

There is probably less than a billion ounces of silver in the world's stockpile and it is being used up rapidly. The supply is being coddled and collected with the greatest of care. At this writing, gold is selling at $215 per ounce and silver at $5.80, so the ratio is 37 to 1. In view of the effects of inflation on the price of gold and the effects of diminishing supply on silver, the race of gold and silver prices will be an exciting one, especially for those sitting on personal stores of each.

Usage and Demand

In economic theory and practice, whenever the price of a commodity gets too high, users will be forced to find alternatives to substitute. The methods of reclaiming and recycling also become much easier to justify and develop. However, this law does not seem to apply to the impending silver shortage since there are many industrial applications where no suitable substitute has been developed.

In photography, silver salts are the only elements with suitable light sensitivity. For twenty or more years, researchers have been trying alternatives, but none will work as well. Projections are that silver will continue to be bought and utilized in photography and x-ray processes even if the prices rise to eighteen and twenty dollars per ounce. The newest inventions in the realm of instant self-developing film processes are not likely to change the picture since there is no recycling potential with instant films. Silver is in the photographic picture to stay and the industry anticipates tremendous expansion over the next decade.

In electronics, silver's utility as a conductor has caused it to be in great demand by manufacturers of circuitry. About 75 percent of the silver used in electrical equipment goes into high- and medium-voltage connections where there are no known economical substitutes for silver. Other irreplaceable uses of silver include catalysts in the manufacture of plastic, reflecting surfaces in mirrors, bearings and brazing alloys, coinage, medicine, and dentistry. New uses are being added constantly in spite of the irreversible loss of the world's silver supply.

There is currently a yearly deficit between production and consumption of approximately 100 million ounces. This difference is made up by sales from existing stockpiles that have dropped from 2 billion ounces in 1968 to less than 1 billion at the present time. Although there is some debate about these figures and their meaning, it appears obvious that the demand for silver can be met only when prices are sufficient to encourage the current holders to part with their treasure. Consequently, I expect silver prices to have a bullish future for the next decade.

Geologists estimate that in every million pounds of the earth's crust there are 50,000 pounds of iron, 80,000 pounds of aluminum, but less than 2 ounces of silver. To make matters worse, we know that silver is always found near the surface of the earth and all the available large silver sources have been mined. The future for silver discovery is not promising—even according to the most optimistic of authorities.

When any commodity grows scarce, the price goes up and spurs the search for substitutes. It's already happened with silver. No suitable substitutes have been found and the price continues to rise. The higher the price, the more incentive there is to start up new production. Yet, the new production of silver is not so much a matter of demand as a question of availability. At some price level, supply usually comes to equal demand. But, given the collision courses of growing demand and shrinking availability, the final balance can be achieved only at a phenomenal price level.

Gold Versus Silver

There is some feeling that silver may be a better investment than gold in the next few years because silver has so many demands in the industrial world and because the historical ratios are somewhat out of kilter. Gold is affected more by speculation than silver is. As a result, there will almost always be wider swings in the gold market, but the prospects for silver values cannot help but be bright.

Metals are generally safer than any other commodity investments. But, for those who are looking to gold and silver as "stashing agents" they can hardly be beaten. And now, after years in which the decision between the two hinged on their portability and relative values, it appears to me that silver offers more stability, but gold affords more inflation protection for the period immediately ahead. While silver is cheaper than gold (and therefore more flexible as a bargaining commodity during economic chaos), it also involves considerably more storage and transportation problems. It takes only twenty Krugerrands to equal the value of a fifty-five-pound bag of silver coins.

As chaos money, silver remains number one for day-to-day exchange and for purchase of the necessities of survival. Gold remains the sure thing for holding and adding to value invested in large amounts. You will need both to have a well-rounded preparedness.

Ways to Weave Your Silver Lining

There are four basic ways to invest in silver. The same principles apply in silver purchases as in gold purchases, though some of the specifics will differ due to the mere bulk of silver required to equal the same value as gold.

You can buy stocks in a silver mining company. They are available on the major stock exchanges throughout the world. The problem, in fact, is that there are too many companies on the stock exchanges that are involved in silver mines. Only a few are worth considering, and they are questionable. These companies rarely mine silver only. They usually are after copper, lead, and zinc with silver as a by-product. Copper, lead, and zinc are all plentiful so the companies are not usually aggressive. You can buy their shares quite inexpensively but there is little likelihood that you will be getting dependable, high dividends or capital appreciation in the near future. You don't have to worry as much about the mining being in South Africa or Russia (as with gold mining stocks); on the other hand, it will take much higher prices to make the mining of silver only highly profitable. I would not advise silver mines as a short-term stock investment, but, if you have money for the long term, the prospects for the eventual resumption of lucrative silver mining are quite promising in light of the dead-end course of current silver supply and demand.

You can buy silver futures contracts if you are interested in speculating in short-term silver price movements. The same principles apply here that we discussed in the section on gold futures. For your investment strategy, you will be more interested in purchasing and holding silver instead of in these speculative "paper markets" where you rarely will see any actual silver. If you are interested in some short-term speculations you can get into futures by checking with any stock broker who is represented on the Commodity Exchange, Inc. (in New York) or on the Chicago Board of Trade. While this is primarily a market for full-time professional traders with nerves of steel and reflexes of silver, small-timers who can tolerate substantial risk have made substantial returns in this manner.

You can buy silver bullion in America or Switzerland. If you do not plan to take physical possession of the silver investment or if you are apprehensive about the U.S. government confiscating your precious metals, you can contact the American representative of a Swiss bank and order a specified amount of silver either by weight or by dollar amount. You can also write, phone, or wire a Swiss bank directly if you prefer. Your privacy is more likely to remain protected in this manner. The bullion will be set aside and labelled with your name and account number. While you will have to pay a small storage fee, you will not have to be concerned with costs of assaying or insurance.

If you intend to take possession of your silver, you will be better off buying it in this country and storing it in a private vault or in a nonbanking safe deposit box. Bullion is available through banks, coin shops, and through some specialized companies like North American Coin & Currency, Ltd., Monex, or major banks. Owning bullion is the most direct and low-risk way to profit from the expected long-term price advances in silver. There are some storage and exchange problems for the survival buyer, but even these may be more than offset by the promise of silver's skyrocketing future. As will be quickly apparent, however, my personal preference is that your basic stock of silver be stored in the form of coins since they will be so much more recognizable by the grocer after the economic system comes unglued.

You can buy silver coins. United States dimes, quarters, and half dollars minted prior to 1965 are 90 percent silver. If by some quirk you get one in change, hang onto it because it is already worth almost four times its face value. Almost any silver coins you own will have to be bought from a coin dealer and you will have to pay a premium for them. The traditional way to buy this "junk silver" (meaning without numismatic value) is in large canvas bags about the size of a bowling ball but weighing over fifty pounds. You order one of these bags from your supplier. The coins will have combined face value of $1,000 and, of course, always will be worth at least that much—even in the unlikely event that the bottom should drop completely out of silver.

Bags of silver coins with $1,000 face value are currently selling for around $4,200. In my opinion, the very best investment for those with small assets would be bags of silver coins. It is a basic inflation hedge for the small investor. While silver coins can be bought from almost any dealer, it pays to shop around. Anyone who is interested in this ought to call three or four of the numbers listed in Appendix C. Check prices and delivery terms carefully. Unless you know someone personally who is involved in silver sales or live in a city that is large enough to have a major dealer, I would recommend sticking to an established organization that has a history of performance. There are a number of very reliable dealers who perform this service and you may have some reasons for preferring to work with them.

A reasonable goal is for you to have one bag of silver coins for each person in your family or survival group. While it is a very good investment, I view it more as a survival kit. When I talk later about your investment portfolio, I will stress that the most basic component of a portfolio is *sur-*

vival. If you don't have enough money to need Krugerrands, then silver coins can be extremely helpful. As I mentioned earlier, a 1964 dime is worth more than forty cents today. Silver coins are an investment that will continue to appreciate, be readily recognizable, and fairly easy to acquire. For most people, silver is much more easily managed for day-to-day purchases than gold coins. Purchasing, taking possession of, and storing a bag of silver or two is your first investment priority. Do this before you begin to look at any of the other investment opportunities discussed in this chapter.

No Way But Up?

No matter how you come into possession of silver, you have something of value that is not likely to lose its value. Gold can protect your big bucks. Silver can keep your daily bread on the table. And diamonds, as we will soon see, win the prize for being able to store the greatest amounts in the smallest areas without loss of value.

ARE DIAMONDS A SURVIVOR'S BEST FRIEND?

Except for a brief respite in 1978, Wall Street has been gloomy for the past few years. While brokers have been depressed, diamond merchants around New York's West Forty-seventh Street have scarcely been able to conceal their excitement. Between 1976 and 1978, the wholesale price of a one-carat, high-quality diamond ("D" color, internally flawless) stone has risen from $5,600 to approximately $16,500 per carat. Normally these stones are purchased immediately as soon as they hit the diamond market, but if they were sold retail the price might be twice that amount. Diamond merchants assert that the price of their product has never declined and has always moved ahead of inflation. Moreover, history is filled with examples of wealthy people and royalty who have survived natural and political calamities because they possessed the world's most concentrated form of wealth.

An acquaintance of mine was a Jewish diamond dealer in Berlin before the Hitler regime. When he saw the handwriting on the wall, he took a snuff can full of quality diamonds and beat the SS troops to the border. His cannister was worth about $100,000. It enabled him to travel about the world until eventually he reached the United States. He settled in San Francisco with less than half of his original horde. Now he is a retired millionaire living on the Monterey peninsula.

The Diamond Sheiks

The major reason, in addition to their historical survival potential, for the tremendous appreciation in diamond prices comes from the control exercised by one of the world's most powerful cartels. Long before the Arabs organized their petroleum cartel, the South African company DeBeers Consolidated Mines staked a claim to most of the world's diamonds. Although their own mines produce less than a third of the worldwide production of uncut and unpolished stones, they virtually control worldwide rough prices. They are the sole distributor for almost every other major producer of rough diamonds, including the Soviet Union.

Through their subsidiary arm, the Central Selling Organization, they distribute stones to around 250 to 300 key clients throughout the world. They decide how many diamonds will enter the market and at what price. If demand weakens, DeBeers simply cuts the supply and maintains the price. When diamond demand peaks, they release larger amounts of the stones. During the 1978 investment fever in diamonds, DeBeers slapped a forty percent premium on their stones to reduce the speculation. Diamond brokers were selling (mainly to Israeli speculators) uncut diamonds at 30–40 percent above the going rate. Russia was getting upset that they were not getting their fair share of the profits. DeBeers also felt they should get more of this profit; therefore, the surcharge was placed on these goods as a warning to the speculators.

In addition, DeBeers has started purchasing cut goods from the market and there is some speculation that they may start marketing them as well as uncut goods.

Evaluating Diamonds

Diamonds are evaluated or graded on the basis of the four famous C's: color, clarity, cut and carat (weight). Their total value is determined in an overall evaluation of these four factors.

Color—In diamonds, the absence of color is ideal. These

Table 6—1
Diamond Grading Scales

GIA COLOR SCALE

INVESTMENT QUALITY

D	E	F	G	H	I	J	K	L	M	N	O	P	Q	R	S	T	U	V	W	X	Y	Z	
Colorless			Near Colorless				Faint Yellow			Very light Yellow					Light Yellow								Fancy Yellow

GIA CLARITY SCALE

INVESTMENT QUALITY

FLAWLESS	VVSI-1	VVSI-2	VSI-1	VSI-2	SI-1	SI-2	I-1	I-2	I-3
	Very, Very Slight Inclusions		Very Slight Inclusions		Slight Inclusion		Imperfect		

"blue-white" (technically called colorless) stones are virtually transparent. Less than 1 percent of all diamonds have this characteristic. Poor-quality diamonds have a distinctly yellowish cast. The Gemological Institute of América trains jewelers to be more knowledgeable about grading diamonds, if they desire to become registered gemologists. The Institute is one of the most highly respected for their grading criteria. This organization classifies colors into twenty-three variations as shown in the preceding exhibit. Investment-quality diamonds are "H" or better. "Z" is distinctly yellow and is at the bottom of this spectrum.

Clarity—The number of inclusions or imperfections in the diamond determines its clarity. The fewer the imperfections, the rarer and more valuable the stone. A perfect stone would be free of all blemishes, flaws, or specks. Although some retailers are prone to advertise their diamonds as flawless, the FTC regulation limits this claim to diamonds that show no blemishes or inclusions under a magnification of ten times. As shown in the preceding table, clarity ranges from flawless through imperfect and is divided into ten categories. If you can see flaws in a stone without magnification, the stone is probably graded imperfect and is not a good investment. If you have to use a magnifier to see the imperfections, the stone would probably rate a "slightly imperfect" grade. Generally, diamonds from grades flawless to VSI-2 (very, very slight inclusion) are generally recommended for investments. In reality, any stone bought at the right price is a good investment. For example, a VIS, "H" color, ½ carat diamond that sold for $550 per carat in 1976 would sell for $1200–1500 per caret in 1978.

Cut—Most investment diamonds have fifty-eight facets and are cut out to precise calculations. Style, fashion, and preference will affect the desirability of various cuts. Less desirable cuts are often utilized to avoid wasting a flawed stone.

Carat—Each cut and polished diamond is stated in carats. A diamond described as 1.53 carats means that it has one and 53/100 carats. The larger the stone, the more rare it is. Depending on color, clarity, and cut, one-carat stones can go anywhere from $400 (at your local pawnshop) to almost $30,000.

For investment purposes, seek out the best stones available. The novice investor should watch out for diamond imitations.

Modern technology has made it sometimes difficult to spot a fake. You don't need to worry about this if you purchase through reliable channels. Stones appraised by the GIA (Gemological Institute of America) are generally required for investment purposes. A jeweler's appraisal certificate should not be taken for investment purposes. The GIA certificate is accepted in all the cash markets around the world.

The Advantages of Diamonds

While most of the advantages of diamonds as an investment medium have been suggested by the preceding paragraphs, we can summarize these key concepts: durability, portability, stability, and appreciation potential.

While many people have heard that diamonds are the hardest of all substances, they cannot comprehend the degree of its superiority. A sclerometer, an instrument that measures the hardness of materials, gives corundum (rubies and sapphires) a hardness value of 1,000. With a hardness value of 140,000, it can be said that diamonds are 140 times as hard as their nearest competitor. The reason for this significance is that if a gem breaks in half, it will lose much more than half of its value. You should not expect to survive any type of holocaust and find that your diamonds have been destroyed.

Because of the portability of diamonds, demand has grown dramatically in France and Germany during periods when citizens feared that the communist party might come to power. In the United States, diamond specialists estimate that more than 20 percent of the diamonds now sold are for investment. There are over 200 firms in business whose sole business is selling investment diamonds to the public. One of the most successful, North American Diamond, reports that it is grossing about $1 million a month.

Investment-quality diamonds have demonstrated steadily accelerating price increases over forty-three consecutive years. In the last ten years, diamonds have dramatically moved ahead of inflation. Since 1970, the smallest yearly gain for diamonds has been 18 percent. The average yearly price increase during the 70's has been approximately 30 percent. During the first eight months of 1978, the average increase was about 60 percent.

With this impressive historical performance, the potential for diamonds continues to be real. Increasing worldwide interest in investment diamonds, as well as the strong and growing international jewelry market, constitutes a healthy demand situation. George Switzer, Director of the Mineral and Gem Department of the Smithsonian Institution estimates that known diamond supplies will be exhausted by the year 2000 or shortly thereafter. There is little likelihood that any large new deposits will be discovered in the future. Further political unrest in South Africa, which supplies over 80 percent of all rough carats produced annually, could produce a drastic reduction in the availability of diamonds. In Angola, production has dropped from a high of 1.5 million carats to about 300,000 carats per year.

Disadvantages of Diamonds

Although diamonds have many factors that recommend them as investments, there are some problems. Dealers agree that individuals buying stones as an investment should exercise extreme caution. It is very difficult to buy from a retail jeweler and sell it back to him at a profit. The retail markup is anywhere from 30 to 100 percent of the wholesale price. Investors must also pay local sales taxes and usually an annual insurance charge that may be 5 percent of the stone's value. Selling isn't simple either. The retail jeweler would probably offer even less than the current wholesale price.

These high markups in the usual market places have provided an opportunity to the diamond investment firms. These firms claim to sell their stones at the prevailing wholesale price plus 10 percent. A number of them, however, are selling at twice the wholesale price. I have reviewed price lists and found some of them to be ridiculously high. For example, one firm was selling nine ⅓ carat stones at $2400 per carat—about double the true wholesale price for that specific quality. It is easy to get in touch with these firms. They advertise aggressively in the major financial publications. Many maintain WATS lines with a staff of personnel who aggressively work their prospect lists. Despite GIA certificates and insurance, I am still dubious when a high pressure salesman says, "If you'll send me ten or twenty thousand dollars I will pick out the very best diamond we have available." It's a nice offer, but it requires more trust than I can afford to exercise with my family's survival money.

In summary, diamonds pay no interest or dividends and

are not likely to experience a stock split. You must be responsible for insurance and storage costs as well as the expense in selling the diamond. Despite the promise of many firms to buy them back at their original investment price or better, these promises are only valid as long as the firms survive and there is no sweeping political or social upheaval in the country.

Diamonds do have a place in any significant investment portfolio, but their greatest advantage is to the wealthy individual who needs to conceal or carry large amounts of wealth in an inconspicuous manner. It is very difficult to carry $100,000 in gold without being a prime target for a hernia or a holdup. Yet a million dollars in diamonds can be carried without notice. Unlike gold, they do not show up on X-ray scanners that are used at most airports.

The DeBeers control of the market protects the diamonds from depreciating in price during a depression. Inflation and the historical track record of diamonds protect the buyer on the up side. In my opinion, anyone with an investment portfolio of about $50,000 should consider putting a small amount of their resources in small, high-quality stones.

How to Buy and Sell

As we have indicated earlier, one of the major disadvantages of most diamond dealings is the difficulty of making purchases at acceptable prices. Most people buy their diamonds at retail prices and sell them at wholesale. Small stones (anything under a full carat) usually have a markup of at least 100 percent. The larger your purchase, the smaller the markup you should be able to negotiate. If you are going to invest a quarter of a million dollars, you should investigate the possibility of buying a box of assorted rough-cut stones from one of the DeBeers brokers. The various diamond brokers, investment firms, and auction houses are possibilities that may provide alternatives for smaller purchases. Regardless of which approach you use, check the reputation of your seller and insist on a GIA certificate. However, you need to know your dealer to make sure that you are getting the diamond that the certificate describes. Most of the reputable dealers will allow you a five-day appraisal period. Unfortunately, local appraisals are seldom objective. If you take a stone to most local jewelers, there's a strong possibility that they will downgrade your acquisition in hopes of replacing it with something from their own stock. Plan to spend some time in shopping before you make your initial purchases. After several sessions with a jeweler's loop, you will be able to tell what constitutes a top-quality stone. My best experience has come from looking in the telephone directory under "Diamond Wholesalers." Talk to two or three dealers before you make a decision. After considerable shopping, I have made most of my purchases from the nearest representative of SIDIAM (Society International Diamonds), a Belgium diamond company. This firm imports and purchases directly from diamond-cutting factories.

A Sparkling Review

The international speculation in diamonds became so great during 1978 that DeBeers added a 40 percent surcharge on the prices it quotes for rough stones. About the same time, one of the world's largest and most famous diamond retailers, Tiffanys, warned the public that diamonds were priced much too high.

Massive speculation is always a dangerous specter. If you feel that your financial situation warrants this type of investment, the following guidelines summarize the main points that we have discussed.

1. Diamonds have appreciated faster than most other investment media. Of the over 2,000 separate categories of stones, only 1 percent—the finest quality gems—have historically appreciated faster than 15 percent per year. Recently, however, practically all diamonds have doubled in value within a two-year period.
2. Be sure that your diamond has been graded by a bonded and insured gem laboratory such as GIA.
3. Shop and compare prices and grade categories. Do not buy a one-carat stone just because it is cheaper than any other diamond of that size you have seen. Insist on inspecting the diamond under magnification and make your purchases only from established companies whose references you have checked. Buy only from firms that agree to repurchase your stone within a specified time period if you are not completely satisfied.
4. Pick a stone that fits your financial requirements. While most advisors recommend buying the largest and

highest-quality stones available, I believe that one-third to one-half-carat diamonds are probably the best choice for individuals with less than $100,000 to put into gems. It is true that the large, top-quality diamonds appreciate faster, but these are very difficult to find and are usually not very liquid. Good-quality gems between one-third and two carats are the most liquid when you need to change your stone for a more commonly accepted medium for exchange.

INVESTMENT STRATEGY

Without knowing a great deal about you and your personal situation, I cannot make specific recommendations about how you should invest your wealth. Yet there are some general principles that will help you finance the voyage through the troubled waters ahead.

In approaching this challenge, your strategy should reflect a combination of three important variables: the amount of your wealth, your station in life as reflected by your age or family responsibilities, and your assessment of the immediacy of a major depression. Table 6-2 at the end of this chapter summarizes my basic recommendations by breaking your portfolio into three types of dollars you will be investing.

Survival dollars: The first order of priority is a good food supply. If your "getting ready" capability is no more than $10,000, then you are going to deal first with that six-months supply of food and a bag of silver coins. You'll also put some of your money into the services of a locksmith to make your residence as secure as possible and purchase a gun for hunting or protection. The lower your income level, the larger percentage should be allocated to survival needs and the fewer investment concerns you will need to worry about. It is important for you to recognize that some of the items in the "survival" category are really "depressionproof" investments. Diamonds and silver will appreciate; gold coins will buy more each year; and any money that has been placed in the right kind of retreat will be an investment that will pay off more than traditional real estate investments. This is true since your consideration of water, weather, and fertility of the land in choosing retreat property will become key determinents of land values during the depression even more than they are today.

Traditional Investments: Beyond survival needs, you will need a couple of months' income in a savings account. If your assets are limited, you may want to put some of this into a Swiss bank account (see Chapter 8). By doing this you accomplish dual goals of having ready liquidity in a depressionproof medium. Even if you share my reservations about the long-term safety of savings institutions, you should keep some of your funds where you can get to them quickly in the event of a personal crisis.

After providing for your liquidity needs, I would recommend that your next group of traditional investment dollars go to buy some stock in a company, preferably local, that you know well. As your income increases, you will probably want to shelter some of your investment earnings from income taxes by purchasing some municipal bonds. As suggested in Chapter 5, this can be tricky since many of the nation's largest cities will be experiencing grave financial problems during the next decade. As a short-term consideration, I think you can make some good choices with the debt obligations of some healthy medium-sized cities. When you start moving most of your resources out of the traditional into the depressionproof categories, your municipal bonds will be one of the first categories to cash in.

Until you have assets in the quarter-million-dollar category or extremely high earned income, I would recommend that you avoid traditional real estate investments. In my opinion, it is almost impossible for the small investor to make a significant return in real estate. With adequate resources and the principles identified in the previous chapter, you can enjoy some excellent (and partially tax-sheltered) returns from properly situated real estate holdings.

Depressionproof Investments: While most other writers who recognize the probability of imminent economic chaos will disapprove of my recommendations for traditional investments, I believe that there will be substantial profits to be made in these investments in the predepression period. Government officials and financial executives will do everything in their power to keep the sinking system afloat. Their efforts will create some excellent opportunities in the investment area.

These recommendations are being prepared in late 1978

with an eye toward the situation I expect to exist in mid-1979 and early 1980. With each passing year, you will probably want to move more money out of traditional investments. As the signs continue to confirm the predictions throughout this book, you will want a larger and larger proportion of your wealth in depressionproof investments. During any period of relative stability as we approach the brink, take advantage of every opportunity but only on a short-term basis, never diluting your security and depressionproof investments. In deciding how to balance the amount of commitment in traditional versus depressionproof investments, ask "What is the probability that the crash will occur during the next two years?" Anytime you think there is more than a 50 percent probability of disaster within twenty-four months, multiply your estimate of that probability times the total amount you have to invest in nonsurvival categories—and move in that direction. In other words, I now believe that there is approximately a 50 percent probability that the crash will occur within two years after the publication of this book. Consequently, I have recommended that you place approximately equal amounts of dollars in the two major nonsurvival categories. As I become more convinced that the depression is closer at hand, I will want to move more of my assets in the depressionproof category.

Amount of Wealth: Obviously, a person's investment strategy will be determined by the amount of his wealth. Until a person's investment portfolio approaches $25,000, survival will demand the largest share of his wealth and attention. I have provided percentages of the various investment ideas that should hold true between the categories identified. For instance, if your investment portfolio is $75,000, I would recommend that you use the percentages recommended for a $50,000 portfolio. Above $100,000 you can use the recommended percentages as guidelines, but I would suggest that you sit down with a specialized advisor from each of the purchase areas to help you select optimal choices within that category.

Typically your portfolio should exceed $100,000 before you should begin to think in terms of a retreat that is separate from your major residence. Consequently, you may want to plan your major residence with as many retreat considerations as possible.

If you are able to sell your house in the city, try to make

your housing investment in a safer location. This would, of course, provide more flexibility in your financial planning. The retreat figures I have suggested do not take into account the basic cost of primary housing.

Your "monetary depressionproof" investments might be acquired and held in the following order of priority:

1. A small account in Swiss francs so that you have money that will help protect you against further dollar declines. The Swiss franc is gold backed and is therefore likely to continue to appreciate in relation to the dollar.
2. Watch for downward movement in the price of gold futures. Only when they are less than 90 percent of their past year's high, should you consider making investments.
3. Small diamonds should be added whenever your investment resources reach the $50,000 level.
4. If gold prices move as I expect them to, before this book is published you will not be able to purchase 100 troy ounces for $20,000. Wait until you *can* afford 100 troy ounces before getting into gold bullion. The rising price of gold will provide its own barometer for your own ability to get this investment with safety.

A Summary of Principles

1. Your life and security come first. Your first available dollars should go to make your home secure and to provide a basic food supply.
2. Be sure that you can buy a quart of milk. One bag of pre-1965 silver coins should be safely stored where you can have ready access to them before you put money in the stock market or even a savings account. Don't worry about losing interest. Silver coins will probably appreciate faster than a savings account and will have much greater interest during a crisis.
3. Invest in the future and not the past. A company's record in the stock market may be important, but not nearly as significant as what you see as its prospects. I'd rather buy stock in a company that has had some difficulties but has turned them around, than a firm that has been successful for twenty years but is now coasting on the laurels while losing market share and returns on investment. The same principle applies to any investment

TABLE 6-2
Sample Investment Portfolios

PORTFOLIO SIZE	SURVIVAL	TRADITIONAL INVESTMENTS	DEPRESSIONPROOF INVESTMENTS
$10,000	50%	25%	25%
	Food Supply (Up to 6 months supply) $500	Up to two months' income	Swiss Francs
	Portable Retreat 500		
	Locks & Guns		
	Silver Coins One bag		
$50,000	40%	30%	30%
	Food Supply $3,000	Savings 6,000	Swiss Francs 5,000
	Retreat 7,000	Municipal Bonds 4,000	Gold & Silver Futures 5,000
	Silver Coins 10,000	Local Stocks 5,000	Diamonds 5,000
$100,000	36%	32%	32%
	Retreat & Food 15,000	Savings 6,000	Swiss Francs 12,000
	Silver Coins 12,000	Bonds 12,000	Gold & Silver Futures or Options 10,000
	Gold Coins 9,000	Stocks 14,000	Diamonds 10,000

TABLE 6-2 Cont'd.
Sample Investment Portfolios

Portfolio Size	Survival 30% / 14%		Traditional Investments 35% / 43%		Depressionproof Investments 35% / 43%	
$250,000	Retreat & Food	50,000	Savings	10,000	Swiss Francs	20,000
	Silver Coins	11,000	Bonds	30,000	Gold/Silver Options	23,500
	Gold Coins	13,000	Stocks	30,000	Bullion	20,000
			Real Estate	18,500	Diamonds	24,000
	14%		43%		43%	
$1,000,000 and Over	Retreat & Food	100,000	Savings	20,000	Swiss Francs	20,000
	Silver Coins	14,000	Bonds	140,000	Gold/Silver Options or Futures	100,000
	Gold Coins	26,000	Stocks	140,000	Bullion	130,000
			Real Estate	130,000	Diamonds	180,000

medium. If gold were to have a couple of years like most blue chip stocks, I wouldn't hold on to it just because of its fantastic record.

4. Don't worry about hitting the highs and lows, but try to move with the market. It is important to get all the good advice, but then trust your feelings. I would not recommend investing in anything that makes you rush to the newspaper every day with trembling hands to check the latest quotation. Whether it is stock prices, mutual funds, or gold futures, you want to maintain your peace of mind. If you can buy *toward* the beginning of an upward market movement and sell *near* the onset of a decline, you'll do much better physically and financially than if you stay tensely poised waiting for the peaks and valleys.

5. Stay up to date. No matter how good your research is at a given point, circumstances can change very rapidly. So, you need to seek out the kinds of news sources that will enable you to monitor the significant developments on a daily basis. If you don't have time to keep up, then you need to be willing to pay somebody to do this for you.

6. Don't be afraid to pay someone for help. If you are a plastic surgeon who charges $5,000 for a simple face-lift that takes an hour of your time, you will probably be wise to pay some one else to do your investment research. It's not likely that the best researcher in the country will cost $5,000 an hour. Find a professional advisor—perhaps several—and make sure that you recognize when their advice may be serving their own purpose. You may be wise to let them know that you are buying the advice from them but intend to go somewhere else for the actual services they recommend. (It works with auto mechanics—it ought to work as well with other diagnosticians and prescribers.) If your assets or income warrants professional assistance, check with a member of the rising profession of "financial planners" who charge on an hourly basis for a complete assessment. Only as a last resort would I ask a stock broker or insurance agent to evaluate my investment program. The broker knows stock and the insurance agent knows policies. But only *I* know my personal priorities.

Section Three

HOW TO SURVIVE ADVERSITY IN LUXURY

CHAPTER SEVEN

Yourself:
The Best Investment

One of the major purposes of this book has been to evaluate several important types of investments in view of their probable performance during a period of economic turmoil. As you might expect, most of this investment advice has been directed toward your money and how to use it.

I don't mean to imply that money can bring happiness. I have known people with $9 million who were just as happy as the people with $10 million. But I can't help but remember the words of the great philosopher Sophie Tucker, who said, "I've been rich and I've been poor—and I'm here to tell you that rich is better!"

Much of my advice is predicated on the assumption that rich is better than poor. I won't even try to make you believe that poverty is just a state of mind. Money (especially real money) has a great deal to do with concept such as poverty and riches. One of the real tragedies of poverty is that people have to spend so much time worrying about money. Even P. T. Barnum recognized that "Money is a terrible master, but an excellent servant."

I hope you will have invested some of your hard-earned money according to the principles identified in Chapters Five and Six. Now, I am about to describe the best investment you can ever make. Investment in your own knowledge or well-being is more stable than gold and will shine brighter than diamonds when the stock market collapses and the dollar explodes.

Investment for Pleasure and Profit

Some authorities recommend investments in jewelry and art because they can bring pleasure along with their potential for appreciation. I have not dealt with these as investment media because of the specialized knowledge it takes to evaluate acquisitions and because there is a very limited market for these items during a period of economic depression. Nevertheless, the concept of enjoying your investments is a very important one. Where can you put your money that will provide more pleasant returns or be more valuable than by investing in that person who smiles back at you in the bathroom mirror each morning?

An investment in self-sufficiency pays dividends regardless of the economic environment. Diplomas and other paper evidences of achievement may become worthless, but skills can never be confiscated. There is a Chinese proverb that suggests, "Give someone a fish and you teach him to steal because he will be hungry tomorrow. Teach him to fish, and he need never be hungry again."

In order to gain the maximum benefit from this chapter, you may have to rearrange your thinking about the Christian virtue of humility. None of the cardinal virtues is more widely misunderstood. You remember how St. Paul wrote to first-century Christians in Rome not to think of themselves more highly than they "ought to think" (Romands 12:3). Many ministers have utilized this verse to prove that people ought to be self-effacing. They fail to notice that Paul continues by saying that each person should recognize that "God has given to every man a measure of grace." Rather than endorsing the practice of depreciating your abilities, the apostle was really saying, "Be honest about the gifts you have been given." A street corner philosopher has expressed it, "God don't make no trash."

In the Broadway musical *The Unsinkable Molly Brown* the lead character finally admitted, "I mean more to me than to anybody else I know." You will be able to avoid considerable guilt if you can make this same declaration for yourself. You are important. You deserve respect and attention—most of all from yourself.

The Virtue of Selfishness

Selfishness is the second virtue that is widely misunderstood and abused. Nothing could be more arrogant than for an individual to assume that he is so important in the total scheme of things that he must put the happiness of other people always ahead of his own. When you get right down to it, everyone is basically selfish. One person spends every available hour helping underprivileged children. Another becomes the Mafia's most proficient "hit man." Still another develops a new drug that she hopes will relieve suffering and earn several million dollars. In each case, the motivation is the same. Each individual is choosing, without force or coercion, to do whatever he or she believes will provide the greatest happiness and satisfaction. The difference lies in the paths they have chosen to achieve this goal.

The sermons on self-sacrifice assume that there are only two roads to happiness. One requires that you give up what you enjoy for the benefit of others. The other option is to take advantage of others and exploit them for your own good. Fortunately, there is a third avenue that provides a greater potential for genuine contentment. This requires that you accept the responsibility for your own well-being and grant other people the right to plot their own course through life. No one has the ability to provide happiness for you. Similarly, no matter how great you are, you cannot give happiness to someone who is unwilling to seize it for himself.

This is one of the most difficult concepts that parents have to accept as their children grow up. No amount of formal planning, investment, or cajoling can provide happiness, good grades, or wise marital decisions. You can tell your child how much he or she should enjoy a concert, a good book, or a trip with you. Your assurance will, however, provide no guarantee. Enjoyment, success, and happiness can only be achieved by the person who wants them for himself. If you really want to make someone happy, my best advice is to use your time, talent, money, and effort to help the one person you know well enough to make good decisions about his or her happiness—yourself. The remarkable thing about this formula is that if you are able to gain true happiness and contentment for yourself, other people gain much more pleasure by being around you than if you are constantly trying to manipulate them into having a good time.

Ayn Rand uses a dramatic illustration to show how her selfishness would lead her to actions that many people might describe as heroically unselfish. If someone were about to shoot a husband whom she loved dearly, she admits that she would readily stand between him and the bullet in order to spare his life. A noble gesture? According to Rand, this would be the most selfish thing that she could do. Life would be difficult without this person whom she truly loved, especially if she had to live with the knowledge that she could have spared his life. On the other hand, by stepping in the bullet's path, she dooms her husband to suffer the feelings of loss, pain, and guilt. Instead of a noble act of altruistic concern, her heroism would be the easy way out and the most selfish thing she could do.

When you make any purchase, you are deciding that you prefer that item to the money that it takes to acquire it. Similarly, the merchant wouldn't sell you the item unless the price seemed fair. Under the basic values of a private enterprise society, no one has to sacrifice himself or his possessions for any other person. Exchanges are made only when they are mutually beneficial. The same thing ought to be true in human and social relationships.

People who practice enlightened selfishness will not be insensitive to the needs or feelings and desires of other people. Neither do they accept those wishes as absolute demands. In most instances, the wishes of other people can be seen as opportunities for potential exchanges that are mutually beneficial.

Planning for survival in a changing world does not require that you sacrifice your own needs for other people. It cannot be built on the assumption that other people will forfeit their own best interest for you. Yet it is possible, even probable, that several people will find that their own self-interest will lead to extensive cooperation via mutual investments in property and protection.

A NEW YOU

The American Dairy Association recently sponsored a major advertising campaign that stresses the theme, "There's a new you coming every day." Based on the idea that the body generates millions of new cells each day, these ads stress the importance of proper nutrition in creating this new you.

Today, we find dinosaurs only in museums because these marvelous creatures lacked the adaptive powers to survive in a changing environment. Because they could not adapt, they became extinct. Our way of life faces a similar challenge today. The old you may have functioned efficiently in a world of economic growth and prosperity. But unless you can acquire new skills and new attitudes, new realities could create insurmountable obstacles to survival.

A New Mind

A great deal of what modern psychology has discovered is summarized by the great king of Israel, Solomon, in the proverb, "As a man thinketh in his heart, so is he." For centuries, scholars and philosophers have attempted to establish a definition of reality. Still, the most brilliant argument will not convince a miserable man that he ought to be happy. During the past decade, several mystical writers, such as Carlos Castaneda and Jane Roberts, developed major underground markets by explaining the transient nature of personal reality. An eight-ounce glass with four ounces of water is half full or half empty depending on your perspective. So it is with our financial resources. Many of the discouraged financiers who jumped from window ledges during the crash of 1929 were far from penniless. Life just didn't seem worth living without the wealth they thought they possessed.

A former colleague who taught economics at Columbia University conducted a long-term research project in which he asked groups of people ranging from students to successful business executives how much money they thought it would take for them to be truly happy. He found that it made very little difference how much money the people were making. They seemed to consistently report that they needed about 15 percent more than they currently were earning.

A New York attorney gave an interesting example of this principle of need. For many years he had handled a very large trust for a young man who received $2 million a year in income. Since this individual had expensive tastes, he was able to spend the entire proceeds of his trust. In a few years, the value of his inheritance was reduced because of economic conditions and eventually his income dropped to approximately $200,000 per year. The attorney reported that he received many phone calls from his distraught client who complained, "Life just isn't fair. It's impossible to live on $200,000 a year!"

Before you judge that individual's greed too harshly, ask what life would be like for you if you were to be suddenly receiving 10 percent of your current income. Doubtless, it sounds like a pretty bleak picture; but in all probability, you can remember a time when you made only 10 percent of your current income. I would even be willing to bet that you were about as happy then as you are now and maybe even saved a larger percentage of your income. Abraham Lincoln was very perceptive when he commented, "I have about decided that people are just as happy as they decide they want to be."

There is no truth that exists apart from the perception of the person who is experiencing it. While you have only limited control over your future environment, you have absolute control over your attitude about it. Norman Vincent Peale has become wealthy by preaching the gospel of the power of positive thinking. More importantly, he has helped many other people become wealthy by following the simplistic formula that he outlines.

Events always grow from thoughts. We can view these thoughts as seeds and the events as harvest. Whatever happens to you is a consequence of your conscious and unconscious thoughts. Accept circumstances as a result of your own thoughts and actions rather than blaming them on greater outside forces, and you can reduce your dependency and open up new options to change your life.

You cannot increase your strength, awareness, potential, or happiness by thought alone. It takes determined effort. Deal with circumstances by concentrating on what you may have done to create the situation. More importantly, focus on what you can do to make things better.

Don't spend too much time in your analysis of the past. Accept your mistakes and your limitations. Adversity and pain almost always create new strengths if you have the will to win. Invest in a new attitude by thinking of your strengths and abilities. Concentrate on the opportunities for improvements that exist around you. You can collect dividends for many years from these investments of time and money.

In the Biblical account of Creation, man was given dominion over the earth and everything within it. We have the power to overcome disease, poverty, war, and crime. Power over these and other problems exists only for those people who feel self-sufficient. Without this attribute, we are dependent on our ability to exploit or emulate others. As Arthur Schopenhauer has said, "We forfeit three-fourths of ourselves in order to be like other people." The person who is dependent and must rely upon the crutches of other people can go no faster or farther than those crutches will carry him.

Obviously, self-sufficiency must be developed. Children

come into the world with a total dependence upon others. The degree to which they achieve maturity can be measured by the extent to which they overcome this dependence and are able to rely upon their own skill, ability, and judgment.

Unfortunately, many individuals learn at an early age to manipulate others into taking care of them by appearing to be dependent. We do our children a disservice when we do for them those things that they are perfectly capable of handling. Similarly, we do a disservice to the poor and perpetuate their poverty by giving them things rather than opportunities.

The greatest gift that any parent can give a child is independence. It is also the greatest gift that you can give yourself. Self-reliance has been a constant thread throughout the fabric of this book. The need has always been evident in every society, but it is becoming more apparent as the clouds of hardship gather around us.

One technique that many people have found useful in creating a more positive outlook and instilling self-confidence in their ability to handle problems is called autosuggestion or subliminal programming. Drawing on the techniques of transcendental meditation, Yoga, and bio-feedback, the positive programming of your subconscious can enforce your belief in goals and yourself. One approach to subliminal programming involves sitting quietly in a darkened room and allowing yourself to move to a dreamlike state by focusing your attention on a picture of yourself in an extremely pleasant environment while consciously relaxing each part of your body from head to toe. After three to five minutes of this form of relaxation, your brainwave activity has moved from an active conscious state to what psychologists describe as the "alpha level." This state of calm relaxation reduces anxiety and provides a receptive environment for positive suggestions. Impressive results have been achieved by people who merely repeat precisely worded statements of personal objectives five or six times. A series of up to eight statements can be effectively repeated in this manner.

These exercises focus concentration and, in controlled experiments, have proved to enhance recuperation, create self-confidence, help decrease stress, and overcome destructive habits. I realize that many people will find the simplicity of this description somewhat distracting. It all sounds just a little bit hokey. Nevertheless, the somewhat stuffy *Harvard*

Business Review has reported on the positive effects of these meditative efforts. Why not invest fifteen minutes a day for one month in your own private research project?

A New Body

Perhaps you have heard the axiom, "You are what you eat." If this is true, and I believe that it is, Americans are becoming a thoroughly processed, packaged, and preserved people. In 1971, we bought more processed food than fresh food for the first time in history. Since that time, the proportion of healthful, natural food has declined steadily. We now spend $100 billion each year for convenience foods that provide little nourishment and are potentially damaging. The average citizen consumes almost five pounds of chemical preservatives, stabilizers, coloring, and other additives each year. The use of artificial substances has tripled in the past twenty years to a total of over 1 billion pounds per year. Today there are more than 3,000 chemicals that are deliberately added to your food. The long-term effect of these chemical additives on your body has not yet been determined, but a significant number of nutritionists feels that this chemical feast accounts for the almost epidemic increase in cancer in the United States.

Food: The devaluation of foods began when people began to leave their farms and move into cities. As part of their "progress," they turned their back on the nutritious, wholegrain bread that they associated with their rural heritage and replaced it by more elegant, refined, white bread that was associated with wealth.

To make bread more attractive, the nutrients of the grain contained in the germ were removed and fed to cattle. The livestock grew healthy on it. The remainder of the hull (largely starch) was bleached chemically and fed to people, who grew ill from it. Eventually, the national health was so affected that a national program of "enrichment" for white bread was begun. Chemical vitamins were put back and most people relaxed. More cautious nutritionists remained concerned.

These scientists continued to look for relationships between diet and health. Dr. Weston Price embarked on a major study of what healthy people around the world ate. He found pockets of exceptional health in the Swiss Alps, Northern Italy, and isolated locations within Australia, New Zealand, Central America, the Soviet Union, and certain northern portions of Canada and the United States. These people stood straight and tall, had exceptional physical endurance, and good dispositions. There was no evidence of most of the diseases modern civilizations experience. Some of their diets emphasized yogurt. Others drank goat's milk. Some emphasized whole-grain foods. A few had eliminated animal meats.

There were only two things that their diets had in common. First, they were nutritionally balanced. Secondly, and perhaps more importantly, none of these healthy cultures knew how to refine foods. They ate them in their natural state.

Today, the United States has become one of the most overfed, undernourished nations in history. Of the approximate 8,000 products on the shelves of the supermarket, over 5,000 have been "invented" by biochemists in the last thirty years. We now "enjoy" synthetic flavorings, synthetic foods such as eggs and cream, synthetic colorings, and chemical preservatives. In many instances, chemistry has provided food that is more attractive to the eye than the real thing. But remember that your eye is more easily impressed than your stomach by appearances.

When you begin to stock your survival larder, don't overlook the importance of good nutrition. Even better, start practicing it now. In some instances, health foods may cost a little more, but if you eliminate the junk food, you will find that your total grocery bill remains about the same. There will be an added dividend as well. You will feel better, be healthier, and have lower doctor bills. Within two years of adopting a program of healthy eating, I've seen doctor bills for families drop to less than a third of their former level.

Just for the fun of it, take out some of your old doctor's statements. What are you billed for? You will probably find charges for Billy's bronchitis, Tommy's tonsilitis, and Freddie's flu. Do you find a single item on any of the statements that promotes good health, for avoiding colds or coronaries, or for making you feel healthy, happy, and vigorous?

Unfortunately, the economic incentive for physicians is backwards. We don't pay doctors to keep us in good health. We pay them to make us feel better after we get sick. The ancient Chinese had a much more practical system. They paid their physicians to keep them well. As soon as they got sick, the physician went off the payroll. Since we are not likely to win the endorsement of the American Medical Association for this compensation program, good health for your family is up to you.

If you are looking for a simple formula for healthy eating, let me propose a two-sentence recommendation for nutrition and health. First, eliminate everything from your diet that has refined flour, sugar, or chemicals in it. Secondly, eat as many natural foods (especially fruits, vegetables, and nuts) as you can and two teaspoons of miller's bran per day.

There are some excellent books that have been written on the subject of healthy eating. Obviously, my simple summary cannot provide the detail that these more thorough analyses will offer. Another excellent investment would be to purchase a couple of the nutrition books described in the bibliography. Jane Kinderlehrer's *Confessions Of A Sneaky Organic Cook* offers a concise but slightly more involved summary than mine:

HOW TO HAVE A HEALTHFUL KITCHEN
(No harmful things and all of the essentials)

The "Good-Nutrition" cook rids her pantry of these foods:
1. Bleached white flour
2. Refined sugar
3. All shortenings that are solid at room temperature
4. White rice
5. Maraschino cherries (they're loaded with harmful preservatives)
6. Any product loaded with BHA or BHT (freshness preservers)
7. Fruits canned with sugar syrup (there are some that are not)
8. All synthetic sweeteners and products sweetened with them (Saccharin as well as cyclamates)
9. All sugared dry cereals
10. Hydrogenated peanut butters (use the natural)
11. All candy made with refined sugar
12. Commercial breads that are loaded with emulsifiers and preservatives
13. Refined table salt

The "Good-Nutrition" cook keeps on her pantry shelf:
1. Raw honey

2. Raw sugar
3. Date sugar
4. Soy flour
5. Whole wheat flour (stone ground)
6. Carob flour (chocolate substitute)
7. White germ (in the refrigerator)
8. Wheat germ oil (in the refrigerator)
9. Soy and sesame oils (cold pressed) in the refrigerator
10. Nutritional yeast (sometimes called brewer's yeast)
11. Sesame seeds (unhulled)
12. Sunflower seeds (raw)
13. Pumpkin seeds
14. Kelp (as a salt substitute)
15. Unsweetened coconut
16. Seeds for sprouting (wheat, rye, oat, mung beans, alfalfa, etc.)
17. Raw nuts

Another simple rule of thumb is to never purchase a product that has any ingredient listed on the label that you can't pronounce. With this restriction, William Buckley might have a more extensive diet than most of us, but almost without exception, those complicated words and strange initials signify a chemical that isn't going to do you any good.

Fat: Maintaining a proper weight level is easier for people who eat well. Obesity is not an evidence of too much of a good thing. Typically, it means that there has been too much of some bad things. Today, combating fatness has become a $10-billion-a-year industry. There are over 30 million people in this country who are seriously overweight and 15 million obese Americans. If you'll pardon a pun, obesity is becoming very widespread. Unnecessary weight puts a strain on most of the body's organs and is a contributing factor in a large number of serious illnesses.

Losing weight is not incompatible with enjoying life—or food. If you are willing to invest a little extra effort in developing a healthy body that will serve you more efficiently, consider the following simple suggestions:

1. Take time to learn a little bit more about the requirements of good nutrition.
2. Study your own eating habits and requirements. Do you have to eat at precisely the same time each day? Could

you eat four nutritious snacks rather than three large meals?

3. Don't eat leftovers. It is no more wasteful to dump something in the garbage than it is to dump it into your stomach. If you are really hung up about waste, get a dog or start a compost heap.

4. Always eat a nutritious, high-protein breakfast to get you started. This may be simply a glass of milk fortified with a tasty protein compound.

5. Never eat empty calories. Don't eat anything made with sugar or refined flour. This especially includes donuts, macaroni, frosted cereal, and chocolate candies.

6. Never eat until you are comfortable. Eat slowly and give hunger pains a time to subside.

7. Keep plenty of carrots, radishes, and cucumbers ready for between-meal snacks.

8. Be sure to include lecithin in your diet. Lecithin helps you feel well fed with less food. It also helps to avoid some of the health problems associated with dieting, such as cholesterol deposits and gall bladder complications.

9. Avoid coffee. Drinking black coffee during a diet leads to added production of insulin and actually increases hunger pains.

10. Don't use artificial sweeteners in an effort to reduce calories. One of your objectives should be to retrain your taste buds so that you no longer crave sweets. Moreover, artificial sweeteners of all kinds are highly suspect from a health standpoint. If sweets are absolutely required, use honey as a substitute. With most recipes and for most purposes, you can substitute one unit of honey for three units of sugar.

11. Weigh yourself every morning. In this manner, you can observe the close relationship between food intake and weight.

12. Start an exercise program. An exercise program combined with good nutritional habits is essential for permanent healthy living. More about the exercise regime later.

Fitness: One positive aspect of contemporary life is the current emphasis on physical fitness. It doesn't make a great deal of difference what program you use as long as you have a regular routine that provides a workout for your respiratory and circulatory systems and develops some degree of efficiency and endurance. The best exercise you can do is the kind of exercise you will do.

Finding something you enjoy that gives you a real workout is the only rule you have to remember. The benefits are numerous. Regular exercise makes you look and feel infinitely better. It reduces your chance of heart attack or other circulatory or respiratory ailments. It enables you to work harder and more efficiently. It tones up muscles throughout the body, improves general circulation, muscle tone, skin appearance, and overall well-being.

Before jumping into the middle of a rigorous program, you probably should check with your family physician—especially if you have a history of medical problems that might conflict with the exercise. If you are over thirty, you should have a check-up that includes an electrocardiogram (EKG). If you are over forty, you should request a Master's EKG, that monitors your heart while exercising. A regular EKG determines if you have experienced cardiac damage. The second records the conditions of your heart under stress.

Try to choose a regular time for your workout and make it a part of your daily routine. Physicians recommend that you wait a couple of hours after a meal. Before your evening meal is an ideal time. Don't try to start off with too rigorous an activity the first day. Stiff muscles discourage follow-up exercise. Start off with just a few minutes of exertion and add as your fitness improves. George Burns used to say that he got his exercise from serving as a pallbearer for his friends who tried to exercise too hard. Try to keep a chart showing your progress. It will not only help you remember where you are, it will serve as a motivator.

Perspiration isn't a danger sign, but you shouldn't push past the point of discomfort. Signs of overexertion during exercise includes tightness in the chest, severe breathlessness, dizziness, and nausea. If you experience these, you should stop exercising immediately. Count your pulse about five minutes after you have completed your workout. If it is still over 120, you are pushing too hard for a person in your condition. Ten minutes after the end of your exercise, the pulse should be below 100.

Don't get discouraged if you don't make immediate progress. It took a good while to get out of shape. Getting back in shape will take a while too.

Most people recognize the importance of a warm-up period. Unfortunately, few people understand that the body also needs a cooling-down period after exercise. Moving into complete relaxation immediately after exercise can cause dizzy spells, fainting, and even more serious problems. Five minutes of walking will ease the transition between vigorous exertion and relaxation.

Many fitness specialists suggest that your goal should be to keep your heart beating at about 60 to 70 percent of your maximum heart rate for close to fifteen minutes. A person below forty can view 140 to 125 as his optimal range. The younger you are, the higher sustained heartbeat you should tolerate. For individuals between forty and sixty, the range will be between 110 and 125 heartbeats per minute. Again, the older you are, the less stress you should plan to experience. For those above sixty, a heartbeat between 100 and 110 should be viewed as reasonable maximum level of exertion.

Remember, there are practical reasons for developing the type of health habits described in the preceding paragraphs regardless of your economic environment. It only follows that good health will be even more important during a period of unusual stress, tension, and independence than ever before. With a new, improved body and mind, you will be able to cope with the challenges of a chaotic future with calm, confidence, and strength.

NEW RELATIONSHIPS

We live in a world of transient relationships. Friendships, jobs, and marriages are frequently viewed as short-term commitments. Dr. Eli Ginsberg of Columbia University has predicted that we are all on the verge of becoming metropolitan people without ties or committed long-term friends or neighbors. In a scholarly paper entitled *"Friendships of the Future,"* psychologist Courtney Tall suggests that "stability, based on close relationships with a few people, will be ineffective due to high mobility, a wide interest range, and growing capacity for adaptation and change found among members of a highly automated society. Friendship patterns of the majority in the future will provide for many satisfactions, while substituting many close relationships of shorter duration for the long-term friendships formed in the past."

While many Americans have a pool of acquaintances ranging from 500 to 2,500, most have only a limited number of people who can be referred to as friends. One study of middle-class couples in the Midwest found that the average couple listed approximately seven friendship units. Jess Lair, Professor of Psychology at the University of Montana, has suggested that it is far better to have six good friends than it is to have a host of casual acquaintances. As we will discuss in Chapter 13, unique meaningful friendships will be far more valuable in your quest for survival than an impressive list of mere acquaintances. When you get right down to it, how many people do you feel free to talk to candidly about your concerns for the future? If you are embarrassed to share your anxieties with an acquaintance, that is pretty good evidence that you don't have a genuine friendship. There are practical as well as psychological reasons for having a few people you can depend on in any emergency rather than a multitude of fair-weather friends.

A key test of the quality of a relationship is whether the advantage and benefit is mutual. As we have stressed before, some of the best relationships are practically selfish for both parties involved. Openness, honesty, and integrity are the foundations of strong relationships. If you are afraid to talk to someone about your concerns, it is probably because you fear rejection. Fear of rejection really means that you do not have much confidence in the strength of a relationship. In all cases, close relationships require considerable effort and honest, open communication.

According to Dr. Ari Kiev, "Human misery usually results when we encounter unexpected events unprepared. At times of crises, people with a natural affinity are drawn to each other as if they had prepared for the eventuality." In a very similar way, people who are inclined to prepare for certain eventualities are naturally drawn together. If you don't already recognize that you share concerns with some of your acquaintances, I believe that the material contained in this book can serve as an important catalyst in strengthening your relationships.

PERSONAL INVESTMENT STRATEGY

The same principles you employ in handling your financial investments are appropriate for personal investment. The serious investor will not put a great deal of money in the stock market without checking the financial pages of the newspaper on a regular basis.

If you are interested in personal survival, you'll want to do a great deal of research and reading. A complete library of important resources is contained in the bibliography of this book. I have even added an asterisk to the ones I think are practically essential.

In addition to the survival library, you will want to stay on top of current events that affect your social and economic environment. Subscribe to at least one of the major newsletters reviewed in Appendix B. Subscribe to a couple of practical periodicals or financially oriented newspapers, such as the *Wall Street Journal, Business Week,* or *U.S. News & World Report.* These sources will often help you read between the lines written by the more traditional press.

Get involved with your reading and approach every subject from a practical standpoint. Don't read to be discouraged, read to decide how you can best cope with situations as they arise. Make notes and underline freely. Check sideheadings and topics to select those that you feel are more important to you. Few magazine articles and books are written in such a way that every page is equally valuable for you. Look for the items that will make your reading more challenging and rewarding.

No matter how long you have been out of school and regardless of the advanced degrees you may hold, your education isn't over. It had better not be. Once a person has finished learning, he or she is really finished!

Call your nearest university or community college and find out what types of courses are offered through continuing education. Make a list of all the courses you think would help you achieve self-sufficiency. Plan to take at least one course each term until you have increased your arsenal of survival skills. Most of these courses will meet only once a week. It is worth trading an evening of mind-deadening television for stimulation and practical learning.

I am probably the world's worst handyman. Some time ago, I decided that I needed to correct this deficiency in case the services I was dependent upon were to become unavailable. I made a list of the courses that I felt would be useful to me during the coming decade. Mine was a rather extensive list, and I am still taking classes. I don't expect to complete this project before I am forced to start using some of the things I have learned. Already, many of the concepts have proved valuable.

My first course was a standard first-aid program offered by the Red Cross. It dealt primarily with the type of skills that are required for accident prevention and the treatment of minor accidents. It helped provide preparation to treat several injuries and to meet most emergencies when medical assistance is not readily available. This course took only one day of my time and was one of the best investments I've ever made.

Next, I moved through a program on home repair. The knowledge provided by this course would be virtually essential in the kind of society I envision. This expenditure has already returned many times the original modest tuition investment because of the newly acquired ability to solve minor problems without calling for the friendly neighborhood plumber and his gold-plated invoice pad.

My original list of courses included small engine repair, automotive repair and maintenance, home remodeling, organic gardening, living off the land, wilderness experience workshop, environmental education, landscape design, basic gardening, furniture upholstering, self-defense, and speed reading (just to stay up with all the new areas I am interested in). I have not finished with working my way through the original list, but have discovered at least a dozen new courses that I am anxious to add.

If you are involved in team preparations, practice division of labor. If you are working as a couple or an extended survival community, try to split up the responsibility for areas of knowledge or types of expertise. In this manner, some people can specialize in the area where they are most interested or skillful. It will also allow you to accomplish your goals more quickly. In many instances, my wife and I would enjoy taking some of the classes together. Unfortunately, I don't feel that time provides us the luxury of this type of duplication.

My final investment advice is to begin immediately practicing the concepts we have talked about. Invest a little time in acquiring your skills and keeping those skills up to date. The worst mistake you can make in reading this book is to agree with the concept, but to decide that there is plenty of time to prepare when things get a little less hectic for you. Your life will not become less crowded until you rearrange your priorities or until circumstances rearrange them for you.

Even with food prices becoming more exorbitant every day, I still believe that I can receive a larger financial return by writing another book or conducting another seminar than practicing my organic gardening skills. By short-term return on investment analysis, I can't justify the time I spend with the garden. Still, I don't want to face the coming crisis with only some excellent books and pamphlets about survival. Right now, it is fairly easy to find people who are able and willing to offer advice and assistance. Supplies are readily available and less expensive than they will be again until after the crash.

Today's mistakes are not catastrophic. Learn to trust your hunches and rely on your intuition. For important issues, this may solve more problems than logic or intelligence. Learn when to seek the counsel of others and when to ignore advice that doesn't convince the jury of your own judgment. Don't assume that other people have better insight about what your objectives should be or how you should go about achieving your goals.

You are your very best investment. Respect that investment, and your dividends will be generous and long lasting.

CHAPTER EIGHT

Setting Up
a Foreign Haven

When I was an undergraduate, there was one professor who stood out from the rest in that he really seemed to be headed for the big time. His boundless energy always had a number of projects whirling. Within a few years, he used his technical expertise to create a product that was in great demand. Today, that product is in almost every school in the nation. The professor no longer works for the university but is employed by his own company, which is headquartered in the Bahamas. Though you are likely to see him anywhere in the States, a majority of his earnings flow through the Bahamian company.

That innovator has done what many others only dream about. When the conversation turns to talk of rising taxes and increasing government control, there is always someone who pipes up to say that he has heard that, with the right legal maneuvers, a person can shelter his money by the use of some other country's special tax laws, banking system, or unique concessions to the money from outside.

Most people, however, conclude that such arrangements are too good to be true and that, if they were for real, everybody and his brother would be making use of them. And so my guess is that while you may like to joke about having millions stashed safely in a Swiss numbered bank account or setting up a business in some exotic tax haven, you haven't done much checking into the matter.

REASON FOR INTEREST (AND PRINCIPAL) ABROAD

In actual fact, there *are* foreign havens for your money. They *do* provide situations in which you can profit while keeping your money secure. As our own nation's economy continues to worsen, the impetus for setting up protective foreign custody for part of your wealth is increasing. Some chapters in this book talk about the ways you can realize the highest possible increases in your wealth through investments. This chapter is not primarily about the highest return on your money. That can (and often will) occur when the world monetary situation has taken a surprise turn and given overseas investments a serendipitous increase. But the primary thought in setting up foreign havens is rarely to make a killing through high interest on deposits. Rather, it is to *protect* the principal and gain a respectable return that is safer or less subject to taxations than U.S. institutions.

The people who have brought the greatest fame to "numbered Swiss accounts" are the Nazi officers who remained alive and well heeled after World War II on money that they had stolen and stashed in secret accounts. There were, however, even more Jewish merchants who were able to use funds they had wisely put away in Switzerland to arrange a new life in a new land when they accurately read the signs of decay in the early days of the Third Reich. In more recent years, Mafia bosses have revived the intrigue of the numbered account. While secret numbered accounts really do exist, they do not constitute the strength or even the primary attraction of the Swiss banking system.

All accounts in Swiss banks are secret and the Swiss have irritated other governments on many occasions by simply refusing to divulge information about the accounts of foreign depositors. But the fabled *numbered* accounts are even secret from the Swiss bankers themselves—except for one key bank officer! The accounts can be opened without a name, and deposits and withdrawals made by the number and some prearranged code words. It is possible to keep the money completely anonymous, though the Swiss are going to demand to be satisfied about its sources. For the most part, numbered accounts remain the domain of those who have something to hide. There is still the overwhelming majority of holders of Swiss accounts who obey every law and make full disclosure of all interest received. Why then, if there is no secrecy advantage, would anyone go to the trouble of setting up and maintaining a "long distance" bank account?

A Place to Hide

There are several major reasons for you to set up any of a

variety of potential foreign havens. First, they can serve as a place to put some of the money that you would like to hide from someone. Secondly, a haven opens many doors for your expanded business interests and activities or to shelter some of business income from confiscatory taxes. Finally, they may offer the possibility of a safe haven to hide yourself!

Europeans who survived the financial devastations of World War II almost invariably did so by adhering to an age-old principle of money management: "Never keep all your wealth in the country where you live because *anything* can happen—and usually does." Given enough time, almost any nation is likely to let go of its conservative principles and embark on shortsighted economic programs that end up eroding the financial strength of its citizens. Already in our relatively short national history, the United States has made rich people out of many whose holdings were not dependent on U.S. economic integrity. Do not misunderstand the message of this chapter. It is not that our system is all bad and the Swiss system is without flaw. For many reasons, I still choose to live in the United States. My implication is that no matter what economic environment you live in (even in Switzerland itself) you will be wise to make sure you have part of your wealth abiding under one or more other systems.

A Perspective on U.S.

The last time I was in the Bahamas, I spent some time with the chief executive officer of a local branch of a major Swiss bank there. He had grown up in Switzerland, but spent a major portion of his banking career in Brazil, where he had lived through some scary inflation experiences. His concern about the future of the United States was a sense of moral bankruptcy in the country—that the national character is greatly flawed so that neither the dollar nor the American commitment is respected abroad. He pointed out our total lack of willingness to bite the bullet when necessary to solve economic problems. He also suggested that, while most of his investments were in hard currency such as gold and silver and primarily in Switzerland, he would never be without enough gold to get him anywhere in the world he might want to go in an emergency. He had one child in Europe and another in Africa and he wanted to be assured that he could get to either of them no matter what set of circumstances might develop.

This cosmopolitan banker argued that it was a mistake to keep the majority of your wealth close at hand. I would agree with this opinion if I lived in the Bahamas but, even though I'm not optimistic about the future of the United States' economy, I still prefer to remain reasonably close to a significant portion of my assets.

There are some ways to make big money through international buying and selling. However, most of the pros who know the ropes of international commodity costs are not going to be reading this book. They will have long since opened their foreign corporations and bank accounts. My assumption is that you are interested in the basics of the question: whether, why, and step-by-step how. These answers occur in the next section. If you want more details, I'll suggest additional resources for you in the Bibliography.

YOUR SECRET BANK ACCOUNT

Throughout this book, I've stressed the idea that only you can design the unique combination of financial arrangements that's right for your resources and economic objectives. This is no cop-out but merely a restatement of a basic truth: I can give you information; only you can decide which parts of it are "truth" for you.

Still a Live Option—Despite Rumors

Regardless of what you've heard, Swiss* bank accounts have not become historic relics. The recent boom in their popularity has made Swiss bankers less enthusiastic about opening small accounts. Still they remain currently hot and are likely to remain so because their history and popularity are based on the integrity of the Swiss banking profession, which had been around for centuries before the colonies gained their independence. From time to time, we Americans get the word through news releases that a "potential new treaty" will result in the agreement of Swiss banks to disclose

* While this section deals primarily with Swiss accounts, many of the principles of secrecy apply to any country with "Swiss" laws concerning bank secrecy.

information about funds held in their accounts. While there continue to be negotiations, developments, and news stories, you can be sure that the Swiss are not going to give up the confidential nature of their banking relationships. Not only is the revealing of bank information against Swiss law, it is the mark of distinction that gives the reputation of absolute integrity to the Swiss. When you *do* see headlines about agreements to disclose information, the fine print will reveal that the agreement applies to cases where a court order has been negotiated because of overwhelming "probable cause" that the money was stolen or extorted.

You may also get the word that Swiss banks no longer welcome deposits from Americans because of the dying dollar and its tendency to drain the blood out of the Swiss franc. It is true that the dollar is sick and it is true that the Swiss would do quite well without every Tom, Dick, and Harry who want to deposit $1000 against the steady decline of the dollar. However, the Swiss have been international bankers since long before the U.S. dollar. They have appropriate legislation to control the influx of huge sums to exploit currency changes. There is actually a "negative interest" charged on some accounts and words like that can be blown out of context in news stories to convince Americans that all the loopholes of Swiss banking have been closed.

The advantages of a Swiss account do live on and will continue to live. They result from basic philosophical stances of the U.S. government and the Swiss government. They will not be treatied out of existence. Next time you see a story about the end of Swiss bank accounts as worthwhile devices for Americans, keep reading between the lines until you discover who released the story. Nine times out of ten, it will reveal itself to be from a government agency that stands to gain if Americans are convinced that one more loophole has been closed.

In 1978, the Swiss began to be more serious about discouraging dollar movement into their banking system. After a sensational nonstop seven-month vertical climb, the Swiss instituted some tough new restrictions. While this created what I believe will be a temporary adjustment, it still made foreign accounts a little more difficult. You can, however, open or maintain a Swiss franc account of up to SF100,000 without being subject to the negative interest. You can even earn interest on accounts up to the first SF20,000 (that's about 10,-

000 U.S. dollars as I write this). You can also buy Swiss francs and put them in a safe deposit box. Harry Schultz recommends buying Swiss domiciled mutual funds, provided that 80 percent of its assets are invested outside of Switzerland. These shares are denominated in Swiss francs so you still accomplish your objective.

In almost every case of imposed obstacles to foreign use of Swiss accounts, there is a way to circumvent the problem. It should be remembered that Swiss bankers want to do banking business and are unlikely to establish restrictions to prohibit their own progress. However, there is one lesson our country needs to learn from the Swiss. Current profits, which are valued, are still not the overriding motive for any and all policies. The Swiss will forego a profit today if they see that it will weaken their position in the future. That is why the Swiss franc remains backed by gold. This is also why the Swiss have kept their inflation in check and progressively reduced their trade deficit. The Swiss account you open will hold its value because, in spite of the fluctuating values of world currencies and political underpinnings, the Swiss understand the basics of economics.

The Benefits of a Swiss Connection

There are several advantages for you to consider in a Swiss bank account. To begin with, you will have some money outside your own country where it cannot be confiscated by a new government policy. As I have emphasized before, arrange your money in concentric circles, keeping some in liquid forms for emergencies and other categories in ever-widening circles and in ever-increasing productivity. Some of your overseas money should remain in highly liquid forms as mentioned earlier. Other amounts can be invested at higher interest, less liquidity, but equal safety from government intervention.

A Swiss bank account will allow you to deal in foreign currencies, which has become more than a matter of speculation. It is equally important to anyone who travels or deals internationally. One of the truly innovative items of Swiss banking is the multicurrency checkbook. This allows you to deposit your money in a Swiss checking account and then write checks in any type of currency. Your banks will make payment in the currency you specify on the check and deduct

John Loeb

David Alexander

<u>for the USA</u>

kind Julia & June

the equivalent amount from your Swiss account. You avoid the headaches and exorbitant charges of transferring from one currency to the next at each border.

If you intend to really take action in arranging your financial affairs to survive and prosper regardless of the coming crash, it is a certainty that you will want to open one or more Swiss (and other international) accounts for a well-rounded personal financial program. Should a miracle occur and the crash be avoided, you will still be in a stronger position for making investments anywhere in the world, utilizing the financial advice of the experts in international finance, and maintaining your fiscal privacy.

Finally, the Swiss banking system does something that young American bank employees would have difficulty even believing—they do not use your money to make money for them. They *will* of course be happy to invest your money if you so request, but they will not loan out your deposit to someone else before you can get out the door. American banks automatically and by policy keep all money working. They could not possibly pay off all their depositors at the same time, but most Swiss banks could. They earn their profits from rendering the services connected with handling your money . . . not by using your money while you're not. No banking system is absolutely sound. The Swiss have some unfortunate chapters in their banking history but, overall, their banking system is the soundest in the world. Even so, if I lived in Switzerland and carried a Swiss passport, I would still expect to keep some of my wealth in another country.

The Problems

Just for balance, let me note a few of the factors that many would consider deterrents from opening and utilizing Swiss accounts. To me, none of the objections is of sufficient weight to rule out the Swiss connection, but I do want to give you all the facts.

First, a Swiss bank account is likely to be less convenient because it is in Switzerland instead of a half mile from your house. Even though writers are fond of waxing eloquent about the shrinking nature of our world, your money in a Swiss account is going to be several days away from you. Our modern communications *will* allow you to get your Swiss banker on the phone for about $6.75 for three minutes, but the turnaround time for the transaction and completing of business remains limited by human clerk speed and the turtles who deliver the U.S. mail. Even if you decide to use the direct dial powers available to you, there are only two or three hours each day when your work day overlaps the 9 to 5 of Swiss time zones. You *can* move the money a little faster by having it wired between your Swiss bank and one of its correspondent American banks, but the cost of the wire is ten dollars or more, the messages can often be garbled, and your confidentiality goes out the window since a record is kept of every wire. Convenience is an insurmountable factor and the obvious conclusion is that you don't try to use a foreign account as you would a local account. Keep the number of transactions few, simple, and economically self-supporting. Don't put money in Switzerland that has to be home for Christmas—unless its trip home can pay for itself!

There's no FDIC in Switzerland. There is no government agency that exists to insure the safety of bank deposits as our Federal Deposit Insurance Corporation does. The Swiss have less government on every score than we do and their hesitancy to gamble with depositor money makes such a safeguard unnecessary. As previously stated, we don't really have deposit insurance here in the U.S. as we think we do. Even the director of the FDIC has admitted that his fund could in no way expect to pay back major runs on a large number of banks. So, while Swiss bankers cannot offer you the promise of FDIC security, American bankers may offer you the promise but not the reality.

Swiss bankers are going to pay you lower interest rates than you get in lots of other places. They will require advance notice of withdrawals in many cases. And, as stated before, they will even charge you part of your interest in some cases. These are disadvantages that you can live with if you are committed to the importance of having some of your money beyond the grasp of governmental regulations. Actually, the Swiss withholding tax on interest paid is not overwhelming and can be regained if you are not afraid to lose your anonymity. You see, the tax was instituted to try to discourage secrecy among those unwilling to pay for the privilege. The way it works is that when your money earns interest, 30 percent of it is withheld and mailed to the Swiss government by your Swiss bank—not with your name but in one check along with everyone else's withheld tax. If you want to stay anonymous, you wave goodbye to the 30 percent of your interest and consider it the cost of privacy. If, however, you are reporting all interest earned (as the IRS requires) there is no need for your high-priced anonymity and you can get a large part of your 30 percent back. All you have to do is file a form R82 with the Swiss government, which will remit to you 5/6 of the withheld money. It's your decision: if you value the secrecy, you can forfeit the 30 percent withheld from your interest earned, or, if you figure the IRS already knows everything you do anyway, the forms R82 are available from the Swiss bank where you are doing business.

The negative interest tax was instituted to discourage international speculators from rushing large sums of money (like a million dollars or more) in and out of Swiss francs just to make quick profits as various national currencies fluctuated. But, unless your investment is likely to be in excess of $250,000 you are not in much danger of trouble from the negative interest tax. While the Swiss do have a few rather inconsequential taxes on foreign banking transactions, they are unlikely to hinder you as long as you are not making a large number of transactions unnecessarily and are availing yourself of the advice and counsel of the branch manager of the Swiss bank in your own city.

The remaining problems result from human error—both yours, the Swiss', or a combination of both. When you are delivering detailed messages over thousands of miles between people who speak different languages, the stage is set for all kinds of misunderstandings and gaps in communication. For starters, the Europeans often use commas where we would use periods and use periods where we would put commas. If you anticipate this reversal, it won't stump you. But if you don't know it's coming it can do amazing things to your deposit or withdrawal. Also, the European dates are written with the number of the day first. In America, December 5, 1980 is written 12/5/80 while the European would write it 5/12/80. It could make a significant difference in checking on your interest computations!

When you correspond with your Swiss bank, a typewriter is your best friend. For some reason, we Americans who have more typewriters than any other nation on earth will undoubtedly try to hand write a quick note to our Swiss bankers. It is an invitation to misunderstanding. Always type your communications to Swiss banks and keep them as simple and direct as possible. Whatever you do, avoid explaining things with figures of speech—the Swiss are not dumb, but neither are they educated in U.S. television lingo.

The final area of human error results from the noncomputerized nature of Swiss banking transactions, the rapidly changing values of many currencies, and the time lag inherent in international transactions. If you initiate a transaction today to buy gold with dollars, there are the variables of the cost of gold now and when the instruction is received, the value of the dollars now and when your message is received, and natural time lags. If you make the request on Wednesday and it arrives after the gold transactions close on Friday, it will be handled on Monday or Tuesday—nearly a week after you issued the instruction. The Swiss have tried to computerize their operation but so far it has not been possible to develop programs that are acceptable. Transactions are still manual and therefore are still subject to the problems of human error. This is complicated by the fact that Switzerland's policy restricting immigration is keeping specialized banking personnel from entering the country freely. The result is a gradual lessening of efficiency and professional care from the transactions of Swiss banks. Even so, the average mistake that you think you find in your statement will eventually prove to be your own failure to take into account some minor fluctuation of values or some incidental charge by the bank because of the method you chose to achieve a certain objective.

In spite of these few problems, a Swiss bank account remains a bargain in a time when you cannot be optimistic about American political and economic direction—or the lack of it.

Types of Accounts

There are a number of kinds of accounts that you may choose from. As you might expect, they offer the ever-present balance between security and interest. If you choose an account that can deliver higher interest, you can expect somewhat reduced safety for the investment and considerable reduction in liquidity.

A *current account* is what the Swiss call a checking account. Unlike your neighborhood American bank, they will not issue a neat little checkbook since the use of your current account will be more select than paying the light bill and the PTA dues. Most often, you will send a letter or a wire to inform the bank of deposits and withdrawals from your current account. The name refers to the fact that the balance may be changing at any time. Usually there is no interest paid on such an account, though most holders of current accounts have made significant gains during the recent past by merely having their money stored in Swiss francs while the dollar was being devalued. Some Swiss banks *do* pay small interest (½ percent to 1 percent) on current accounts if the balance remains high and the number of transactions stays low.

A *deposit account* is similar to an American savings account except that there are some restrictions on the amounts that may be withdrawn. Ordinarily, you can withdraw up to $3,000 each month with no advance notice, but if you want to withdraw more, you need to give up to three months prior notice. The amounts vary but the basic idea is similar to the Certificates of Deposit available in U.S. banks, except that you make small withdrawals. If your deposit account is kept in Swiss francs, the bank will pay you about 3 percent interest, not "compounded semiannually," but paid once a year. You can get higher interest if you ask the bank to keep your account in some currency other than Swiss francs, but, by doing that, you lose one of the primary values of the Swiss account.

What the Swiss call a *savings account* usually pays 4 percent interest but requires six months notice for withdrawal of more than $1,000. Here again is the similarity to the American Certificate of Deposit except for the ability to make withdrawals and the low interest.

The *investment savings account* raises the interest a little and tightens the liquidity. Interest is about 4½ percent if you have $3,500 or less in the account and 5 percent if you have more than $3,500. You can still make withdrawals, but you are limited to no more than $350 for any six-month period. If you suspect that you are going to have a sudden need for more than $350, you probably should not consider an investment account.

The *fixed deposit account* closes the periodic withdrawal option out completely. You agree to place a fixed amount of money in the account and leave it for three months, six months, or a year at a time. Interest rates hover around 5

percent, with a higher interest going naturally to the money
that is committed for the longer periods of time.

Cash bonds are similar to the fixed deposit accounts in that
money is committed for a longer period of time with no in-
terim withdrawal options. These are usually bonds issued individually by each bank and the interest runs between 4¼
percent and 5 percent.

A *custodial account* is the place to put your gold bullion or
your original Rembrandt. It is quite similar to the American
safe deposit box in that *you* pay the bank for the storage
service and they give you no interest and lay no hands on
your possessions. It is unlike an American safe deposit box in
that it will still be available without complications even if
American banks have a sudden declared bank holiday as they
did following the stock market crash in 1930. If you can
store cash, gold, silver, or art objects in your custodial account, the bank will keep it secure and, even if the Swiss
bank should fail, your possessions will not be considered part
of the bank's holdings. If you are looking for the closest thing
in the world to 100 percent financial security, buy gold or
Swiss francs and store them in a custodial account in a Swiss
bank. More likely, you will want to include this absolute in
your *balanced* financial plan, putting your emergency funds
there and then launching into the higher-risk ventures with
other portions of your money.

Trust accounts are another way of using the Swiss banking
expertise. Like trust funds anywhere, these are arrangements
where you *trust* your money to the management of some experienced, professional investor. Though the Swiss are fine
bankers and of unquestionable ethics, they are not, on the average, much better investors than any other nationality. My
advice is to do your homework and manage your own investments if they total less than one-half million dollars. Above
that, you still need to do your homework but your research
should be directed to finding the right advisors. If you've
made substantial money as a physician, business owner, or
farmer, you'll be better off to do what you do best and pay
someone else to help manage your investments. You still
need to stay on top of your financial management.

Some Swiss cities sell *municipal bonds* just like American
cities sell bonds. One major difference is that the cities don't
seem as likely to go bankrupt in Switzerland as they do in the
States. A second, equally significant difference is that these

Swiss bonds are denominated in Swiss francs, which have regularly increased in value relative to the U.S. dollar over the last few years. The bad news is that Swiss law prohibits the sale of these bonds to nonresidents. However, your Swiss bank can buy one of these bonds for you if the bank happens to be selling it for another customer. These government bonds are tax exempt as in the United States and there is no withholding tax on your interest. The interest varies from about 5½ percent to over 6 percent depending on the sources of the issuance and the length of time of the investment.

Swiss stocks and mutual funds are also available to nonresidents with restrictions, but they are really no better or worse than American stocks and mutual funds. If you are going to get into the stock market, do it in one that you can check daily.

Eurocurrency accounts are for your use in buying and selling amounts of currency in any country other than its native country. For example, your Swiss banker could establish such an account for you if you wanted to purchase and hold 10,-000 of the Dutch guilders. In such a case, you are the one out on the limb since the Swiss bank acts only as a broker for you. You have to be the one to know *why* one currency in another country is likely to be a particularly good buy and just how long you ought to keep it. In any case, don't hold it a full year since the U.S. Interest Equalization Tax applies to contracts of twelve months or more. Interest on dealings in Eurocurrency fluctuate between 6 and 15 percent and are pretty risky for the novice. They certainly do not need to be listed under the safer and more secure aspects of Swiss banking. However, with your security established, they may prove to be a useful and exciting area of investment productivity.

Certificates of deposit are used in a way similar to Eurocurrency, with the Swiss bank purchasing for you a specified amount of the currency of a given nation. There is no withholding tax and no negative interest tax. The Swiss bank is not responsible for the outcome of your investment or for the failure of the bank where the investment may be made. Interest rates can vary between 5 percent and 10 percent.

Types of Banks

The banks of Switzerland fall into three categories: the big banks, the private banks, and the other banks.

Five banks qualify as the big banks. They are the Swiss Credit Bank, the Union Bank, the Swiss Volksbank, Bank Leu, and the Swiss Bank Corporation. These are the retail banks with much larger assets than other banks in the country. To walk into them, the American would feel more at home since they have much the same appearance and services of the American bank. They are the go-getters of Swiss banking and the first three have offices in major U.S. cities. These retail banks are the most likely to give the American novice the kind of understanding service and Swiss philosophy that will accomplish his purposes in opening a Swiss account in the first place.

My personal feeling is that the Bank Leu is probably most responsive to the needs of the small investor (i.e., people with accounts under $100,000). Bank Leu provides a good variety of services and is solid and reputable. I have dealt with Bank Leu and its branches both in Switzerland and in the Bahamas and have found them to be dependable and reliable.

The private banks are rather unlike anything familiar in American banking. They are less like banks as we think of them and more like the private lending capability of one rich individual. The private banks are not incorporated. This relieves the owner of the obligation to publish financial statements and therefore allows the owner to get into many types of lending endeavors that might never even be considered by other banks. However, since the private banks are not incorporated and the liability is therefore not limited, the banker himself must stand behind each loan. His personal fortune is on the line every time he agrees to a deal. The chances of your becoming involved with a private bank on your first Swiss account are remote. They have to choose their customers carefully because of the potential risk in each and every decision. While the private banks *do* perform all the same services that the big banks perform, you might do well to think of them as the "country clubs" of Swiss banking, with participation by invitation only.

There are a number of *other banks* in Switzerland. These are, of course, branches of major American banks as well as branches of banks representing other countries. They tend to be like the private banks in that they cater to specific groups—often the non-Swiss population. Various ones of the other banks have their unique advantages but, overall, I have not found that their strengths ever compensate for their weaknesses. For example, the Swiss branches of American banks are sometimes subject to American laws concerning availability of information. My feeling is that, if you are going to the trouble of having a Swiss bank account, you ought to go all the way and have your account with a *Swiss* Swiss bank.

Opening Your Swiss Account

Anybody who can really afford to open a Swiss bank account can probably afford to make a trip to inspect and talk with a few alternative banks. A person can legally carry out $4,999 without reporting it to the U.S. customs authorities. This doesn't include the cost of your ticket and you can charge most of your expenses on American Express, Master Charge, or Visa.

If, however, you are not concerned about total secrecy, forget that $4,999 and take as much as you like in a cashier's check. Obviously, opening your account in person is the best way to do it—and involves an enjoyable vacation to one of the world's most beautiful countries. There is something to be said for the face-to-face contact when it comes to gaining clear understandings and accurate information.

If, however, you are unable or unwilling to make the trip in person, the entire transaction can be handled by mail. Allow yourself plenty of time. Don't rush into opening a Swiss account in order to make some sale or purchase. Dig the well before you need the water and make sure your Swiss account is running smoothly before you begin using it extensively.

To open an account by mail, drop by the local library. The reference room will have the American Bankers Association's *Directory of Foreign Banks* and you can jot down the names and addresses of the specific banks you think you might want to deal with. Type a simple one-line letter requesting current information on types of banking services available and current interest rates. Don't give any information beyond that since it cannot help and may serve to confuse the issue.

When the response comes back, you can compare the answers on an equal basis and make your decision. Write another simple letter to open your account and send it along
with a bank money order in U.S. dollars. For example, you
might write:

> Gentlemen:
>   Enclosed is a Cashier's Check for U.S. $0,000,000.
> Please open a Swiss franc deposit account for me in the
> name of ————————————. Please send all correspon-
> dence to me in English at the above address.
>
>   Thank you for your assistance.

When your Swiss bank opens your account, it will temporarily hold the money while it returns several things to you
to make it all legal. You should receive (1) a credit slip
showing the amount of your initial deposit in Swiss francs;
(2) a legal-length paper with statements of Swiss banking
policies and procedures (you will probably be asked to read
this, sign it, and return it); (3) a signature card on which
you should place any and all signatures you wish to be able
to transact business in the account; and (4) an application
form with information about ways you want the account
handled.

The bank will assign you an account number that you will
use on all future transactions. However, this is an additional
identification, not the only one, and you do not have one of
the infamous "numbered" Swiss accounts. Once your account
is functional, you can make deposits, withdrawals, or transfer
transactions by mail. It's about like banking by mail in your
own hometown except for the time lag.

Your money is safe once it's in Switzerland. No matter
what happens in this country's economic system, your money
will always have a welcome passage back *into* the U.S. and,
if things turn out to oppose the exit of money from the U.S.,
yours is already safely across the border and cannot be
forced to return.

How to Use Your Account

This book can only give you advice and information. It is
not my purpose or responsibility to tell you how to use your

Swiss account. There are some people who intend to utilize the secrecy of a Swiss account to intentionally *evade* the payment of U.S. income taxes that would normally be paid. There are others whose purpose is to protect their wealth and *avoid* by skillful maneuver all the taxes they can legally avoid. Avoiding is legal—evading is against the law and the IRS is well known for its never-say-die pursuit of money it suspects may be owed to it. To the IRS, "it's not the money, it's the principle" and they will literally spend $100 to regain $10. Considering that set of mind on the part of the IRS and adding in the myriad sources of information and cross-checking that flow into IRS computers, you need to make your decision carefully and be fully advised of the adversary if you decide to try evasion of U.S. taxes. For my own affairs, I am convinced that the amount I might save through evasion would not be worth the constant anxiety that a fatal flaw might occur in my concealment. That's a personal opinion for me—you will, of course, make the decision for you.

If you are not likely to be a focal point for IRS scrutiny, you are the kind of person whose Swiss account might accidentally never be recorded on Stateside records. If you've never had a Swiss account, it is understandable that you might simply overlook checking that little box on your income tax form. Few accountants ever think to ask about Swiss accounts when they are doing your tax return for you. It is simply an oversight, not a blatant effort to deceive, and the IRS is not likely to be very vigorous in pursuing a small-timer unless the source or amount of money tends to attract attention of other government agencies.

After the first draft of this chapter was written, I learned that the U.S. is beginning to take a tougher stance on banking secrecy. Citizens who have bank accounts abroad are now being asked to file a new form 90-21.1, which is sent directly to the Treasury Department rather than the IRS. The significance of this move is that the names of foreign account holders will be centralized at the Treasury Department in Washington. The Treasury has added an important warning; failure to file a report can, "under certain circumstances," result in a fine of up to $500,000 and imprisonment of up to five years. Many experts believe that the purpose of this new regulation is to allow the Treasury Department to collect information and set up criminal prosecution where the IRS cannot obtain enough information to prosecute a tax-evasion case. This clearly means that the United States is beginning to "get tough" about foreign accounts. A recent study showed that 60 percent of tax returns failed to check the box on whether or not they had a foreign account. The new form requires the name of the bank and account numbers, as well as the address of the branch if the accounts are valued at more than $10,000. In my opinion, this is a very ominous sign that shows that financial privacy in this country is nonexistent. As any government attempts to make foreign holdings less attractive, it is a certain sign that there are some very good reasons to have some foreign holdings. Each individual must assess his or her own situation to decide if the risk of a secret account is justified. If the decision is yes, then it is imperative that you maintain an absolutely low profile. A little paronoia in covering your tracks can be quite helpful. And, by all means, be sure that the stakes are worth the risk.

HAVENS NEARER HOME

Both the Bahamas and the Cayman Islands operate under Swiss banking laws. In other words, the privacy aspect of Swiss banking is also available just off the Florida coast. Some of the Swiss banks have branches in the Bahamas. For large accounts, the Swiss Credit Company is probably the best option and for smaller accounts (under $100,000), stick to the Bank Leu. Although they paid interest in the amount of 4 percent through the first part of 1978, the interest rate was lowered in March because of the decline of the U.S. dollar relative to the Swiss franc. Even so, people who have been keeping their accounts in Swiss francs enjoyed considerable appreciation because of the dollar decline.

For people in the United States, the Cayman Islands tend to be the best all-around tax haven. Here, we are talking about a person who has business interests arranged so that he can spin off some of the activities to a foreign operation and build up some wealth in it as a means of avoiding taxation—or, at least, postponing it until the time when he might want to bring the money back into the United States.

Tax havens also represent the basic economic wisdom of never putting all your nest eggs in the same basket. There is just as great a chance that money sheltered in the Bahamas or Caymans will be endangered as that it will be sucked into American economic disaster. However, the chance of the bottom falling out everywhere at the same time is relatively small. The political risk in the Caribbean is obviously greater than in Switzerland, but there are also some tax advantages. So, hedge your bets, spread your money, be prepared, not just for *anything*—but for *everything*.

Choosing a Tax Haven

If you own and operate a company, you may wish to consider basing that company in one of the small countries of the world that is easily accessible and makes a good deal of its national income by allowing businesses from other nations to do business taxfree.

You do not have to *live* in the haven country to have your company incorporated and doing business from there. In fact, there are ways that such an arrangement can be set up for you by mail for a cost of as little as $2,000, which includes the legal fees of attorneys in the shelter country as well as nationals who are paid $100 or so a year to serve as your rubber stamp Board of Directors. For the details on how to set up a foreign corporation in the Cayman Islands and other places around the world, you should see *How to Do Business Tax Free* by Midas Malone or Robert Kinsman's *Guide to Tax Havens*.

As is true of foreign bank accounts, tax havens must be given constant, careful, and cautious attention lest the pennies saved be swallowed up in dollars lost through oversight. The *Inflation Survival Letter* has provided an excellent check-list of factors that ought to be considered as you try to touch all the bases in evaluating a potential tax haven selection.

1. *Income tax rules* vary from low to no taxes at all. Others have high taxes for income earned outside the haven—which is your most likely situation.
2. *Remittance tax* refers to the country's policy of withholding a percentage of money you are trying to bring home from your haven. Balance these costs with the income tax situation.
3. *Estate taxes* are especially significant if the entire haven corporation is in your name. Some havens have low income tax but really sock it to your estate if you die. If you are in a partnership or a larger-than-you corporation, don't worry too much about estate taxes.

4. *Corporate law* of the haven can make a big difference. For example, can changes be made easily or do they literally require the country's legislature to act? Do all directors' meetings have to be held *in* the country?

5. *Trust laws* will determine how business may be transacted. Make sure your haven uses English laws as most civil law countries who do that do not recognize the trust.

6. *Treaties* between the haven country and your homeland could nullify all the tax shelters you thought you were creating. Know the implications for you of all treaties between the haven and your homeland.

7. *Secrecy* varies both within the haven itself and between the haven and the IRS's demands for information.

8. *Costs* need to be all listed at the front end. Tax havens make their revenues from establishing enterprises but you need to be sure you know all initial and continuing fees.

9. *Geographic accessibility* can be important when you *do* need to visit your company away from your country.

10. *Climate* can be of major interest if you plan to take advantages of your haven's vacation offerings in connection with your regular business trips there.

11. *Residence and immigration* restrictions could be important if you have any anticipation of ever moving to the tax haven. Some countries allow it . . . others do not.

12. *Communications* are an obvious necessity if you expect to transact business with the haven.

13. *Language.* You are at an obvious disadvantage if you do not speak the language of your haven—either the official language or the language used for commercial dealings.

14. *Political climate* is of great significance when considering some of the Caribbean tax havens. Some small nations are on the brink of chaos which could well nationalize your holdings. Be sure you check this variable out.

15. *Local counsel* will be needed by your haven corporation sooner or later. Make sure of their skill and willingness to be of assistance to you.

16. *Banking facilities* make an important difference be-

cause you are going to be moving funds in and out of the haven.

17. *Currency in use* may be that of other countries or it may be a local free-floating variety. You need some certainty about ranges of monetary value and exchange rates.

18. *Remittance controls* may cancel the other positive features of a tax haven. It won't matter how much your company makes if you can never take it out of the country!

19. *Permissible activities* should be investigated in case your corporation expects to form a bank, insurance company, or real estate development company. Some of these are restricted in some havens.

20. *Available data* is a significant factor. If you find that answers and assurances are impossible to obtain before the fact, imagine what it will be like after your operation is in business.

The *Inflation Survival Letter* has also provided an excellent chart that places the basic information about the havens of the world in a clear, concise, and usable form for the businessman beginning his investigations. Check the chart, write lots of letters, but do not set up a tax haven until you have dug your toes into the sand of the haven's beaches.

Exodus Movements

There are a number of people who are exploring the alternatives of an exodus from the United States. Some find Australia rather attractive to their specific requirements. Others plan to follow their money into some tax haven. These groups are growing and various newsletters are published regularly (most of them from addresses outside the United States) that promise to capsule the latest political and philosophical developments with impact on any person's need to move to protect his wealth. Consultant services are also regularly advertised to assist individuals who need answers to specific questions regarding living conditions and financial climates in the nations contemplated as destinations for modern Exodians.

A little over ten years ago an organization called the Phoe-

Tax Havens of the World

Country	Tax Structure	Most Popular Uses	Legal System	Currency	Language
BAHAMAS	no corporation or profits tax; no personal income or capital gains tax, and no estate or inheritance tax. But real property tax on value of improved property.	banks and trust companies	based on English common law	Bahamian $ = US $	English
BERMUDA	no direct taxes on individuals or companies. Annual fee of $650 for companies	banks, trust and insurance companies	based on English common law	Bermudan $ = US $	English
CAYMAN ISLANDS	no taxes at all on income or capital: 'exempt' companies and trusts have freedom from tax guaranteed for 20 to 50 years respectively. Incorporation fees payable	banks; trust companies	based on English common law	Cayman $ = US$1.20	English
CHANNEL ISLANDS	personal and corporate income tax at flat rate of 20%: no wealth or gift tax, no capital gains tax and no estate duty; companies not carrying on business there and not controlled from there may be exempt from any tax but L 300 annual fee	banks; insurance and trust companies	unique customary law but in commerce and tax, English law followed	L sterling	English and French
HONG KONG	standard rate 15%, main forms of direct taxation: property tax, salaries tax, profits tax, interest tax	trading companies and trust	English common law	Hong Kong$(HK$ 5.085 = US $1)	English and Chinese
ISLE OF MAN	standard rate 21-25%; no capital gains, wealth tax or estate duty, no company tax on foreign source income if control outside island	trust and unit trusts	similar to English common law, but with local variations	L sterling	English

		Tax Havens of the World Cont'd.			
Country	Tax Structure	Most Popular Uses	Legal System	Currency	Language
LIECHTENSTEIN	corporate net worth 0.2% of capital (0.1% for holding and domiciliary companies who pay no profits tax); coupon tax on dividends 4%	'anstalt' and 'stiftung'	Austrian civil code; Swiss property law	Swiss franc	German; English and other languages used
LUXEMBOURG	based on German tax laws, rates between 21% and 41%; holding companies exempt except for annual tax of 1% or assessed value of securities	holding companies	civil law; commercial law based on German law	Luxembourg franc-Belgian franc	German and French
MONACO	no direct taxes on bona fide resident; no withholding tax on income from funds invested in Monaco paid to non-residents; businesses deriving at least 75% of turnover in Monaco pay no tax	administrative offices and trusts	Monaco law	French franc	French
NAURU	no taxes or duties of any sort	trusts	English common law	Australian $	English
NETHERLANDS ANTILLES	basic corporate income tax rates of 27-34% with municipal surcharge of 15% on the tax; special facilities reduce effective rate to 2.4-3% for finance, patent holding, shipping and aircraft companies	investment and holding companies	Dutch law	Neth. Ant. guilder	Dutch, English and Spanish
NEW HEBRIDES	no direct taxes, value added tax on land subsidiaries		English and French law	Australian $ and New Hebrides franc	English and French
SWITZERLAND	basic cantonal rates between 25 and 35% plus federal rates, concessions for domiciliary, holding, service and international sales companies	holding and domiciliary companies	Swiss civil law	Swiss franc	German, French and Italian

nix Foundation was formed. It was created by a group of individuals who believed in the concepts of private enterprise, personal freedom, a strong gold-backed dollar, and limited federal government. Since these values were difficult to find in most existing countries today, the foundation decided to exert its efforts to help with the creation or support of small countries striving for independence. Members of this group hope to be able to create a country that would offer a kind of lifestyle they are seeking.

For individuals who are interested in considering the characteristics of life or business ventures around the world, Doug Casey's book, *The International Man*, is a valuable resource. While Casey reviews the benefits and dangers associated with foreign business ventures, the key to the book is a detailed analysis of five nations that are identified as "last frontier" countries. An additional forty-five nations are analyzed with a view to financial and personal freedom, taxes, costs of living, and other aspects of residence. Even if you, as I, choose to remain in the United States, it certainly is a worthwhile exercise to consider potential alternatives in the event circumstances should change dramatically.

While I believe there are psychological and political advantages to maintaining a loyalty to one nation, it is hard not to argue the philosophy advanced by John Milton over 300 years ago, "Our country is wherever we are well off."

CHAPTER NINE

How to Protect
Your Person and Property

You've seen it in the movies, but no one under fifty has any real basis for even imagining the kinds of shortages and value changes that follow major civil conflicts or upheavals. Perhaps, if you multiply the public paralysis during the Arab oil embargo by the supply loss of a national transportation strike by the way things were in the worst blizzard or flood you ever saw, then you are approaching an understanding of the kinds of shocks you are going to experience.

As we consider in this chapter the various aspects of providing for and protecting your family and property, you might recall in your mind's eye scenes from classic movies, like the *Grapes of Wrath* or *Gone With the Wind*. Will you find yourself like Scarlett O'Hara, gnawing on a peppery radish found in the dirt next to the hollow shell that had once been the most stylish home in the region? Will you be clinging to life and trying to work through the shocked disbelief of what is happening? And will you find yourself unbelieving as you pull the trigger to blow away a renegade soldier who will most certainly kill you if he doesn't get what he wants? All things are possible and the probabilities are high enough to warrant preparatory action.

REASONS TO BE CONCERNED ABOUT PROTECTION

If you recall Chapters 1-4, and if the warnings mentioned there had the ring of truth to you, then the necessity for basic protection of your loved ones and the things you have provided for them is obvious. Even a slight possibility of a period of massive civil disorder, unrest, or lack of food following a natural economic disaster is ample motivation for anyone to give serious thought to the methods of protecting the things that are important to him. Even if *none* of these predictions come true—and I hope they will not—the rising U.S. crime rate within itself is significant enough to demand that some precautions be taken. The chances of your being exposed to some type of crime in this country are already high. Almost three out of every ten citizens are victims of some type of crime each year.

Violence in Black and White

There is an unfortunate tendency on the part of most people to overreact to the problem of racial violence today or the prospect during the social trauma that will follow an economic collapse. We made it through the violent summers of the 1960's, and the more naive among us have decided that all the problems of the ghetto have been ironed out (or bought off). This is not true. The central city of all major urban centers is seething with unemployment, hunger, frustration, and impacted anger. The only reason the terrifying "burn, baby, burn" days passed into history is that minorities learned that those actions tended to hurt them more than they hurt anybody else. The frustration remains, however, and while a little of it is being worked out in lobbying and demonstrations for larger and larger pieces of Federal largess, the anger is real and dangerous. In fact, the federal giveaway is making the problem worse instead of better. By conditioning a significant number of people into habitual dependency on Uncle Sam, we have locked them into a frustration cycle with high expectations being met with higher inflation and unemployment. The cycle is heating up and getting ready to blow a fuse.

The last chapter on the history of the riots in this country has not been written. Just wait and watch the 1980's. All the frustrations that existed in the '60's will be doubled when New York City is unable to borrow more money from the U.S. Treasury, bankrupts, and demonstrates for all the other cities in hock that the future is a downhill spiral of loans they can't get, employees they can't reward, bills they can't pay, and fires they can't put out. There will be killing and burning and areas that will be completely out of control. Some observers predict that the war between black and white is going to be the bloodiest and most devisive in history.

As suggested in Chapter 4, this is hard to accept when viewed in the light of simple numerical realities. Where are the guns in America? Well, the ghetto seems to be replete with "Saturday night specials" that are likely to blow your hand off the thirty-ninth time you shoot them. The real firepower in America, for better or worse, is in the suburbs. The middle and upper class can afford more guns and they buy more of the kinds of weapons that can be turned into effective warfare. Hunting rifles, shotguns, and more expensive hand guns will outlast the "Saturday night specials" and sawed-off shotguns anytime.

However, long before we reach the point of comparing the fire power in the urban arms race, we need to stop and realize how completely unlikely it is that (1) the ghetto troops will make it to the suburbs and (2) that they will do great damage when they get there. If you live between ten and thirty miles from the center of a major metropolitan center, and *all* the looters from your city's center take off in all directions, their numbers are going to quickly diffuse. By the time they are twenty miles from the center city, the percentages have whittled their "presence" to something like fifteen or twenty raiders to the square mile. Stop and think how many people live within a mile of your house. Then think about the number of high-powered deer rifles in your area. And then picture a bunch of looters riding through your subdivision firing at random with red-hot hand guns—a suicide mission at best.

Preparation Is Better Than Worry

People who have been in combat tell me that, while war definitely *is* hell, the anticipation is even more devastating psychologically. Often the nightmares and fears we have are much worse than the actual situation during a crisis. You simply do whatever you must do next rather than agonizing over all the myriad possibilities. If it comes to you and you are prepared, you will do what you can. If it comes to you and you are not prepared, you will still do what you can. The point is to stop picturing the gory details of everything that might possibly happen—and prepare for eventualities.

You should neither ignore the probability of riots, looting, and civil chaos, nor overreact and turn your home into a fortress with steel-plated shutters and arsenals. *Preparation* is one thing—ruining every day of the present because of potential dangers of the future is something else again. Be sane as you prepare.

The likelihood that acts of terrorism and vandalism will affect you indirectly is probably more significant to your planning than threats of direct aggression. The possibility of your house being attacked is not as great as some other dangers. The chances of your electric power source being under siege are quite high. Utilities are not prepared to defend against guerilla warfare and you can almost count on being without electricity, gas, water, and telephone service while reason and order take a recess. You should also anticipate the absence of some services that you seldom notice today. Sanitation and animal control workers are not likely to continue their thankless jobs when the chances of their being paid are low and the odds of being injured are high. Retreat consultants report that police and firefighters are the most active group (next to Mormons) in making extensive plans to escape the turmoil that seems just over the horizon. More than almost any other segment of society, these individuals have an opportunity to observe how slender the thread is that holds order together in our society. You should be prepared to keep your household warm, well fed, and protected while the rest of the world runs around frantically trying to settle things.

The Family that Prepares Together . . .

This kind of preparation is going to mean a much greater commitment than the purchase of several cans of food and a checker board. You and your family will need to start now practicing the kinds of skills and self-discipline that will be needed. If you have trouble making it through a whole Saturday with the family together, then you need to start systematically working up to the kinds of family understanding, honesty, and togetherness that will enable you to endure a time of crisis. One key question is whether you see your family surviving *because of* the cooperative efforts of all members or *in spite of* nagging and troublesome behavior.

The changes required to get ready for the time of crisis will not be easy changes to make. They will most certainly not be changes that are encouraged or facilitated by the society around you. Your home environment should emphasize quality resources rather than the products of planned obsolescence in our throwaway society. You will have to change the personality and value system that Madison Avenue has given you over the past thirty years. It may sound romantic to think of bucking the tide and being a true individual, but nobody likes to be laughed at. Being seen as an eccentric millionaire is even tougher when you are a long way from having a million dollars.

Coming out of the Closet

An unusual degree of commitment is required to make private preparation for catastrophe and an even greater challenge comes when you recognize the importance of involving some friends or neighbors in cooperative planning and preparing for traumatic times. At this point, you must take a major emotional risk. If you want to get results, don't mention your ideas tentatively and expect other people to reinforce your timid expressions of concern. Many individuals who are deeply worried about the future are afraid to admit this concern. Before putting your own convictions on the line, you need to spend a significant time with yourself. Get to know your own value system and decide whether you are really willing to accept the inevitable slings and arrows of social abuse for physical and emotional security in a time that is not inevitable, only highly probable.

At the same time, you need to be careful about creating antagonism. Many people simply do not wish to hear about your vision of the future. They have too much invested in their status quo. When you first mention your concern, you may anticipate some polite kidding. If you continue your persuasion, the kidding will begin to lose its politeness. Unless you want to alienate some friends and become known as a hopeless paranoid, you should simply state your views once and then let your example serve as a gentle reminder for your friends who may be open.

All of this talk about commitment is not idle conversation. The steps to total preparation are numerous and expensive in energy, time, and money. Unless your value system tells you to take these steps, it is unlikely that you are going to convince other people or carry through to ultimate personal success. Remember though that each improvement in your readiness will bring an equal rise in the quality of your family's life today and tomorrow. This, of course, is simply my opinion—until it becomes part of your commitment.

RX FOR SURVIVAL

Don Stephens started out to be an architect in Los Angeles. But, because he was tuned in to what was happening in the world around him, Don became interested in the most effective and systematic way of preparing for the upheaval he saw on the horizon. Eventually, Don Stephen's interest in preparedness and retreats for the duration took over as his prime business interest. Today, Don is the unquestioned expert in the field of preparing your home—and your retreat—to withstand shortages and hardships. His booklet *Personal Protection Here and Now* is the most concise and readable breakdown of defensive approaches, which range from survival lockers to automatic weapons.

I recommend Don's books. If he is ever in your area to conduct a survival seminar, take advantage of a valuable opportunity. Don has a style that is serious and direct, while maintaining a sense of perspective. With regard to self-defense, he recommends:

1. *Learn to use common sense* in keeping a low financial profile and staying out of places where you are more likely to encounter personal danger.
2. *Forget about depending on others* for your protection. You cannot pay enough taxes to have public protection available whenever and wherever you may need it.
3. *Practice being alert.* Most people need to force themselves to become more alert to the indicators of danger that are quite imminent. You have probably learned "defensive driving." You need to get in the habit of reading your environment continuously as a hunter does as he walks through the woods.
4. *Pre-think the levels of force* you might be willing and obligated to use in a specific situation. Like a defensive driver, be thinking ahead at all times about the best response you would make in situations that potentially could evolve. If you resort to force, you want to use the least possible necessary to neutralize your attackers, but too little could be disastrous.
5. *Weaponless defense* is quite possible for those who choose not to carry weapons. The first and best is to run. The next is negotiation. Others include the use of keys, combs, or aerosol sprays to disable or distract an

assailant long enough to give you a head start at running away.

6. *Arming yourself* opens many possibilities. There are several nonlethal defense tools such as blackjacks, yawara sticks, tear gas, and mace. Knives are not recommended since you have to use them at close range and are likely to be doing so with someone with far more experience at "cutting and pasting" than you. Somebody always loses in a knife fight—and nobody may win!

7. *Handguns* are available for every level of defense. Stephens recommends a light high-standard two-shot .22 Magnum derringer concealed in a wallet for close-range single attackers and a Colt .45 automatic combat commander or lightweight commander for any other circumstances. His rationale is that no other handgun is so perfectly designed to stop an assailant completely with one hit. Other handguns will wound or slow down, but even lethal hits will often leave the intruder with enough time and energy to do considerable damage. Only the .45 will cause immediate unconsciousness 95 percent of the time, due to general system shock to the brain.

8. *Shotguns and rifles* are more likely to be used in defending your home or retreat. While hunting rifles have plenty of power and impact, the shotgun is more likely to stop an intruder without the misses going through the wall and into the residence next door. One suggestion is to use a shotgun with a flashlight mounted on it in such a way that whatever is in the light is in the sight.

Later, we will talk about the variations of defensive weaponry for your home and for your retreat. Of course, a major value of having a working knowledge of guns is the role they can play in providing meat for the table.

Location, Location, Location

There's an old retailing adage that, "There are three important principles for success. They are location, location, and location." The same thing is true in terms of survival. There are some locations in our country where the problems of survival are going to be greatly intensified regardless of preparation.

High-danger areas have been identified previously in the book. However, if you live in a large metropolitan area of 1.5 million or more, your anxiety is well justified. If you must keep a business location in this type of area, planning a separate retreat is even more essential than for more fortunate folks. If you can buy even a small amount of property in an isolated area you should be able to rest easier. Small towns—especially those with an agricultural base, should avoid the worst of the chaos. At the same time, most small towns have less than a two-week supply of food in the grocery stores and warehouses. They too are dependent upon regular shipments of food from major distribution centers. Towns that are dependent upon factory employment will be only slightly better off than large cities—unless you prefer to be robbed by someone you know.

Try to avoid large cities with obvious financial and social problems where you are likely to be subjected to a paralysis of supply for food, fuel, and services. My personal suggestion is that you go south because of the warmer weather—southeast for agricultural strength, southwest for isolation. Other experts recommend the inland northwest and intermountain areas that they believe will be less populated because of very cold climate. With adequate planning and the use of greenhouses these areas should be able to provide an adequate food supply. Much of your decision will revolve around personal preference and your current location. If you currently live in Baltimore or Atlanta, the Pacific Northwest is not a viable option for your retreat.

If you are extremely mobile, I believe it makes a great deal of sense to find what you believe to be your own optimal location. I know one successful physician who left a $200,000-a-year medical practice in Orange County, California and moved to a small town in northern California. While his income has dropped dramatically, his living standard has improved immeasurably. Additionally, he has been able to make provision for an uncertain future that would have been impossible in his old practice.

If you do not have the flexibility to find another location, then the development of a "pure" retreat is an almost essential insurance policy. In this chapter, we will talk about things you can do to improve the security of your existing house, develop self-sufficiency in a primary residence, or plan an isolated retreat for your fall-back insurance.

It seems a drastic move to sell out, load up, and move to another location. The decision is yours. If you firmly believe that the bad, bad times are coming, then no change is too drastic if it helps you prepare. If you are still only marginally concerned, it is unlikely that you will follow through with relocation—just yet.

Move up to Less

One other note on location and relocation. When you relocate, avoid the temptation to buy a more expensive home for your family. There's always a tendency to try to "move-up" in status and storage space. You can use the storage, but that extra status is just going to use up dollars that you'd rather have in gold in downtown Zurich. Keep reminding yourself that this relocation is not like the others. You are not trying to move up the homeowner's ladder. Increasing your monthly mortgage payment is going to make it even harder for you to make preparations. A far better course would be to drop down one or two mortgage notches (which should be easy if you are moving from urban to suburban or rural) and invest the saved dollars in the kinds of future security described throughout this book.

As you choose a new home, force yourself to think in terms of living there in the midst of a chaotic social upheaval. What are the *walking* distances? What storage facilities exist or can easily be added? What about protection of the site? Is there room to farm or put in a garden that is not next to a public highway? Are there alternate methods for obtaining heat, water, and power?

You won't find all the requirements in any home unless you pay too much for it. It is wiser to find a place that you can purchase cheaply and renovate into a self-sufficient sanctuary for the crisis. The first and most important step in this process is finding the right location with regard to the small town, and with regard to your own family's needs.

PROTECTION OF YOUR HOUSE

Throughout this book, my approach is to help you start where you are and gradually add successive layers of protection. Each layer will be of use in the present as well as in the future. This principle is even more applicable when it comes to protection of your house because so few American homes have taken that number one step—the fire detector.

Even the most skilled burglar is not going to carry off everything you have, but a fire will. Most robbers will avoid homes with people in them—but a fire won't. You and your loved ones can sleep through a burglary and survive—but it doesn't work that way with smoke and fire.

Make sure your family is protected from smoke and fire. Don't fall for expensive smoke and fire alarm systems that are peddled with scare tactics (unless you have extensive wealth in your house and get the smoke and fire component as part of a more elaborate total protection system). There are many serviceable alarms on the market that will do the job for under thirty dollars. Make sure you get one that is approved by Underwriter's Laboratory, or you may just be buying a wall decoration. Install your detector and try it out periodically to be sure it is still sensitive and to be sure all family members know the appropriate reflexes in a fire. These detectors can be powered by your house's regular electrical system or by batteries. That decision is yours. If you are a slow battery replacer you may be better off going with household current. On the other hand, if your fire starts coincidental to (or as a result of) a power outage, you have no more protection. The ideal system works on both systems—household current until it runs out, then, rechargeable batteries—but that costs more money. Whichever style you choose, get the fire protector today. You need that protection regardless of what the economy does.

While you are at it, purchase some inexpensive fire extinguishers and position them where fires are likely to start—in the kitchen, next to the fireplace, in the workshop, in the automobile. Make sure each member of the family knows how to operate them and check them periodically to be sure they are charged and that all chemicals remain active.

PROTECTION FROM OTHERS

Now that your house is safe from *you*, we need to look at some of the things you should do to make it safe from others. Ideally, you should hire a burglar to come in and tell you what needs to be done to foil his efforts. Since this procedure might have undesired side effects, try checking with your local police or locksmith. You need a professional, objective eye to point out the things that need doing.

On all doors, get locks that cannot be opened from the outside without a key. Pin tumbler and dead bolt locks offer the best protection for outside doors. Try to avoid locks that require a key on the inside since they can trap your family in case of a house fire. Be sure that your windows cannot be forced. Make provisions for those sliding glass door panels that lift out too easily. Modify the way things are built, always remembering that while you want to keep others out, you don't want to trap your family inside.

Once your home is locked and secure, move out to the yard. Put a fence around it with one or more ferocious-sounding dogs inside the fence. A prowler can say he was just taking a short-cut through your yard, but when he climbs the fence to do so, he appears a bit more committed than a casual neighborhood stroller. You may also wish to run a trip wire along the top of your fence that will sound an alarm when anyone starts over the fence or cuts the wire.

Make your house an unattractive target for anyone considering a burglary. Rich Italians today are learning the virtue of looking poor. Theirs is a model for us to consider. Always make your house look like you are inside. Inexpensive twenty-four-hour timers will turn on lights and radios at various times of the day and in different parts of the house so that someone watching your house for a long time still won't be able to be sure you are away. Stop all regular deliveries so that a pile of newspapers or milk bottles doesn't invite an intruder. Have a neighbor mow your grass and pick up your mail—you can return the favor. Keep curtains closed on first-floor rooms—make it hard for the burglar to know what will be encountered inside the house. Vary your routine of coming and going as much as possible. Don't leave notes on the door about how long you'll be away. Don't leave recorded messages that say you are away, just that you will return the call as soon as possible. And—should you return home and suspect that you have been burglarized or that someone is still in the house, don't go in, go next door and call the police and wait for them to enter. This is not only safer, it also assures that fingerprints and evidence will be preserved.

Budgeting and Building a Security System

The experts in electronic warning devices give the following rule of thumb about the appropriate amount to spend. Add up the value of items in your home that might be resalable and spend about 2 percent of that total figure on electronic warning and/or surveillance systems. The simplest device I know of is a sonar alarm that can be placed anywhere in the house, aimed at any space, and depended upon to sound a terrible alarm if anything moves in that area. These clever devices can be set so that they overlook the movements of pets or a book falling over on a shelf, but go off immediately if any other movement lasts longer than one-half second.

Beginning from this basic unit, you can add on indefinitely to include wired windows and doors, multiple sonar units that "report" to a master unit, systems that are tamperproof and power-failure-proof, systems that sound alarms, turn on lights, lock windows or doors, and even call the police. A fire and burglar alarm specialist will jump at the chance to explain his wares and provide you with estimates and proposals. Remember to be a careful consumer in this field, especially as there are many ways to get "robbed" by the experts who make your home burglarproof.

You will need to give consideration to the differences in protecting your regular home and your retreat home if you have one. Things stored in the retreat ought to be well hidden as a first option, locked up securely as a second choice. Remember that anybody who is nosing around your retreat can do it at their leisure since you will probably have chosen a place that is isolated. Plan a retreat that can be locked and secured, but think more of the clever ways to store things in hidden areas.

Should the worst expectations come to pass and you have to defend your family's life and possessions in an actual attack by lawless groups, there will be a significant difference in the firepower necessary, assuming you have decided to fight rather than give up the things the attackers want. For the person who is serious about building up an arsenal for defense, Mel Tappan's *Survival Guns* is a comprehensive analysis of the kinds of batteries that might be appropriate in various circumstances.

If you are attacked at home, there are likely to be only a few intruders to deal with, a brief time of attack, unarmed burglars, short-range shooting situations, and nearby neighbors to be considered. If, however, you are attacked at your retreat, there is a greater likelihood that it could be by a larger, organized band of well-armed and experienced looters. Your shooting will be at longer distances, for longer periods of siege, and with less prospect of nearby neighbors rushing to help.

None of us likes to think about the need to actually take another person's life. For my part, a protective system is preferable to violence. Isolation and camouflage can also reduce the danger of violence. But, regardless of your defenses, there can come a point where the safety of your family is at stake. Each individual should evaluate his or her value system, in advance, to determine how this confrontation is to be handled.

Protecting Your Valuables

Assuming that a thief gets into your house and ready to load up a pillowcase or two, you should rest easy and know that you have placed the really valuable things where he (1) can't find them or (2) can't get at them.

One of the oldest and best security practices is *hiding* things. Forget about the top shelf of the closet or under your socks. Think more along the ancient architectural lines of secret compartments, sliding panels, and floor boards that can be lifted up. Use also the places that a burglar is unlikely to look, like a buried strongbox under the ground in the back corner of the basement or crawl space. Try hiding valuables in hard-to-get-to places, like under the insulation in the narrow eaves of the attic. Unless the burglar has come with a purpose of finding a certain thing that he knows to be in your house, your best bet is to put it where he will never see it and if he does will think that it is something else. David Krotz's book, *How to Hide Almost Anything,* is a valuable resource for the amateur carpenter who wants to know how to build secret compartments and hidey-holes.

If you are storing articles of high value, you may want to investigate the installation of a safe or vault. I say "installation" because if it is something that you personally can carry in and set in the corner, you can be sure that a burglar can carry it out almost as easily. A cheap vault is useless and the thief can probably turn the whole thing over on its impressive front and drill through the back in a matter of minutes. If you decide you need a vault, then go all the way with imbedding in concrete and steel, shearproof bolts, and a recessed head for concealment under a floor or carpet or behind a wall.

My advice, however, is that you depend on your own ingenuity for hiding your household valuables and "chaos money" in a fireproof, burglarproof way, and then put the really heavy stuff in a safe deposit box that is not under the control of a bank. These are available in most cities in the financial district or the companies that provide armored cars. These are more likely to be available should there be an extended bank holiday. They are not as likely to be locked up for an IRS audit in the event of one of the box-holders' death.

SUPPLIES FOR THE DURATION

Most people can survive for only about three minutes without oxygen. In severe weather, they can survive about three hours without protection. Three days without water is usually the limit that the human body can endure. Three weeks without food is a difficult but endurable hardship. Unless there is an unusual medical malady, most people can survive from three months to three years without the services of a physician or most of their pharmaceutical requirements.

While the foregoing approximation of limitations is subject to many individual differences, they do suggest a heirarchy of needs in your planning activity. Clean air, protection from the elements, water, and foods should rank very high on your list of immediate concerns.

Food for Survival

The Mormon church has encouraged all of its members to have two years' supply of food on hand. Regardless of what happens in our nation, this is an excellent recommendation that would stand a family in good stead in the event of natural disasters or loss of employment. Church officials estimate that only 10 percent of Mormons have actually followed through and stored this much food.

Two years' worth of food seems extreme, especially for people who have the capability of growing some food. A six-months' supply would be a reasonable length of time to begin your purchases with. There will be a short period when no food is available. Then, there will be another time period when food will be available in stores at very high prices and through the black market. There are, however, some excellent reasons for the two-year supply. If it became necessary for you to move to your retreat in early summer, over a year would elapse before you could hope to begin harvesting your own food. This assumes that you would have a supply of seed already on hand, will make no major mistakes in learning, and experience no adverse weather. The pilgrims who first came to this country suffered great hardships because it took three years for them to become self-sufficient. A two-year supply will be a good investment if you can afford it. You are certainly not going to *lose* any money by nailing down any food in a spiraling inflation era.

When you begin storing food, you will need to do it in stages. The first stage is to provide immediately for a survival situation. There are companies in every major city that stock and supply dehydrated and freeze-dried foods packed in cans so they can be stored for long periods of time. While regular canned goods will be some of your larder, you will find that these take up a great deal of space. You are also paying far too much for water and sugar. You can add those later when you are ready to prepare the food. But—remember that weight is important since it is possible that you may have to move everything you have set aside. Incidentally, when stored at a temperature of between 50° and 70° Fahrenheit, most canned goods have a shelf life of approximately a year. If storage temperature is 80° or more, the shelf life is cut in half.

The freeze-dried and dehydrated kits are expensive and occasionally too low in nutrition to keep an adult healthy. You may select kits that come packaged and labeled and even organized for your systematic use. In mid-1978, I received a brochure offering a fourteen-can trial kit for $35.15, a nine-case starter unit for $127.50, the standard kit for one person for one year for $394.75, and the deluxe one-year kit for $492.10. The standard and deluxe prices also included some valuable things like a water purifier and equipment for growing nutritious sprouts. I mention these prices to give you some feeling for the kind of cost and bulk involved. Today, one person can plan to survive for approximately $500 per year. You will probably spend considerably more than that just as you do for regular food. You'll also need around fifteen to twenty cubic feet of storage per person. You are never going to have too much food in a society that is uncertain about its monetary system. Food may be the surest barter item for quite some time after the crash.

In buying your food for storage, be sure to compare prices and ingredients. Sometimes a bargain package will be nutritionally inferior to more expensive units. Ask for a list of ingredients before you buy. Many of the more exotic items offered by the storage companies have more chemicals than food. Take the time to examine the complete list of items and order only those that are appropriate for your needs and taste. I have yet to find a single program that I would buy without modification.

GOOD HABITS FOR TODAY AND TOMORROW

Don't make the mistake of buying a big cupboard of freeze-dried survival food and then ignoring the rest of your food storage habits. Build some common sense positive habits of food usage. Buy in bulk when possible, even for daily use. Rotate cans and packages to use the oldest first. If you are going to eat a case of something this year and you can make the room, buy the whole case in January instead of one can at a time. You might as well transfer some of the nation's food supply to your house now—it won't be there for the transferring when the panic hits. Start from the assumption that all the stores *are* going to close and you will have to feed your family anyway. Once that basic assumption is made, the other procedures follow naturally.

Get your family out of the junk food habit. You don't have to become a health food addict to realize that half of our food today has as much nutrition in the wrappers as in the food itself. Become sensitive to the useless dollars in your grocery budget and the wasted calories consumed by your family without equivalent nourishment. Wean your family from the American sugar diet and reeducate them to the solid taste and nutrition of real food. There's a lot of similarity between junk food and dollars as they relate to solid food and gold. The hollow commodities keep us feeling full but give no substance. When the showdown comes, whole, healthy foods will be even more important than they are today.

Long before the crisis, transfer your family over to the habits of eating that will be useful when all of us are forced "back to basics." You'll be able to reduce your medical bills, too.

Rotate your stored food by having regular "survival meals" to get your family used to the program. Otherwise, you could all end up with adjustment problems that could cancel all the advantages you had worked to assure.

Try to eliminate sugar and fried foods. Emphasize farm fare—vegetables and fruits. You'll need some animal fat for stamina, but think more in terms of tuna protein and bean protein. With your emergency store in the closet or basement, be sure the cupboards are crammed full of things you can use repeatedly, then fill the freezer with meats and fish and other things. When the crunch comes, eat your way from one to the other. Empty the freezer first, because the power may go off. In that case, a small smoker unit can give thawed food three or four additional months of shelf life. When the freezer food is gone, move to the kitchen cabinets and eat from them. Save your light, portable survival food until last because you may need to make a move or may even see the crisis ease before you get down to a regular diet of dehydrated food.

Be Sure to Add Water

If you decide to make the dehydrated or freeze-dried foods a major part of your security program, remember to store plenty of water. If you have a water purifier ready, you may be able to prepare enough water from local creeks and rivers, but they are, at best, an undependable source. You should have an emergency quantity of water stored—at least twenty gallons for each family member. And, next time you run across a rain barrel at an auction sale, think about it—your roof and gutter system is a ready-made water reclamation device. Dehydrated food goes better with plenty of water! Either make provision for chemical water purifiers, charcoal drip purifiers, or the fuel to boil the germs away. The use of 32 milligrams of iodine per gallon is one of the best antibacterial agents you can use. Of course, running the water through a charcoal silver ion water purifier before storage will be even more reliable. To eliminate the flat taste of storage water, you should shake it occasionally and pour it back and forth between containers before using. A convenient means of storing water is in a quality water bed. A king-sized water bed will hold more than 300 gallons and be functional as well. But remember that this much water will weigh about 2,500 pounds. Be sure your floor construction will handle this load.

At home and at the retreat, you will need to consider the fuel required to keep generators and farming equipment running. If you are about to purchase a car, give some extra thought to a diesel engine. They are not as peppy as your old internal combustion, but they will go a lot farther on a gallon and don't require expensive tune-ups. More importantly, diesel fuel can be stored for relatively long periods of time while ordinary gasoline requires special additives at periodic storage intervals. At the very least, make sure you have provided sufficient fuel to get your car from the house to the retreat.

Don't forget adequate medical and first aid supplies. If any member of your family is dependent upon a specific medication, you should make necessary arrangements to have adequate (and rotating) supplies of these drugs. Try to decide which medicines are really necessary. If you are like most Americans, there are one or more drugs you ought to "kick"—most likely a nasal spray, pain reliever, or laxative. Does anybody in the family seem blind without his glasses? Better find the money for that back-up pair that won't be available in a crisis.

Everyone in the family should learn first aid. The Red Cross has regular, inexpensive, and highly effective classes for all ages. Even your youngest may be able to save a life—and may have to.

Stockpile items that are essential to your family's unique needs. Special soaps, detergents, and hygiene products may need to be bulk purchased—they'll never be any cheaper. Remember paper supplies, matches, batteries. Have enough of these to last six months.

Practice Personal Adjustments

One of the adjustments that will hit us hardest will be the necessity of staying in one place. Few of us can stand to stay home for a whole weekend without running down to the shopping center for something. It's not something we need—we just want to be with people, to be where the action is. You and your family probably need to recognize your "urge-to-go" habits. It's a habit you can break and one that you should break, no matter what the future holds. Practice. Spend some intentional time at home together. Plan your shopping trips more carefully. Stay in the house, out of each other's way, and productively occupied. Don't count on television. You must build today the kind of family strength, stability, and communication that will allow you to survive the disease that will be rampant even among the prepared—cabin fever.

As mentioned previously, you will want to have some real money for trading throughout the crisis. Bags of pre-1965 silver coins will be ideal for this purpose. Think of this as your "bread and fuel" money. You'll want to have some gold coins available for larger purchases. When you see the economy failing rapidly, try to dispose of your greenbacks as quickly as possible.

If you own several firearms, remember that your guns become useless as soon as you fire your last bullet. Don't count on the sporting goods store still being open for business. Stockpile a six-month supply of ammunitions unless you foresee a time coming when your ammunition may be an accepted trading commodity.

Don't overlook the importance of storing fuel for heating. Wood can be stored easily, inexpensively, and systematically. With the right wood stove or fireplace arrangement, you can be prepared for warmth and cooking power as long as necessary at limited cost. National forests usually have wood you may cut and haul simply by asking. Many farmers and landowners are happy to have you remove timber. And one of the best urban sources is a residential building site just as the framing is completed. Be sure to ask permission. Otherwise, you risk arrest and eliminate the wood-gathering opportunity. This treated lumber burns faster and hotter than logs, but when it is free and there is an unlimited supply, the burning rate is inconsequential. It stacks neatly and squarely and ages well. If you must purchase wood, turn time to your advantage by buying several winters in advance, thus enabling yourself to purchase cheaper, greener wood that will age until you are ready for it.

Once the essentials for food, shelter, and warmth are taken care of, you should look to the supplies that will enable you to make your siege more comfortable and productive. Stock up on lanterns, candles, batteries (batteries last longer if stored in the freezer), kerosene, wicks, lamp oil, alternate sources of cooking and heating, and additional clothing and blankets. Remember that unused material will be valuable when you want to make something for a purpose you have failed to think about. This suggests the need for needles, thread, patches, zippers, and buttons. Tools for all types of repairs will be at a premium when old things have to do because all the new things and replacement parts have disappeared. Make sure there is a way to lock up your tools and other repair equipment.

Traditional sources of energy are not totally dependable today. In planning for the future, you should consider alternative power sources or learn to do without electricity. If your property contains a stream that flows across hilly terrain, you may be able to utilize a relatively inexpensive form of hydroelectric power. You will be amazed at how little power is actually necessary if you do proper planning.

Think of radios as information giving, not diversion producing. There will be nothing to listen to but bad news and propaganda for a while, and you may be able to tell more about what is actually happening by monitoring police, fire, Coast Guard, or military channels. It will also add immeasurably to your communication capability if you learn the skills and equipment of HAM or CB radio operation. However, don't depend on electricity to run your radios. Either have battery capability or provide an electric generator and sufficient fuel. Radios with solar batteries can be purchased. Finally, be sure that you have built your library with the crisis in mind. Not only will you want to stock up on books that will be enjoyable to read in the long hours without television, but you will also need to build up a bank of skill manuals and how-to books about topics you'll need to master. These may range from *How to Fix Plumbing* to *How to Make Candles at Home* to *Recognizing Wild Plants That You Can Eat Safely*. Don't overlook reference books and books for solving human relations problems.

SUMMARY

I believe that hard times are inevitable. The extent of suffering is impossible to forecast. Even so, I am equally sure that the kinds of preparations suggested in this chapter can do nothing but strengthen your body, your personality, and your family whether we face feast or famine. Get ready for the worst and you will do well at handling the best.

First, make the necessary preparations to supply your family with food, shelter, warmth, and water for six months. Subsequently, make provisions to hold out longer, to protect your necessities from those who would steal them from you, and to turn a period of devastation into times of strength, enjoyment, and growth.

I am convinced that storing food and other supplies is the easiest part of your challenge. The greater challenge is to build a family structure that can cope with the social and emotional stresses of the future well enough to survive, prosper, and even enjoy the material provisions that you have made.

CHAPTER TEN

Build Your Own Dream House for Nightmares

Our review of the calamities that cloud the horizons of the coming decade seem inevitably to stimulate a strong urge to run away. Even a wise general knows when it is time to retreat. Fortunately, proper planning can give us the ability to retreat to something that is positive rather than merely running away from negatives.

When the subject of retreating arises, the mind's eye immediately begins to picture a castle with a moat and an inexhaustible supply of everything. While it might be nice for you and your family to enjoy all the luxuries of this type of home while the world outside is looting and starving, only a few of my readers will find it practical to plan towards this end. Such a setup would probably require you to spend more time defending your wealth than enjoying it.

WHY RETREATING?

While the idea of a retreat constitutes many different things to different people, the need for some method of getting your family out of the line of the fire is obvious. Providing shelter, supplies, and safety will require some planning and practicing in the present to make sure that all systems will function effectively in the time of crisis when there will be a scarcity of electricity, gas, food, and water.

Your own resources and personal assessment of the forthcoming social upheaval will determine the extent of the retreat preparations you are willing to make. If you have come to foresee a mild—mostly economic—realignment of our nation's imbalances, with some minor shutdowns and shortages, then your retreat may indeed be a matter of some supplies in a foot locker and a heightened awareness of the ways daily routines may be temporarily altered. On the other end of the spectrum, your scenario of the cataclysm may include total social collapse and up to two years before control is regained. If so, your retreat plans will obviously be more elaborate.

Provisions for retreating are a natural result of the thought sequence that anticipates and tries to prepare for the 1980's. The degree to which you prepare is not merely a matter of finding out the "state of the art" in retreating and ordering "one of each." As you read this chapter, your basic task is to compare each of the alternative descriptions of your own concept of the future. Compare your expectations with the preparations necessary to meet that kind of future.

If you have read the previous chapters of this book and any three of this week's newspapers, you don't have to be sold on the inevitability of major social and economic problems ahead. You know that there's no way we are going to get out of this mess without some national suffering. Now, let's look around for the best ways to prepare your physical settings for survival and success.

If you begin to plan your own retreat and you want more information, there are several excellent resources. As I mentioned in the last chapter, Don Stephens is the leading expert on retreating. Don and his wife, Barbie, started early in the 1960's investigating the various ways of escaping and retreating. They lived through the planning stages and early ventures of some of the theoretical utopian plans and were ahead of the "back to nature" fads that have grown in popularity in the 1970's. Don was the person who originally put Harry Browne in touch with retreating as an approach in planning for potential monetary crisis. He has been most helpful to me in preparing this section of my book. Through Don's training in architecture, and enduring interest in an area with mushrooming data sources, and some good old creativity and ingenuity, this couple has come out knowing more than anybody else about retreating.

As you plan your retreat, just remember that it is a matter of your priorities. You may want to make minor provisions—the kind that can dovetail nicely with your vacation and recreation needs. Or—your expectations may entail the ultimate in seclusion properties and independence equipping. The extent and nature of your preparations remain a personal matter. Whether or not you will need a retreat is, in my opinion, less subject to debate.

THE PROCESS

Once you have finished this chapter and done your initial thinking about the extent of retreat preparation you believe necessary, sit down and spend some serious time committing your plans and timetables to paper. As usual, you will find your activities will become more realistic once they evolve from the nebulous back of your mind to the concrete reality of a timetable and budget.

Your first decision concerns the amount of time you are willing to take to be as ready as you want to be. It would usually prove wasteful—even if you have the money—to rush out and buy everything you expect to need for the emergency. Most people don't have that kind of extra money and so they eventually settle (either by trial-and-error or by thoughtful planning) for a sort of concentric circle plan. This means that they set specific time deadlines to accomplish a limited survival program, then set a subsequent time period for carrying all aspects of the total plan a little further.

The alternative to this coordinated planning approach is to make one major decision and build every other consideration around that. A common shortsighted approach is to purchase the perfect piece of real estate at a cost that weighs the planner down with high payments that nearly prohibit the continued development of a plan. Not only are the payments burdensome and contributing to the nation's inflationary spiral, but, when the economic collapse comes, the retreater will not own the retreat. It won't matter how perfect the retreat is if you haven't planned well enough to protect it from foreclosure.

Your inner circle of planning may be a matter of accumulating the necessary food and supplies to be as ready as possible if the collapse occurs sooner than I anticipate. The one-year plan that follows may include buying a small piece of property and stocking an old house or other dwelling on it while you begin gardening and planning for a permanent retreat. During the next year, you may begin to actually build this retreat while you continue to purchase other items that will be useful in your survival strategy.

Of course, all this timing is going to hinge on your personal projection about how long the country can hold out before it blows out. If you are convinced that things can't last for more than a year, then you might forget the gradual build-up idea and sell what you have and sink the proceeds into immediate preparation. My assessment is that the general crisis is probably two to four years in the future, with a 65–70 percent probability for the end of 1984 and a 90 percent probability by 1986.

A concise summary of some excellent common sense suggestions for things you should consider for inclusion in your early planning stages was suggested to me by Don Stephens. They are things that need to be done right away regardless of crises, but may require the motivation of impending disaster to make you do them. For example, you need to force yourself to go ahead and get that dental work up to date. Get your eyes checked and new glasses ordered. Keep the old pairs in good enough repair to serve as backups. *Think survival* . . . and take a class or a vacation that toughens you up and teaches you how to get by when the soft living stops. Do some hunting and fishing . . . not just to buy up a bunch of expensive and fancy equipment, but to be sure you can feed yourself if you need to. Try some *preservation* methods on meat and vegetables and fruits—methods that don't depend on freezers or microwave ovens. *Plant a garden* and learn how to grow enough of things you will eat; go to the grocery only half as often. Raise some *animals* like chickens, ducks, or rabbits, and learn how to prepare and cook them. Become a *repair* person, gathering the necessary tools and materials and experience to fix things when they can't be replaced. Be sure you make a distinction between the person who *repairs* and one who only *replaces* parts. Talk to your doctor and make provisions for the *medical* and *pharmaceutical* needs of survival should the drug stores be closed or looted. Learn some *first aid* procedures and how to splint, lower a fever, or deliver a baby.

Get your *finances* arranged by removing money from banks and putting it into gold, silver, and other commodities that grow with inflation. Get your investments into places that are highly and quickly liquid. Determine what happens to your home when the mortgage is called in. Reinvest in depressionproof places and store these investments out of reach of governmental snooping and illegal grabbing.

Store essential equipment, like firearms, ammo, spare parts, seeds, old clothing and new fabric, a sewing machine, used furniture and bedding, tools to do things you need to do, and books to tell you how to do them. The specifics of your preparation will follow naturally once you have worked out the timetable by which you feel compelled to accomplish preparedness.

The key to success in making your preparations is to plan and proceed in a way so that you are always ready—no matter when the warning buzzer sounds. Once this readiness has been established, you will have the feeling of security from which you can calmly continue to get "more ready."

You and Your Ark

Some retreat writers suggest the use of recreational boats as getaway and survival vehicles. My opinion is that boats might *limit* rather than enhance your flexibility and ability to escape and survive. There are a few people who have the kinds of equipment and skills to retreat by water, but to me the problems of securing fresh water and food if you are on salt water—or of navigation to safety if you are on a lake or river—will cancel the few advantages. The one exception I can see would be a houseboat that might be used as a retreat cabin. Even here, if it remains in the same location, it becomes more a cabin than a boat, and if it moves around, it consumes extremely wasteful amounts of fuel, which is likely to be scarce. Mobility *is* a desirable option in your retreat planning, but my opinion is that true flexibility is harder to accomplish on the water than on land. If you are interested in sea mobility, because you are an expert sailor and you live close to some major body of water, you may want to investigate this subject in greater detail. If you choose this method, you will want to make sure you make regular trial runs and even arrange strategic stashes of food, water, and fuel in places where you are sure it will be safe and you have easy access to it.

LOOKING FOR LAND

Far too many people make the largest single purchase of their lives on the basis of luck or chance. Whether you are buying a home or a retreat location, don't let yourself be forced into taking less than you had hoped for simply because an easy-to-buy property happens to come available at the time you are eager to buy.

Perhaps the first rule in buying a place is to get yourself in a position of not needing the things you are going to buy. This sounds contradictory but it *is* true that you can be most methodical and careful about the land you are inspecting if you are not needing it as a place to unload your truck! The same principle holds true with houses and retreat properties—let your six-month plan provide temporary comfort and security that allows you some leisure to consider several alternatives.

Purchasing a site for a retreat is very tricky. While your retreat may offer you many happy hours of vacation relaxation, you should avoid some of the qualifications one usually seeks in a traditional vacation home. Remember that your retreat has to afford a self-sustaining environment and should not depend on the station wagon load of supplies you customarily bring in for a weekend.

Be systematic in the choice of land. Start by deciding where you want to live. As we have suggested previously, you may need to approach the impending crisis by a well-planned move to a more temperate climate. If that is needed, do it before you begin to look for your retreat. It will be dangerous for you to have 500 miles of chaos and marauding bands between you and your well-stocked retreat.

Get your home where you want to be during the crisis. For some, your new residence may also serve as a retreat haven. If you can arrange your work or profession in such a way that this is possible, you are most fortunate. If you must still maintain a base of operations in a large metropolitan center, begin to look around at the possibilities for a safe retreat site. Don't rush. Make your list and check it twice. In making that checklist, be sure to include the following items:

1. *Climate*—All the beauty in the world can be canceled if the climate is too harsh. Why would you want to provide twice as much firewood and insulation when you could avoid these by starting in a warmer location?

2. *Cost*—You are caught between the need to ignore cost and concentrate on getting what you need and the need to maintain your financial independence. Don't consider cost first, but don't buy until you have explored every possible alternative within your allocated budget. For example, you may be able to make the land pay for itself by making a small down payment and selling the timber to pay the mortgage.

3. *Community*—Do you plan to create your retreat as a single family locale or are you thinking in terms of a place where several families may work together? This could make a huge difference in what you buy (i.e., how much space, the cost, the ways of paying for it, and the possibilities of dividing the tasks required for survival and maintenance).

4. *Commitment*—Signing on the dotted line is quick and easy compared to the hard part that comes when you start digging stumps and building fences. Spend some time working on a farm before you buy your retreat. It can make an enjoyable and enlightening vacation and can help you to be more realistic as you decide how many blisters and backaches you are willing to endure. There is always a tradeoff between dollars and sweat— you can spend more of one if you are unwilling or unable to spend the other.

5. *Choice*—Once you are in the area that you have found through careful research, be sure to choose a piece of property according to *your* interests and not by the opinions of real estate agents, chambers of commerce, previous owners, or community consensus. Other people may be able to give you valuable input, but they cannot see things from your viewpoint.

6. *Isolation*—Avoid the charming country places that are frequent weekend haunts for city people. These are the first places they will go when they have to "get out of town." Stay away from main highways and out of view from any public roads. Stay away from residential developments and never buy land downriver from a dam or nuclear power facility that could become the target for sabotage in a national emergency.

7. *Neighbors*—Get a good idea of the kind of neighbors you will have. It is more important to picture them in the event of a national crisis than just seeing how they act when you make a social visit. Do they seem like the kind of secure people who will remain self-supporting and calm in such a calamity—or might they become your nearest enemy?

8. *Environment*—Don't buy land just because you like the view. There are many more important things to consider. Some are: soil conditions, flood plains, extremes of cli-

mate, thunderstorms, salty air, and insects and plants that may be hazardous to your health.

9. *Topography*—Mountain cabins are colorful but they are hard to get to, exposed to the elements, and invariably uphill from the water supply. Choose land that can grow food *naturally*, perhaps without the aid of a gasoline tractor. You need some level land with enough slope for effective drainage without erosive run-off.

10. *Water*—No other element is quite so important. You have to have it probably without the county water works or dependence on electric or gasoline pumps. Is there running water? Where does it come from? Is there a water table that will facilitate digging a well? How does the drilling rig get in and out? Are there adequate slope and stoney soil to facilitate sanitary disposal of sewage and waste? How does the waste disposal path relate to the supply of fresh water? Is there sufficient natural water to irrigate your crops? How much money or sweat is required to accomplish the irrigation?

11. *Natural Shelter*—Warm air rises to hilltops and ridges. Cold air sinks to valleys and canyons. You will want to know exactly where your house will go before you buy the land, and you ought to see the sun come up and go down on that spot and have a good idea which direction the wind blows most of the time.

12. *Fire*—Fire travels fastest uphill through brush. If you build on a hilltop, clear the brush and make sure you have an escape route. Keep a fifty-foot section of ground plowed as a firebreak around your property. Fire-retardant shingles on your house may keep your house from burning when your neighbor's property is burning and filling the wind with sparks. Lightning is a potential cause of fire. A lightning rod costs little and provides a lot of protection.

13. *Vegetation*—The trees and shrubs already on the land can tell you what other crops are likely to grow there. Beech, sugar maple, hickory, black walnut, and white oak trees indicate rich land. White pine, scrub oak, and scrawny trees are typical of poor land. Willows, poplars, and elder bushes may suggest too much water and the need for drainage. Weeds are even more indication than trees and bushes because they follow cultivation, whereas trees usually precede it. It's not really important to know

the *types* of weeds. What does count is what they look like. Dark green, lush, leafy growths mean those plants are well fed and there's plenty of nitrogen in the soil. If the growth is sickly, scrawny, or pale, and apparently eking out a miserable existence, then it's likely that your crops are going to have to do the same.

Speaking from experience in buying land, my feeling is that you get more good buys from knowing people who may be thinking of putting a piece of property up for sale than reading some aggressive real estate agent's listing in the newspaper. I have been successful in placing ads requesting land for sale in a weekly smalltown newspaper near the area I was seeking. You should be willing to spend a little more for an ad that will be noticed. Here's an ad that helped me find the land I was seeking:

SELL YOUR PROPERTY AND STILL FARM IT.
City man wants to bring his family back to the country. Would like 40 to 100 acres of land with woods, crops, pasture, and water. You can live on the land as long as you wish. Send details to Box————.

It is not terribly difficult to find an older farm couple whose children have the left the nest and who would like to get their money out of the land without saying goodbye to the farm. If you can make an arrangement like this, you should be able to negotiate a better price and have somebody to teach you some of the things that you may not know about farming.

The old adage, "Your terms, my money or my terms, your money" simply means you can offer somebody a great deal more money if they are willing to spread it out over a long period of time. If you pay more than 29 percent of the total price as a down payment, the seller will probably encounter some tax problems. In negotiating this kind of transaction, it's important to remember the advice mentioned earlier about not pledging your other assets in buying real estate and involving a good attorney in drawing up the details of the agreement.

When you buy a farm or a retreat property, it is important to try and buy one with a creek or spring on it. If that's not possible, be sure that water is available by digging a well.

YOUR HOUSE

One of the greatest challenges in designing and building a structure for retreat survival and comfort will be shaking loose from the kind of decision reflexes society has given you about housing. It's easy to worry too much about factors of status, style, and appearance more than the factors that will really make a difference in how you live.

You may have the option of renovating an existing farmhouse. This can be a good intermediate step, but should not be allowed to color your evaluations of available properties. Don't value a farm more highly because it has an existing structure. You may end up paying more to weatherize and remodel it than you would spend to build from scratch a retreat home perfectly matching your specifications. The farmhouse may prove valuable as a place to live while finishing your retreat home, but it is not likely to be designed for the kind of services you will want it to supply.

Buy, Build, or Contract

The best place to save money on a retreat home is by doing much of the work yourself. If you fear that your amateur carpentry and plumbing will cost more in the long run, you have two options: either get the tools and necessary practice to do better work or resign yourself to the necessity of paying the price for tradesmen to do it for you. If you do decide to serve as the contractor on the job (and almost everybody has to subcontract some part of the job), you will need larger doses of patience and persistence. Experience will soon teach you that you get more value from small companies and individual craftsmen who are likely to be doing the work themselves rather than delegating it to a passing laborer or a major construction firm.

Bargain carefully and ask every question twice before the project begins. Be on the lookout for hidden costs and overruns. If you have the time but not the expertise, try to be on the job most of the time. Even if you are not looking over the workman's shoulder, your presence will have a positive influence on the quality and pace of the work.

If you find yourself having to subcontract the majority of the work, you may need to give a little thought to whether or not you have the self-reliance and drive that will be essential for surviving in that retreat when it is finished. You need to discover the satisfaction that comes from the attitude that "if anybody can do it—I can learn, too!"

Your new skills may begin at the beginning with the excavations and ground-moving stages. Why hire a bulldozer driver when you can rent a small dozer and learn to drive it yourself? You may even want to consider puchasing a small, used, $3,000 to $5,000 bulldozer, as it will never lose its value to you as long as you work the land. Some jobs are too big to "learn on," but you should not just consider cost if a skill is involved that you need to learn for survival. Better to take a little longer and become a more skilled person. Besides, if you put in the septic tank and drain fields yourself, you are going to be the one who knows most about repairing them.

When you design your house, don't fight the land or the weather. The house you see frequently in an area may present a clue to the type of structure for the local weather and temperature extremes. Give thoughtful consideration to the traditional styles and building materials, but don't accept anything without asking "why?" and coming to your own design decisions. In some instances, early settlers gave up the use of energy efficient natural materials as soon as they could afford to build the kind of houses associated with "modern civilization." Consider stone where stone is plentiful, adobe in the desert, and unfinished wood in the forest and in the shelter of trees where cooling is a major challenge.

The Modern Cave Dweller

The underground house in an idea that has become more and more popular as costs of energy and maintenance have risen. Such a house can now be designed and constructed for about the same initial cost as a house of similar size above the ground. The advantages are tremendous, ranging from no maintenance (except mowing the roof) to low heating costs ($1.29 for a winter in one case I am familiar with). Since the earth's temperature does not fluctuate as much as the outside air, an underground house need only be warmed a little to be comfortable year round. Once the temperature is right, an underground house has perfect insulation all around. At a depth of eight feet, the winter earth temperature will approximate the average yearly air temperature of the area. Architect Malcolm Wells, one of the pioneers of underground housing, reports that his underground office is a comfortable 67° in the summer when the air outside is 95°.

Many designs are available with specifications that solve problems of dampness, mildew, and other concerns of the uninitiated. Such homes not only are cool in the summer and warm in the winter, but they are tornado and hurricane protected, extremely quiet, and can be designed with large windows in some parts and skylights in every room to reduce any claustrophobic problems. Rather than needing maintenance, they can only get better with age since the concrete gets harder and harder with passing time. There is little to burn so insurance rates are low. The underground house may be the perfect retreat home for you, but don't expect a local builder to figure it out for you. If you see the values and get the underground bug, send off for the plans described in the bibliography and get the detailed plans and the benefit of someone else's trial and error. Then, settle in for a gradual step-by-step evolution of your own cave. You can utilize the services of local subcontractors, but you need to be ready for them to make light of such an unorthodox approach to home design. However, the indications are that the underground dwelling is likely to become more and more common since the utility companies seem intent on driving their customers out of traditional structures.

Whatever design you choose—above or below the ground—you should make sure that you allow sufficient storage space. If you are building from scratch, you may find it efficient to first construct your storage barns and tool sheds. This will allow you to proceed in a more orderly fashion on the house and give you more opportunities to learn about the terrain and character of the setting.

When you build your retreat home, make it small. If you have extra money to put into it, let it go into quality materials instead of into extra space or luxury appliances. Do you really need a separate dining room or both a den and living room? Insulate the house, over, under, and all around, including double panes in the windows and doors. Overinsulation is a better mistake than underinsulation, especially in view of the predicted Ice Age of the Eighties.

By all means, have a place to burn wood, but do not let that place be a beautiful but inefficient masonry fireplace. An open-front masonry fireplace pulls more heat out of your house than its fire can put in. Either add glass-front fireplace doors, or, better still, add a free-standing iron stove or metal fireplace to the house. If the stovepipe has to be exposed all the way to the ceiling of the house, it will produce even more heat.

Make maximum use of the sun's warmth in the design of your house. And remember the principle that warm air rises when ventilating for summer coolness. When you are designing for function rather than appearance, you can do some desirable things, like connecting buildings so that you can go from one to another without stepping out into the snow, grow food in your solar-heated greenhouse all year round, or bring in the dry firewood without changing to your boots.

Your retreat home becomes a unique extension of your own personality. Your design will naturally amplify the aspects that you value most and leave off some things that others might consider to be necessities. It becomes in that sense a self-actualizing project as well as one that can provide safety and comfort for your loved ones in case of a disaster, or in case of a regular vacation.

YOUR FOOD

It may be that the last thing on your list of wishes is to become a farmer. A few years ago, our society discouraged us from growing food unless we were willing to commit fully to a farming career. Already rising food prices have prompted almost a third of all U.S. families to start "victory gardens" to help them survive the war against inflation. During the times of uncertainty that will come in the 1980's, there will be plenty of motivation to plant and grow food for survival. Who can produce food will become richer than almost anyone else.

Surprisingly enough, the survival motivation to learn how to grow your own food very quickly gives way to the excitement and satisfaction that comes from eating food that tastes better, costs less, and is demonstrably more nourishing. You may look with condescension on those wild-eyed organic food nuts you meet more and more often these days, but don't be too critical until you have compared doctor bills. You don't have to become a hippie to get your first taste of self-sufficiency satisfaction. Even the simple experience of growing tomatoes in your window box may hook you with the joy of growing your own food.

As you are looking for your retreat property, you should give special attention to the lay of the land and its appropriateness for becoming a self-perpetuating ecological food factory. In our plastic society, we quite naturally begin to absorb the idea that man grows plants inspite of the dirt—that the main service of the soil is to prop up the plants so that the farmer can dump on the fertilizer and insecticides. This is an unnatural approach and only leads to the plants making greater and greater demands for the petroleum-based fertilizers, which are becoming more and more expensive.

Keep the same plant in the same soil year after year and you will have to do all the work. Learn to rotate your demands on the soil and you can soon sit back and let the soil do most of the work. Moreover, the soil will do the work gladly if you will set up your food production facility in a way that you help the soil live and let live.

One of the most admirable traits of the old farmer is his patience and harmony with nature. It only takes time and a little attention to the basic laws of agriculture. Remember, the basic laws of farming were in action long before man invented tractors or fertilizers. There are steps you can use that will reinstate natural cycles that allow the soil to feed the animals, the animals to feed the soil, and human beings to enjoy the overproduction of both by understanding and facilitating these natural processes.

The Lowdown on High Farming

The Europeans of the last century practiced what they called "high farming," in which they established some principles of sequence and rotation that allowed them to turn tiny land areas into no-waste ecological wonders. For years, our nation has had land to spare and we have foolishly wasted, exploited, and even fought the principles of natural farming, trying to force the land to yield things it did not "want" to grow. Yet the principles of "high farming" remain valid and are perhaps even more valuable as we begin to cross the threshold of a time when your family will survive by growing its own food.

Even if our world were not in economic trouble, it would still be facing a resource shortage and an insecticide proliferation that could drive us all to self-sufficiency anyway. The fact that our society is being gradually buried under its own garbage is a further reminder of the wisdom of the old, natural ways when there was no such thing as garbage—only fuel for the continuation of the growing-feeding-nourishing chain.

High farming is a systematic, natural approach to the use of small farms by dividing the available land into four sequential categories that are alternated by season. By this method, the soil is not drained or depleted by unnatural demands. In high farming, the land that has grown a demanding crop is given a subsequent season of growing a crop that builds up the soil's nutrients. During the next season it can lie fallow or serve as grazing pasture for animals who fertilize the soil with their manure. Even the grazing sequences can be arranged in a way that the life cycles of the animal parasites are interrupted, and the land is grazed from pasture status down to an "almost plowed" condition by the time the pigs have had their turn.

The excitement and order of a self-sufficient system can become a great hobby for you as you purchase the land for your retreat and initiate the growing processes. Even if you have to put off beginning construction until later, you can begin cooperating with the land immediately. Plant your slow-maturing crops immediately. Fruit trees and vineyards should also receive your immediate attention. It is better to have a tent home on a self-sustaining farm than a beautiful house on retreat property that has not yet cut the cords of dependence on the food and service that will be unavailable when the crisis begins.

The Small Retreat

While a significant degree of self-sufficiency can be acquired on very small amounts of land, unless you are a vegetarian, total self-sufficiency will require enough space to grow hay and grains that you need for livestock. You'll also need wheat to make bread. At the outset, you will have to accept the fact that some of the things you need will have to be bought outside the microcosm of your retreat.

Your supply of silver coins will be helpful to you in making necessary purchases. You may decide to store some of the necessities you require in advance. Be careful in using gold coins. Because of their high value, gold may attract more attention than you want. In the initial days of the crisis, barter will be your best medium of exchange. Through arrangements with friends and neighbors, you should be able to trade skills or possessions that you have in abundance for items that you require.

If you are able to live on your retreat property, I strongly urge you to stock a few animals. Since they require daily care, you are going to have to live on the property, have someone there who can help with these chores, or "board" your animals with a neighbor. When the time comes for the retreat to be your home all day long every day, the chores of keeping the farm will provide diversion as well as food.

The pioneers who have studied the concept of self-sustaining farming almost unanimously recommend the keeping of one or more cows. No other single farm item will so completely supply the good health and natural pacing as that of a cow's machinery. The cow's body is a natural processing plant that eats food that is inexpensive, produces food that is healthful and expensive (milk, cheese, butter, yogurt, and cottage cheese), and leaves behind that which is absolutely essential to farming on limited amounts of land (rich manure for fertilizer). If you have a very small piece of property and are quite isolated, you should consider goats or sheep as alternatives to a single cow. Cows require regular "freshening" if they are to produce milk. A couple of goats or milk sheep may be easier to keep on a small retreat. In addition to milk, they can provide the self-sufficient retreater with meat, wool, and leather.

Get a cow (or a goat or two), a couple of pigs, a few hens with a rooster, and a couple of rabbits. Set yourself up to confine them in movable pens that will allow you to control the fertilizer supply for any section of your land at any time. Remember also that you are wasting effort any time you harvest and transport feed to the animals when you can move the animals to the food and leave them to harvest it as they graze.

With only an acre or two, you will probably only be able to graze your animals during the summer and will need to plan to bring in feed for the winter months. (Obviously, the extra preparations for cold weather provide further reinforcement for the earlier advice that you move toward the Sun Belt for your retreat home.) You will need to provide a small barn or shelter for your cow (and perhaps some other animals) during the winter months. If you keep a steady supply of good, clean straw underfoot, your cow will mix it with rich manure that will make better fertilizer than money can buy.

Caring for these animals is a simple matter for those who know how, but it can be puzzling if you are doing it page-by-page from a manual. For this reason, you will want to begin now arranging opportunities to familiarize yourself and your family farmhands with the sights, sounds, smells, and pleasures of animals and their care. While you will certainly want your retreat library to include books that can guide you as you develop your farm, you will also want to begin establishing friendships with your neighbors who may have years of experience in working with animals and crops in the exact climate and setting you are taking on.

It is likely that your desire to spend time at your retreat will increase steadily as you become more and more captivated by the natural symmetry of life in ecological balance. Even while you remain in your city home, you can begin enjoying the delicious fruits of your weekend and vacation labors at your retreat. This growing ability to avoid the spiral of food costs can also enable you to have additional funds to prepare for the time when goods and services halt. In short, your small retreat farm offers you cheaper, more wholesome food and a chance for your youngsters to establish contact with food that grows on plants instead of in plastic containers.

If you only have an acre, begin by dividing it in half. Put half in garden and half in rough pasture. These two halves can be alternated every four years, or you can leave the grass half in pasture and transport its supplies of manure to the garden half as it is needed. If you are going to keep pasture, it is wise to further divide the grass half of your land into four parts so that you always have some freshly sown pasture, some two-year-old pasture, some three-year-old pasture, and some four-year-old pasture. The farm will be more productive if you rotate it this way.

Sow a grass, clover, and herb mixture and alternate your grazing animals on it. You may wish to graze them on tethers or along strips inside a "run" created with an electric fence that can be moved easily. Jersey cows are well adapted to tether grazing since they were bred for this purpose in the Jersey Islands of Britain.

On the other half acre, you will want to do your best possible intensive gardening. If you made good use of space and of the natural fertilizers produced by the grass half acre, then you should be able to feed your family well on a half acre and have some produce to store, sell, or use for barter.

Divide the garden into four plots. If you are rotating the full acre each year, turn one quarter of your grass land into garden land and one quarter of the garden land into grass land. The first year after grass, put in potatoes. The next year, after potatoes, put in cabbages and cabbage-type vegetables. After the cabbages come the year of root plants. These are the ones whose roots are the part you ordinarily eat. The year after the land grows roots, it should grow peas and beans and then return to grass land for four more years of strengthening. If this rotation seems too troublesome to you, mulch gardening may present a simple solution. Be sure to check Ruth Stout's books in the bibliography.

If at all possible, a garden should be or become a part of the place where you live. Even if your space is limited, you can become accustomed to growing times, space required, varieties preferred, seeding procedures, and the relationships of one set of plants to another. If you have restrictions that will keep you from purchasing retreat land immediately, you should still be able to arrange to begin your self-education in farming through swapping some farm labor time for experience, by growing a garden in your yard or a friend's yard, or even planting a remote garden plot on a bit of unused public land somewhere. Time is the essence of successful farming. Farming takes time, but so does the learning process. You should begin your learning immediately and, if possible, short circuit some of that learning time by cultivating some farm friends who have already been through several cycles of seasons.

I didn't believe that almost total self-sufficiency could be obtained on only one acre of land until I became acquainted with Raymond Murphy of Chatham, Massachusetts. Murphy has fashioned his house lot into a beautiful and productive acre that includes his own greenhouse, an astonishing array of livestock, seventy-four hives of bees, five kinds of fruit trees, four kinds of nut trees, strawberries, raspberries, grapes, and a quarter-acre vegetable garden. Discharged from the Marines in 1948, Murphy migrated to Chatham, bought his acre in 1958 for $1,300, and has since paid for everything as he added it. There's no mortgage on the house and the Murphys need only about $3,000 a year for living expenses not supplied by their acre. This amount is easily gained by sales of things grown on the farm—honey, pheasants, and peacocks. Raymond Murphy's acre doesn't have to be an exception. It can be emulated easily on your retreat land with time, sweat, and careful planning.

Five Acres or More

There are, of course, advantages to having all the extra property you can afford. If nothing else, it can afford you extra privacy and allow a place for hunting. If you have five acres, you can support your family and leave plenty of quality produce to sell to folks who don't grow their own.

With five acres, you will do things by the same principles and rotations as on your one acre—but in larger chunks. Assuming that one acre is set aside for house and buildings, orchard, and garden, the rest can be involved in a high-farming-type rotation of animals and crops except for four half-acre plots for rotation and two acres for the grass and grain growth to support the rest of the farm and its animals.

The productivity of four acres of carefully cultivated and naturally cycled land can easily support your family and supply an inexpensive but lucrative roadside vegetable and fruit stand where your children can learn about private enterprise. They will learn that good products are always in demand. Their customers will find that the food is better since it is not picked green to provide time to travel through a long marketing channel. Because your naturally grown products will be better and tastier, repeat business will be common. This applies also to eggs, honey, and other surpluses.

A Retreat Within a Retreat

When I am convinced that the depression is really beginning (see Chapter 12), I plan to move immediately to my own retreat, which I have been working on since 1976. This property consists of forty-eight acres with a small stream that has been damned up to provide a lake where we are able to water our stock and stock the water with fish. Although there are a couple of acres that are intensely cultivated, there are also wooded acres that can be used for hunting and for fuel supply. In addition to a small, well-planned house that has been built according to the principles we discussed earlier, we are also developing a retreat within a retreat.

The ultimate retreat is an office (it could be a studio for an artist or a guest room for someone else) that is relatively close to the main house but built underground with a single large room and a couple of small compartments. It could be used in the case of a major calamity. It is furnished for my purposes as an office but with two couches that make into beds. It has a kitchenette and a compact bathroom. There is ample storage space for our food supply that is safe from spoilage because of the temperature control. It is a combination retreat, food and wine cellar, storm shelter, and office. Because of the way it has been built all the construction costs have been capitalized as a business expense. Since it is (1) totally separate from the house, and (2) not used for any other purpose, it meets the stringent 1976 IRS regulations concerning a home office. Though technically it isn't used for any other purpose at the present, it will be a very attractive ultimate retreat in case the worst of all possible worlds should evolve.

SUMMARY

For those interested in developing self-sufficiency, the *Mother Earth News* is an intriguing publication. John Shuttleworth put together the first issue of the magazine on his kitchen table in Hendersonville, North Carolina, in 1969. Since then it has grown to a point where it has been described as the "most powerful medium for change in the whole alternative life style movement." It comes out bi-monthly, costs $12.00 for one year, and includes articles on alternative energy, organic food growing, and stories of people who have exchanged city life for remote farms and attempts at self-sufficiency. *Mother* has everything from articles on goat keeping and jam making to new construction techniques. During the rapid growth and early success of this periodical, some of the staff was relatively inexperienced. Consequently it was necessary to check the accuracy of some technical information contained in this exciting publication. As MEN gains maturity, the quality of material is returning to its former levels.

Another magazine which may interest you is called *Organic Gardening and Farming*. It costs $6.00 per year and can stimulate your thinking on aspects of food production you are currently interested in. Technically, I have found it to be excellent.

Your retreat plan should be one that allows for a very positive, healthy productive orientation. Even if we somehow avoid the major depression that appears inevitable, your retreat can open the doors to a positive, healthy life style as you use it on weekends and whenever you have an opportunity. At the same time, it is a good investment, providing for peace of mind, family togetherness, and an ark in the event of a flood of troubles.

CHAPTER ELEVEN

Setting Up Survival Teams

When Benjamin Franklin was attempting to stir his fellow revolutionaries to united action against the oppressive government controls and confiscatory taxes of Britain, he summarized the situation in the immortal phrase, "We must all hang together, or else we hang separately." About the same time, Patrick Henry was proclaiming the policy, "No taxation without representation." Two hundred years later, we are finding that taxation *with* representation is not so hot either. Today, the quiet revolutionary who seeks relief from confiscatory taxes and oppressive government control frequently finds fundamental wisdom in another of the colonists' mottos, "In union, there is strength."

WHY GROUP RETREATING?

In the preceding chapter, we looked at some of the pleasant, practical ways of achieving comfortable, independent living. While independence as a goal is to be fervently sought, there are few individuals or families who possess such a complete arsenal of survival skills that they can make it entirely on their own. As John Donne, English poet, suggested, "No man is an island apart unto himself." Most of us must confess that there are certain areas where we need the assistance of others. Although this need not be the kind of helpless dependence that offers nothing in return, it is psychologically and emotionally comforting to feel that there are other people who can be counted upon in times of crisis. Many retreaters are finding numerous, practical reasons for pooling some of their resources and sharing their survival concerns and skills.

Combined Strength

Probably the most significant reason for forming survival teams is to gain the combined strength that comes from working together. To illustrate the importance of group unity, Chairman Mao once presented his strongest associate with a bundle of slender bamboo reeds that were tied together by a single cord. He then challenged his robust young disciple to break the sticks. After the assistant admitted his inability to accomplish this objective, the Chairman untied the cord and gave each of his older associates a single reed. When the challenge was repeated, it was an easy task for each of his assistants, even the weakest, to break each slender bamboo shoot.

Financial Resources

By pooling financial resources, a group of survival-minded families can accomplish objectives that no one of them could do independently. In Chapter 6, I suggested that about $15,000 was a reasonable amount to allocate for food and retreating if an individual has $100,000 in an investment portfolio. Usually $15,000 will not provide a great deal in the way of property or protection, although people who are very skilled have been able to get by for less. How much easier it would be if five families of comparable resources put together $75,000 to purchase a significant piece of property, perhaps with a large farmhouse. By sharing the availability of this property and work assignments, you could have an attractive weekend retreat and a working farm to provide support when the real crisis comes. Even if you have $50,000 to devote to retreating, think how much more complete your surroundings would be if you were able to create a compound with five other individuals so that your total investment would equal a quarter of a million dollars. Another financial benefit that accrues to an individual searching for retreat property comes from the economies of scale. Since one individual can afford fewer acres than several people working together, the group can purchase larger amounts at a smaller price per acre. Land in less than twenty-acre parcels may sell for four times as much per acre as a tract of 500 acres or more.

Diverse Talents

Unless you are a completely unique person who is able to do everything well, there are some challenges associated with retreating (or survival) that will be almost impossible for you. Certainly, it would be comfortable to depend on someone whose special expertise could supplement those areas where you feel less competent. As mentioned earlier, I am currently trying to develop as many survival skills as possible. At the present time, I enjoy creating a retreat that my family can enjoy on weekends and holidays. This individual approach has proved educational and stimulating. You may remember, however, that I had purchased a total of forty-eight acres for this family retreat. Within the next two years, I will add three or four other families to my survival group. My goal is to have a complete survival team assembled by the beginning of 1982. In the event that you may have parallel interests, I will outline the characteristics that I believe are associated with an ideal group for retreating.

1. *Farm management skills:* Several of the most essential skills are those that have to do with growing food, the care of domestic animals, and the management and use of timber resources. In earlier days, these were pretty well associated with the typical farm family. I was fortunate to find an elderly couple who wanted to sell part of their farm while retaining possession of the other portion. In addition to gaining an option to buy additional property in the event this couple should decide to sell their remaining acres, I gained an immeasurable amount of information through the accumulated wisdom and knowledge that they have gained in their fifty years in a farm setting. Neither of these individuals have ever taken a course at an agricultural college, but they know more about the practical aspects of allowing the earth to work for them than any professor of agricultural science that I have ever known. You may be able to find an individual who has other practical skills but remembers lessons learned while growing up on a farm. Some people are even able to gain an adequate working knowledge of these concepts through written

resources. However these skills are acquired, they are actually essential for an optimal retreat setting.

2. *Construction and Repairs:* Even if you buy property with an existing house, substantial construction skills will be required in order to renovate to meet your survival needs. There will be shelters and pens that need to be constructed. If your roof begins to leak during the siege, you will not be able to call a neighborhood repairman. Consequently, the more of these types of skills you can have in your group, the more pleasant your retreat will be. The ideal background for this individual is architectural or construction/civil engineering. Hopefully, this person will have some practical experience in the construction business. An associate of mine with no technical skills feels very fortunate in being able to work out an arrangement with a retired Navy man who had spent many years in the Sea-Bees. Don't overlook the need for the ability to repair engines, rig water pumps, or unclog drains. Generally, a person who is good in one of these technical areas will be able to extend this expertise to perform similar duties.

3. *The Healing Arts:* When you are in an isolated location for any period of time, basic medical skills are vitally important. You can learn to deal with some emergencies through the Red Cross training mentioned in Chapter 7. Your group will be immeasurably strengthened, however, if you are able to bring a practicing physician into it. While an M.D. with a specialty in general practice or internal medicine is preferable to a dermatologist or plastic surgeon, anyone who has gone through medical school has been exposed to the basic concepts of medicine. I particularly feel that physicians of the Seventh Day Adventists faith are uniquely qualified because they typically have a better background in nutrition and preventive medicine than many of their colleagues. Of course, an experienced nurse would have 90 percent of the medical skills required for survival in a retreat setting. The ability to prescribe or to perform open heart surgery is not likely to be as critical as the ability to treat simple infections or accidents.

4. *The Ability to Teach:* If your group can have one individual who is a knowledgeable and inspirational teacher,

this ability will prove a valuable asset for your children as well as for the entire group. Youngsters who may be growing up or spending some extended period of time in a rather isolated environment need to learn basic academic and study skills that will enable them to become productive members of society when it is time to move forward from the retreat. Adult members of your clan will also benefit by the presence of an individual who can draw practical and inspirational lessons from a knowledge of the past and the experiences of the present. This need not be a Ph.D. or a university professor. Frequently, we tend to become too specialized or esoteric in our approach. A person with a wide range of basic knowledge is more valuable than the world's leading scholar on the mating habits of the South American bumblebee.

5. *Legal Liaison:* Although legal training may be relatively useless during the height of a crisis, a good attorney can provide invaluable assistance in the preparation period and when order begins to be restored. Tax angles, incorporation procedures, and continuing evolution of government regulations are but a few of the matters that can require legal knowledge. If your group does not include an attorney, be prepared to spend substantial amounts of money in legal fees in order to gain the optimal organization and financial advantage for your team. Legal training will also be of assistance in anticipating the evolution of the new form of order that will prevail following the clashes. Certainly, tax and corporate attorneys are preferable to criminal and international specialists.

6. *Combat Training:* In a recent conversation, Don Stephens recommended that I should suggest the talents of a veteran with combat training and battle experience. This individual could serve as a war chief for the group in the event that they should have to deal with intruders or a group of hostile marauders. While I can see that some defensive skills would be helpful, I have not yet decided that preparation for armed combat should be one of my major priorities.

7. *Charismatic Leadership:* While the dangers of a heavy ego-trip are inherent in the presence of a dominant leader, any group retreat will require some leadership

skills. I would prefer a situation where no individual is totally dominant. The Romans recognized the desirability of having one person who was their political leader and another individual they could ask to provide leadership in time of war. The same thing has turned up in many primitive cultures. Many of the American Indian tribes would have a war chief, a medicine man, and a food chief. This kind of division of authority seems preferable to allowing one individual to become a dictator. A leader who is able to coordinate activities and to establish consensus by drawing people out would be preferable to an authoritative approach. When a number of families are living in reasonably close proximity, it would be important to have a person with the ability to draw out minority opinions and resolve conflicts. These skills should be present in one of the previously mentioned roles rather than an individual recruited specifically for his or her leadership abilities.

Security

If you believe there is a high probability of armed conflict at your retreat, obviously several people will have a better chance at survival than a single couple attempting to protect themselves against a group of enemies. My personal feeling is that a retreat setting can help eliminate the greatest danger of armed attack. Many experts disagree and believe that during the height of an economic crisis there may be several months when retreats may be happened upon at any time by wandering bands of vagabond looters. They urge retreaters to be prepared to maintain an around-the-clock watch to prevent being overcome by a surprise attack. In this instance, a group of responsible adults who can take turns at watching would reduce the hardship imposed on each. Certainly, this scenario would put an overwhelming demand on the strength of two parents in a typical family. Of course, if an attack does come, the presence of several individuals who are able to help in the mutual defense of a retreat would be a powerful discouragement to looters. In such instances, strength in numbers would be a very valuable asset of the group approach to retreating.

There are other advantages of having the combined strength of several people working together. Many tasks are simply too difficult for one or two adults to handle by themselves. There can certainly be advantages to sharing some of the demanding work at planting and harvesting time.

Whether your security concerns focus on armed terrorists or stealthy burglars, people working together can provide better protection at less cost to each family. Fencing, electronic alarms, lookouts, and camouflage are all easier when the requirements are shared.

Building a simple barbed-wire fence is almost an impossible task if you are working alone. If four or five people work together, a much more elaborate fortress can be erected in an almost enjoyable setting. You'll also find that people working together will come up with much more ingenious ideas than a loner thinking in isolation.

Religious Unity

Many of the group retreats that are already organized have been formed along religious lines. In Utah, the Pacific Northwest, and the Canadian Wilderness there are several groups of Mormons who have banded together in this manner. Several conservative religious groups who expect communism to play a major role in the coming crises have also planned for survival in a similar manner. There are also sects that might be described as Christian communists (not communists in the Soviet sense) who have adopted an intense emphasis on the Golden Rule in their retreat planning.

For people who are very committed to their religious beliefs and organizations, the religiously oriented retreat can provide an added catalyst for cohesion. People of similar beliefs tend to work together more effectively than those who share diverse points of view. While not essential, a sense of religious unity among the group is an important consideration.

Pleasant Association

As I suggested in the section on religion, association with people you enjoy is practically an essential for life in any type of setting. Freedom of association is guaranteed by the U.S. Constitution. You should anticipate that attempts will be made to restrict this freedom within the next decade. The loneliness of isolation will be a major challenge for many people during the period of retreating. Most of us have been conditioned for togetherness through the collective nature of our society. At this point, I still enjoy the opportunity to work alone on my retreat. But as I have indicated previously, a limited degree of interdependence will be a very valuable asset within the next three to five years.

The importance of associating with people you like may be especially important for people who are part of large, close families. As we will see in a few pages, there are many advantages for people of several generations within the same family working together because they share a common commitment to their mutual survival.

Division of Labor

More than simply shared effort, the division of labor creates an opportunity for each person to specialize in what he or she does best. In 1776, the father of classical economics, Adam Smith, described the economies of specialization in pin manufacturing. By dividing work into three specialized functions, a unit of three workers could produce almost twice as much as when the same three workers each had responsibility for manufacturing the entire pin. The marvels of mass manufacturing and the high-speed assembly line are testimony to the technical advantages of specialization.

While our society may have carried this specialization too far, division of labor would suggest that a single individual would not be expected to be an expert in each of the important survival skills that have been talked about in this book.

Tax Advantages

Several group retreats have been set up as religious organizations. For many years, established religious bodies have their well-planned retreats where members can go for seminars, meditation, or simple relaxation.

Several survival groups have decided to set up their retreats as nondenominational religious organizations in order to secure tax advantages. In this manner, the property is not taxed and contributions to the retreat by the various members are usually tax deductible. The nondenominational approach is less likely to be challenged by the IRS than those that are associated with an unusual religious viewpoint. As I write this, there is a case pending that involves the Liberation Church of California. They are being refused IRS recognition as a church and appear to have been chosen as a target to challenge nonconventional religious groups that have controversial tenets. With nondenominational groups, the government is left in a more tenuous position. There are at least 100 of these nondenominational retreats throughout the country. Challenges to nondenominational groups or established religious orders are risky for the government because it raises the specter of separation between church and state.

There are three unique approaches that I have seen work very effectively. The first is where the entire property is developed as part of a "religious retreat." The second is where individual members own their own residences and dedicate or contribute a part of the property to the church. This facility can be developed into a group meeting house, guest house, or office for members who want to work at the retreat. Members have access to this and share maintenance equipment or even recreational facilities. In some instances, the money to purchase or construct these items has been contributed by members and deducted as a charitable contribution. In other instances, members have contributed property or equipment and have received a sizeable tax deduction. Finally, some large group retreats have found additional tax advantages from incorporating as a city. This approach will be discussed in greater deatil in another portion of this chapter.

Time Savings

Many concerned individuals find it difficult to make the necessary retreat preparations because they are too involved with their own business or professional life to do the planning, find a suitable site, direct the construction, purchase equipment and supplies, and perform the other tasks that are necessary for a desirable retreat. Very few skilled professionals feel that they can justify taking off the necessary time to become their own carpenter, plumber, or realtor. At the same time, a group may be able to attract individuals with the specialized knowledge required to perform these tasks. Another alternative is for them to hire a specialist and share the cost. It is considerably less expensive for a builder to come in and erect five structures on one site than to build one house at an isolated location. On an individual basis, it is less expensive to excavate for 300 feet of underground water pipe on one site than to do excavation for 60 feet of piping on each of five locations.

Other Shared Economies

As previously indicated, land purchases can be made much more advantageously with the power of group purchases. The same is true in quantity purchase of dehydrated food, electrical equipment, ammunition, or almost anything else you will need in quantity. Prices will almost always decline with volume. When there is a backlog of orders, large purchases receive factory priority. A few years ago, Sears was able to obtain Michelin's new tubeless, steel, radial tire before they were available to Michelin's own dealers because of the tremendous power of their volume purchases.

Additionally, a well-equipped retreat will need many relatively expensive items such as chain-saws, farm equipment, canning supplies, and perhaps even hydroelectric generators or power equipment. If some of these items can be shared by a number of families, this will be much less expensive than if each couple has to attempt to provide a full range of equipment by themselves.

APPROACHES TO GROUP RETREATING

Group Retreating on Wheels

One novel approach to the group retreat is illustrated by the experience of a California-based group called Liber-Vans, which is a mobile group retreat. This is a collection of families who are equipped to function like a modernized gypsy colony. Each family owns its own recreational vehicle. Collectively, the group owns property in two or three sections of the country. At the present time, they enjoy alternating visits to the various retreat properties that they own. In the event of a crisis, they would congregate at the most convenient location. They could set up to remain at this location on a sustained basis, but at the same time maintain the flexibility to move to whatever other location they felt might be more appropriate. The Liber-Vans group has also built in the option to live abroad or set up on unused property that they do not own if this should be necessary.

Another similar group has actually purchased property on the Canadian border of the United States so they can cross in one direction or the other without having to worry about checkpoints and existing bureaucracy. They do not use this ability at the present time because it is illegal and unnecessary. Yet they have created the capacity to deal with a potential problem that might be tied to their survival under a particular scenario.

This type of mobility is especially important for people who expect communism to be a part of the ultimate crisis. There are other groups who fear that some totalitarian form of government may prevent them from practicing their religion. Consequently, they are concerned about their ability to get out of the United States and into the Canadian wilderness.

Obviously, the mobile group retreat, regardless of its equipment or design, has the tremendous advantage of flexibility and mobility. On the other hand, the cost of owning multiple recreational vehicles may be prohibitive for some groups. Others will want more protection for the investment required. Another important consideration is the energy dependency of most recreational vehicles.

The Extended Family

Margaret Mead, one of the world's most famous sociologists, has suggested that one of the major failings of contemporary life is the diminishing dimensions of family life. The current emphasis on the nuclear family with parents and young children eliminated some important dimensions that were previously associated with family living. A generation or so ago, it was not uncommon for a child to grow up in a living environment where grandparents, an unmarried uncle or aunt, parents, brothers and sisters, and perhaps a married older sibling with children lived together in the same house or at least on the same farm. While we tend to think of the lack of privacy and limited space, there are some important advantages that a child gains from this type of environment. Older relatives are able to provide wisdom from the past as well as a tie with the history and traditions of the family.

Young nephews and nieces provide an opportunity to learn some of the skills of child rearing. The presence of several adults of working age furnished much-needed manpower in managing the demands of life in a heartier era. At the same time, the presence of older members of this extended family offered a means of teaching and supervising children who were not old enough to assume their place in the fields.

This type of arrangement was often necessary in the farm-based society a few years ago. Today, variations on such an arrangement have several advantages for survival. Some of the family retreats that I know about today grew out of a concern that an older couple has developed. Because of their years of experience, they may be more concerned about the economic trends of the nation. In many instances, their married sons and daughters are caught up in the excitement of getting ahead and rearing their own families. Since the children have known nothing but prosperity, they may lack the perspective to perceive the need for retreating. In these instances, the older parents who have had more time to accumulate capital resources can build the family retreat with provisions for each of their grown children and their families. This facility may be a retirement home or simply a vacation home. The supposition is that the children are not willing to join in the survival efforts now, but will see the wisdom of their parents' decision when the cities are burning and there is looting in the streets.

Older parents who wish to move in this direction need to be aware of the danger of overselling relatives. Pushing too hard can easily raise suspicion of paranoia. Parents who are able to indicate that this is a matter of importance to them and are willing to share their convictions are more likely to experience a responsive reception that those who are ardent evangelists.

Most middle-class Americans are aware of family compounds that more wealthy citizens enjoy. During the Kennedy administration, the family home at Hyannisport was an exciting model for many families to envy. This type of arrangement could easily double as a vacation and survival retreat. The major danger is that an ideal vacation resort may not be the optimal place for depression survival. If survival retreating is one of your major concerns, you may be more reticent about sharing your facility or its location with vacationers and acquaintances.

In summary, the family compound is especially appropriate where parents are successful and wish to help or be close to their children. At the same time, there is an unusual degree of potential for disappointment if children display no interest or sympathy with their parents' beliefs. The chance for unequal effort (especially among in-laws) has the potential for conflict.

The Two-Family Compound

The union of two families who are willing to share a site, equipment, and other expensive facilities in a survival situation can afford some benefits if the families are compatible. As I have stressed previously, the desirability of sharing expense is an important advantage. If you decide to investigate this approach, I would strongly advise that your arrangements be kept on a businesslike basis to avoid potential conflicts. Be sure to plan a system for resolving conflicts before your first disagreement arises. Generally, shared living quarters are undesirable except in emergency conditions because they impose a tremendous strain on normal family relationships.

The Survival Commune

In every generation, communal living has attracted a number of followers. In theory, the idea has much to support it. Unfortunately, I know of few instances where this type of arrangement has had long-term success.

In my opinion, communal living has been successful only with families. Most everyone is willing to share their resources with their own children. Often, that generosity will extend to brothers, sisters, or parents. When it comes to acquaintances or strangers, trust and generosity tend to be somewhat restrained.

For some people, especially the young, communal living has been an exciting experiment—at least for short periods of time. I must confess to a personal bias against the premise, "From each according to his abilities, to each according to his needs." My personal value system is based on the premise that each individual should be rewarded in direct proportion to his or her contribution. In my experience, this has proved to be fairer and more productive than any other arrangement.

In conducting a research project for the Sloan Foundation, a university colleague of mine had the opportunity to visit the last truly communistic village in the Soviet Union. As he visited the agricultural community, the signs of its ultimate demise as a communistic experiment were already obvious. Cold Siberian mornings produced an unbelievable number of illnesses. People who dreaded facing the demands of the collective farming effort knew that their needs would be met from the community till. Unfortunately, this unproductiveness became so epidemic that there was insufficient food to go around at harvest time.

The same type of experience had something to do with the foundation of our historical Thanksgiving feast. Originally, the colonists had attempted a community farming effort. The harvest was so slim and the winter so cold that many of the original settlers died. The following year, it was decided that each family should have its own plot to cultivate. The result was a harvest so bountiful that the pilgrims were able to invite the local Indians to share in their feast of thanksgiving. While they were appropriately thankful to divine providence, which had sustained them in their efforts, there was also reason to be thankful for a better incentive system that allowed their individual efforts to be rewarded in accordance with their own productivity.

For a short period of time during an intense crisis, the communal approach to sharing responsibilities and resources might be a viable alternative. If this is your interest, I encourage you to read elsewhere. The bias of this book is too much toward the individualistic ethic to have answers to the questions you will raise.

Voluntary Survival Compounds

Having already explored the idea of an extended family gathering for extended survival, it is only natural that people who lack the family unity of interests could develop the same idea among individuals who share common interest values or religious beliefs. The basic idea is for a group of families to share a portion of their resources in the purchase of a particular piece of property. Depending on their own interest, they can erect a major structure that will provide housing for the entire group or they can erect individual residences while sharing a common security system, farm equipment, or a barn.

My first acquaintance with this concept came several years ago when I met with a group of six young professional families near Atlanta, Georgia. These individuals were able to purchase about twenty-three acres of property immediately adjacent to a state park. With the aid of one of the members who is an architect, they designed the entire facility along a common theme. Each family had its own house and small garden plot. The more affluent members of the group were able to build larger and more expensive homes. Collectively, they shared an orchard, a barn, a tractor, two small lakes, and a "church" building that doubles as a recreational building, part-time office, and guest house for the entire group. Individuals who used the facility most frequently for an office were expected to make larger "contributions" to their church. Since all of the individuals were members of a conservative, congregational religious group (Church of Christ) they experienced no difficulty in obtaining official recognition of their tax-exempt status. Since their particular religious group does not require seminary degrees or formal ordination, each family alternated serving in an official ministerial role. This meant that each year, a different family was entitled to receive a $300-per-month taxfree housing allowance.

When I first visited this facility, I was impressed with the aesthetic advantages of this cooperative effort. The entire property was landscaped along the lines of an old southern community. From the road facing this property only one of the smaller houses could be seen. Upon reaching the top of a small hill where this house was located, you could see a narrow roadway leading down into a very large stand of tall pine trees. Along the roadway were numerous pecan and fruit trees, their whitewashed trunks guarding the approach to the compound. As I passed through the pine grove, I saw the remaining five houses built around two small lakes. The roadway led between the two lakes, over a dam where a replica of an old-fashioned covered bridge had been erected. The church building, which resembled no other church structure I have ever seen, was built on a small peninsula that extended into the larger of the two lakes. It commanded an imposing view of both lakes that were rimmed with weeping willow and dogwood trees. The roadway ended with the group of houses, but a pathway led over the hill into another valley where a community barn housed six cows and four horses. Only after I had gained the trust of this ingenious group did they share some of their protective planning with me. By combining resources, they had been able to erect a much more extensive fence than any individual family could have afforded. Two of the peaceful-appearing collies who roamed the property were trained to attack any uninvited visitors who penetrated the area. An almost completely concealed cave had been dug in the rear hill of the property. While this commanded a view of all of the houses, it also contained an extensive food supply and a sizable collection of weapons.

In this instance, the compound served as the major residence for each of the families. Six individuals held full-time jobs in Atlanta, approximately thirty miles away. Car-pooling was used to conserve energy in the daily trips to work and taking the children to school.

A group of individuals with greater financial resources could use the same concept to develop a retreat that was apart from their primary residence.

Commercial Survival Compound

Unless you are fortunate enough to have four to eight close friends who share concerns and interests, you will find it very difficult to develop a voluntary survival compound like I have just described. In this case, your best alternative may be a commercial survival development. To illustrate this idea, I will share the experience of a psychologist in the Midwest who decided to combine the best tenets of retreat planning and private enterprise in his own commercial development.

After examining various pieces of property for over a year, this psychologist was able to find an eighty-acre farm being offered for $32,000. After negotiating with the owner, he was able to secure the property for $24,000 plus an agreement that allowed the owner a life tenancy on the family farm. Through conversations with the Department of Agriculture, this individual was able to secure federal assistance in building a five-acre lake by damming up a small stream that ran through the center of the property. His own expenditure for this lake was slightly less than $3,500. By spending an additional house to the lake. He then proceeded to sell six eight-acre plots with lake frontage for $12,000 each. Next, he made a charitable contribution of eight acres to a nondenominational church, which he had helped to incorporate. The value of the adjoining property had already been established, so he was able to claim a $12,000 contribution. Since he was in a 40 percent tax bracket, this translated to another $4,800 in income for him. In other words, he had spent a total of $31,-700 on the retreat. His income from sales and tax savings amounted to $76,800. Through some simple planning and judgment, he found himself with a clear title to twenty-four acres of property and with over $45,000 to spend for his own retreat. Ultimately, he persuaded the other residents of the compound to help him erect a common facility that served as the church and recreational area. As the "minister" of this church, he received a taxfree housing allowance. Later, he was able to rent the facility at a nominal price for seminars and group sessions at the retreat. While an optimal arrangement as far as cash flow, he lost much of the secrecy that is typically associated with a retreat setting. Your own approach to a commercial survival compound can be as varied as your own imagination and particular situation demands.

Commercial Survival Community

Anyone who has read Ayn Rand's monumental *Atlas Shrugged* has doubtless daydreamed about the desirability of living in a community like Hidden Valley. This, as you may recall, was the community that the producers of society finally retreated to when they became tired of supporting an unproductive majority in their own cities and towns. Although Rand fails to describe the financial arrangements surrounding Hidden Valley, I am confident that this was organized as a profit-making project according to the best tenets of private enterprise.

At the time I was preparing this chapter, Don Stephens and some co-developers were putting together a commercial survival community in the Pacific Northwest. They plan to accommodate sixty communities. "Mountain Haven" is envisioned as a complete survival city. The total property will be broken down into five clusters of eight to twelve families that would live around a common square or circle. Each family within the group will be capable of self-sufficiency in terms of food and other essentials. They also have the potential of trading for things that they choose not to produce for themselves or that someone else could produce better.

Stephens described the basic design of these clusters as a "natural doughnut." While each family has access to five to ten acres, this will not be evenly spaced out over the entire property. Central areas will be developed into homesites and there will be surrounding areas of natural timber and foliage that isolate the entire community from the outside world. If an outsider wandered onto the property for 200 or 300 feet, there would be no indication of developments.

In addition to the obvious advantages of combined strength and proximity to individuals with common interests and values, the concept of a survival city has many additional advantages. First, if a group incorporates as a city, they are able to eliminate a level of taxation. By providing a school, firefighting facilities, and police department, they are not obligated to pay for the same services that may be provided by the county. This obviously is more practical when the group is planning to reside in the retreat area on a permanent basis rather than waiting to move there as a last resort. The possibility of establishing an independent police department has additional advantages for people who are extremely concerned about security. A police department, no matter how small, has access to fully automatic weapons and other firearms that are not available to the general public. Legally, all members of the community can be deputized so that they can carry concealed weapons. The idea of a whole town composed of deputies may be frightening to some, but other individuals have found this reassuring.

If the idea of a survival community appeals to you, you can start from scratch and build your own small community and then apply for incorporation. Another approach is to buy a city. Occasionally, a real estate agent will offer an entire town for sale. Typically, these consist of nothing more than a grocery store and perhaps a small motel with three or four cabins. There may be a post office and a couple of other houses. In my opinion, the difficulty of locating a town for sale plus the likelihood that the location will not be ideally suited to security make this an interesting, but not very practical alternative. There are, however, at least two group retreats that have utilized this approach.

One of the most original approaches to a retreat community is represented by the person who read that the General

Accounting Office of the U.S. Government was offering an obsolete missile site for sale. This individual arranged to purchase this site for less than 10 percent of its original value. To the government, it was simply an obsolete silo with little tax value. The developer decided to maintain the government character of the entire installation. He maintained the original "No Trespass" government signs and attempted to maintain the facility so that it looks like a real government installation. The group even maintains a guard in khakies to discourage intruders. Since much of the installation is below ground, the group has almost an optimal degree of protection.

YOUR STRATEGIC RETREAT

In the military when one person runs for cover, it looks like cowardice, but when a squadron or group of people move back together we view it as a strategic retreat. By using the principles developed in the previous two chapters, you can make your retreat a strategic move that will provide for survival and strength. The biggest battles of the future will be survival. Begin now to develop your strategy, practice maneuvers, and prepare to defend your personal, physical, psychological, and financial resources. The world's oldest form of defense is not kung fu or karate. It is the time-honored tradition of running from a situation that is totally overpowering. I remember hearing of a pragmatic Confederate recruit who refused a cavalry appointment because, "When I get ready to retreat, I don't want no horse slowing me down." Retreating may be contrary to the tradition of the Alamo, yet, "He who turns and runs away, lives to fight another day."

Section Four

HOW TO FACE THE FUTURE WITHOUT FEAR

CHAPTER TWELVE

Countdown to Armageddon

To students of Biblical prophecy, the term *Armageddon* refers to the scene of the final battle between the forces of good and evil as prophesied in Revelation 16 to occur at the end of the world. More generally, the word refers to any decisive battle in which there is great destruction. Certainly, we are entering into a period where there will be a decisive battle between the positive and negative forces in our society. There will be many casualties in this conflict, and the destruction of a way of life.

The purpose of this chapter is to identify a series of steps that will enable you to avoid being one of these casualties. In many ways, this chapter is a summary of everything that has gone before. Recommendations that are made throughout the book will be briefly mentioned here without the support and documentation contained in previous chapters. Several steps are outlined that you need to take immediately. Others can wait for as long as six months. Several signs are suggested that will indicate that the curtain is about to go up on the greatest economic depression of your lifetime. Finally, I will suggest some things you could do to survive this depression and to help you move through it to a new era of prosperity.

TAKE TIME FOR AN IMMEDIATE CHECKUP

In business management, any description of the planning process begins with an assessment of the current situation. Knowing where you are is just as important as knowing where you want to go. This assessment or checkup should include every area of your life that is important to you.

1. *Your health:* If you have not had a complete physical checkup in the past year, make an appointment immediately. Make this examination complete enough that you know that it is safe for you to begin a program of vig-

253

orous physical activity. This activity will be required for you to get in top physical condition and do the variety of jobs that may be associated with other parts of your planning. Critically assess your physical condition and the habits that relate to your health. This will enable you to do a better job of planning for the various supplies that you may need for survival.

2. *Your food and water supply:* How would you survive if your regular food and water supply were cut off? Decide how much and what kinds of food you want to stock. Compare prices and quality of competing approaches and sources. Begin to develop a stockpile immediately. Keep some at your primary residence and a larger amount at a retreat location. After developing your alternative water supply, be sure that you have a means of purification.

3. *Review your physical security:* Contact a member of your police department or a security consultant to evaluate your current residence. Call a locksmith and ask him to make some changes that make your home safer and more secure. At the same time, begin to consider where you want to be during the forthcoming depression. This may involve some basic thinking about moving your principal residence or developing a survival retreat.

4. *Intellectual inventory:* Based on a consideration of the kinds of knowledge you would need to survive an economic catastrophe, what courses should you take as part of your personal preparations? Review the books recommended in the bibliography that follows the next chapter. Decide which of these resources are most important for your well-being.

5. *A psychological review:* Subject your own mental health to the same type of assessment that you give your physical surroundings. You may need to devote special attention to some key relationships. Perhaps some psychological counseling would be helpful for you as an individual or your family. Don't forget about the contribution of a meaningful religious conviction.

In working with business clients, I recommend that the Chief Executive Officer spend a weekend at some isolated setting once each year to review the current status of the organization and to develop plans for the immediate and long-range future. The same type of advice is appropriate for individuals and families. In either case, if you fail to plan, you are planning to fail. I urge you to make a commitment to develop a detailed plan for your family's future within one month of reading this material. If you are unable to spend eight to ten hours on this important activity within thirty days, the chances are very good that you will not get around to taking the steps that could insure your safety and survival. Each of the actions recommended in the following paragraph should bea part of your short-range plans. Ideally, you should resolve to initiate each of the recommended actions within six months of the present time.

PHASE I: DO IT NOW

Fitness

1. Improve your eating habits. As suggested in Chapter Seven, begin to develop good nutritional habits that will enable you to feel better and perform more effectively whether we experience feast or famine in the future. Remember the two-sentence summary of good nutrition, "Avoid foods with chemical additives or refined sugar and flour. Eat as many natural foods (especially fruit, vegetables, and nuts) as you can and two tablespoons of miller's bran each day."
2. Start a regular exercise program. If the physical examination recommended above indicates that you can safely begin an exercise program, you have no excuse for being physically unfit. Remember, the best exercise you can do is the one that you will do. Choose a program that will provide for good muscle tone as well as cardiovascular conditioning.

Finance

1. Buy one bag of pre-1965 coins immediately. Plan to make additional purchases of silver coins (up to one bag per family member) as soon as possible.
2. Watch for additional buy signs. No matter what the price of silver coins when you read this book, you

should make arrangements for at least one bag. Add additional silver and a few gold coins as your resources allow and whenever the prevailing price drops below 90 percent of the past year's high.

3. Set up a foreign account. Begin immediately to explore your preferences for a foreign account. You may want your account to be maintained in Swiss francs or Japanese yen. Decide if you want your account in the Bahamas, Switzerland, or some other haven. Then, take the necessary actions to open the account even it if has to be a very small one at the beginning.

4. Evaluate investment diamonds. If your resources are sufficient, review the principles of diamond selection as suggested in Chapter Six. Explore avenues for purchase that seem most convenient and reasonable for you. Arrange for purchase and storage of your gems.

Your Survival Retreat

1. Start a victory garden. As soon as possible, start to develop some experience in growing some portion of your own food. It may merely involve putting a tomato plant in a window box outside your high-rise apartment. Expand this experience as soon as possible. Consider the advantages of organic gardening in your plans.

2. Check out retreat property. If your previous analysis causes you to conclude that you do need to plan a retreat, start shopping for desirable property immediately. Even if you lack sufficient financial resources at the moment, the experience you gain in learning to evaluate property and prices will be extremely valuable. Having access to a retreat property will be an important foundation when you begin some of the other activities that follow.

3. Buy at least a six-month supply of food. Regardless of whether you decide to utilize a wholesale grocer and purchase cans of conventional food or the preferable route of storing dehydrated foods, secure your basic six-month supply immediately. As your resources and facilities permit, expand this supply to whatever level you feel will be most appropriate for your needs.

4. Stockpile other basic supplies. Make a list of the other items that you feel will be necessary during the du-

ration. Be sure that you have adequate water (and means to purify it), medical supplies, batteries, and eye glasses. Carry a small notebook with you and jot down items that you think of at stop lights or in the middle of the night.

5. Purchase weapons for hunting and protection. Unlike some survival experts, I do not recommend an extensive arsenal for protection. If possible, however, you should have personal access to a 12-gauge shotgun, a rifle, and a handgun (perferably a .45 caliber automatic).

6. Develop provisions for communications. Purchase or adapt your CB or Ham radio equipment for battery capability. Start monitoring police, fire, coast guard, or military channels. In addition to providing good experience, this can substantially broaden your knowledge of what is really going on in society.

Intellectual and Psychological Preparation

1. Purchase a basic survival library. After reviewing the basic bibliography contained at the end of this book, purchase the references that you feel would be most helpful for you. Items marked with an asterisk have my priority recommendation for your basic library. Having these books on your shelves will not help at all unless you actually take time to read them. Books on many of the specialized topics discussed in this manuscript will provide more details than a comprehensive book like this one can do.

2. Start a positive meditation program. Using the principles suggested in Chapter Seven, begin a practice of meditation and affirmation. Meditation will provide relief from stress that accompanies modern life and the affirmation program will help program your subconscious for a more positive approach to living.

3. Monitor key relationships. Guard against the tendency to become so caught up in professional pursuits or preparations for an economic depression that you undermine some of the most important relationships in life. Proper retreat preparations should enhance your family relationships. Yet undue obsession with any aspect of your preparation can alienate your family members.

4. Mention your concern to three or four of your best friends. Don't become so evangelical that you alienate those associates. Mention your personal plans and perhaps give them a copy of this or some similar book as a birthday or Christmas present. This is about as much as you can safely do without endangering the relationships that are important in the present.

5. Enroll in helpful courses. Through the continuing education program of a local college or other community organization, you should be able to identify numerous evening courses that can provide much needed information. To help cope with headaches created by concern about the future, take one or two courses every six months. This will make you a better-informed and more competent individual.

6. Practice your escape plan. If you plan to survive the depression in some retreat setting, don't assume that you will be able to drive to that location on major highways. Get a detailed map of your surroundings and identify secondary roads that will lead to your destination. Earthquakes may make some roads impassable, and civil disorder will almost certainly create obstacles to your usual mobility.

7. Test your plans. At least once a year, I suggest that you and your family plan to live for a week off the supplies that you have provided. This will enable you to test the completeness and palatability of your provisions. Avoid the temptation to prepare for this exercise by extra stocking of the refrigerator. If you plan to retreat with a group of individuals, you should practice this temporary exercise together and compare results. You may even want to try bartering for the items you have overlooked in your planning.

8. Practice your survival skills. Camping is good exercise to provide practice in self-sufficiency. In addition to being a wholesome family activity, it provides you with a chance to practice surviving without electricity and modern conveniences. Your children may even gain an appreciation of bathtubs and running water after a few days of hauling water from a stream. After you have developed the skills of camping and foraging, you might attempt an actual survival trek where you survive on

the resources you are able to find in a wilderness setting.

HOW TO KNOW WHEN IT'S TIME TO MOVE

Have you ever sat in the audience of a musical production waiting for the curtain to rise? You wait expectantly for an indication that the main event is about to begin. The overture to this depression has been an extended one. Astute observers have long recognized that an economic and societal breakdown was likely. I believe that the ultimate depression will not happen until we have lived through another apparent economic recovery and an additional siege of very high inflation. There are several key events that may provide a warning signal that the collapse is coming. While I anticipate that this will be between 1982 and 1985, the presence of any three of the following factors in any six-month period will be a warning to me that I should begin to move aggressively to a defensive position.

1. Double-digit inflation for a period in excess of one year.
2. The Dow Jones average drops below 600.
3. Three major cities are unable to meet their bond issues, and Congress is unable or unwilling to bail them out.
4. Three major banks fold, using up all of the reserves of the Federal Deposit Insurance Corporation.
5. Major crop failures reduce the nation's food stockpile below the 1974 level of a twenty-three-day supply
6. Two U.S. cities are hit by major earthquakes.
7. Rioting and major guerilla activity break out in three U.S. cities.
8. Unemployment rises above 10 percent of the work force.
9. The government outlaws foreign bank accounts or ownership of gold for private citizens.
10. An extended nationwide strike of teamsters, police, firemen, or longshoremen.
11. The federal deficit moves above $80 billion.
12. Winter storms immobilize three or more major cities during a power failure.

In my opinion, the presence of any one of these events increases the probability of a major economic breakdown by 10 percent. Two or more of these events occurring within a six-month period would raise the probability of a depression by 25 percent. Whenever three of these warning signals exist simultaneously, I believe that the chance for an imminent depression rises by 50 percent. Whenever this happens, I plan to move immediately to put my contingency preparations into operation.

AFTER THE CRASH

When the signs mentioned above and your own judgment convince you that the crash has begun, you will need to begin your last-minute preparations with a genuine sense of urgency. Unless you are in the center of an urban ghetto, there will probably be a few days where you can take care of some last-minute details.

1. Eliminate existing financial risk. Despite warnings of the precarious economic circumstances that prevail, most people will still have a significant number of their assets in paper dollars. Additionally, there will be debts that may have some contingent liability. Once the signal for a retreat has been sounded, move quickly to gain as much liquidity as possible to clear up your debt obligations.
2. Move more fully into hard currencies. At this late date, the prices for gold and silver coins will be exorbitant. Nevertheless, when you see that the last obstacles to a full-scale depression have been removed, you should begin trading in your dollars, even if you have to swap a wheelbarrow full of them for a few pieces of survival currency. At this point, I would not be interested in contracts or receipts for silver or gold in some distant location. I will want to take immediate possession of items I have previously trusted someone else to hold. Some people who have made extensive preparations for a depression by purchasing through a trusted financial organization in a distant city may be left with receipts that are as worthless as their paper dollars.
3. Finalize your food supply. Make whatever last-minute adjustments you can. Expect supermarket prices to be

at their highest as other people are beginning to realize what you have been anticipating for some time.

4. Begin your retreat. The decision to leave for your retreat will be one of the most difficult you have ever made. Many individuals will wait just a little too long as they try to earn a few more dollars to see them through the crisis. In some ways, people who lose their jobs early in the crisis or experience a business failure will be fortunate because this will provide them with the incentive to move to their contingency plans. When your city begins to be affected by rioting, looting, and massive civil disobedience, it is a good time to take whatever vacation you may have coming. If you own your own business, close it down for a few days or delegate authority for security and operations to a subordinate. Promise this subordinate a major promotion if the operation is successfully managed during the crisis. If he or she succeeds, they will have earned the promotion and gained some very valuable experience. More importantly, you will be out of the line of danger during a critical period.

5. Prepare to protect your resources. While you will want to delegate authority for protecting resources in critically dangerous locations, you will need to make provisions for other resources as well. Hide the majority of your precious metals and gems where an intruder will not find them. You should keep a few coins handy for your own use and to convince an intruder who may penetrate your other defenses that he has found your reserves. Regardless, whatever defense method you have decided to use, this will be the time to put them into operation. Extreme diligence will be required during the first few days of the crisis. Gradually, the violence will become more sporadic.

6. Keep a low profile. In the first chaotic weeks, you should avoid showing any signs of your comfort or preparedness. It will be far better to look poor while living rich. Ostentatious living will not merely create enmity among the less fortunate, it will move your name to the head of the list for potential robbery or looting victims.

7. Look for co-survivalists. As the initial tensions subside,

a new order of life will be established. If you have not made plans for a group retreat, you will want to identify individuals with common interests. You and these other individuals may be able to swap resources, join in mutual assistance, and provide the basis for restoring order.

8. Look for opportunities. As the new order begins to emerge, there will be countless opportunities for building personal wealth. As has always been true, individuals with good survival skills and a keen eye for opportunity will see many exciting prospects for success. There is no reason to feel guilty about your ability to profit from an unpleasant situation. Society will need producers and doers much more than guilt-stricken penitents. Your opportunities will provide a means of helping individuals. This assistance will not be in the form of giving your resources to the less fortunate. Instead, you shoul plan to exchange some of your resources for the assistance that other people can offer you. This will be the basis on which the new order of society will emerge.

9. Exercise leadership. In the past few years, our society has appeared to be vaccinated by an "antileadership" vaccine. On a national and local basis, we have lacked the strong, vibrant leadership that historically was a part of this nation. Crisis has always brought out the best in exceptional people. The ability to survive and prosper during the coming depression will sharpen the leadership skills that you already possess. Plan to use these skills in a positive, productive manner to help rebuild a civilization out of the economic ruins of our past mistakes.

10. Be thankful. Those individuals who come through the trials of the coming depression will have many reasons to be thankful. You should be thankful for the good sense to have prepared for a crisis and appreciative of the physical and intellectual capabilities that enabled you to prepare for these problems. Be thankful too, to have been spared the unavoidable catastrophes that will strike some well-prepared people. Some individuals will be thankful to God for providing their deliverance. Others will be grateful for their own initia-

tive and insight. Another group will recognize that their survival and prosperity came from their diligent efforts to utilize and expand their God-given abilities and talents.

CHAPTER THIRTEEN

Invent Your Own Future

In our journey through this book, you and I have come a long way together. Most of the scenery on our trip has been rather unpleasant. If you are feeling a little pessimistic, I can't blame you. And yet, I hope you do not view pessimism as the pervading theme of the book.

Let's be honest with each other. There is no way any book can shatter the placid complacency of a truly contented person. You wouldn't have picked this book unless you, too, were concerned about the economic future of western civilization. Now that you have faced up to your own anxiety and discovered that there are valid reasons for concern, I hope that you are left with a determination to use your newly acquired knowledge to make a potentially unpleasant situation as positive as possible.

The kind of pessimism I advocate is actually optimistic realism that recognizes the complexities of our world, but moves on to survival and prosperity.

Richard Lovelace once wrote, "Stone walls do not a prison make, nor iron bars a cage." In a similar way, a declining dollar need not create a personal depression. In the coming crisis, I am more interested in helping you avoid personal depression than economic depression. By this time, I hope you have accepted my premise that a severe economic adjustment is essential.

There is an immutable law that both individuals and nations must reap what they sow. This country has sown the wind of financial irresponsibility, it must reap the whirlwind of economic catastrophe. In the United States, we have been intoxicated with the abundance of our vineyards, but the days of wine and roses have ended. There's got to be a morning after when we awaken to a Herculean hangover with economic headaches for nations, cities, and families.

Do you remember the fable about the ant and the grasshopper? During the warmth of the spring and summer, the grasshopper had a glorious time, while the ant was busy making preparations for the cold, barren days of a winter that he believed was inevitable. This ant must have appeared rather paranoid. While the ant seemed quite happy with his disciplined approach to preparation, the grasshopper was on a perpetual high. With the advance of autumn, the ant's vision seemed more reasonable. But the grasshopper kept arguing that the weather was a temporary aberration. "We had a cool spell last May," he recalled, "but things got warm again. There is really nothing serious to worry about."

That's how it is today. It is no longer summer. Fall is in the air. You can continue to ignore the warning signs or you can begin, even at this late date, to make preparation. Whether you prepare or not, the winter will be cold. No amount of personal preparation will postpone the killing frost, but preparation can make survival possible and perhaps even pleasant.

I believe that the winter will be severe, and I am planning accordingly. If it turns out to be milder than anticipated, so much the better. My retreat will still be a pleasant place to spend weekends. The vegetables I grow will be tastier and healthier than anything I can buy in a store. Investments in gold, silver and diamonds will have held their value and appreciated, and my supply of food will save many a trip to the grocery store to purchase supplies that are certain to cost even more in the future.

THE FUTURE OF THE FUTURE

John McHale has suggested that, "The future of the future is in the present." Individuals have greater flexibility than large organizations, such as governments. Consequently, we can make adaptations much more quickly. This nation's stage is already set for the next act. As an individual, you can still make some adjustments.

There is a Chinese proverb that says, "All the flowers of all the tomorrows lie in the seeds of today." A uniquely human characteristic of man is that we can make the future what we would like it to become. Perhaps not totally, but we do invent our own futures.

Let's pause a moment for a bit of perspective. A noted public figure has said, "Politicians have strained their ingenuity to discover new sources of revenue. They have broadened perilously the field of income and property tax. When I was a boy, wealth was regarded as secure and admirable, but now a man has to defend himself for being rich as if it were a crime." The speaker was not a right-wing businessman. It was Socrates, who lived about 400 years before Christ, speaking as he surveyed the scene in ancient Greece.

· Professor Nathan Adler, a prominent psychologist at the University of California, Berkeley, and an expert on youthful dissent, rebellion, and anarchy has described a particular youth group:

> They were long-haired and young, wore wild, bright-colored clothing, sometimes they frolicked nude in the streets, chanting obscenities at their elders—and consumed generous amounts of dope. Reared during an age of doomsday-oriented crises, they were protesting the growing materialism of their parents' generation.

The description is familiar, but he was not describing college campuses of a decade ago. He was simply discussing the "Bouzingos," a French youth movement in the 1830's. Dr. Adler comments:

> At the decline and fall of Rome, during the Renaissance and the Reformation, during the French Revolution and the Napoleonic Wars—during each of these periods, we find a social movement and a personality style that emphasizes intuition, immediacy, and self-actualization, and transcendences.

A review of history often causes the observer to conclude that people have always been pessimistic about the future. There is a natural temptation to say that since the world has survived other critical periods, why should we worry about the crisis that confronts us today? During each of the periods where there was the kind of breakdown in order such as Dr. Adler has described, we find that it signaled the end of an era. Life goes on. People continue to survive, but the world is not the same.

This book was written to help you understand why things are going wrong and how the ultimate collapse will occur. More importantly, it can serve as a blueprint for an ark that can provide safe passage for you, your family, and your possessions during the flood of imminent calamities. Unlike any other book on the market, it gives guidelines and suggestions in a variety of key areas: personal investment and finance, family protection, health and nutrition, retreat planning, and survival skills. With this outline, you can begin to build your own personalized defense system, you can and must be the master of your fate, the captain of your soul.

If I can convince you that you don't have to be dependent on anyone else to solve your problems, a major purpose in writing this book will be satisfied. Our society has taught us a variety of subtle forms of dependency. We depend on other people to teach our children, cook an increasing number of our meals, perform a multitude of minor services for us, guarantee our finances and even pass judgment on whether or not our life style is satisfactory. No one has forced this dependency on us. We have freely and voluntarily given up our birthright of individuality and self-sufficiency.

There is nothing wrong in letting other people do things for us. The danger is that we may lose the ability to care for ourselves and thus become dependent upon an undependable source of support. The millions who are dependent upon the government for one form of aid or another are a dramatic illustration of this problem. Although many people fail to recognize the symptoms, a very similar problem is the majority of citizens who are dependent upon other people for approval and acceptance. David Riseman calls these the "other directed" people. When you think about it, it is rather absurd to realize how much we worry if other people are going to approve or legitimize our dress, our behavior, our life styles. How far this is removed from nature. Animals seem to accept their stripes or characteristics with no apparent concern. They are what they are. Therefore, they must be what they are supposed to be. No one ever worries that a cat's coloration is definitely lower middle class, or that a dog is only a mediocre barker. Yet we apply those judgments to ourselves and to others on a regular basis.

Self-sufficiency and independency can be the keys to a happy tomorrow regardless of how the scenario of the 1980's unfolds. You will find happiness and contentment only if you feel fully capable of standing on your own two feet. That's really what maturity is all about. No person is a mature adult as long as he or she depends on other people to solve problems and give approval or credence.

For years, I devoted my energies to building a professional

reputation as a business educator and consultant. Why should I take time to care for my yard, reasoned I, when my hourly consulting fees were thirty times what the yard man charged. By devoting every waking hour to my professional activity, I developed an outstanding professional reputation and a bland one-dimensional life. At some point (I don't even remember the catalyst), I decided that if the world I had come to know were to change significantly, I would be totally unable to function. I was counting too much on a professional reputation that would have very little value if my worth were measured for the number of practical things I was capable of doing. As I began to take time to do some things for myself, a remarkable transformation began to take place. First I found that my happiness was no longer dependent upon the approval of other people. I began to practice making decisions that I thought were truly best instead of doing what I thought other people would approve. My worry and anxiety declined and my zest for life grew dramatically.

Make no mistake, this can be a frightful transition. Some of the people that you think are your very best friends may choose to reject you. Even if you held leadership positions in your church, you may find that your involvement is approved only as long as you are so dependent upon the group that you are willing to accept its decisions without questioning. You may find that your parents, spouse, and children prefer a person who can be manipulated in predictable ways. You may find that out of a multitude of acquaintances, you have only a few friends who are worthy of the name. But those friends are the ones with whom you can build a life that matters.

A search for self-sufficiency cost me dearly. A marriage of sixteen years collapsed and with it the financial accumulation of a very successful career. My former wife and children moved halfway across the country, and I started over from scratch in a new town. Despite the initial loneliness and pain, it was invigorating to find that I could establish relationships with people who knew nothing of my professional accomplishments. Moreover, new relationships that were formed on this basis were almost immediately deeper than the so-called friendships developed over the past decade or two.

A key turning point came when I met a woman who had gone through the same type of experience. At our first meeting, we talked for hours about our mutual concerns and dreams. Each of us admitted wanting a retreat where we could provide a degree of independence against potential calamities while enjoying a life style that this would provide. As days went by, an important relationship began to emerge, but I wasn't content with the progress we were making. Casually, one evening, I gave her a copy of two of the best books I had written. She accepted them graciously and put them away. I was a little bit disappointed, but fully expected a report during the next day or two on how superb they were. A couple of weeks later, when I had heard nothing, my curiosity forced me to ask. It was devastating to learn that she hadn't even begun to read them. Evidently my look of hurt disbelief prompted an explanation. "Look," she said, "I want to be impressed with you as a person, not with your balloons."

I didn't know what she meant by the phrase *balloons,* so she explained, "Most people try to get by on their balloons. It may be money, good looks, or achievements. These are really nice to have, but it is dangerous to fall in love with the balloons rather than the real person. The balloons are nice for a while, but they won't support a real relationship."

A lot of things fell into place with that explanation. Balloons look pretty on festive occasions, but when problems arise, balloons don't contribute much to the solution. Only by being independent can you have something of value to offer when you give yourself. Otherwise, you merely offer a pale imitation of the real thing. It may be smoother and prettier, but it doesn't have the substance or potential of the genuine article.

THE MANAGEMENT OF TOMORROW

Several years ago, I was reading the magazine published by the World Future Society and noticed a reference to a graduate-level business course entitled, "The Management of Tomorrow." I contacted the professor who developed the course at Georgia State University and found that his students were exposed to projections about the future of management practice as well as techniques for managing the future. This latter objective is what I want to provide for you. You cannot change the world, but you can have a tremendous impact on your portion of it. With informed judgment and common sense, you can manage the future rather than being ruled by it.

Take a look at that word, *Management.* I had taught the subject and practiced it for years before I ever saw the richness that is contained within the word itself. You remember the little game the children used to play in seeing how many more words they could find in a larger one. The most important concepts of management are contained within the word itself.

The first three letters suggest the importance of the individual. Great business organizations have been described as the lengthened shadow of a single individual. Certainly, this book has stressed the importance that you as an individual will have in inventing your own future and assuming responsibility for the kind of life you seek. It is impossible for me to stress too much the importance of depending upon that individual that looks back at you from the mirror each morning. Ralph Waldo Emerson summed up his "Essays on Self-Reliance" by saying, "Trust thyself, every heart vibrates to that iron string. Accept the place that divine providence has found for you; the society of your contemporaries, the connection of events."

Five hundred years before Christ, Buddha said, ". . . whosoever shall be a lamp unto themselves and a refuge unto themselves . . . shall reach the very topmost height." Neither of these two great thinkers was suggesting that success would come easily. Your intelligence, planning, and effort must be combined with self-trust to make the difference. I agree with Cervantes: "No man is more than another unless he does more than another." This is your challenge: to do more than your contemporaries in anticipating the problems that lie ahead and, by doing this, to provide protection for those who are important to you and thus to be an example for others to emulate.

If you look toward the end of the word manage*ment* you'll notice that successful management involves others. Independence and self-sufficiency doesn't have to mean total isolation. You gain tremendous strength when you know that your success and survival are not dependent upon other people. Yet, life is much more pleasant when it is shared by strong, independent and caring friends. It is also a great deal easier to share work and responsibilities with other people. Chapter Eleven stressed the importance of cooperation and team play in survival planning. True cooperation can take place only between equals, neither of whom has advocated personal initiative to the other. These relationships are not common, but there is no other type that is fit for the human being. I refuse to accept the fact that there can be a good master or a good slave.

The original concept of private enterprise provides an ideal example of the kind of cooperation I am describing. The butcher, baker, and candlestick maker each handles an individual talent, activity, know-how and goal. Their hours and operations may be very different, but each is free to pursue an interest in a way that preference or personality suggests. Each is clearly responsible for the quality of his own product and is entitled to whatever degree of success or failure is generated by these efforts. While this may seem to describe a great deal of independence, each is cooperating with the other since eventually each must exchange goods and services with the other in order to improve his standard of living.

Exchanging ideas, efforts, time, or talent with another person because it is a desirable choice for both of you is a far cry from depending upon someone for charity or feeling responsible for an individual who is unable or refuses to care for himself. There is not room or time in your life for you to truly share the essence of life with many people. Jess Lair described the vast improvement in his life now that he has five or six friends instead of boasting of having five hundred people on his Christmas card list. In his popular book, *I Ain't Well, But I Sure Am Better,* Lair proposes that the ideal arrangement for a human being is to have five or six human beings that are so important that a good job offer in a distant state would not even be a temptation to move away from them.

The first four letters of the word *mana*gement form a Polynesian word used by the Swiss psychologist Carl Jung to describe the aura projected by people who are in touch with themselves and the world around them. I would translate the term *mana* as "the charisma of excellence." Doubtless, you have known people who exuded this quality. Regardless of the situation, they seem to be sufficiently confident of their own abilities that they have provided a rallying point for others.

Charisma is a quality that cannot be bottled, sold, or taught. Yet the assurance that comes with awareness and preparation provides much of the confidence and competence that is associated with this attribute. Once you have taken the steps outlined in this book, I can assure you that you will observe the darkening clouds of economic and social disorder with a kind of serene confidence that conveys to everyone that you are managing your own tomorrow.

Peter Drucker has said that we live in the age of management. Professional managers run most of the large organizations in our society. Few individuals know the names of the chief executives who run giant corporations such as IBM, General Motors, and Exxon. While outstandingly competent individuals, none of them is known in the same way that the dynamic entrepreneurs who founded these organizations were.

As a leading writer in the field of management, Drucker has suggested that the time of talking about management has ended. It is now time to practice it. That is certainly true in the area of business and governmental organizations, and even more imperative when applied to your personal predicament. This book cannot be described as a Distant Early Warning system. As I prepare the manuscript, I fear that our economic problems may accelerate even faster than I have anticipated, causing this book to appear too late to give you a chance to act on my recommendations. Whenever you read these words, I assure you it is time for action, rather than an age of contemplation.

Perhaps the most significant message contained in the word *management* is in the first eight letters of the word. An almost plaintive plea implores manage me! The french novelist Francois Rabelais expressed this sentiment in the 16th century:

> How shall I be able to rule over others if I have not full power and command of myself?

An inscription on the ancient temple at Delphi said, "Know thyself." The Grecian guide to self-knowledge is deceptively simple. The great Spanish novelist Cervantes recognized its complexity and added a key phrase. He said, "To know thyself is the most difficult lesson of life." You obviously know more facts about yourself than anyone else. Yet, the truth of knowledge can elude those who know all the facts. The key to understanding the people in the world around you is to start with yourself.

The maxim "Know thyself" looks good on paper. But if you have tried it, you know that one of the greatest hurdles is

eing able to see yourself objectively. We all have built-in bi-
ses about who and what we are. These biases can color our
elf-images until we really cannot accurately weigh our own
bilities. It is very difficult to see ourselves as others see us.
n the same way, we often cannot be objective about our
motional selves because we have built up defenses that hinder
ccurate self-evaluations.

Our insight about ourselves usually contains a number of
convenient blind spots. The individual who can see, much less
peak freely and honestly, on his faults and abilities is rare.

Several years ago, Frankie Szymanski, a star center on
Notre Dame's football team gained a reputation for humility.
Although he was outstanding on both defense and offense and
ad been named to most of the All-American teams, he was
ever heard to brag or speak highly of his own abilities in
football. One day, Frankie appeared in court as a witness.
The attorney asked if he was on Notre Dame's football team,
and Frankie replied that he was. Next the attorney asked the
young man what position he played. "Center," answered
Frankie without looking up.

"How good a center are you?" demanded the attorney. The
shy young man squirmed a little, but answered confidently,
"Sir, I am the best center in the history of Notre Dame."

Coach Frank Leahy, who was in the courtroom, was
shocked by such a statement from the usually modest boy.
Afterward, the coach asked Frankie why he had spoken as he
did.

Szymanski blushed and responded, "I hated to do it,
Coach, but after all, I was under oath!"

The Notre Dame star center knew his ability and had
tested it on the field. While physical abilities are often easy
to test, elusive inner strengths are difficult to probe. Each of
us must discover who we really are, and we must learn to
like what we find. But how can we overcome both the natural
and the social barriers to self-objectivity?

Nena and George O'Neill in *Shifting Gears*, an important
book about coping with changes, stress the importance of
clarifying life stances to find ourselves in what we believe
and stand for. They identify seven keys to creative self-
management that can help any individual develop a firm
benchmark for coping with life.

1. Don't ask permission	Do it.
2. Don't report	Check things out with yourself not others
3. Don't apologize unnecessarily	This is telling others you are a self-diminisher
4. Don't recriminate yourself	The missed-opportunity syndrome keeps you from moving forward
5. Don't say "I should" or "I shouldn't"	Ask "Why?" or "Why not?"
6. Don't be afraid to say no or yes	Act on what you think and feel
7. Don't put yourself completely in the hands of another	Be a self-determiner

When you take charge of your life, there is no longer need to ask permission of other people or society at large. If there are other people who will be affected by what you do, then you should tell them of your plans and ask for feedback. Listening to feedback and taking this into consideration is important, but it is not the same thing as asking permission. When you ask permission, you give someone else veto power over your life. This is not a noble thing to do. You will always wind up resenting that person and will never achieve your true potential.

The Functions of Management

Every student and practitioner of management is intimately familiar with the basic functions of planning, organization, and control. Managers have many kinds of activities, but their ultimate responsibilities in management revolve around these duties.

Chapter Twelve has provided the essence of a plan for you to follow in getting ready for the greatest challenge this country has faced since the early 1940's. Regardless of your resources, you will need to organize your purchases and preparations with the most essential items to be taken care of most quickly. Other desirable, but less essential items, can be saved in the event there is time to take care of these as well. Whether it be food storage or investment strategy, you should practice regular and careful control. At least once every six months, sit down and review your achievements during the past six months. Identify the specific goals which you plan to achieve during the next half year. Keep your list of goals constantly before you so that you are not diverted by temporary improvements in the economic picture.

WHAT IS THE FUTURE YOU SEEK?

The first step in inventing your own future is to decide what kind of future you seek. I firmly believe in the motto, "Whatever the human mind can conceive, the human spirit can achieve." If you really believe this is a doomsday book, you haven't been reading closely enough. At this late date, I do not believe that it is possible to avoid an economic depression. Yet I feel this coming depression can be a great opportunity for individuals and the nation. Good planning will not eliminate tornados, but planning can enable you to sit comfortable in your storm shelter while the winds howl around you.

Given some bleak economic prospects for the immediate future, what is your personal goal? Do you wish to pursue the dream of total self-sufficiency? Can you and your family live as the Swiss Family Robinson in an isolated setting? Do you prefer sharing hardships with a group of like-minded friends who form an extended family or survival community? What about the possibility of living in a small town that is less likely to experience the severe dislocations experienced by major cities? Any one of these alternatives has several sub-objectives that need to be considered.

The most important thing about goals is having one. The Roman philosopher Seneca observed, "If a man knows not what harbor he seeks, any wind is the right wind." To put it in a more contemporary idiom, "If a person doesn't know where he is going, any road will take him there." As one of the characters in *South Pacific* suggested, "If you don't have a dream, how are you going to make a dream come true?" If you have not formulated your life's goal or your objectives for the coming decade, sit down with several sheets of paper and jot down some ideas. Then, brainstorm these ideas with other members of your family or close friends. Remember, however, responsibility for your goals must remain with you.

Be sure that your goals are worthy of you. Nothing is more frustrating than spending your life in the pursuit of a dream only to discover that the dream is a nightmare. Former advertising executive Jess Lair tells how an almost fatal heart attack gave him a sense of real perspective in determining his life goals. While in his thirties, Lair was president of his own advertising agency. He lived in one of the most expensive suburbs in the United States, sent his children to exclusive private schools, owned two expensive cars, and was clearly a young man on the go. One day, he had lunch with his financial advisor and evolved a plan whereby he would work twice as hard at a job he despised in order to secure enough financial resources to retire at age fifty. On his way back to the office, Lair recalls how his "Norwegian heart said, 'You can go that way if you want to, but I'm not going with you.' " He suffered a massive heart attack and had to give up his thriving business.

The Lair family moved out of their upper-middle-class ghetto and rented a rundown house on ten acres outside of Minneapolis. Jess enrolled in a graduate psychology program while the family income dwindled to about one-tenth of what it had been before. Strangely enough, the family found they enjoyed their reduced circumstances more than the frantic race to stay ahead of everyone else. The irony of life was brought home to them when their landlord, a successful Twin-City attorney, would come out to his property about once a month and walk across his investment. He would look longingly at the children riding horses and at the fresh vegetables growing in a garden. Then he would return to the city and work harder than ever in order to make sufficient money to some day move to the farm and live like the Lairs. Today, Jess and his family live in Bozeman, Montana, where he teaches an occasional class at the University of Montana, conducts a few seminars, does some writing, and spends most of his time hunting and fishing with friends who are so important that nothing could lure him away. The heart attack taught him that riches could not be obtained by money alone. In a similar way, poverty cannot be eliminated by money.

One of my purposes in writing this book is to help you gain or hold on to all your riches. I want to help you to have sufficient money to see you through the depression of the 1980's, but this will not guarantee your prosperity. Money has no brain, but a dollar in one person's hand is very different than it is in another's.

A long time ago, I saw a play in which the main character

said to her child "Be careful what you set your heart upon, for it will surely come to you." Don't wait to begin your survival program until you have accumulated enough money. If you feel poor now, the feeling of poverty is probably bottomless. You cannot quench this thirst through the accumulation of possessions or awards. It is like a shipwrecked sailor who tries to quench his thirst by drinking seawater.

Make the financial provisions that I have suggested, but always remember that prosperity depends more on wanting what you have than having what you want.

THE JOURNEY ENDS—AND BEGINS

In our journey together, we have documented the decline and fall of the American dream. We have explored the reasons behind these problems and assessed a variety of projections about the immediate future. I have described my vision of how we are moving toward an inescapable monetary and economic collapse within the next few years.

Despite this gloomy background, I have attempted to paint a cheerful picture of how planning and discipline can provide for genuine prosperity for you while, for the majority, survival will be the issue. We have explored investment strategy, ranging from positive thinking to diamond selection. Proven techniques for timing and choice have been identified for your evaluation. We have also looked at a variety of techniques that can be used to protect your person, property, family, and health.

One of the major rewards that I have experienced from writing this book is that it has helped me crystalize a blueprint of how I plan to cope with the challenges that confront me. If my plan is not totally suitable to you, there are numerous sources that can provide additional direction and assistance.

Success is a journey, not a destination. I hope that the portion of the journey we have shared together has been successful for you. The ultimate measure of your success will be the degree to which you are able to spend your life in your own way.

I hope you will be concerned about the problems of our future, but not so concerned that you fail to enjoy the pleasures of today. I want you to begin immediately to make preparations for economic depression, but not with such anxiety that you suffer personal depression. Don't procrastinate beginning your survival program, but don't proceed with such desperation that you fail to savor the good that still survives in our society.

If one advances confidently in the direction of his dreams and endeavors to lead the life which he has imagined, he will meet with success unexpected.

—Henry David Thoreau

Appendix A

Bibliography

This bibliography will attempt to accomplish two major objectives. First, I want to provide credit for the distinguished authors who have helped shape and influence my own thinking. In working with my publisher, we agreed that extensive footnotes would make the book appear too scholarly. While most of my readers will not be interested in reviewing my references, I do want you to be able to identify some of the sources I have read in preparing the manuscript. Secondly, I want to share the books that I have found to be most valuable in planning for the future. These are marked with an asterisk and are recommended for your personal library. In most instances, I have indicated the price of the book and a little bit about it if it was not reviewed in the body of the book. If you have trouble locating one of these references, any library can give you the address of the publisher.

An even more extensive listing of appropriate references is contained in Don and Barbie Stephens' book *The Survivor's Primer and Updated Retreater's Bibliography* (Spokane, Washington, Stephens Press, 1976), 122 pages, $12.00. Harry Browne calls this the most useful retreat volume available by the most knowlegeable professionals in this field. It discusses possible reasons for concern, potential hazards, choices for course of actions, plus over 950 annotated listings providing the details about responsible crisisproofing through advance preparation.

Chapter 1

This chapter was put together after an extensive reading of newspapers, periodicals, government reports and foundation studies. The references suggested below are useful for an overview of the entire subject matter discussed in this book.

Harry Browne, *How You Can Profit from the Coming Devaluation* (New York: Avon, 1975), 189 pps., $1.75. Originally written in 1970, this is a classic description of monetary manipulation and its consequences. Although Browne has updated this book twice, it still remains an important starting point.

*Harry Browne, *New Profits from the Monetary Crisis* (New

York: William Morrow and Company, Inc. 1978) 480 pages, $12.95. As a follow-up to his previous works, Browne describes an emerging "third investment era" and outlines a recommended investment approach that analyzes such investment media as the stock market (especially warrants), real estate, gold, silver, foreign currencies, fixed interest, commodities, and collectibles.

*Harry Browne, *You Can Profit from a Monetary Crisis* (New York: Bantam, 1975), 395 pages, $2.25. An expansion and updating of Browne's original work.

James Dines, *The Invisible Crash* (New York: Ballantine Books, 1975), 489 pages, $1.95.

Barry Goldwater, *The Coming Breakpoint* (New York: Macmillan Publishing Co., Inc. 1976), 206 pages, $8.95.

Robert Preston, *How to Prepare for the Coming Crash* (Salt Lake City, UT.: Hawkes Publications, 1973), 121 pages, $2.00.

John C. Raines, *The Illusions of Success* (Valley Forge, PA.: Judson Press, 1975), 128 pages, $5.95. An excellent documentation of how the middle class in America is losing ground. Although the data is somewhat dated and Raines believes that a redistribution of wealth is the solution to the problems he identifies, this is an excellent overview.

*Howard J. Ruff, *How to Prosper During the Coming Bad Years* (New York: Times Books, 1979), 325 pages, $8.95. Describes Ruff's view of the future on how to provide for a breakdown in the delivery of goods and services. A summary of the ideas, recommendations, and philosophy contained in his newsletter.

E. F. Schumacher, *Small Is Beautiful: Economics as if People Mattered* (New York: Harper and Row), 305 pages, $2.45. In an important break with traditional growth economics, Schumacher describes his view of emerging hazards and presents ideas on possible solutions to them.

Herbert N. Woodward, *Capitalism Can Survive in a No-Growth Economy* (Stanford, Conn.: The Brookdale Press, 1976), 261 pages, $7.95.

Chapter 2

History

Crane Brinton, *The Anatomy of Revolution* (Englewood, N.J.: Vintage Books, 1965), 310 pages, $1.45.

*R. E. McMaster, Jr., *The Cycles of War: The Next Six Years* (Kalispell, Montana: War Cycles Institute, 1977), 217 pages, $11.00. A former instructor at the U.S. Air Force Academy and commodity trading advisor for Hornblower and Weeks, McMaster reports that he has spent the last thirteen years in researching this book. It documents the large number of business, weather, and other cycles that point to an extremely high probability of war, national revolutions, rioting, and other conflicts in the very near future.

Gordon R. Taylor, *How to Avoid the Future* (London: Secker & Warburg, 1975), 339 pages, $4.90.

Arnold Toynbee, *A Study of History* (abridged by D. C. Summerwell) (London: Oxford University Press, 1947), 1031 pages, $19.95.

Futurists

Dennis Meadows et al, *The Limits to Growth* (New York: Universe Books, 1972), 205 pages, $6.50.

*Alvin Toffler, *The Eco-Spasm Report* (New York: Bantam, 1975), 117 pages, $1.50.

*Robert Vacca, *The Coming Dark Age* (New York: Doubleday & Company, 1974), 221 pages, $2.50.

Economists

Robert L. Heilbroner, *Business Civilization in Decline* (New York: W. W. Norton & Company, Inc., 1977), 127 pages, $6.95. An expansion of Heilbroner's previous work that focuses on the deterioration of a market system in the world of the future. While I agree with Heilbroner's assessment of emerging problems, I disagree with his assessment of the way to cope with these problems through collective planning.

*Robert Heilbroner, *An Inquiry into Human Prospect* (New York: W. W. Norton & Co., Inc., 1974), 150 pages, $2.25.

*David Rhoads, *How to Survive a Spastic Economy* (San Diego, CA: J. D. Press, 1977), 174 pages, $8.50

James B. Schuman and David Rosenau, *Kondratieff Wave: The Future of America Until 1984 and Beyond* (New York: Dell Publishing, 1974), 234 pages, $2.95.

Earthquakes

Jeffery Goodman, *We Are the Earthquake Generation* (New York: Simon and Schuster, 1977, 265 pages, $10.95. Dr. Goodman has used his background in archeology and engineering to develop an interesting description of the potential impact of earthquakes affecting the world in the period between 1980 and 2000. His research centers on the predictions of psychics concerning the changes to be affected but supplements this data with scientific sources.

John R. Gribbin and Stephen H. Plagemann, *The Jupiter Effect: The Planets as Triggers of Devastating Earthquakes* (New York: Vintage Books, 1975), 178 pages, $1.95.

Astrology

Geoffery Dean and Arthur Mather, *Recent Advances in Natal Astrology—A Critical Review 1900–1976* (Isle of Wight, England: Para Research, Inc., 1977), 608 pages, $17.00.

Francis Sakoin and Louis Acker, *The Astrologer's Handbook* (New York: Harper & Row Publishers, 1973), 461 pages, $11.95.

Climatology

H. H. Lame, *Climate: Present, Past and Future* (London: Methuen, 1972), $55.00.

*The Impact Team, *The Weather Conspiracy, The Coming of the New Ice Age* (New York: Heron House Publishing International Limited, 1977), 234 pages, $1.95.

Religion

Hal Lindsey (with C. C. Carlson), *The Late Great Planet Earth* (New York: Zondervan Publishing House, 1970 and Bantam Edition, 1973), 192 pages, $1.95.

Chapter 3

*Henry Hazlitt, *The Inflation Crisis, and How to Resolve It* (New Rochelle, N.Y.: Arlington House, 1978), 192 pages, $8.95. In an updated version of a 1968 classic, Hazlitt covers, in very clear and understandable terms, the nature of the problems we now face, ways we could solve them, the policies that we will probably actually use to make them worse, and ways that individuals can try to protect themselves.

Abba O. Lerner, *Flation* (New York: Quadrangle Books, 1972), 184 pages, $5.95.

*J. Houston McCullough, *Money and Inflation: A Monetarist Approach* (New York: Academic Press, Inc., 1975), 121 pages, $5.00.

Harvey W. Peters, *America's Coming Bankruptcy* (New Rochelle, NY: Arlington House Publishers, 1970), 222 pages, $7.95. Peters estimates that government, private, and business debts totaled more than $1.5 trillion in 1970. When the national wealth is computed in terms of constant dollars (1947–49), these debts may equal 98 percent of the total wealth.

Franz Pick, *The U.S. Dollar: An Advance Obituary* (New York: Pick Publishing Corp., 1976), 74 pages, $42.22.

M. Martin Rom, *Nothing Can Replace the U.S. Dollar . . . and It Almost Has* (New York: Thomas Y. Crowell, Co., 1975), 244 pages, $7.95.

Murray N. Rothbard, *What Has Government Done to Our Money* (Santa Anna, CA.: Rampart College, 1972), 49 pages, $1.00.

Sidney Rutberg, *The Money Balloon: Inflation and How to Live with It* (New York: Simon and Schuster, 1975), 220 pages, $7.95.

Chapter 4

The best scenarios of how an economic collapse might occur or the challenges of survival under any form of serious catastrophe are typically presented in fictional form. Some of the sources identified below help explain how a collapse may occur. Others suggest some of the ways that people will approach the challenges of survival.

John Brunner, *The Sheep Look Up* (New York: Ballantine Books, 1972), 461 pages, $1.75. The author assumes that humans are killing the planet with chemicals, drugs, indifference, stupidity, and greed. A frightening description of how people are forced to come to terms with their impacted environment.

*John Christopher, *No Blades of Grass* (New York: Avon/Equinox, 1975), 190 pages, $1.95. A gripping description of how one British family attempts to reach a safe retreat during a period of worldwide famine. This classic story of survival has been made into a motion picture that you may occasionally see on late television.

John Christopher, *The Ragged Edge* (New York: Simon and Schuster, 1965), 254 pages, $4.95. Another survival story—this one focusing on the challenges of coping with widespread earthquake activity. An epic account of a divorced father searching for his daughter as the world around him collapses in terror, disease, starvation, and a desperate longing for the orderly past. A graphic description of people faced with the problem of survival—some meeting the challenge with savagery with others attempting to build on the foundations of law and justice.

Paul E. Erdman, *The Crash of '79* (New York: Pocket Books, 1976), 428 pages, $1.95. Written by a former Swiss banker, this book describes a worldwide collapse brought on by a nuclear misunderstanding in the Middle East. A frightening picture of the power of petro-politics.

Ayn Rand, *Atlas Shrugged* (New York: Ballantine Books, 1972), 461 pages, $1.75. This monumental work of objectivism describes a breakdown in society brought on by a revolt of the producers against having to bear the burden of the lazy majority. Many of Rand's predictions have already taken place.

*Benjamin and Herbert Stein, *On the Brink* (New York: Simon and Schuster, 1977), 370 pages, $5.95. Written by a former White House speech writer and Wall Street Journal columnist with his father, who is a former member of the President's Council of Economic Advisors. While not great fiction, this is a detailed de-

scription of economic collapse brought on by uncontrollable inflation. The book provides a superb picture of potential economic
reality.

Chapter 5

*Gerald Apple, *Ninety-Nine Ways to Make Money in a De-
pression* (New Rochelle, N.Y.: Arlington House Publishers,
1976), 238 pages, $8.95.

Harry Browne, *How You Can Profit from the Coming Devaluation* (New York: Avon, 1975), 189 pages, $1.75.

*Harry Browne, *You Can Profit from a Monetary Crisis* (New
York: Bantam, 1975), 395 pages, $2.25.

Boyd Crabtree, *How to Drop out of Social Insecurity* (Para-
dise, CA. 95969: Boyd Crabtree, 1977), 51 pages, $5.00.

V. C. Myers, *The Coming Deflation: Its Dangers and Opportunities* (New Rochelle, N.Y.: Arlington House Publishers, 1976),
218 pages, $8.95.

Chapter 6

The Apple and Browne books referenced in the previous chapters have helpful material about depressionproof investments.

Daniel Cohen, *Gold: The Fascinating Story of the Noble
Metal Through the Ages* (New York: M. Evans and Company,
Inc.), 186 pages, $6.95.

E. J. Farmer, *The Conspiracy Against Silver* (New York:
Greenwood Press, 1969), 144 pages, $10.75.

*Anthony S. Sutton, *The War on Gold* (Seal Beach, CA.: 76
Press [P.O. Box 2686], 1976), 232 pages, $9.95.

Bill Tonelli, *Gem Investments* (Random, Pa., Jeweler's Circular
Keystone [Chilton Way], 1978), 48 pages, $10.00, originally
published in the July, 1978, issue of JCK, the jewelers' trade magazine. Shows the positives and dangers of gem investments.

Chapter 7

*Williard and Marguerite Beecher, *Beyond Success and Failure:
Ways to Self-Reliance and Maturity* (New York: Pocket Books,
1971), 159 pages, $1.25.

Herbert Benson and Miriam Z. Klipper, *The Relaxation Response* (New York: Avon Books, 1976), 158 pages, $1.95.

Harry Browne, *How I Found Freedom in an Un-Free World*
(New York: Avon Books, 1973), 107 pages, $1.95.

*Linda Clark, *Get Well Naturally* (New York: Arco Publishing
Com., 1965), 406 pages, $1.95.

*Kenneth H. Cooper, *The New Aerobics* (New York: Bantam Books, 1970), 191 pages, $1.25.

*John Henderson, *Emergency Medical Guide* (Third Edition) (New York: McGraw Hill Book Company, 1973), 651 pages, $3.95. The author recently retired as corporate director of medical affairs for Johnson & Johnson. This book provides an excellent, thorough, yet easy to understand description of how to deal with a wide variety of medical emergencies from infectious disease to burns and accidents.

Beatrice P. Hunter, *Food Additives and Your Health* (New Cannan, Conn.: Keats Publishing, Inc., 212 Elm St. 06840, 1972), 116 pages, $.95.

D. C. Jarvis, *Folk Medicines* (Greenwich, Conn.: Fawcett Publications, Inc., 1958), 192 pages, $1.50.

Ari Kiev, M.D., *A Strategy for Success* (New York: MacMillan Co., Inc.), 136 pages, $6.95.

*Jane Kinderlehrer, *Confessions of a Sneaky Organic Cook* (New York: Rodale Press, Inc., 1971), 206 pages, $1.50.

Marjorie Miller, *An Introduction to Health Foods* (New York: Dell Publishing Co., Inc., 1971), 196 pages, $.95.

Anne Moyer, *The Fiber Factor* (Emmaus, PA: Rodale Press, Inc., 1976), 140 pages, $1.50.

*David S. Viscott, *Feel Free* (New York: Peter H. Wyden, 1974), 246 pages, $5.95.

Roger J. Williams, *Nutrition Against Disease* (New York: Bantam Books, 1971), 370 pages, $1.95.

Chapter 8

*Harry Browne, *Complete Guide to Swiss Banks* (New York: McGraw-Hill Book Co., 1976), 535 pages, $9.95.

*Douglas R. Casey, *The International Man* (Alexandria, Va.: Kephart Communications, Inc., 1978), 113 pages, $14.95. Described as the complete guidebook to the world's last frontiers for freedom seekers, investors, adventurers, speculators, and expatriates, this book analyzes the opportunities, costs and risks of doing business in fifty-three countries around the wrld.

T. R. Fehrenbach, *The Swiss Banks* (New York: McGraw-Hill Book Co., 1966), 280 pages, $9.95.

*Robert Kinsman, *Guide to Tax Havens* (Homeward, Ill.: Dow-Jones-Irwin, 1977), 283 pages, $17.50.

Robert Kinsman, *Your Swiss Bank Book* (Homeward, Ill.: Dow-Jones-Irwin, 1975), 283 pages, $9.95.

Midas Malone, *How to Do Business Tax Free* (Wilmington, Del.: Enterprise Publishing Co., 1976), 158 pages, $14.95.

Franz Pick, *The Numbered Account* (New York: Pick Publishing Co., 1972), 73 pages, $45.00.

Harry D. Schultz, *What the Prudent Investor Should Know about Switzerland* (New Rochelle, N.Y.: Arlington House, 1971), 215 pages, $7.95.

Chapter 9

William Hanson, *City Survival—City Resistance* (Hillcrest Publications, P. O. Box 395, McDonald, Ohio 44437), 116 pages, $4.00.

David Krotz, *How to Hide Almost Anything* (New York: William Morrow & Co., 1975), 157 pages, $5.95.

Ira A. Lipman, *How to Protect Yourself Against Crime* (New York: Atheneum, 1975), 202 pages, $9.95.

*Howard J. Ruff, *Famine and Survival in America* (Target Publishers, P. O. Box 172, Alamo, Calif. 94507, 1974), 196 pages, $4.95.

*Don Stephens, *Personal Protection Here and Now* (Stephens Printing Company, P.O. Drawer 1441, Spokane, Washington, 99210, 1975), 50 pages, $3.00.

Mel Tappan, *Survival Guns* (The Jenus Press, Inc., P.O. Drawer 75455, Los Angeles, Calif. 90075, 1977), 458 pages, $7.95.

Chapter 10

Bradford Angier, *Survival with Style* (New York: Vintage Books, 1970), 320 pages, $2.25.

M. G. Cains, *Five Acres and Independence* (New York: The New American Library, 1973), 401 pages, $3.00.

James E. Churchill, *The Homesteaders Handbook: Guide to Independent Living* (New York: Vintage Books, 1974), 224 pages, $2.95.

James B. DeCorne, *The Survival Greenhouse: an Eco System Approach to Home Food Production* (El Rito, New Mexico: The Walden Foundation, 1977), 165 pages, $7.50. (P.O. Box 5, El Rito, New Mexico, 87530)

Jethro Kloss, *Back To Eden* (Santa Barbara, CA.: Lifeline Books, 1975), 680 pages, $2.25. An updated version of the original classic by Jethro Kloss presents his recommendations based on forty years of experience with American herbs for health and healing. Natural nutrition with detailed recipes and instructions for living off the land.

Sidney Ragsdale, *How to Plan and Develop a Survival Retreat* (Carmel, California: Ragsdale Press, 1976), 89 pages, $9.95. (P.O. Box 6566, Carmel, CA. 93921)

Patrick Rivers, *The Survivalists* (London: Eyre Muthuen, 1975), 224 pages, $4.95.

*John Seymour, *The Guide to Self-Sufficiency* (New York: Popular Mechanics Books, 1976), 256 pages, $11.95.

Ruth Stout, *How to Have a Green Thumb Without an Aching Back* (Birmingham, Al.: Cornerstone, 1974), 195 pages, $1.95.

Ruth Stout and Richard Clemence, *The Ruth Stout No Work Garden Book* (Emmaus, PA.: Rodale Press, Inc., 1971), 218 pages, $6.95. Based on articles originally appearing in *Organic Gardening and Farming,* this summarizes Ruth Stout's many years of experience with mulch gardening.

*Survival Homes, Inc., *Design Criteria for Total Self-Sufficiency* (Provo, Utah: Dana Press, 1971), 81 pages, $15.00. Part of a self-study course for self-sufficiency offered by Survival Homes, Inc. This is an excellent booklet that provides an overview of the types of changes that will be required and helpful hints in dealing with retreat planning. A comprehensive fifteen page appendix provides a checklist for self-sufficiency preparation.

*John Tole, *Living Off the Land* (Ontario: Greywood Publishing, Ltd., 1973), 400 pages, $1.25.

*John Vividan, *The Manual of Practical Homesteading* (Emmaus, PA.: Rodale Press, 1975), 340 pages, $5.95. This has been described as almost the ultimate book on practical gardening and rural living. An excellent and comprehensive summary for the novice and expert alike.

Underground Housing

Alternatives in Energy Conservation: the Use of Earth-Covered Buildings (Washington, D.C.: Superintendent of Documents, 1975), 353 pages, $3.25. This is a copy of the proceedings held in Forth Worth, Texas, sponsored by the National Science Foundation. Stock number on this valuable booklet is 038-000-00286-4.

Malcolm Wells, P.O. Box 1149, Brewster, ME. 02631

In-Earth Designs, P.O. Drawer 1441, Spokane, Washington 99210.

Davis Caves, Inc., Armington, ILL. 61721

Chapter 11

Spencer MacCallum, *The Art of Community* (Menlo Park, CA.: Institute of Human Studies, 1970), 118 pages, $2.00.

Melford Spiro, *Kibbutz: Venture in Utopia* (New York: Schecken Books, Inc., 1971), 266 pages, $2.75.

*Don Stephens, *Greenpapers* #4 (Reprints of 4 articles), (Spokane, Wash.: Stephens Press, 1976), 8 pages, $2.00.

Chapter 12

Since this chapter summarized much of the information contained throughout the book into a series of action steps, no specific references are recommended. Two rather detailed checklists of supplies are suggested, however.

*Don and Barbie Stephens, *The Survivor's Primer and Updated Retreater's Bibliography* (Spokane, Wash.: Stephens Press, 1976), pages 92-93, $12.00.

*Survival Homes, Inc. *Design Criteria for Total or Partial Self-Sufficiency* (Provo, Utah, 1977), Appendix A, 15 pages, $12.00. This book may be ordered from Dana Press, P.O. Box 163, Provo, Utah 84601.

Chapter 13

Williard and Marguerite Beecher, *Beyond Success and Failure* (New York: Pocket Books, 1971), 157 pages, $1.25.

*Jess Lair, *I Ain't Well, But I Sure Am Better: Mutual Need Therapy* (New York: Fawcett World, 1975), 205 pages, $1.95.

*Nena and George O'Neill, *Shifting Gears* (New York: Avon Books, 1974), 281 pages, $1.95.

Henry Thoreau, *Walden and Civil Disobedience* (New York: New American Library, 1973), 255 pages, $.95.

Appendix B

Review of Selected Financial and Survival Newsletters

PUBLICATION NAME	FREQUENCY	SIZE	COST	CONTENT
HARRY BROWNE'S SPECIAL REPORT Harry Browne Special Reports, Inc. Box 5586 Austin, Texas 78763	Ten per year	25 pages (average)	$175.00 for ten issues	Regular features include vital statistics of major currencies, prices and economic indicators, and investment news summaries. Plus reports on a variety of investment topics with recommendations.
DOW THEORY LETTERS, INC. P. O. Box 1759 LaJolla, CA. 92038	Every other week	6 pages	$150.00 per year	Market trends, investment advice on stocks, bonds, gold. Discussions on inflation and deflation.
EXODUS Box 7032 4000 Dusseldorf 1, Germany	1-2 issues per month	4 pages	$150.00 per year or $10 per copy	Newest of the Schultz Newsletters, not an investment letter. Covers subjects such as gaining a new citizenship or passport, opening foreign bank or investment accounts and tax havens.
THE FORECASTER John Kamin 19623 Ventura Blvd. Tarzana, CA. 91356	Weekly		$28.00 for 11 issues	Forecasts money movements and gives strategy and checklists on how to take advantage of these movements, as well as sound business advice. Gold, silver, and rare coin coverage detailed, unavailable elsewhere.

PUBLICATION NAME	FREQUENCY	SIZE	COST	CONTENT
GOLD AND OTHER CURRENCIES Box 2523 Lausanne 1002, Switzerland	1-2 issues per month	4 pages	$150.00 per year or $10 per copy	A Harry Schultz Newsletter tells how international events affect the gold market.
THE GRAHAM LETTER Basil Investment Corporation Richboro Professional Center Richboro, PA. 18954	Monthly	4 pages	$100.00 per year	Basic analysis of U.S. and World economic situation; strong on fundamental patterns and trends. Specific advice in U.S. stock, gold, currency, and Eurobonds.
IMAC Economic Newsletter 79 Wall Street, Suite 501 New York, New York 10005	50 times per year	8 pages	$150.00 per year	Currency, bullion and gold, Wall Street, and international stock markets plus influential political economic comment—subscribers worldwide.
INTERNATIONAL INVESTORS VIEWPOINT 610 S. W. Alder Street Portland, OR. 97205	Every four weeks	16-24 pages	$100.00 per year	Sophisticated review of economic monetary trends, investments, tax shelters, with an emphasis on gold and gold stocks. Detailed monthly analysis of 50 gold mining stocks.
IMI BULLETIN Institute of Money and Inflation Suite B-1, 314 East Capitol Street Washington, D. C. 20002	Every two months	4 pages	$50.00 one-time tax-deductible membership	Institute on Money and Inflation publishes this newsletter. Written in crisp, concise format, articles often deal with effects of congressional legislation on economy.
THE INTERNATIONAL HARRY SCHULTZ LETTER FERC SA P.O. Box 2523 Lausanne 1002, Switzerland	Every 3 weeks	6 pages	$258.00 per year	Currency, gold markets; political editorials written in abbreviated spelling for quick scanning, Schultz's view of U.S. and other economies. A review of worldwide economic and investment opportunities.

PUBLICATION NAME	FREQUENCY	SIZE	COST	CONTENT
THE INTERNATIONAL MONEYLINE 25 Broad Street New York, New York 10004	Twice per month	4 pages	$90.00 for six months	Investment and trading advice on long- and short-term holdings in foreign currencies and gold, plus monetary and international economic analysis as applied to U.S. stock markets.
THE L. T. PATTERSON STRATEGY LETTER P.O. Box 37432 Cincinnati, OH. 45237	Monthly	6 pages	$75.00 per year	Discusses censorship of economic and financial matters in America. Harassment of private savers, retirees, and investors are explained in detail.
PERSONAL FINANCE Kephart Communications, Inc. Post Office Box 2599 Landover Hills, MD. 20784	24 times per year	8 pages	$48.00 for 24 issues	Investment ideas to hedge against inflation; excellent range of topics covered along with superb review of other sources. Formerly "Inflation Survival Letter."
PERSONAL SURVIVAL LETTER P.O. Box 598 Rogue River, CA. 97537	12 times a year	12 pages	$100.00 per year	"Conceived as a postscript to the hard money newsletters." It concentrates on techniques, skills and products for long-term survival following a monetary collapse.
THE REAPER P.O. Box 39026 Phoenix, AZ. 85069	Weekly	4 pages	$195.00 per year	Makes commodity recommendations using economic analysis to make economic forecasts; explains the principles of markets as they apply to one's personal and professional life.
REMNANT REVIEW 713 W. Cornwallis, Suite 105 Durham, N.C. 27707	22 times a year	6 pages	$60.00 per year	Conservative-Christian outlook, pro-gold, anti-Federal Reserve System stance. Concentrates on price controls, "alternative" markets and investments.

PUBLICATION NAME	FREQUENCY	SIZE	COST	CONTENT
THE RHOADS CONCLUSION P.O. Box 22674 San Diego, CA. 92122	Monthly	4 to 8 pages	$48.00 per year	Articles concern economic events, their meaning and impact on investments and the business community.
RUFF TIMES Target Publishers P.O. Box 172 1451 Danville Blvd. Alamo, CA. 94507	Twice per month	6 pages	$96.00 per year	Articles deal with how current events affect individual investors and attempt to identify stress points in the U.S. economy before they are obvious.
SILVER & GOLD REPORT P.O. Box 325 Newtown, CT. 06470	Twice per month	20 pages	$144.00 per years or $10. per 2 months	Coverage of precious metals markets and factors that influence gold and silver prices.
THE SURVIVOR Atlan Formularies P.O. Box 438 Eureka, CA. 95501	Monthly		$10.00 for 12 issues	Keyed toward survival in an uncertain world. Emphasis on practical, "how to" nonfinancial techniques.
WELLINGTON FINANCIAL LETTER P.O. Box 1287 Honolulu, HI. 96807	Monthly	12 pages	$87.00 per year	Analysis of internal investment and economic trends, specializing in foreign currencies, precious metals, and investment vehicles for inflation hedging.
WORLD MARKET PERSPECTIVE ERC Publishing Company #204-1760 Marine Drive West Vancouver, B.C., Canada V7VIJ4	Monthly	8 pages	$96.00 per year	Emphasis on monetary affairs, the value of money and the inevitability of very serious inflation in the future.

Appendix C

Gold and Silver Merchants

	Ten Krugerrands*	$1,000 Face Value pre-1965 Silver Coins*
BRAMBLE COINS 1064 Michigan National Tower Lansing, Michigan 49833 800/248-5952	$2,385.00	$4,500.00
COLONIAL COINS 909 Travis Houston, Texas 77002 800/231-2393	$2,380.00	$4,600.00
DEAK & COMPANY 1800 K Street, N.W. Washington, D.C. 20006 800/424-1186	$2,395.50	$4,507.00
FIRST NATIONAL MONETARY CORPORATION 26555 Evergreen Road, Suite 406 Southfield, Michigan 48076 800/521-2409	$2,378.00	$4,464.66
FIRST NATIONAL BANK OF CHICAGO One First National Plaza Chicago, Illinois 60670 800/621-4156	$2,325.00	$4,442.00
FRONTIER METALS INTERNATIONAL 4075 Westheimer, Suite 670 Houston, Texas 77056 800/231-3666	$2,410.00	$4,500,00

Gold and Silver Merchants

	Ten Krugerrands*	$1,000 Face Value pre-1965 Silver Coins*
MONEX INTERNATIONAL 4910 Birch Street Newport Beach, California 92660 800/854-3361	$4,763.00 (20)	$4,386.00
NORTH AMERICAN COIN & CURRENCY 106 W. Washington Street Phoenix, Arizona 85003 800/528-5346	$2,398.50	$4,370.26
PREMEX 21700 Northwestern Highway Southfield, Michigan 48075 800/521-2950	$2,553.00	$4,694.75
T. E. SLANKER COMPANY 610 S.W. Alder Street Portland, Oregon 97205 800/547-0146	$2,417.50	$4,400.00

*November 1, 1978 delivered price quotations

Selected Diamonds Merchants

	Color	Clarity	Carats	Cost
*AMERICAN DIAMOND COMPANY Box 2800 LaJolla, California 92038 800/854-2288				
*THE DIAMOND GUILD OF AMERICA, LTD 521 Fifth Avenue New York, N.Y. 10017 800/221-4702				

Selected Diamonds Merchants

	Color	Clarity	Carats	Cost
DIAMOND NETWORK ASSOCIATES	G	VVS1	1.04	$ 7,930
3660 Wilshire Blvd.,				
Ste. 340	G	VVS1	1.09	8,311
Los Angeles, California 90010	G	VVS2	1.00	6,250
80/421-8482	G	VS2	.47	2,687
KOHINOOR INTERNATIONAL, LTD	G	VVS1	1.00	6,400 (includes 5% commission)
1 Lincoln Plaza				
New York, N.Y. 10023				
212/595-6282				
NORTH AMERICAN DIAMOND	G	VVS2	1.01	6,427 + 10 percent
Suite G-2	G	VVS2	.57	1,628 + 10 percent
100 W. Washington St.				
Phoenix, Arizona				
602/257-7800				
RELIANCE DIAMONDS	G	VVS1	1.03	7,854
Box 2000	G	VVS1	1.47	13,009
Alamo, California 94507	G	VVS2	.51	1,536
800/227-1590				
THE SIDIAM	G	VVS1	1.09	7,200
Suite 1216	G	VVS2	1.08	6,200
2670 Union Ave., Ext.				
Memphis, Tennessee 38112				
901/452-0188				

NOTE: THE QUOTATIONS WERE RECEIVED DURING NOVEMBER, 1978. *SOME FIRMS CHOOSE NOT TO REVEAL THEIR PRICES FOR PUBLICATION.

Index